SUCH BIG DREAMS

"Cynical, street-smart Rakhi...is a sharply drawn protagonist [who] gives this novel power and zest."

—*Kirkus Reviews*

"Debut novelist Reema Patel vividly portrays the many strata of Mumbai, from the streets to the slums to the upper echelons, through the eyes of a young woman seeking control of her own future."

—*Booklist*

"Patel's riveting debut examines the exploitive class structure in Mumbai and the pitfalls for those on the lower rung....With a captivating arc and solid character development, the story highlights the impact of greed in a poverty-stricken Mumbai. It's a powerful debut."

—*Publishers Weekly* (starred review)

"*Such Big Dreams* is a haunting, gutsy novel. I rooted for Rakhi, I grieved for her. A heartbreaking yet hopeful story about the resilience of the human spirit in the face of insurmountable odds. Loved it!"

—Etaf Rum, *New York Times* bestselling author of *A Woman Is No Man*

"An astonishingly gifted storyteller, Reema Patel writes with a confidence, insight, and skill that belies her status as a debut novelist. A smart, haunting, compulsively readable novel with a tightly woven plot and an unforgettable narrator, *Such Big Dreams* is a gripping story you'll want to simultaneously race through at breakneck speed and slow down to savor every word."

—Amy Jones, author of *We're All in This Together*

"From the very first page, *Such Big Dreams* grabs you by the throat and doesn't let go. Patel's prose jumps with energy, plunging the reader into a page-turner of a story that doesn't shy away from exploring hard and painful truths about the way people navigate the systemic conditions of society. With assured writing, Patel explores themes ranging from societal elitism to the nuances of interpersonal betrayal. Visceral and kinetic, *Such Big Dreams* is a splash of a debut."

—Zalika Reid-Benta, author of *Frying Plantain*

"*Such Big Dreams* charts the ambitions, disappointments, and dreams of two people who are improbably thrust together as they try to find their way in—and make their mark on—a bustling Mumbai that's indifferent to their struggles. Unflinching yet written with compassion and insight, *Such Big Dreams* is a richly textured and powerful novel that, like Mumbai itself, pulsates with humanity. Patel is a writer to watch. I absolutely loved this book."

—Bianca Marais, author of *Hum If You Don't Know the Words*

"Mumbai has inspired many great novels about the city, and now we can add Patel's *Such Big Dreams* to that list. Her portrayal of Mumbai is fresh, vivid, and personal, in part because of the book's charming and perceptive narrator, Rakhi. I finished the book with a sigh of regret, feeling already the loss of Rakhi and the gift of Patel's Mumbai."

—Shyam Selvadurai, author of *Funny Boy*

SUCH
BIG
DREAMS

SUCH BIG DREAMS

.... *A Novel* ....

Reema Patel

BALLANTINE BOOKS

NEW YORK

2023 Ballantine Books Trade Paperback Edition

Copyright © 2022 by Reema Patel
Book club guide copyright © 2023 by Penguin Random House LLC

Published in the United States by Ballantine Books, an imprint of Random House, a division of Penguin Random House LLC, New York.

BALLANTINE is a registered trademark and the colophon is a trademark of Penguin Random House LLC.
RANDOM HOUSE BOOK CLUB and colophon are trademarks of Penguin Random House LLC.

Originally published in hardcover in the United States by Ballantine Books, an imprint of Random House, a division of Penguin Random House LLC, and in trade paperback in Canada by McClelland & Stewart, a division of Penguin Random House Canada, in 2022.

Library of Congress Cataloging-in-Publication Data
Names: Patel, Reema, author.
Title: Such big dreams: a novel / Reema Patel.
Description: First edition. | New York: Ballantine Books, 2022. Identifiers:
LCCN 2021051756 (print) | LCCN 2021051757 (ebook) | ISBN
9780593499528 (trade paperback; acid-free paper) | ISBN 9780593499511
(ebook) Subjects: LCGFT: Novels.
Classification: LCC PR9199.4.P3775 S83 2022 (print) | LCC PR9199.4.P3775
(ebook) | DDC 813/.6—dc23
LC record available at https://lccn.loc.gov/2021051756
LC ebook record available at https://lccn.loc.gov/2021051757

Printed in the United States of America on acid-free paper

randomhousebooks.com
randomhousebookclub.com

1st Printing

Book design by Caroline Cunningham
Flame ornament: iStock.com/bonezboyz

For my parents

SUCH
BIG
DREAMS

1

THIS TIME, THE FLAMES ARE everywhere—licking the walls, sweeping across the tin roof of my one-room hut.

I bolt upright in the dark, a full-body scream ready to erupt from somewhere deep inside my lungs. My hands reach for my throat as I gasp for air. Panic courses through my body while I try to recall Dr. Pereira's bad-dream exercise, the one she told me to do each time this happens.

"When you wake up," she said, "sit on the edge of your bed and put your feet on the floor." I had to tell her I don't have a bed, just a thin mat. "So sit at the edge of your mat cross-legged," she replied, patiently. "Then, name out loud the objects in the room."

Trembling, I fold one leg under the other and try to focus on the dim outlines of my belongings scattered around me.

In the corner of the room, my heavy, steel cabinet. "Almirah."

Beside it, the cooking vessel I never use. "Pot."

Drenched, sweaty clothes plastered to my back. "Kurta," I mutter.

Then I notice the damp, heavy weight tickling my neck. "Hair."

I slide a cautious hand toward the little blue Nokia that Gauri Ma'am gave me when I started working for her. "Phone." I clutch it tight. The small screen oozes a dull green glow, which I hold up in front of me to illuminate the room.

Shining the light on my cassette player, I press the eject button with a trembling finger and retrieve the tiny crystal elephant from its hiding spot. "Elephant." As I say the word and cradle the figurine in my palm, I can sense the flames of my nightmare start to recede.

And now for the last, most stupidest part of Dr. Pereira's night terror exercise: "I am awake," I whisper into the shadows. "I am safe."

My shoulders tense as I wait for flames to climb back up the walls, sparks to burrow into my clothes. None of that happens, though. I let out a deep breath and flop back onto my mat, dank and musty from my sweat and the humid monsoon air.

The nightmares started eleven years ago, after the paanwala incident. Just after I lost Babloo. They used to come almost every night. They've since tapered off to a few times a week, but they're just as vivid as ever. Most nights I try to stay awake for as long as I can, fighting the lull of the dead air and emptiness of my one-room hut, before drifting into broken sleep by two or three in the morning.

Behrampada slum sprawls out over seven acres in the middle of Bombay—or Mumbai, if that's what you want to call it—an island city flooded with too many people with too-big dreams. By the time I come home in the evenings, the slum roars with noise: The hiss and flare of gas cooking cylinders being lit; tawas and kadais clanging on stovetops. Women shouting at their husbands, who in turn shout back. Someone's shrieking child is always chasing someone else's bleating goat. And when India wins a cricket match, firecrackers burst in the lanes like fistfuls of corn popping. By midnight, though, people retreat inside and switch off their television sets, and the pressures that build up in Behrampada's crowded huts and narrow lanes fizzle out until dawn. Except for the squeals of horny rats and the occasional bottle smashing, all goes quiet—and that's when the night terrors come for me.

Letting out one of those big yawns that almost unhinges my jaw, I roll onto my side. Last night, flash rains banged down on my leaky tin roof like a herd of sharp-clawed cats. The steady sound of water dripping into a plastic bucket would drive anyone else to tears, but I was grateful to be kept awake for a little while longer. As the storm died down, though, so did the noise, and I eventually fell asleep. If I had the secret weapons that important people do, like loud English or proper Hindi, I'd command the nearby Garib Nawaz Masjid to keep the call to prayer going all night, crying out "Allahu akbar" and "la ilaha illa-Allah" on loop from their tinny loudspeakers. "We have to help Rakhi keep the night terrors away," the muezzin would reply flatly, if anyone complained about his six-hour azaan.

Already, I hear the clamor of the people of Behrampada as they start to stir, which means it's just past five. By six, the sun has risen, and by seven, I've used the stinking public toilet and bathed. By eight, I've drunk a cup of tea and gotten dressed, and am ready to leave for work.

On this muggy July morning, the main road from Behrampada to Bandra Station glistens with a slick layer of oil, water, and dirt. I take careful strides over the puddle-filled potholes dotting the street, but the cotton ankles of my clean salwar end up speckled with mud anyway. "Dressing smart tells the world you think our work is valuable," Gauri Ma'am told me during my first week at the office, after I wore the same salwar kameez for three days straight. She handed me a stack of her daughter's old clothes the next day.

It's only as I pause on the station bridge to inspect the mud splatters on the backs of my pant legs that I spot my train pulling into the station. The people who have been waiting on the platform are already getting inside, which means I have less than fifteen seconds before it departs. By the time I fly down the stairs to the platform, the train has started to move again. The slanted green-and-yellow stripes of the ladies' general compartment are exactly two cars away.

I haven't chased after a moving train in a long time. During our years living on the street, Babloo and I were always running. Running away, that is—from policewalas, shopkeepers, and passengers who'd had enough of us. While other children had their hair oiled and combed, rode in autorickshaws to school, and ate proper lunches and dinners, we were leaping onto moving trains, traveling ticketless up and down the railway lines, looking for something to put into our growling bellies.

The train picks up speed, so I do, too. There's only one way on now, and it's to jump in the open door closest to me—the first-class ladies' compartment. I don't have a first-class pass, but that's never stopped me before. I reach out for the pole in the doorway, the tip of my middle finger grazing the cool metal, but it's inching away from me. I'm going to have to leap for it. Bracing myself, I lurch forward, stretching for the pole with my left hand, this time gripping it firmly. Quickly, I suck in my breath and vault over the gap as the train gains momentum, and my outer hip takes a sharp blow from the pole while my feet slam down onto the metal floor. Out the open door, the city rushes past me. I am inside. Panting like a dog on a summer day, but inside.

The train roars down the Harbour Line toward the next stop, Mahim Station. I'll hop out there and switch into the ladies' general compartment. The total fine for ticketless travel would come to three hundred rupees if they caught me right now. I only have seventy rupees in my purse, and the Railway Police holding cells swell with ankle-deep sludge during monsoon season.

The wind from outside undoes most of the curls from my pony-tail, which blow about in a thousand directions. I must look like some deranged woman, the kind whose uncle or husband drags her to a temple so a priest can beat the evil spirits out of her. As I twist fistfuls of hair into a massive bun at the back of my neck, strong gusts continue to hit my face, and the curls around my forehead whip at my temples.

When I finally turn away from the door and toward the inside of the car, I am struck by the emptiness, the quiet of first class. Nobody is inching in front of me, threatening to steal my breeze. On the bench facing me are a tall college girl in a pink T-shirt and a squat lady in a faded yellow salwar kameez with white embroidery. Between them are two whole inches of empty space. In the general compartment, four or five women will squash onto one bench together. The last one to jostle in will tell the others to "shift, please," until at least a third of her behind is on the seat. And she'll hang off the edge like that, straining her hips and thighs, because if she doesn't sit there, someone else will.

Seats by the window with maximum airflow are in high demand, like gold at Diwali, or a fair price for onions. At this time of day, the ladies' general compartment is so packed that nobody who boards at Bandra gets breeze. Only a few months ago, in the pre-monsoon heat that drives the entire city into random fits of rage, some fat, middle-aged woman with green glass bangles thought she could elbow me out of a seat I was about to squeeze into. She didn't know who she was dealing with. Somewhere in the scuffle, her glass bangles snapped, scraping into my wrist, cutting deep enough to leave a mark. I got the seat in the end.

Apart from the extra room and the softer seats, there's not much difference between the compartments. First-class ladies pay ten times more so they can buy space for their first-class hips, I guess—and more air for their first-class noses, too.

Outside, the city flies by, followed by the mangrove swamps that protect the city from storm surges, then Mahim Creek, choking on thickened blue-black sewage. Now we're passing a row of squatting bare bottoms. The pink-shirt college girl wrinkles her nose, but the naked bums greeting the Harbour Line passengers in the morning light make me smile.

The first time I laid eyes on Bombay was like this, from the window of a train. That was sixteen years ago, when I was seven. The city had only just been renamed Mumbai, and I was merely hours away from being renamed Rakhi myself.

Our train rolls into Mahim Station, and only three women board the first-class compartment. I peek out onto the platform to see thirty or so women fighting their way into the general car. I duck back into first class. One more stop in this breezy compartment can't hurt. As soon as we start to move off, one last woman hoists herself into the first-class car, leaning back on the wall opposite me.

Shit. It's Gauri Ma'am. We're moving too fast now for me to jump out. I slouch down, lowering my head. She hasn't seen me and I intend on keeping it that way, at least until I can slip out at the next station.

Gauri Ma'am, or Gauri Verma as she's known in the newspapers, is the executive director of Justice For All, the NGO where I work. Ma'am is one of India's biggest human rights lawyers. I know this because when she gives interviews to the papers, it's my job to cut the news stories out and keep them in a big yellow folder. Gauri Ma'am leads a team of lawyers who argue human rights cases and do social justice campaigns, fighting for the rights of Dalits, Hijras, blind people, children, prisoners, women, that sort of thing. "Champion of the Exploited," they sometimes call her in the papers.

Lately, Gauri Ma'am has been talking about how we have to focus our efforts. When I say "we," I don't mean me. I don't get involved in this social justice funda. That's for the lawyers and interns. My job is photocopying important papers I'll never understand, and boiling tea for everyone several times a day. Accepting deliveries, going to the post office, organizing things here and there. And, of course, taking care of the foreign interns, who somehow require more attention than small children. Ma'am calls me her office assistant. Most people would just say "peon" or "office girl," but Ma'am says our office doesn't endorse classist language. Still, I take home less than a quarter of what the others earn per month.

Gauri Ma'am dabs the sweat from her upper lip with a starched white handkerchief. With her wire-framed glasses and cropped peppery hair, she stands at least a head taller than me. Her broad hips and bulky shoulders are swathed in a gray handloom-cotton salwar kameez. Standard Indian intelligentsia look. Pulling her BlackBerry from her purse, she punches at its tiny keyboard with her thick thumbs.

Trying not to make any sudden movements, I hold my breath and drift farther away inside the train, but she glances up from her phone and frowns. "Rakhi?" Her eyes narrow. "What are you doing, riding in first class?"

"Ma'am, by mistake—"

"If the ticket inspector comes, you'll be fined for traveling without a pass." She presses her lips together. "How much is the fine these days?"

"Two hundred fifty rupees penalty, Ma'am, plus the first-class fare . . . So, three hundred."

"That much, only?" Gauri Ma'am tilts her head forward, raises her thick, black eyebrows, and pauses as if she has just made a closing argument in front of the Bombay High Court, before lowering her eyes to her BlackBerry screen once more. She doesn't have to say anything else. She's good like that.

Rubbing the back of my neck, I return to the doorway without a word, ready to switch compartments at the next station.

"Accha, listen," Gauri Ma'am says. "There's a new intern starting this morning. A Canadian. He's a Harvard graduate student. We've never had someone from Harvard before."

What's Harvard? And why is she telling me now, only? Usually I spend a good month preparing for a foreign intern's arrival.

"He can sit at the empty desk in the corner. And when we get to VT, fetch a bottle of mineral water for him. I don't want to hear any this-that about loose motions in the first week."

The train rattles on. I scan the advertisements plastered all over the car's interior. Most of them are written in English. Gauri Ma'am made me take lessons when I first came to work for her. "Your spoken English is slow and choppy, but you read and understand well," my tutor told me. "You just have to converse more." I told him I got plenty of practice while babysitting the foreign interns at the office, which was a lie, because those firanghis mostly talk to each other, only. I read over a sign with big black block letters: "Ramesh Balakrishnan, astrologer, offers help with all problems in the life: marriage, infertility, in-laws, divorce, health, disease, accident, evil eye . . ."

Before I can finish the list, I feel two hard taps on my shoulder. Then an unfamiliar, stern voice says, "Ticket."

I glance back. It's the squat woman in the yellow salwar kameez who, moments ago, was sitting with her hands folded in her lap. Now she's got an ID card around her neck and the smug sneer of an undercover ticket inspector on her face.

"Ticket," she says again, her lips curling.

"Wait one second." I rustle through my bag, pretending to search for a ticket I don't have, clinking coins together for dramatic effect. If Ma'am wasn't here, I could stall the inspector until the train slowed into the next station, then hop out and sprint down the platform. Nothing I haven't done before.

But Gauri Ma'am is here, and she's staring me down. What would she do if I made a run for it? Scold me? Force me to pay the fine? Send me to Dr. Pereira every day instead of once a week, when I already hate having to go at all? Or worse, would she fire me for cheating the railway? I'd be jobless. Nobody would hire me. I'd have to live on the street again. And then what?

I shove those thoughts back into a distant corner of my head while I continue to push coins around in my purse.

"This ticket must be in here somewhere," I mumble.

Gauri Ma'am clears her throat, then steps forward and wedges herself in between me and the inspector, her legs planted wide.

The inspector ignores Ma'am and starts to scribble a ticket with a blue pen.

"Put that away, right now," Ma'am demands.

The stone-faced inspector glances up from her notepad, oblivious that the woman towering over her has argued twelve different cases against the government at the Supreme Court of India, and won eleven of them. "If I don't see her ticket, she pays the fine. Three hundred rupees."

Gauri Ma'am raises her voice now. "The only reason she is riding in first class is because these damn trains are stuffed beyond capacity. What is she supposed to do, let ten of them pass her by until she can get in? Tell me," Ma'am bellows, "is being on time for work only a privilege of the rich?"

When the other women on the train start to peer up from their newspapers and mobiles, Ma'am calls out to them. "Ladies! Are any of you bothered that this girl is riding in here?" The women glance at one another, but none of them answers Gauri Ma'am.

"You see?" Ma'am turns her attention back to the inspector. "Go on. Deal with actual problems instead of troubling yourself with who's traveling in which compartment."

Unmoved by Gauri Ma'am's rant, the inspector finishes writing the ticket and tears it from her notepad. That's when Ma'am snatches the paper from the inspector's hand, crumples it in her palm, and flings it out the moving train. Then she lowers her voice and leans in very close to the inspector's face. "If you try and write another ticket, I will lodge a formal complaint about you with the BMC. And you know none of the goondas who run this city will bother defending you."

The ticket inspector takes a step back.

"Thousands of people are waiting for a job like yours to open up," Ma'am adds. She holds out some creased bills. "Take this."

Without missing a beat, the ticket inspector seizes the money and slips it into her pocket. Cracking her knuckles, she steps off the train at King's Circle Station.

My ears burn from embarrassment. India's top human rights lawyer just offered hafta? For me?

"That was a tip, not a bribe," Ma'am grunts at me. "And how many times must we go through this? You must work at undoing all these bad behaviors with Dr. Pereira, or you'll keep finding yourself in situations like this."

"Ji, Ma'am."

Frowning, she pulls out her handkerchief again and wipes her forehead. "I can't keep bailing you out, Rakhi. You have to behave like an adult now. Nobody lives a life without consequences."

"Ji, Ma'am."

Ma'am eyes the rest of the women on the train and then glances back at me. "This city is mutilating itself with these bloody class divides. If they did away with this first-class nonsense, there would be more space for everyone."

Now is not the time to point out that she herself travels in first class.

For the rest of the journey down the Harbour Line, we travel in silence, until our train rolls into VT station, its final stop. The inside of VT is a drab warehouse filled with soaring ceilings, old trains, thousands of people, and a few extended families of crows who glide from beam to beam, raining shit everywhere. On the outside, though, it looks like a grand palace. The kind of place where firanghis stop to click photos.

Gauri Ma'am says that fundamentalist governmentwalas renamed Victoria Terminus as Chhatrapati Shivaji Terminus after the Maratha warrior king, even though it was the Britishers who built the station. That was in 1996, a year after Bombay became Mumbai and VT became my new home. A lot of names changed then, but no one I knew called the station CST, so neither did I. Babloo, the other street kids, and me, we knew the building inside out, all its main arteries and hidden veins. We learned who was allowed to go where, who wasn't, and how to get there anyway. We named all the gargoyles on the outside of the station after famous movie villains— Gabbar Singh, Mogambo, Kancha—and we steered clear of the beedi-smoking older boys who also lived around the station, dodging their violence, offers of hard drugs, and attempts at sex. Well, we tried, anyhow.

I hop out of the car before the train grinds to a halt, waiting on the platform for Gauri Ma'am to descend with the other first-class ladies. She plods toward me, hands me twenty rupees, and waves her handkerchief, motioning at me to keep going without her. "Go buy water for the new intern. I'll see you at the office. And make it quick, haan?"

I weave past slow-walking older women, sinewy porters with large parcels atop their heads, and half-asleep stray dogs sprawled on the ground. A little girl with a tangled ponytail, sun-bleached yellow T-shirt, and tattered orange shorts steps out in front of me.

"Just one rupee, didi," she moans, her cupped hand outstretched my way. "Didi, didi, one rupee."

I shake my head no and she pivots to the woman behind me. I could teach that girl a few things. You have to relax your eyes, for one. Droop your upper eyelids, specifically. But no dramatics. Quiet crying can double or triple your earnings with firanghis. And don't take no for an answer. Following someone closely—but not too closely—also works.

"You have big eyes, and you're a girl, so you'll make good money begging," Babloo told me the day I arrived in Bombay. So, when a particularly good target came along—a firanghi, usually—I would walk up to them and release big, fat, silent tears. Pocket change fell freely into my outstretched palm. Once, I built up to a carefully timed whimper and managed to squeeze a five-hundred-rupee bill out of an old gora with beige socks pulled up to his pale, freckled knees. I told only Babloo about the money. We hid it behind a pile of bricks in our little laneway and spent it, bit by bit, on movies and food. That was after we finally managed to find a shopkeeper willing to take such a large note from us.

When I was twelve, Babloo and I were picked up by the police, and that was the end of my time on the streets. I haven't seen any of the other kids we ran with since. I heard some girls ended up in the brothels of Kamathipura, to no surprise. Most of the boys got involved with local gangs. One of them became a political goonda, terrorizing Muslim shopkeepers and taxi drivers from Uttar Pradesh. A couple of them are dead now. But I never heard anything about Babloo.

When I returned to Bombay five years ago, I circled around the city for weeks, asking if anyone knew Babloo's whereabouts. Nobody around VT had a clue. Not the beediwala, not the poori bhaji guys, not even the old ticket-selling uncles waiting for retirement. I still scan the faces of thin-limbed beggars to see if any are his.

The road outside VT crawls with morning traffic. A chauffeur-driven jeep honks furiously at the bicycle delivery boys carrying four-foot-tall stacks of newspapers. Sidestepping a bullock cart that appears out of nowhere, I turn three corners to Sai Krishna Vegetarian Lunch Home. Outside the restaurant, potato vadas crackle and hiss in a huge black kadai filled with hot oil.

"One Bisleri," I say, motioning toward the large water bottles in the fridge behind the counter. Ma'am prefers me to buy this brand for firanghis because the plastic bottle is sturdy enough for them to reuse, even though they end up chucking them anyway. I count out some of my own coins and point to the kadai. "And one of those."

Even though Gauri Ma'am is waiting for me to hurry back, freshly made vada pav is impossible to resist. I tear off the paper wrapping and sink my teeth into the soft white bun and then the crispy fried potato inside. The tamarind chutney is sweet and tangy. I wipe my oily fingers on the hem of my kameez and grab the cold, sweaty water bottle for the intern.

As I turn a few more corners to reach the Justice For All office, beads of cold water roll off the bottle and onto my hands and down my wrists. I dab the wetness onto my throat. It is refreshing for a few seconds, but then the water dries, leaving my neck hotter than before. I roll the bottle against my cheek, behind my ear, shaking my shoulders a little to help the water roll farther down my back.

Mid-bottle-rub, I hear a foreign-sounding voice behind me. "Hi, excuse me?"

I turn around, yanking the bottle out of sight. A light-skinned man in a pressed white shirt and shiny brown shoes walks up the street toward me. A dark blue BMW idles behind him, too wide to pass by a small lorry blocking its way. The driver squints out at the buildings on either side of the narrow lane. Using the back of my hand, I try to brush the vada pav crumbs from the corners of my mouth.

Up close, the man's face shines like buttered toast and his brown hair is neatly combed. "Excuse me? Speak English?"

I nod yes.

He breaks into a wide smile and holds out a small piece of paper with an address written on it. "Do you know the Maarrr-tray-eeya . . . no, May-treeya Building? My driver thinks it's on this street." His voice has that familiar firanghi drawl where they stumble over and then spit out Indian names they've never heard before.

I nod again and point down the lane toward our office, which sits on the second floor of the Maitreya Building, an old four-story structure with monsoon-blackened outsides, fungus-dashed ceilings, and a lift that's always out of service.

Before I can tell him that I'm going there myself, Gauri Ma'am's voice cuts through the air: "Ah, this must be our new intern from Canada." She plods down the lane toward us, beaming.

Ma'am and the firanghi exchange greetings, and she tells him that the office is a few steps away and she'll be ready for him in an hour. She trudges along and calls out to me in Hindi. "Take him upstairs and get him settled in. And show him around the office, introduce him to the others."

The firanghi jogs over to the BMW, bends down so his head is level with his driver's, then points my way. Once the car disappears, he jogs back to me. His eyes are a muddy green, and his eyelashes are thicker than mine. Pleasant-looking, in that Jawaharlal Nehru sort of way. Tall, like so many firanghis are.

"What's your name?"

"Rakhi," I say, rubbing my arm.

"Alex Lalwani-Diamond," he says, his hand hovering over his chest.

I want to laugh. A name like that, and he couldn't figure out how to say Maitreya?

GAURI MA'AM'S HUSKY VOICE THUNDERS from across the office. "Rakhi! Have you cleaned up the empty desk for the new intern?"

"Ji, Ma'am. Almost done."

With a damp blue towel, I wipe specks of dirt from what's supposed to be Alex's computer mouse. Bombay grit gets everywhere. It blows through the windows daily, caking furniture, lodging itself under your fingernails.

She calls out to me again. "Where did he go?"

"Sitting in the waiting area." I peek out from behind the computer to see him standing before a faded prisoners' rights poster by the front door, stroking his chin. We printed those posters a few years back, when we still had money to waste on things like that.

Gauri Ma'am grunts something about how the new intern was supposed to arrive much later in the morning. "So eager, these Canadians."

I set down the mouse, now several shades lighter than how I found it. A vinegary scent swells as I wring the towel out in the morning light. Last Monday, one of our other foreign interns, Saskia, found five newborn kittens taking shelter beneath her desk. I used this same towel to scoop the kittens up while a raging Saskia shrieked about everything that was wrong with India. I left the kittens outside on a piece of cardboard behind a parked bicycle, hoping their mother would turn up before the rats.

Showing the foreign interns around when they first arrive is one of my jobs. This year, we have Saskia and Merel, two Dutch graduate students who have been with us since the middle of May. For Saskia, the office is too hot, the tea is too sweet, and she complains of employee abuse whenever one of the senior lawyers asks her to go to court to file documents. Merel is always taking photos of herself with her digital camera. A few weeks back they returned from a mini holiday in Rajasthan, and Merel showed everyone pictures from their trip: Saskia winking beside two villagers in bright pink turbans; Merel raising an eyebrow and frowning into a beer bottle by the hotel pool in Udaipur; both girls in the middle of the desert, riding creaky old camels dripping with faded multicolored pompoms.

I work the musty towel over the computer screen, leaving sideways streaks that won't go away no matter how hard I wipe.

"Hey, Rakhi?"

Startled, I turn around to find Alex behind me. Who told him to come in?

"Are there other interns working here? Or is it just going to be me?"

"Yes," I say. "Two girls."

He lowers himself onto an office chair a few feet away. It's off balance, so he tilts down on one side. In his starched white shirt and shiny leather shoes, he looks like he should be working at a bank with sparkling white tiles and glass doors. Not a human rights law office cluttered with lopsided chairs and stacks of yellowing papers bundled with string, and dusty cobwebs fluttering from the ceiling fans.

"Where are these girls?" he asks, fiddling with the knobs under his seat.

I shrug. How should I know where they are? I haven't spoken to

Merel and Saskia since the kitten drama. "Pata nahin," I mutter to myself.

"Sorry," he says with a laugh. "My Hindi's a little rusty. Can you say that in English?"

How do I reply? *I am not know? I do not know?* "I . . . no know," I offer.

Alex gives me one of those polite nods that's meant to show he understands, even though he doesn't. Firanghi classic.

Lately, Merel and Saskia have been showing up three days a week only. A year ago, Gauri Ma'am might have cared. These days, though, she has more to worry about than a couple of unpaid interns bunking off. Her funding agency in England is only giving her half the money she needs for the next year. Back in April, one night after everyone had left, I overheard Ma'am on her phone. "I understand you want us to make cuts," she said, her voice straining, "but the need for our work is critical—I simply cannot scale back." The conversation ended soon after, and Ma'am stayed at her desk for a long time, rubbing her temples. The next morning, she fired three of the junior lawyers, shut down our satellite offices in Assam, Gujarat, and Tamil Nadu, then lectured everyone else about something called "efficiency." I didn't bother asking what it meant.

"Rakhi," Gauri Ma'am shouts from her office. "Show him around the office, na? Do I have to tell you how to do everything myself?"

"Ji, Ma'am," I call back. Turning to Alex, I stand up. "You come? See office?"

"Sure, that's great."

"Building old. Lift no working," I say, opening the doors leading into the corridor. "Men's toilet this way."

He peeks his head out into the hallway.

I lead Alex back through the waiting area and into the lawyers' workspace, a U-shape formation of desks pushed up against the wall at the front of the office. It's separated from the interns' workspace—a unanimous request from the lawyers once Justice For All started hiring firanghis to work for free.

"All lawyers working this space," I say, and a few of them turn their heads toward us, eyeing him.

I've steered Alex back to his workstation and left him there when Bhavana, the lead lawyer in Justice For All's anti-human-trafficking cases, calls me to her desk. "So," she says in a low voice. "Who's that guy?"

"I don't know. Some firanghi."

She studies me carefully, flipping her shoulder-length hair to reveal a gray streak that grows wider every week. "Arre, you were talking to him, weren't you?"

"He's an intern from Canada, I don't know anything else."

"The interns always start in May. Why would Gauri Ma'am hire one in July?" Bhavana asks, resting a finger on her chin. "And why wouldn't she tell any of us?"

How should I know?

"Is Vivek Sir aware of this?" Bhavana continues impatiently. "Gauri Ma'am would at least tell him, na?"

"Tell me what?" an amused voice asks from behind us.

It's Vivek, the second-most senior lawyer at Justice For All and the kindest person in the office. He's slogged away on all Gauri Ma'am's major cases since she founded Justice For All twelve years ago. He used to have his own practice, a tiny office in the central suburbs, but he gave it up to join Gauri Ma'am, who consults with him on all her decisions, big or small.

"Sir," Bhavana says, rising to her feet. "Did you know there's a new intern here? Look—see that gora sitting over there."

Vivek peers at Alex through his old-fashioned round frames. "How do you know he's an intern? He could be a guest. Some journalist, perhaps."

Bhavana points to me. "Rakhi said it."

Vivek's already-rounded shoulders slump a little more. "Gauri Ma'am hired another intern? What for?"

Sensing a slew of questions that only Gauri Ma'am can answer, I walk away to see if she is ready for Alex, but her office door is still shut. By the time I return to his desk to finish cleaning, Saskia and Merel have finally arrived for work and have pulled their chairs up beside him.

"We're doing the fieldwork portion for our master's in international development studies at the University of Amsterdam," Merel says. "We're here to research how people use the legal system to protect informal housing settlements. What about you?"

"Well, I'm starting my master's in public administration in September."

"Where?"

"Harvard," he says, with a hint of a smile.

Merel and Saskia trade looks, clearly impressed.

It took me about a week to tell the girls apart. Saskia is shorter, has a silver nose ring, and gets angry a lot, while Merel is taller, has a Hindi tattoo that says SHAKTI on the inside of her lower arm that she is always trying to conceal, and is often happy to let Saskia fight their battles. Now they are both twirling their stringy blond hair around their fingers as they lean in toward Alex, their eyes bright and full of longing.

"You're only here for two months, then?" Saskia asks.

"It was kind of a last-minute thing."

"And where are you staying?"

"With my aunt and uncle in Pali Hill," Alex informs them.

"How do you have family here?"

"My mom's side is Indian."

"Ohhhhhhh," they say, in unison.

"Now that you say it, your face is kind of Indian," Merel says.

"And your skin color, too, a little bit," Saskia chimes in. "But your name isn't."

As Alex tells them his long last name, I reach past Saskia for the keyboard on his new desk, turning it over in my hands and thumping its backside. A few months' worth of crumbs, little black and brown hairs, and a dried-out spider fall out. Saskia huffs, rolls her chair to the right so she can see Alex again, then resumes drilling him about where he's from ("Toronto, that's in Canada"), how long he's been in India ("About a month"), if he speaks Hindi ("Here and there"), and what he wants to do after Harvard. ("Is it cliché of me to say I want to make a difference in the world?")

As Alex, Saskia, and Merel continue chatting, I slip between his computer monitor and the wall, dusting at the cobwebs that coat the tangle of wires behind the desk. I don't talk much to the interns. For one, they hardly talk to me. And the English lessons Ma'am made me take were only good for reading and writing, not speaking. I'm slow to form full sentences, and if I make a tiny error, like "you is a lawyer," people snicker, if they understand me at all. Speaking English feels like sinking into the slowest of quicksand while nobody can be bothered to hold out a hand.

"So, where's Pali Hill?" Merel asks Alex.

"It's a little neighborhood in Bandra. It's a suburb. Close to the sea."

"What an amazing location," Saskia purrs. "We've been up to Bandra a couple of times for dinner."

"Yeah, it's nice. Lots of trees, relatively quiet."

"Quiet? You can't be serious," Saskia says, raking her fingers through her hair. "I'm convinced there's not an inch of peace to be found in this city."

Merel turns to me and says, "Don't you live in Bandra, Rakhi? You're practically Alex's neighbor, no?"

When I don't reply, she repeats herself, slow and deliberate: "Neighbors? You and Alex, side-by-side homes, you know?"

I know what *neighbors* means, kuthi, I want to say. But not only are we not neighbors, we are so many worlds apart. Pali Hill is a hi-fi part of Bandra West, with flamboyant gulmohar trees, lime green parakeets, and luxury flats by the sea. Behrampada, on the other hand, is open sewers, monsoon floods, and seventy thousand people crammed into multilevel hutments east of the train station.

I give Merel a polite nod, though. "Yes, close only."

"Come, Rakhi, sit with us," Alex says now, leaning back in his seat. "So where do you live?"

I perch warily at the edge of a chair. "Me, near Bandra Station. East side."

"East, eh? I've been visiting my aunt and uncle here since I was a kid, but I've never been to Bandra East. What's it like?"

What's in Bandra East? I swallow, unsure of how to respond. "Highway is there . . . flyover . . ."

He stares at me, waiting for more.

"Bazaar . . . vegetable and fruit bazaar . . ." What else do people sell? "Clothing bazaar . . ." I'm not sure what more to tell him. Big cowsheds? Tiny temples? Rows and rows of political signboards still wishing everyone a happy Navratri, nine months later?

"So, same as everywhere else," Alex offers.

"She lives in the slum by the train station," Saskia blurts out, clearly bored by the pace of this conversation.

Alex fixes his large green eyes on me. "Really? How long have you been there?"

"Five years," I say, scratching at my cheek.

"Where did you live before that?"

The three interns wait for me to respond. I take a deep breath. "I coming here, to Bombay. Gauri Ma'am, she taking me to stay there."

Saskia smirks. "Job perk, is it, living in a slum?"

"This office pays your rent?" Alex says. "That's pretty amazing."

"No, I paying."

Saskia turns to Merel. "I doubt it would cost much more to just live in a shitty apartment."

"She'd probably live somewhere better if she could afford it," Merel replies. "Perhaps she could put some money away. Or go to one of those microcredit banks?"

"I thought those banks are set up for, like, people who are actually poor by Indian standards. She has a steady income, at least," Saskia says.

"Saskia!" Merel elbows her friend. "If she lives in a slum she's obviously poor."

I grit my teeth while they continue to talk about me as if I'm not even there.

"I'm sure the slum isn't that bad," Alex says to the Dutch girls. "I read an article recently about how living conditions in slums vary. Some are kind of nice, right?" He glances at me hopefully, as though I'm going to reassure him that I, his neighbor, live someplace decent.

Merel sighs. "Have you ever been in one? Vivek took us to one a couple of times to meet with clients. It's awful, even by Indian standards. Crowded, dirty . . ." She twists her face like she's tasted sour milk.

Alex turns to face me, as though he's giving me a chance to respond.

Seizing my dirty towel, I stand up to walk away from this bhenchodh conversation when, without warning, Gauri Ma'am appears behind us, clearing her throat. The girls spin back to their computers and flip open notebooks. I give the table a final, useless wipe.

"Alex," Ma'am says, "we're very pleased to have you here all the way from Canada. Come, let's have a chat." She gives him a tired smile, even though it is barely ten-thirty in the morning. Alex springs to his feet and follows closely behind her. The interns always start off keen like that.

Before disappearing into her office with Alex, Gauri Ma'am calls out for me to make tea.

"Ji, Ma'am," I call in response, scrambling to the tiny kitchen at the back of the office, where I fill the large aluminum pot with one part milk and two parts water. It sits flat, barely warm yet, in spite of the flame it's sitting on. I wish I could feel that undisturbed. Instead, I'm seething, trying to brush off the interns' stupid comments.

Why do you live in a slum? Why don't you go to a microcredit bank? What must it be like, being a starched-shirt Pali Hill rich boy like Alex? Or these white girls with yellow hair, all of them coming to

India to dip their toes into our shit, pretending like our problems are their problems, then going home and never coming back?

I tuck an escaped curl behind my ear, then grip the steel can of tea leaves sitting on the counter as I stand at attention at the gas stove, scanning the watery milk for signs of a boil.

And why should they care about my life? Who asked them to? Maybe it's Gauri Ma'am's fault, always using my life story as a teaching moment for new staff. Especially the foreign interns when they start complaining about how demanding the work is. "There is always hope," Ma'am will say, "even when a positive outcome seems impossible." And then she'll tell them about how her very own assistant ran away from an abusive uncle in Bihar, grew up on Bombay's dangerous streets, and then was taken in at the Asha Home for Destitute Girls, where Gauri Ma'am was a trustee. "You see Rakhi, over there? She learned to read and write, she learned English, and now she is a productive member of society. A self-reliant, independent woman," she'll declare, her voice triumphant. And the firanghis listening to the story will turn to gape at me if I'm nearby, and I'll nod a couple of times and then back away, because it's embarrassing to be invisible one minute, and then completely exposed the next.

Ma'am doesn't tell people the entire story, though. She doesn't tell them about the begging, the stealing, the beatings, and certainly not about the paanwala. Or Magistrate Kapure. Or Babloo.

Hot milk froths over the pot and onto the stove with a loud hiss. Startled, I turn off the gas.

Vivek pops his pudgy face into the kitchen. His modest paunch peeks in, too. "Head in the clouds, Rakhi?" He chuckles, handing me a cloth to wipe down the milk dribbling down the sides of the single-burner stove. "Still haven't heard why we're taking on a new intern all of a sudden, have you?"

"No, sir." I start the tea over again. The kitchen smells like burned milk.

Vivek leans against the doorway, scratching the part of his neck where a spray of tiny, dark brown moles sticks out from his collar. "It's unusual, isn't it? To hire someone out of nowhere."

"Sir, interns are unpaid, na? What's the problem?"

"You have a point there. And Saskia and Merel just told me he's a Harvard student. We don't get many people from American Ivy Leagues through here. I suppose there's no damage done."

Sick of talking about these interns, I try to change the subject. "Sir, how are your daughter's marriage plans going?"

I've heard Vivek tell Bhavana about the mounting costs of his eldest daughter's wedding to some Marwari businessman. Even with his salary and his wife's small income from making lunch tiffins for office people, he's already taken out two high-interest loans to pay for unexpected demands from the groom's family—a deposit for a flat and a new motorbike. Bhavana referred to this as dowry, but Vivek was quick to dismiss it as "part of our culture."

"Well, we got the pandit to examine their horoscopes and he's found a date in October."

"So soon? That's only three months away."

"My wife refuses to question the stars. Tell me, Rakhi, how auspicious can a wedding date be if you can't even rustle up the money to pay the expenses by then?"

I don't say anything. The milk reaches a violent boil, but this time I bring it back down to a quiet simmer without a mess. The tea buds release inky beige clouds into the burbling pot.

Vivek appears lost in thought for a moment, then puts on a smile. "Make mine without sugar, okay?"

"Of course, sir."

Once, I tried to count how many pots of tea I'd made at the office. Twice a day, two hundred and sixty-one days a year, for five years. I thought I should subtract at least ten days for Independence Day, Republic Day, and Gandhiji's birthday, and six or so days for Hindu festivals, both Eids, and Christmas. Then I remembered to subtract more days for periodic political riots, that time the terrorists shot up

VT and the Taj Hotel, and all the other times Gauri Ma'am instructed us to stay home. Not that she ever takes time off herself. She is unmoved by the constant fataak of fireworks at Diwali, or the human traffic jams of Ganesh Chaturthi, or fear-mongering from political goondas.

After distributing the tea to the lawyers, I return to Gauri Ma'am's office with the last two cups.

"Oh no, Ruby Aunty isn't my *real* aunt," Alex is saying as I push the door open with my hip. "But she's close friends with my aunt and uncle here in Mumbai."

"Well," Ma'am says, clearing space on her desk for the tea. "Rubina tells me you are very keen to learn about the work we do, and you're pursuing graduate studies at Harvard University in September, is it?"

"Yes, I'm starting a master's degree in public administration in international development at the Kennedy School in September."

"Marvelous," Gauri Ma'am says. "We like clever people around here. You know, my daughter, Neha, was accepted to Harvard for her doctorate. To study engineering."

Any chance to brag about Neha. I set the tray down slowly so I can listen to more of this conversation.

"How'd she like it?"

"She turned it down. She got a full scholarship to study in Rochester."

"I guess that makes sense," he says.

"It'll be so valuable for you to have this experience before you begin your studies. I'm glad Rubina Mansoor could connect us on such short notice."

Rubina Mansoor? Did I hear that correctly? The actress from the nineties who used to go by "Ruby M"? What is she doing sending firanghis to Justice For All? There's hardly any buzz about her these days, besides the odd picture of her posing like a peacock on page three of the *Mumbai Mirror,* with that developer husband of hers, the one whose billboards are plastered all over the city.

Alex takes a loud slurp of his tea.

"Rakhi," Ma'am says, "there must be a fresh packet of biscuits in the cupboard. Bring a plate."

I hurry out to the kitchen to find two closed packets and an open one. Ma'am serves fresh biscuits to important guests only. And in the Justice For All rankings, interns are only one step above me. I fish a biscuit out from the already-opened packet, snap it in half, and cram both pieces in my mouth. These ones don't taste too stale. I place six of them on a plate. "Never serve more than three biscuits a person," she once told me, after I put ten biscuits on a plate. "I'm not running a langar hall." With a plate of hardly stale biscuits in my hand, I rush back into her office.

". . . I've been in Mumbai since April, actually. I wanted some international work experience, and my uncle has a business here in the city, but once Ruby Aunty mentioned your office, I decided to go for something more aligned with my interests."

"What kind of business does he do, your uncle?"

"He exports leather goods to Europe."

"Aside from that, have you ever worked internationally before?"

"I helped build wells in Honduras, actually. In my third year of undergrad, for some clean-water project my university was connected with. Basic construction work. But we were so bad at it," he says, chuckling, "that each night the villagers had to rebuild the structure so that we wouldn't know what we'd built was unsound. When I found that out I felt so foolish. Like, what was the point? Why were we there in the first place?" He shrugs as though none of it was his fault. "I didn't know any better."

Gauri Ma'am folds her hands together in her lap. "It's rare to hear a Westerner acknowledge the futility of their work in developing countries."

"I'm Indian, too, don't forget," Alex says.

"Aap Hindi bolte hai, kya?"

"Thoda thoda," he says, smiling sheepishly. "I try, but my Hindi's pretty weak. We never spoke it at home, since my dad isn't Indian."

Gauri Ma'am nods along, as though his explanation is perfectly acceptable. Imagine if I'd said the same thing to her about English. *We never spoke English on the street, that's why I'm so bad at it.* I set the plate down in front of them.

Ma'am watches Alex take a biscuit. "You realize we can't pay our interns, yes? I stressed this to Rubina several times when she asked if I'd take you on."

"I know. It's okay, I've got enough money saved up to last me until September, and my room and board are free, so . . ."

"Tell me, why a master's in international development? Why not go to law school? Or get an MBA?"

"Well, it's a pretty prestigious program. And there are a lot of professors there whose work I follow. I want to learn about complex public problems and find the tools to design solutions that work."

"What kind of tools?"

"That's the question, isn't it? Do we find ways to shape public policy and law from inside government? Or do we come up with more entrepreneurial fixes? From what I've read about your work, you're firmly on the side of the latter solution."

"When our governments neglect their responsibility to protect human rights, what choice are we left with?" She turns to me and frowns. "You're still here, Rakhi?"

I dip my head and make my way slowly to the door.

"India is not like Canada," I hear her say. "When you go searching for justice here, you have to work twice as hard."

That's her classic line for all the interns when they first meet her. And they always eat it up. As I shut the door, I see Alex nodding vigorously and scribbling in his notebook, hanging on her words.

Once Gauri Ma'am takes Alex away to introduce him to the lawyers and set him up with some reading, the rest of the day drags on. The ceiling fans whir, churning steamy air around the office. Even though my hair is pulled back in a thick knot, my neck stays hot and sticky. Gauri Ma'am only turns on the AC when it's over ninety-five degrees outside, usually in May and September. The rest of the time, like today, the office is hotter inside than it is outside. "It's a waste of money. Money we don't have," she once barked at a sluggish Vivek, whose sweat stains bloomed big under his arms and all over his back.

I put on afternoon tea, forgetting to make Vivek's without sugar, but he slurps it back without a word, smacking his happy lips. Merel and Saskia vanish by two o'clock, so I drink their share over the kitchen sink. I sink into an afternoon daze while rearranging all the English books in the library by subject.

Gauri Ma'am said this task would benefit me more than it would the office. "Each time you read a book title, ask yourself what it means. Flip through the pages. Scan the table of contents. Practice your reading comprehension. Believe me, this will help you more than it helps me."

Yawning, I pick up three books, running my fingers over their embossed spines. In the heat, they feel heavier than usual. *Workers' Rights and Labour Laws. Right to Shelter: International Instruments, National Policies, Judgments. Against Mandatory Pre-Marital* HIV *Testing.* The HIV book's pages are damp, and speckled with black dots of mold. I place it and a few others into a separate pile to show Ma'am. She should know her books are rotting.

After some time, I trudge to the kitchen to wash everyone's empty teacups. They clink and clatter in the sink. Peeking out to make sure nobody is heading my way, I lower my face under the tap and gulp down mouthfuls of cool water. Gauri Ma'am once told me I shouldn't drink from the tap like this because this is not how people behave in an office. Vivek pointed out that I should be careful with tap water, since waterborne diseases peak during monsoon time, when the gutters overflow and the streets flood up past your knees and high tides threaten to crash over the seafront walls. But I can't be bothered to switch on the wall-mounted purifier and wait three minutes for it to debug and sputter out a tiny dribble of slightly cleaner water. It's not like Behrampada's communal taps have purifiers. Anyway, people like me have iron stomachs.

Mid-drink, I nearly hit my face on the tap when I hear the loud crack of a phone slamming down hard. A long, muffled scream rings out. Wiping my chin with the back of my hand, I wander out of the kitchen to find the lawyers gawking from their computers and notebooks, eyebrows raised. The sound has been sucked out of the room so hard I can hear how dry Bhavana's throat is when she swallows.

Then a noise comes from inside Ma'am's office, like a wall is being kicked. "Bastards!"

Vivek's muted voice emerges from the office as well. "Gauri, we can try to—"

"Someone must have paid them off. It's outrageous!"

Her shouting continues, and Alex eventually gets up from his chair, motions to Ma'am's office, and asks if someone should go in. Bhavana puts a finger to her lips and glares at him the way my neighbor Tazim does right before she gives her son a tongue-lashing.

After fifteen minutes of muffled shouting, Gauri Ma'am emerges with her bag on her shoulder, her face tight. Vivek walks out behind her, staring at the floor. Standing in the middle of the lawyers' workspace, Ma'am clears her throat. "Everyone, pay attention, please. Phones and books down. The Bombay High Court has turned down our petition for leave to appeal the Chembur slum decision."

The shouting makes sense now—the Chembur case was Ma'am's biggest one this year. Nobody says a word until Bhavana breaks the silence with a bark of nervous laughter. Along with Vivek, she's been working closely with Gauri Ma'am on it. "H-how? This must be a mistake—"

Ma'am speaks up again. "I know you all have questions, but I'm late for a meeting. Vivek is in charge until I return. He will tell you what you need to know." We all watch her turn on her heel and storm out the door, letting it slam behind her. I wonder if she really has a meeting or if she just needs to go somewhere she can scream loudly.

Vivek looks as startled as the rest of the lawyers, but he takes a breath and turns to face them. "For those who don't know what Gauri Ma'am means"—and here he glances at Alex—"the Bombay

High Court won't let us appeal the Chembur decision to the Supreme Court."

"What's the case about?" Alex asks. Some of the lawyers wince at this firanghi's ignorance. The Chembur case even made international news a few times this year.

"It's a public-interest litigation case that we filed against the state government last year after they bulldozed a slum in Chembur, an eastern suburb in Bombay. They wanted to take the land back to build a new bus depot."

"Did people die?"

"Nobody died. But many lives were uprooted."

"Not just uprooted, *destroyed*," Bhavana adds.

"Yes, like our clients the Prasad family," Vivek continues. "They had invested all their savings and pinned all their hopes on their eldest daughter, Tulsi, who was studying for her medical school entrance exams. The government scheduled the demolition two days before her exam, without giving any notice, which is expressly prohibited under international law. We're arguing for fair and just compensation, and resettlement for the family and for the rest of the slum-dwellers who were displaced unfairly."

"And the High Court decided not to compensate them?" Alex wrinkles his forehead.

"The Bombay High Court found that the government gave adequate notice, which they very clearly did not. And now the High Court is saying they won't let us appeal the decision."

"Okay, and the girl who missed her exam—"

"Arre, you can get the details later," Bhavana snaps, banging her fist on her desk. "Vivek Sir, why did they deny the appeal?"

Vivek's gaze wanders for a moment, then he sighs. "I don't know. We weren't expecting this to happen. We were really counting on this appeal, not just for the slum-dwellers but also to raise our public profile."

Bhavana holds both palms to her cheeks, her eyes wide.

I don't understand why these lawyers get so dramatic about their work. It's not like it was their homes that were demolished.

"What does Gauri Ma'am want to do next?"

"Well, procedurally, our next step is to file for special leave to appeal directly to the Supreme Court, which they can do when a High Court refuses to give a fitness-of-appeal certificate."

Bhavana sits back in her chair. "How do we know if that will work?"

"Gauri Ma'am will find a way. You just have to trust her on that. We all do."

....

When Gauri Ma'am finally returns to the office, most of the staff have already left for the day. She marches straight into her office and slams the door shut. I can tell she's still furious.

Moments later, Alex, who has been making calls outside in the dingy stairwell, comes back in clutching his silver mobile phone and, picking up a pen and notebook from his desk, heads straight for Gauri Ma'am's office. From my desk in the library, I scramble to stop him, but before I can reach him he's already opened her door and entered without permission. I stand helpless at the threshold of her office, bracing for Ma'am to give him a piece of her mind.

"Ms. Verma? I don't mean to disturb you, but where's the nearest taxi stand?"

I can see Gauri Ma'am raise her eyebrows. I'm sure she's about to throw him out of her office, but instead she peers up at him. "It's on M.G. Road. You know where that is?"

"Afraid not." He holds out his notepad. "Could you draw a map for me? I'm not familiar with this area."

Ma'am sets her wire frames on her desk and rubs her eyes. "Rakhi, take this boy home in the taxi tonight," she says in Hindi. "Pali Hill's not too far from you. You can take the bus back to Behrampada."

Take Alex to Pali Hill? My heart sinks. I promised Tazim I wouldn't go back there.

"Yes, Ma'am," I mutter, since I really have no choice in the matter.

"And make sure he knows we're not paying his taxi fare."

After I give her a nod, she switches back to English. "Rakhi will accompany you in the cab." Then she slides her glasses back on and starts shuffling through a stack of papers on her desk. A cue for us to get out of her office.

Outside, the sky is a dusty pink, like the tissue paper we keep in the office latrine for firanghis.

"I usually don't need someone to escort me home," Alex jokes, as he trails behind me on the way to the taxi stand.

I ignore him and keep walking so we don't delay any further. Tazim was going to make chana for dinner tonight. It'll be cold by the time I get to her hut.

"No, really," he continues, "I was only asking for some help with directions. Not a babysitter."

I lead him under an enormous banyan tree, its ancient roots snaking down toward the pavement. Even after I hear him stumble into the banyan's dangling branches, I don't slow down.

"When I was working with my uncle," he calls out, "I'd get chauffeured to and from the office with him. But they only have one driver right now, so I have to share—"

"Only one driver, is it?" I say, coolly.

"The other one went back to his village. His sister was getting married, or something."

"Accha . . ." I don't think this boy realizes I'm mocking him.

"Anyways, I got a ride to the office today, but from now on I'll have to take taxis for this internship. The problem is that my aunt and uncle are so protective. They're convinced I'll get lost or kidnapped if I go anywhere else on my own."

Kidnapped? The idea is so absurd I can't help but snort out loud. Most of the firanghis I've met take taxis and autorickshaws everywhere. They even learn to take the trains, if there's someone willing to show them how.

"My aunt and uncle have lived in this city their whole lives, and they've never taken the local train. They're always talking about how it's not safe. I mean, how bad can it be?"

I suppose his aunt and uncle are right about this. One of the first things I learned from Babloo was how to choose a target. White-skinned people with black-snouted cameras dangling from their necks were the best for pickpocketing because they were too intimidated by crowds and traffic, so you could lose them easily. Distracted or stoned college students were next. Then it was rich ladies with small purses and big sunglasses, but they could be deceptively aggressive and usually came with a driver, so you had to be ready to run for your life.

At the taxi stand I wave over a driver, and Alex yanks open the cab door for me while peering up the road. "Where's the train station?" he asks as I slide across the faded orange-and-black fabric seat cover.

"There only," I say, pointing up the road.

His eyes light up as he leans down to face me. "Forget this taxi. Let's take the train. It'll be good to experience local travel."

No way. Not at this hour, when millions of people are leaving the VT area to go back home to the suburbs. I summon all the English in my brain to push back against this bakvaas. "Too much of crowd in trains. You getting hurt."

"I'll be fine."

"No, no, people are falling from train. Real Mumbaikar people, they are falling every day."

"I promise I'll stay away from the doors."

He doesn't stop, does he? "You know bombs? Sometimes bomb is on train." The last time it happened was five years ago, in 2006, but he doesn't need to know that.

"I doubt that will happen today."

"Gauri Ma'am getting angry. She is telling to me, 'Take Alex home, make sure Alex safe.' If you hurt, Ma'am . . ." This is exhausting. What's the English way to say it? "Gauri Ma'am mera dimaag kha jayegi."

"Say what?"

"She eating my head." I make food-scooping gestures with my hand and mouth as he frowns, clearly confused.

Alex takes a step back from the taxi to stare at VT Station. "Look," he says, "I'm taking this train with or without you."

The taxiwala, who has been eyeing me all along in the rearview mirror, smacks his hand on the steering wheel and yells at me to get out of his car.

At the VT ticket counter, Alex rejects my suggestion to buy a first-class ticket. "A regular ticket is fine."

"Too much of people in general, you going first class."

"Do you travel in first class?"

"No," I say, even though I did this morning.

"Then why should I?" He steps in front of me and buys his ticket, saying, "No first class, no first class, general ticket, please."

Ma'am will fire me on the spot when she finds out I let this boy die on the local trains. On the first day of his internship, no less. Still, I don't have the energy to fight in English with this firanghi today.

"Bandra Station," I mumble, irritated, when the ticketwala asks Alex where he's traveling to.

I say a quick prayer as the train rolls into the station, pulling Alex back by the arm as a dense crush of men struggle into the general compartment, seizing seats. When the other passengers have shoved in, Alex and I board the crammed train, sliding in between the other hot, tired bodies. I am the only female in the car, and the tip of my nose is barely two centimeters away from the yellow armpit stains of an older man who gives me a severe glare that says I shouldn't be occupying valuable space in the general compartment when there's space for me in the ladies' car. I tell him I'm accompanying the gora behind me, and he grumbles to himself as he sucks in his stomach and gifts me an extra inch of space.

Our train climbs north, up the Harbour Line. Squinting, Alex gazes out the door, watching the outside world go by. When we pass people walking by the tracks, he cranes his neck and then his body to catch a better glimpse. The passengers beside him shove back against him, clearly annoyed at his taking up more space than he needs. Do people not walk on train tracks in Canada? You can tell a lot about a firanghi's home life by the things they gawk at in India.

At Wadala Road Station, the compartment fills with twice as many people, and Alex's back presses hard into the front of my body. I hollow my chest to make it less awkward.

"How many more stations left?" he asks, twisting backward to meet my eye.

"Three. You are okay?"

"I'm good," he says, as two men push past him.

When we roll into Bandra Station, I put my hand on Alex's back and direct him toward the door before the train grinds to a halt. His once-crisp white shirt is now rumpled, sweaty, and half-untucked, and his muscles tense when I touch him.

"Stay close," I shout as we are lifted off the ground by a mad crush of men barreling out of the train.

Alex extends his head back to search for me, and his body jerks forward while someone elbows him in the side. "Oh shit," he yells, a slight tremble in his voice.

"Arre, keep moving," I shout.

General compartment crowds are like the sea waves at Juhu Beach: if you fight the current, you sink. Passengers get trampled by the people boarding the train from time to time. They're usually fine in the end, but when that kind of thing happens to a firanghi, the driver will stop the train and people will scream and make a big deal, as if everyone with brown skin has a duty to keep the white people safe. And if Alex takes a tumble getting out of a general-class compartment at rush hour, Gauri Ma'am will skin me alive. So I grasp the damp underpart of his arm to keep him afloat.

But then someone wedges between us and I lose my grip on his arm.

"Jesus Christ," Alex says, as he struggles out of the train with a pack of other men. His stiffened shoulders hike up to his ears. "Rakhi," he yells.

"Someone help him," I shout out, as I watch him falter. The next few seconds drag on forever as he tries to regain his footing. Finally, a small man with a thick moustache offers him an arm and he seizes it, white-knuckled.

Alex continues to shout my name as we stumble onto the platform. When our feet are planted back on the ground, I pull him by the elbow to the snack vendor booth so he can catch his breath while the other passengers shuffle up the stairs.

"He is okay?" the man with the moustache asks, inspecting Alex, who is panting hard.

I nod. "It was his first time on the train."

The man scowls at me. "What's the matter with you? You shouldn't take these people on trains. Not nice for them, or for us." He marches off.

Slumped against a wall post, Alex untucks the rest of his shirt, flapping it back and forth against his body. He stares me in the eye and breaks into whooping laughter. "I thought I was going to have a heart attack," he exclaims. He gathers himself, then waves at the small crowd on the platform that's formed to gawk at him. "I'm fine," he calls out. "Never been better."

He thinks this is funny? I cross my arms over my chest and take a step back. "Your flat is where?"

"My aunt's building is called Blossoming Heights. Not sure what street it's on. I'll try calling them again for directions," he says, reaching in his pocket for his phone.

Blossoming Heights? It can't be. My mouth goes dry. "Fountain?"

"Yes, a fountain, with some Greek-looking statue. Lots of flowers on the outside."

That's the one, with its high stone compound wall draped in thick fuchsia blooms.

My heart pounding, I hail down an autorickshaw outside the station, and we slide onto the torn, blue-vinyl foam seat. I instruct the driver, a tiny man with a mouth full of tobacco, to take us to St. Andrews Road.

Taking a deep breath, I brace myself as we zoom through traffic toward Pali Hill. If I can just get to and from Blossoming Heights without being spotted, Tazim will never know I was there.

THE LAST TIME I WAS in Pali Hill was in January. I had gone to help Tazim clean Persian rugs for this rich Sindhi family, the Motianis. Tazim cooks and cleans for the Motianis every day but Saturday, but this was a special job. A weekend job. She had been instructed to bring "someone trustworthy" with her, along with some proof of good character. I brought a quickly scribbled letter from Vivek, verifying that I worked for him as an office assistant and if there were any questions, to call him directly. Gauri Ma'am had gone to Delhi at the time, and there was no need to involve her.

A tiny white dog in a purple-sequined collar snarled at me when I rang the doorbell. "O-ho, Tango, that's enough!" Mrs. Motiani snapped. The flat was filled with naked sculptures, big vases filled with dead branches, and paintings the size of my entire tin roof. Tazim had warned me not to stare too much at Mrs. Motiani's things, but as she was giving us instructions on how much soap to use on the pile of carpets by the door, I noticed a little display case filled with tiny crystal animals. In that miniature sparkling zoo, I spotted a small elephant, its trunk outstretched. It reminded me of the pendant gifted to me on Chowpatty Beach so many years back.

Drawn in by the elephant's dazzling light, I placed a finger in the hollow of my throat, where the pendant had once sat all those years ago.

"Tazim, tell your friend I'm not going to repeat myself," Mrs. Motiani said, and Tazim elbowed me in the side.

Tazim and I had to carry the rugs down to the courtyard of Blossoming Heights. We washed them all day, brushing back and forth, before rinsing them clean, beating out the excess water, and laying them flat to dry. Outside in the yard, there was a stone statue of a woman holding a vase that poured a constant trickle of water, and I watched the soft, golden sunlight peeking through the tall, coiffed trees. Except for Mrs. Motiani surprising us with an inspection every hour, it hardly felt like work at all.

I didn't think Mrs. Motiani would see me pocketing the crystal elephant when I went up to the flat to collect my payment—and I was right. But a few days later Vivek got an angry call from Mrs. Motiani. Quick to understand that I was in trouble, he somehow convinced her that I had escaped town with a band of thieves and would probably never return to Bombay again. He was so believable she agreed not to go through all the drama of calling the police.

Vivek wasn't pleased at having to spin lies for me. Things got worse when Gauri Ma'am returned from Delhi and he told her what I'd done. That's when I had to start seeing Dr. Pereira every week.

Tazim didn't talk to me for months. When I passed by her hut she would ignore me. "Ammi, see, see, Rakhi Khala is here," her five-year-old son, Ayub, would say to her, thinking we were all playing a game where we pretended not to see each other. It carried on like that until Ayub caught chickenpox in April and I offered to take some days off work to stay home with him while she went to clean the Motianis' flat.

"Just keep away from Pali Hill," Tazim said, when I returned from the chemist with medicines and calamine lotion. "If Mrs. Motiani finds out you're still here, I'm dead."

"Why would she be mad at you?"

"She kept asking me if you had really run away with gangsters. I just said your hut was empty and someone else was living there, and you hadn't bothered to tell me you were leaving."

"Right." I laughed. "Because that tiny elephant was so priceless it was enough to run away and start a new life with?"

"Arre, you're not going anywhere unless you take Ayub and me along with you."

"Of course," I said, squeezing her shoulder.

In spite of the fallout, nobody—not Tazim, Vivek, Gauri Ma'am, or Dr. Pereira—ever asked about the crystal elephant. Sometimes at night, when I'm lying in the dark, waiting for the night terrors to fade, I remove the elephant from its hiding place in my old cassette player, and cradle it in my hand. I like to admire its finely cut tusks, the way it splits the light into little glints of rainbow. Memories flicker in my head of Babloo and me running down Chowpatty Beach, miles of shoreline stretching out in front of us, and I remember what it felt like to be completely free.

3

AFTER I DROP ALEX OFF, the autorickshaw struggles through the swollen intersection at Pali Road to take me back to Behrampada. Once we make it through traffic, we speed farther away from Blossoming Heights and I let my shoulders relax, resting my elbows on my knees. When I glance up, the autowala is staring at me in his rearview mirror. He's probably trying to piece together why a tall, handsome firanghi who disappeared past the gates of a luxury building was sharing an autorickshaw with a girl going to Behrampada. I would wonder the same thing, too.

I should have taken the bus home, like Gauri Ma'am instructed, but Alex pressed a hundred-rupee note into my hand before he got out and told me to take the rickshaw back.

"I don't have anything smaller," he said, thumbing through the cash in his leather wallet, after I explained the ride back to Behrampada wouldn't cost more than thirty rupees. "Don't worry, a hundred rupees is like . . . three Canadian dollars. The cost of a coffee in Toronto."

The interns always justify overspending in India by converting the price of things back into their home currency.

I hold Alex's hundred-rupee note up to the sky to check its watermark, but the light is fading, and the sky is a dull purple bruise over the city. The bill is clean and crisp, waiting for thousands of hands to crumple it in their pockets, sweat into it, drop it in a puddle, or slap it down on a table, all before it finally weathers away into a cobweb with Gandhiji's face on it.

By the time the autowala drops me off in Behrampada, it is almost dark, the mosquitoes are out for blood, and the gullies are lit up by televisions and crackling tube lights. In the first laneway, five homes in a row are all watching the same serial, the camera zooming in on the vicious, heavily mascaraed family matriarch before cutting to a close-up of her frightened-looking, heavily mascaraed daughter-in-law.

Around the corner, a giant billboard hovers not far away. It's all black, and features only seven swoopy words in sparkly silver:

The Marquis Bandra (E)
Status Redefined
Coming Soon

"What does that say?" Tazim asked me when it first went up. This was in May, shortly after she started talking to me again. Although I could read the words, I didn't know what they meant, so I wrote them down and asked Gauri Ma'am about them the next day.

Ma'am raised an eyebrow. "The Marquis? That's an international hotel chain. Why do you want to know?"

When I told her about the new signboard, she shook her head. "Because that's what Behrampada really needs—a giant luxury tower next door, and international business travelers complaining that the slum is ruining their view as they sip champagne from their balconies."

Farther down the lane, women wash pots and pans on their doorsteps. Hiking up the bottoms of my salwar, I hop between dry spots to avoid the mud running down the narrow walkway. I turn the corner to my lane only to see my landlord, Munna, waddling my way. His too-short shirt reveals the strip of flesh where his belly kisses the top of his crotch. He stops in front of me, thrusting his chest out. "Rent is due next week."

"You think I don't know that?" This chutiya is always after money.

"Rent was late last month, so you'd better pay early this time." His eyes travel down my legs, and linger on my bare ankles under my hiked-up pants.

I swiftly kick the hems down while staring him in the eye. "You can't collect rent early. Gauri Ma'am already told you that twice now."

He sneers, revealing stubs of gutka-blackened teeth. "Always with your Gauri Ma'am."

I try to slide past him but he blocks my way.

"You know, if it weren't for Gauri Ma'am, you'd be out on the street." He flicks his bright pink tongue against his bottom lip.

"Arre, move," I shout, and push past him.

"I want my money on time!"

"And I want my roof fixed," I call out, not bothering to turn around.

Gauri Ma'am knows Munna through one of the Behrampada community leaders. She fought a lawsuit for them against some big developer who forged a bunch of signatures saying some of the slum-dwellers agreed to giving up their land rights. Ma'am won, of course. And then there were the Bombay riots in 1992, when the whole country went mad after some Hindu mobs tore down the Babri Masjid up north. I was only four years old then, but Gauri Ma'am says that the governmentwalas and their Hindutva pitbulls started spreading rumors about Behrampada being a den of Muslim criminal activity, so hordes of angry young men ransacked the whole place in a brutal display of nationalism. They slashed throats and beat people to the ground while the police did nothing. A few years later, Ma'am helped many of the Behrampada slum-dwellers give statements to the Srikrishna Commission that investigated and condemned all that nonsense. So now, most people in Behrampada who survived the riots know Gauri Ma'am and feel indebted to her. Whatever their history, it works for me.

When I first started working at Justice For All, Ma'am came with me to sign my lease. After Munna mentioned that a single girl living on her own should be careful how she behaves, Ma'am marched right up into his face and told him, "If you let anyone touch Rakhi, I will personally see to it that your life is ruined. Do you understand?" Munna replied quickly, "Yes, yes, Gauri Ma'am. This girl will be safe. We will protect her like she is our own sister, I swear." Ma'am also made Munna give me the place at a discounted rate. When she wasn't paying attention, though, he shot me a dirty look.

In the five years I've lived in Behrampada, nobody has tried anything with me. Tazim has told me stories about women being attacked in our slum—people's sisters, daughters, wives. My door has a heavy iron deadbolt, but I've picked enough locks to know *that* is not what is keeping people out.

I walk up to Tazim's hut, which sits squarely beneath mine. When the people of Behrampada ran out of space, they just built on top of what already existed. There are even a few hutments that are now three stories tall, but they're not too common.

Tazim and her husband, Hanifbhai, left their village in Uttar Pradesh seven years ago. Hanifbhai was promised a job as a night watchman at a seaside hotel in Juhu, but when they got to Bombay all they found at the address was a sari shop and an angry watchman. So Hanifbhai found odd construction jobs here and there, while Tazim got work as a maid in Pali Hill.

Last monsoon, Hanifbhai left for the Middle East with a pack of young men from our slum. They were going to Dubai, they said. It was supposed to be like Bombay but with less rain and more money. Rumors churned over how many thousands of rupees these men had handed over in exchange for passports and visas. There was a farewell party in the little square in the middle of Behrampada. I stayed at home, but Tazim brought me a small plate of chicken biryani when the party was done. Soon after the men left, Tazim heard whispers that they weren't in Dubai at all, but in another desert called Saudi, working eighteen-hour days as manual laborers on blazing-hot construction sites, sleeping shoulder to shoulder on dirty kitchen floors. Passports were confiscated, wages withheld, and lashes doled out.

Gauri Ma'm told me it was probably worse than that. "At this point, they're likely just trying to borrow money for a ticket back to India. And if they run away, their employer will press charges and the police will fine them or threaten them with jail time. Or worse." I chose not to relay her thoughts back to Tazim. Like most of the families who sent their men away, Tazim refuses to believe anything is wrong. "He'll send money when he can," she says, though she hasn't heard from him since the new year.

With Hanifbhai trapped in the Gulf, Tazim supports herself and Ayub on the three thousand rupees Mrs. Motiani pays her each month. That's five thousand less than Gauri Ma'am pays me.

Tazim is sitting on a straw mat on the concrete floor, with a cloth rag slung over her shoulder, trying to force a piece of roti into Ayub's clamped mouth. "There you are," she says, as I hover in the doorway. "I was wondering when you'd be back."

"Got held up at office," I lie, sitting down on the floor, avoiding eye contact.

Ayub gazes up at me and whimpers like a tired puppy. "Rakhi Khala, give me chocolate," he moans.

Tazim lets go of him, and he bolts from her lap and zips in circles around the one-room hut yelling, "Choklitchoklitchoklit." She slumps against the wall, her arms resting on the floor. "I don't know who gave him sweets, but now he says he won't eat anything else."

"He'll eat when he gets hungry," I say, slapping at a fat mosquito feasting on my ankle. "Trust me."

Tazim gets up and makes me a plate of chana, roti, green chilies with salt, and a little bowl of lumpy curd. I pay her five hundred rupees a month and she feeds me dinner each night. Thirty meals should cost far less than what I give her, but with that money she buys better vegetables than she could usually afford, and I don't care to learn how to cook. Also, when I join her for dinner, Tazim likes to divulge the real-life masala stories she hears from the other Pali Hill servants: bored, rich wives sleeping with the delivery boy, their bored, rich husbands sleeping with the same delivery boy, that kind of thing. I can't stand to think how furious she'd be if she knew I had just come from Blossoming Heights.

"Any word from Hanifbhai?" I ask, stirring out the lumps in my curd with a piece of roti.

"Still nothing." Tazim's eyes follow Ayub as he darts in and out of the hut. Her voice thickens. "International phone calls are expensive." She doesn't have a mobile, so she checks in every day with one of the wives of the men who left with Hanifbhai.

I tear off a piece of roti and change the subject. "Tell me, how's your Motiani Memsahib?"

Tazim clasps her hands in her lap, half smiling. "Same, same. She has some big party tomorrow night. Had me press twelve saris."

"So many? Why?"

"Because she couldn't decide which one to wear."

We both roar with laughter. Ayub peeks into the hut, his eyes gleaming at the sight of his mother like this.

She carries on. "A sari in every style. Heavy Benarasi silk ones, net saris with crystals, georgette with large prints. Took me hours to prepare them all so she could lock the door and set out all her matching jewelries." Tazim loves to tell me tales of Mrs. Motiani's excess. I like that it gives us something to laugh about, especially since that woman tried to call the police on me for something as stupid as a useless crystal elephant.

"You know," I say, plunging some roti in dal, "she may have more money than we could ever dream of, but at least we can decide what to wear every day."

Tazim chuckles. "Even her nephew had the same problem today."

I dip a green chili in some salt and then bite into it. Tastes as bland as capsicum. "Who sold you these? There's no heat to them at all."

"The chilies? I got them at Santacruz Market." She grabs my half-eaten one, breaks off the stem, and takes a bite from the other side. "They're just a bit mild. What, you think this is some top-class hotel where you can just complain and get a new plate?"

Grinning, I snatch the chili back from her. "You were saying something about Mrs. Motiani's nephew?"

"Accha, this boy from Canada. I told you, didn't I? Came to work for Motiani Sahib, then quit because he wants to work with poor people."

I cough and a bit of chewed-up chili goes down my windpipe, where I can finally feel its heat. Could Alex be the Motianis' nephew?

"He didn't know what to wear to his first day of work," Tazim continues. "Mrs. Motiani told him to wear jeans-pant because he shouldn't dress too nice if he's working for poor people, but Sahib told him to wear formals so people would know to show him respect."

The chili is now singeing the insides of my throat and I hack violently into my hand.

"So I had to press—Arre, Rakhi! Drink something, na?" She thrusts a steel cup of water at me and I gulp the whole thing down.

"Chilies not so mild after all?" Tazim says, as I hand the cup back, gasping for air.

I shake my head, wiping tears from the corners of my eyes, my mind spiraling. If the Motianis are the aunt and uncle Alex is staying with, surely he will mention Vivek to them. And then it's only a matter of time before Mrs. Motiani finds out Tazim lied to her about me. This can't be happening. There's no way I can tell Tazim that Mrs. Motiani's nephew works at Justice For All. She'll panic about what Mrs. Motiani will do if she finds out Alex is working at the same place as me. And it took Tazim so long to start talking to me again after the crystal elephant incident.

As I'm rubbing my nose and sniffling, Ayub dashes back into the hut, launching himself back into his mother's lap. "Why is Rakhi Khala crying?" he asks, settling against her.

"Your ammi fed Rakhi Khala the spiciest chilies in Santacruz Market," I say, grateful for the distraction. "So mean your ammi is." I pretend to gasp for air and he giggles.

"Listen," Tazim says, pulling her braid from under Ayub's body and resting her chin on his head. "I saw some good karela in the market, your favorite. I'll cook it tomorrow for dinner. Be on time so it's nice and hot."

I smack my palm against my forehead. "Arre, I'll be late. I have to see that stupid therapywali then."

"Isn't your head fixed yet? How long will it take?"

"Gauri Ma'am will never let me stop," I say, tickling the bottom of Ayub's foot with my finger. "As long as I'm the problem, she doesn't have to deal with any of her real troubles."

THE FIRST DEAD BODIES I ever saw belonged to my parents. They lay stiff, side by side, on a sheet in our thatched-roof hut in Umaid-pur, white cotton balls plugging their ears and noses. They had been traveling on a bus to a nearby town, looking for work, when it rolled over. I had just turned seven.

People wailed all around me as I sat on my aunt's lap a few feet away from my dead parents. My aunt's tears fell on my head, wetting my scalp. Eventually, she fainted, and I crawled out of her lap to pick the cotton balls out of my father's nose. "Bansari, no!" someone screamed at me as a pair of hands yanked me away by the waist. Others joined in to slap me and call me a shameless girl, and I cried that I was only trying to help him breathe.

Soon after, my aunt packed up some of my clothes in a cotton sheet, knotted it at the top, and brought me with her to the city of Patna. My aunt and uncle's house was dark and small, and sat next to a butcher shop. Big flies flew in and out of the windows.

When my cousin-sister, Sita, who was three years older than me, wasn't at school, we would roam around the neighborhood together. Sita said she had overheard my uncle telling the neighbors that I should have gone to stay with my father's family, but they refused to take me in. I told Sita she was wrong, but what if what she said was true? I didn't have any memories of ever meeting my father's family. Still, had I done something to upset them?

One evening, my uncle cracked a tooth because there was a stone in his dal. Sita, my aunt, and I looked up from our plates when we heard a hollow popping sound. My uncle's face scrunched up, his eyes went big, and he moaned in agony. After he spit out the stone and some fragments of tooth into his palm, he lunged at my aunt, smacking her hard across the face. Dal and rice splattered on the floor.

Reeling from the blow, my aunt hunched against the wall, then jabbed her finger in the air toward me. "Blame Bansari," she whimpered, as he loomed over her. "She cleaned the dal today."

My uncle spun around to face me. "One more mouth to feed, and gives me nothing but trouble. You, come here," he roared. "When I'm done with you, I'm taking you to your haraami father's family."

I sprang to my feet and dashed out the door, grains of rice flying off my hand. My uncle followed me for a while, down laneways and through traffic, but I lost him in a sharp turn toward Patna Station, where the trains rattled in and out, sucking up and spewing out bodies as they went. I kept running through swarms of people at the station, afraid he'd catch me if I stopped, and leapt right into the first compartment I saw, before crawling underneath a vacant berth. The train started to move, but I stayed hidden there for two nights, watching feet shuffle through the aisle, listening to a concert of snores, farts, and rattling phlegm. When the conductor announced we were approaching the final stop, I crawled out and sat quivering on a hard, wooden seat by the window, dehydrated and delirious, watching the mangroves fly by. Without knowing it, I was seeing Bombay for the first time.

Once I got off the train, I sat alone at the far end of the strange, enormous station platform, my back against a concrete pillar. The air here tasted smokier than the air in Patna and Umaidpur. My parched throat felt as though it was coated in sand and nails and red chilies. When I coughed, it burned.

I longed for my mother to stroke my hair, or pick me up so I could fall asleep in her arms. I pressed my scabby knees up against my chest. Fatigue weighed down my head, eyelids, fingers, and feet.

Two policemen with thick moustaches strolled onto the far end of the platform. Their boots clicked like smooth stones hitting concrete. One policeman hooked his fingers in his tan belt, thrusting his pelvis forward. The other dug his pinky into his nose, scanning the station through dark sunglasses.

Up, up, get up, Bansari, I told myself. *The police will help you.* I put my weight on my hands and launched myself up, until my knees buckled and I stumbled back against the pillar.

A loud voice rang out from behind me: "Don't bother."

I turned to see a boy emerge from behind the pillar. He was skinny, with sharp shoulders. His stained white banyan had more holes than fabric, and his dusty blue shorts hung dangerously by a weak elastic waistband.

"Stay away from the Railway Police," he said, tipping his head toward the nose picker and the pelvis thruster. "They will only give you more headache."

"Who says I'm going to the police?" I said, turning away from him.

The boy smirked. "Look at yourself."

I gazed down. Bare toes covered in a muddy film. Green dress torn at the hem.

"All alone in this big train station, filthy, lips are chapped, hair is tangled. And now you're staring at those two gaandu policemen like they're going to give you a nice home, a bath, and some lunch." He laughed, dragging the back of his hand across his nose. It left a yellow stripe of mucus along the top of his wrist.

"Leave me alone."

"Did you come to make it in the movies? Become a big film star?" He cackled.

My stomach tightened. "No. My parents died. I ran away from my uncle."

"Why?"

"He's bad."

"What kind of bad?" The boy raised one interested eyebrow.

"He hits."

The boy frowned like it wasn't a big deal. "Just for that you ran away to Bombay, then?"

"To where?"

"You know that old filmi song, 'Yeh Hai Bombay, Meri Jaan'?" He threw his hands up. "Mumbai, Bombay, Bambai, whatever you want to call it, this is it. You just got off the Mumbai Superfast Express. Didn't you know that?"

Bombay? The city from the films? This big, dirty train station was Bombay? I pushed my hair out of my face and pointed to the police. "Are you sure they won't give me food?"

"I already told you they won't."

"But why? At least a biscuit? Some water, even?"

The boy sighed. "Chalo, let's see what they say. Don't say I didn't warn you." He took my hand and dragged me down the platform. "Arre ey, police! Police!" he called in a voice too big for someone so thin.

The startled policemen bolted upright, spotting the boy and me. Fingers dislodged from noses and curled around lathis. Pelvises jerked back into position. They began to walk quickly toward us.

"Want to feed us lunch?" the boy yelled. "This chokri is hungry! She'll have—what do you want?"

"Roti?" I suggested. I didn't know I had a choice.

The boy smirked at me again and continued calling out to the police. "She'll have one masala dosa! And I'll have mutton biryani! Extra chilies! Make it quick! Fatafat!"

The police started running our way, and I realized they weren't taking the boy's order. "Rascal saala," they shouted. "Come here! You're not supposed to be on the platform!"

The boy pulled me in the other direction. "You see?" he said as he led me past the ticket booth, out the doors, and into the blinding sunlight. The hot sun beat down on my head as we ran down a massive road, the biggest road I'd ever seen, filled with lanes of bicycles, motorbikes, honking cars, and lorries. I glanced over my shoulder as I followed the boy. The police were close behind us, waving their big, wooden lathis in the air, stomachs heaving.

Left right left right left left, we wove through side streets and cramped laneways. I couldn't believe how fast my legs were moving when I could barely stand just moments ago.

Finally, we reached a dark, narrow lane between two tall buildings. The boy slowed down and let go of my hand, panting. "Looks like we lost them."

The lane smelled like old soo-soo. A dog with three legs and one tattered ear sniffed at our ankles. The boy kicked at the dog, which yelped before hobbling away.

The boy stuck his arm behind a blue tarp nailed to the wall and pulled out a scratched-up plastic bottle of water. "Drink," he said, thrusting it at me.

I tilted my head back and drained the bottle. The water was warm, foul, and wonderful. When I finished, he grabbed the bottle from my hands, walked to the end of the block, and turned on a small tap sticking out of the wall. It sputtered a bit and filled the bottle only halfway before drying up. It was like he was milking a dry brick cow. He handed me the bottle again. The water felt cool on my cracked lips.

"Like I said, the police won't help you. They'll throw you in Dongri for loitering in the station."

"What's Dongri?"

"Jail. For children."

My face felt cold in spite of the heat. "Jail? What have I done?"

He shrugged. "You exist."

This didn't make any sense. Who was this boy? "Where are you from?" I demanded.

"Here. Bombay, only. You?"

"Umaidpur. I left from Patna."

"Where's that?"

"Bihar."

The boy rolled his eyes. "Unless your uncle files a report with the police, nobody here will help you. Trust me. They'll just throw you in Dongri so you're no longer their problem. They will pretend to search for a home for you, but they won't. And you'll have to stay there, in lock-up, until you turn eighteen. How old are you?"

"Seven."

"I'm eight, so I'm your elder. When I tell you nobody cares about kids like us, you should listen to me."

"And how do you know all this?"

He squared his shoulders and didn't answer.

My stomach growled. I looked the boy in the eyes. "Can you give me some food?"

"Does it look like I have food?" Then he spat at the ground and walked away, snarling.

I didn't know what to do. Should I find a train back to Patna? To the sure promise of broken teeth? I sat down against the wall and put my head between my knees. I wanted to cry but running from the police had left me light-headed. I closed my eyes so that the soo-soo laneway would disappear. It did, eventually, and I dozed off despite the never-ending sound of horns honking.

I woke up to someone kicking my leg.

"Leh. Take this." It was the boy, holding out a small glass of hot tea and a piece of pav. Light steam licked my nose as my shaky hand lifted the glass to my lips. I crammed the soft white bread into my mouth between slurps of tea.

"Listen. I've decided," the boy said, crossing his arms. "You can be my friend, but you have to pull your own weight. Or else you have to leave. Understand?"

I nodded in between bites.

"And I make the rules around here. Got it?"

"Yes."

The boy ran to the end of the laneway. "Salman, Pappu, Kalu, Devi, come!" he shouted. The power in his voice was startling. Two boys and a girl came racing around the corner, tumbling over one another. Another boy hobbled slowly toward us on an old crutch. They were all skinny and barefoot, like the first boy.

"My name is Babloo," he said, hands on hips. "And this is my gang. We stay in the lanes around that street over there, Mint Road."

"Mint Road?"

"It's some English name."

Besides *hello*, I didn't know a word of English.

"This is Salman, he's from Lucknow." A short boy with a thick nose stepped forward and puffed out his chest. He scratched his head, vigorously, then peered at his fingernails before wiping them on his T-shirt.

"And this is Kalu. He came from—"

"Jabalpur!" Kalu volunteered.

"Yes, some dump called Jabalpur. Look, see how dark he is. That's why we call him Kalu." He grabbed for Kalu's arm, but the boy jerked his arm away and hissed a "bhenchodh" under his breath.

"Her, Devi," Babloo said, "and him, Pappu." The girl and the boy on the crutch looked like brother and sister.

"So, what's your name?" Babloo asked me.

"Bansari Kumar," I told him.

"Accha?" He laughed. "Bansari Kumaaar?" Babloo repeated, mimicking me in a thick Bihari accent. Then he straightened up and made a serious face. "No. That name won't do."

Devi giggled, then leaned down and whispered "Bansari" to Salman, who slapped her on the arm. She slapped him back and he yelped. Babloo told them both to shut their bhenchodh mouths.

"I'm changing your name," Babloo said, as though the matter had been decided.

"Why? What's the matter with my name?"

"Well, for one, it's a buddhi's name. You can be anyone you want to be on the street. My father named me Mohammed, but I changed it to Babloo."

"What's wrong with the name your father gave you?"

"My father's a chutiya." A layer of sweat broke out over his face. Then he pushed his hair from his eyes. "Anyway, Mohammed is a holy name. For guys who go to mosque and pray five times a day. My life is too haraam for a Mohammed."

Salman piped up. "I am Salman Khan, biggest hero in all of India!" He flexed his thin arms and the others giggled.

Babloo said Salman's name was actually Khalid Siddiqui, but I shouldn't tell anyone that because his elder cousin had recently come here all the way from Lucknow to search for him.

I stared down at my feet. Should I keep my name? What if my family in Bihar wanted to find me again?

As if reading my thoughts, Babloo leaned forward with his hands in his pockets. "Nobody is going to come looking for you. Trust me." He stepped back, scratching his chin. "You have big eyes. Like Rakhi Tilak."

"Who's that?"

"Rakhi Tilak, filmi item girl number one! You don't know who she is?" He opened his eyes wide. *"Bhutan ki Baby?* She dances in the mountain song. You haven't seen it?"

I shook my head.

"Kidding me? Number one best movie this year. No, number one best movie ever. You know what Bhutan is?"

I told him I had never heard of Bhutan.

"Are you dumb or what? Bhutan is paradise. It has mountains and space to run around and momos to eat and waterfalls to swim in." He kicked a ball of crumpled-up newspaper lying near his feet. "Not like this garbage dump. I'm going to go there one day, to live. Get away from Bombay and the cars and these nasty people. And Rakhi Tilak is best. Anyway, that's what we're calling you. Rakhi."

Rakhi. I repeated the name in my head. *Ra-khi*. It didn't seem so bad. And this Babloo seemed to think highly of whoever this Rakhi Tilak was, which was probably a good thing for me.

Then I said it out loud. "Rakhi. Okay, I—"

"Listen," Babloo said, "you should know it's not easy out here on the street. But we do what we want."

"Complete freedom," Salman piped in.

Babloo nodded. "We earn, we eat. That's it."

He said they sometimes sold hair clips or nail polish or trinkets on the trains, or begged, or dipped their hands in people's pockets. "You'll learn as you go. Just be careful of three things," he continued. "Number one, the police. They're always looking for criminals to lock up."

"Are you a criminal?"

"To them, yes."

I thought about how the police had run after us, waving their lathis, like they were chasing rats out of the station.

"Number two, the older boys who also live around VT Station. They're always high on solution."

"What's that?"

"Drugs. Little bottles called Eraz-ex they buy from the xeroxwala. When they're not high, though, they'll want your gaand. If you give it to them, they own you. You'll have to do things for them."

"What things?" And why would anyone want someone else's gaand?

Devi snickered at me, nudging Kalu.

Instead of answering me, Babloo kept talking. "And number three, be careful of the cars."

"The cars?"

Babloo laughed and motioned to Pappu, leaning on his crutch. "When you sleep on the footpath, you're bound to get hit once in a while, no?"

.... **4** ....

THE DAY AFTER ALEX'S ARRIVAL, I'm sitting on the floor of the library sorting through the books in the environmental justice section. I run my finger over the rough fabric of *Green Democracy (First Edition)*. The title is embossed in a dull gold, like the slightly bent bangles Gauri Ma'am wears on her wrists. I lean forward to shove the volume into its new home on the sagging bookshelf.

The change from yesterday's rickshaw ride makes a faint clinking sound in my pocket. The coins are warm and the bills are soft when I pull them all out. Forty-four rupees is enough for a kilo of bananas, now that the prices have jumped. Or five average-tasting vada pavs from outside Bandra Station, which have somehow managed to stay the same price over the years, unlike those of the other vada pav stalls across the city. I doubt Alex would want the change from the rickshaw ride, but the one time I kept change from Gauri Ma'am, which was only twelve rupees from buying a pack of felt pens, she made me handwrite the definition of the word "accountability" a hundred times in my notebook. I stopped at eighty because I knew she wouldn't actually count the lines.

Through the empty space between the library shelves I can see Alex at his desk, bent over a book. He's alone in the intern workspace, Saskia and Merel having left the office earlier that morning after twenty minutes of clicking around on their computers and flopping back in their seats. He laces his fingers together and pushes them up toward the ceiling, stretching his body. The thin band of his bright yellow underwear peeks up over his brown khaki pants, like a sunrise. He doesn't notice his chaddis showing, and arches his back, pushing his hips out. Exhaling loudly, he snaps forward, releasing his arms. Then he gets up from his desk and heads out the front door and down the stairs.

Now that he's gone, I hurry over to his desk, stacking the change from the rickshaw ride beside the book he's been reading, *Community Mobilization in Slum Upgrading*. I flip it over and see he has underlined an entire paragraph:

> The urban poor's overreliance on social networks for security and support is derived, in part, from the erosion of their trust in government, which is usually warranted. Evictions, demolitions, and removals, as well as patronage and corruption, have all served to undermine the establishment of robust urban governance. Together with rising land prices, and poor-quality and crumbling services, they have given rise to a sense of insecurity and social exclusion, which can erode social connectivity.

Penciled in the margin, in messy capital letters, he's written, *ASK RAKHI ABOUT THIS*. And as if that's not enough, his computer screen lists search results for "Slum + Bandra East."

Is he trying to find out where I live? What if he makes the connection between me and Tazim, or me and the Motianis? With an eraser from the supply closet, I remove all his pencil marks from the page, pressing so hard the paper crumples. Gauri Ma'am would be furious to see one of her library books defaced. The book slams shut when I drop it on the desk beside his change.

Eventually, Alex returns to the office with a large, sweaty bottle of cold water. He takes a long swig and then sets it down next to the money I left on his desk. He turns the notes over, counts the coins out, and wrinkles his forehead, then scoops it all into his cupped palm and gets up from his chair. I turn my attention back to the stack of books on the floor.

Unlike the tip-tip noise of the shiny shoes he wore yesterday, his leather sandals make a muffled slap against the floor. "Rakhi, did you leave this money for me?" he asks, peeking into the library.

"Yes," I say, not looking up. "From autorickshaw."

He smiles and edges closer to the bookshelf. "I told you to keep it."

I carry on sorting books, waiting for him to leave.

"Listen, can you tell me where I can get some lunch around here? Looks like the other interns have gone off without me."

"I am busy," I say, pointing to the pile of books on the floor, just as Vivek walks by the library.

"Arre, show him where Sai Krishna is, at least," he says in Hindi. "She'll take you," he tells Alex, switching to English.

"Vivek Sir, I don't have time," I protest.

"Rakhi," he says, in his kind, fatherly way. "Supporting the interns is part of your job, too, remember? You have to learn how to balance your priorities."

"Teek hain, Sir." I get up, slide past Alex, and pop my head into Gauri Ma'am's office.

She grunts when I appear in her doorway. "What is it?"

"Ma'am, the new intern wants lunch so I will take him to Sai Krishna and come back."

"Why can't those Dutch girls take him?"

I scan the interns' workstation behind my shoulder to check if Saskia and Merel have returned: computers still off, purses still missing, chairs still pushed in. "Ma'am, they left, I think."

She takes off her glasses. "Where to?"

"Lunch, perhaps?"

She snorts, folding her arms over her stomach. "Those girls have taken enough time off to cover the rest of their lunch breaks for the next month."

I hadn't realized she noticed.

"Rakhi," she says, picking up a pen and pointing it at me. "Take Alex to Sai Krishna, then go find those girls and bring them back here. I have to give them a research assignment for the Chembur appeal. If they're not back in an hour they're finished here. They can hitchhike back to Europe, for all I care."

Back at my desk, I dial both Saskia's and Merel's mobiles, but neither of them respond. I pick up my little handbag and call out to Alex. "Come. I taking you Sai Krishna. Lunch."

He springs to his feet and shoves his wallet in his pocket.

As we weave down two small lanes and through foot traffic, I keep checking behind me to make sure I don't lose him. He stops to gawk at everyday things, like a crow sitting on top of a cow's back, or a wiry man in a checkered blue lungi pushing a wooden cart piled high with thick metal rods.

"Should have brought my camera," he says, walking past a dog poking through plastic bags in a rubbish heap on the side of the road.

Sai Krishna, with its bright orange sign and yellowed walls, buzzes with the weekday lunch crowd. Downstairs in the outdoor eating area, office workers hunch over South Indian thalis. Past a glass door and up a flight of stairs is the air-conditioned upper level of the restaurant, where the same food costs five rupees extra. A lanky teenage waiter with a thin moustache hands Alex a menu.

"Join me for lunch," Alex says.

"No, you stay. After thirty minutes I am coming back."

"If you're going to eat elsewhere, why don't I just join you?" He backs away from the confused-looking waiter.

For lunch I usually eat a leftover roti and two bananas in the office kitchen (three if I'm really hungry), but I don't tell him that. "You stay here. Dutch girls gone. Gauri Ma'am is saying I am finding them."

Alex sits down on a bench and slaps his menu in front of him.

"God, it's hot here." After a short pause: "What will she do if you disobey her?"

What is he going on about? "Means?"

"At my uncle's office, I once saw the accounting manager take off his shoe and hit his assistant with it. His actual shoe. Whacked him on the shoulder."

"Arre, no, Gauri Ma'am not hitting me." I slap my palm to my forehead. What kind of imagination does this firanghi have? I adjust my bag on my shoulder. "I am going."

"Just stay for lunch," Alex says, flipping the menu open. "I'll pay. We'll eat fast and I'll help you find those girls."

"No." Why won't he let me leave?

"Up to you. But if you want to know where a couple of white girls would go to hang out, you might want my help." He turns the menu to the next page. "Just eat with me first."

My stomach hardens. He's probably right. I sit down on the bench beside him.

The waiter comes back and asks me if Sir would prefer to sit upstairs, in the air-conditioned portion.

"Actually, I wouldn't mind," Alex says, wiping sweat from his forehead.

Upstairs, in the mostly empty, chilled room for people who don't mind paying more money for the same food, the waiter sits us next to a man with a moustache digging into a giant cone-shaped dosa. Hanging on the peeling wall above Alex's head is a foggy portrait of some rosy-cheeked white child eating an ice cream cone. I drain both metal cups of tap water on the table and order Alex a Bisleri as he studies the menu, sounding out the appetizers to himself.

"Medu vada, rasa vada, sambar vada . . . You'd think they'd have pictures so people would know what's what."

I pretend not to hear him and tell the waiter to bring us two South Indian thalis. I haven't eaten in a sit-down restaurant since Ma'am took Vivek and me out for lunch on her birthday a few years ago.

In less than five minutes, two big steel plates arrive with little bowls of pumpkin sabji, fried potatoes, shredded carrots, rasam, sambar, cold curd, a tiny spoonful of lime pickle, and a creased papad, still hot from the fryer. The rice in the middle of the plate is soft and light, like grated coconut. It's nothing like the fat, starchy rice Tazim cooks.

"God, this is so good," Alex says, between mouthfuls. "Do you cook like this at home?"

"No." For a moment, I feel guilty for eating out in a restaurant when I'm supposed to be working. Then I tell myself I shouldn't feel bad. For one, I'm not even paying. Second, minding the interns is also my job. In a way, eating a thali with Alex is work.

He licks sabji off his spoon. "The maid makes food like this at home, but nobody really eats it. My aunt says her food is too oily."

I try not to grimace. "You are throwing food? Bin?"

"I don't really know what happens to it. It's not like we deliberately don't eat it."

I push rice around on my plate as he tips his head back and downs a big gulp of water from his bottle. As I watch him wipe his mouth with a napkin and dig back into his thali, my shoulders tense at the thought of Tazim paying for Ayub to stay at a crèche while she works an extra hour at the end of the day to prepare dinner for the Motianis.

"My aunt and uncle just like going out for meals, especially to non-Indian restaurants. A couple of weeks ago we went out with their friends to some new Italian place in Andheri. They all loved it. Ruby Aunty raved about how the pasta was better than anything she'd eaten in Rome."

Right. Rubina Mansoor, friend of Mrs. Motiani and now Gauri Ma'am.

As he goes on about how moved she was by the tomato sauce, I interrupt. "Food was not oily? You say they not liking oily food."

"Oh, right." He pauses for a second and dabs his mouth with the napkin again. "I don't know. People feel differently about olive oil.

Anyway, there was a long wait at the restaurant and my uncle bribed the waiter to give us a table. Just slipped him a bill." He stares at me, waiting for me to be as stunned as he is.

"This is India," I tell him. Even someone like Gauri Ma'am, whose whole life is about fighting this bribery-corruption stuff, slipped a ticket inspector some cash so I wouldn't get booked for traveling in first class without a ticket.

"So," Alex says, through a mouthful of rice, "what did you do after you dropped me off last night?"

I tell him the truth: I saw my friend, ate dinner, went to bed.

"Does your friend live in your . . . area?" He glances up at me, his spoon hovering over the pumpkin sabji.

"Behrampada?" I scan his face for any sign that he recognizes the name of the slum, but there's nothing. He hasn't even referred to Tazim by name, so how would he know where she lives?

"Is that what it's called?"

"Yes. She living downstairs to me."

"Do all your friends live near you?"

If Tazim is my only friend, then yes. I nod and mix the pumpkin and rice together with my fingers.

He stirs his rasam slowly. "Until I came to Justice For All, the only real conversations I've had in Mumbai have been with status-obsessed people who drink imported wine and get driven around in air-conditioned cars. I mean, I've been here three months and yesterday was the first time I've taken the local trains. It's like I've been sleepwalking, barely scraping the surface of this city."

"Means?"

"I've never eaten at a place like this, for example." He eyes the table, the ceiling, and the waiters as if they're covered in spiders.

"Sai Krishna? What is problem here?"

"Nothing! But you know what my aunt calls little restaurants like this?" He lowers his voice. "Diarrhea shacks. As if I would get sick from eating here."

"Arre, what diarrhea, you have clean Bisleri—"

"I'm not saying I agree, but listen: my family and their friends in Mumbai live in a small bubble. I want to see what I'm missing out on. You get what I mean?" Alex wipes his mouth again and rests his elbows on the table. "What was it you said about my uncle bribing his way into that Italian restaurant? 'This is India,' right? I only have two months until I head back to start my master's program, and I want to use this time to soak up as much of the real India as possible."

It's only his second day and already he's in his Real India phase. Most of the foreign interns go through it, but usually a little later on. Gauri Ma'am will send them to a small town or village to do some public education with the junior lawyers, and when they return to Bombay they toss their English guidebooks aside and start to wander the city, befriend strangers on the street, even trade their cigarettes for hand-rolled beedis. That's when Ma'am tells me to keep a closer eye on them. "They think they're invincible," she says. Worst case, they end up in the hospital for a few days because they were brash enough to ask for ice in the lime soda they bought at a roadside stall.

"This probably sounds strange to you," Alex says. "But I'd like to see the India you live in."

"Me? Why me?"

"Well, for starters, you live in a slum," he exclaims, loudly.

I focus intensely on picking up the last grains of rice on my plate. "Slums is everywhere."

"Where I come from, people don't live in housing like that and still hold down jobs and stuff."

You've made your point, I want to say to him. *Your family is rich. You are rich. You think you're trapped, but you'll never understand how lucky you are.* Instead, I push my empty plate away and tell him to eat fast, because we still have to find Saskia and Merel. He gives me an obedient nod and dips a spoon of rice into curd, then into his rasam, which drips all over the table.

"Why do you have to find them, again? Can't they make their own way back to the office? They're adults, after all."

"You are adult, na? But I am taking you home yesterday. Also, I am taking you to Sai Krishna."

He takes a big bite of the shredded carrots. "True. But it seems like Gauri treats you like her maid. I mean, she tells you what to do, and you do it, even if it doesn't make a lot of sense."

The English words flow quicker, easier, this time. "Gauri Ma'am telling Vivek Sir what to do. He also is maid?"

"Sorry. I didn't mean it that way. It's just that my aunt treats her servants like that. Like yesterday, she got her maid to iron, like, five outfits for one party because she couldn't be bothered to make a decision ahead of time."

Twelve bhenchodh saris, I want to say. Instead I examine my fingernails.

Alex relaxes his shoulders. "So how long have you worked at Justice For All?"

"Five years."

"That's a long time. How much longer will you stay?"

I shrug. "Don't know."

"Did you ever go to school?"

"I am high school pass."

"Any plans for college?"

"College?" I snort. "No."

"Higher education is a means of economic empowerment. Especially for women." He takes another sip out of his bottle, eyeing me. "You go to college, you get a higher-paying job, you make more money, you have more choices in how you live your life."

"Who is telling this?"

"Everyone. It's well known that the earning potential of a college graduate is much higher than a high school graduate, anywhere in the world. Did you know that in Kerala, the state government started investing in training and education for women selling vegetables in the market, and—"

"You are reading," I interrupt. "But you are not living here. You know nothing about India." I wish I could tell him he's no different than the other foreign interns who come here wanting to fix India and leave after two stomach bugs, whining about how much they miss clean air and something they call almond milk, which is apparently nothing like badaam doodh.

Alex holds his hands up. "You seem smart, and you're assertive. And you speak English. All I'm saying is you could do so much more than taking orders and playing hide-and-seek with Dutch interns."

"I no speaking good English."

"Are you kidding? Your English is fine. The key is to practice. Do your friends speak English?"

I shake my head. Tazim couldn't string together a sentence in English if she tried.

"Why don't you practice with me? We could hang out after work and just talk. And I could even help you apply to college if you change your mind." He gestures at the waiter to bring us the bill. "What do you say?" Alex prods. "It's a fair trade. You help me, I help you."

I stare down at the streaks of oil and curd on my plate. Of course the answer is no. Where would I find the money to pay for college even if I got in? And where would Alex and I spend time together? Not Behrampada, that's for certain. There would be all kinds of drama baazi about me entertaining single males in my hut. And Mrs. Motiani would absolutely call the police if I showed up at Blossoming Heights. Not to mention that Tazim would never speak to me again. And we couldn't meet at the office. Gauri Ma'am would find out and think I was disrespecting her if I applied to college without her involvement, especially after everything she's done for me.

The air in this chilly upstairs room makes me shiver. I clear my throat. "No," I say.

Alex shrugs and pulls a wad of cash from his pocket, throws some down on the table, and stands up. "Let's go find these Dutch girls," he says, swinging open the glass door to the humid afternoon.

On the road, I scan the distance for any sign of yellow hair, while Alex pauses to examine books laid out neatly on a purple sheet on the footpath. Rubbing the back of my neck, I shudder at the thought of what Ma'am will do if I return to the office without Saskia and Merel. Gauri Ma'am has less patience with foreign interns than she does with the rest of us. Last year, we had a British law student who suggested Justice For All provide her with a small stipend for her internship. Ten thousand rupees to offset expenses. "Did you hear that?" Ma'am called out loudly to Vivek from her office, in English, so the firanghi would understand. "They exploited our people for how many centuries? Stole our wealth, starved our people, butchered our borders, and now they want us to pay them 'a small stipend'?" Within a week, the student found another internship with some NGO in Delhi.

It's not that I care what happens to Saskia and Merel, but when Gauri Ma'am gets angry, her rage can spin out of control and there's no telling who else will take the hit. A couple of years ago, she lost a case—some public interest litigation about compensating acid attack victims. After the decision came out, she announced to the office that anyone who showed up for work later than nine in the morning would be sacked immediately.

"Maybe they're on a coffee break," Alex suggests as we walk past Fabindia, with its colorful stacks of overpriced handloom-cotton kurtas for tourists and Gauri Ma'am types. He steps into the store and asks the woman at the cash register if she knows of any nearby cafés, "something a European would like." Without hesitation, she points us toward the lane near Rhythm House. Fifty meters from the record shop is a stark white building with a stoop and big glass windows, revealing a narrow café with small tables and large paintings hanging on bright white walls. Sure enough, Saskia is there, leaning back against a dark wooden bench, stirring a tiny spoon in a fat white cup.

We walk up to the window beside two human-sized jungle-looking potted plants flanking the entrance. Alex waves at Saskia and her face lights up. Her smile wilts when she sees me trailing behind him. Inside the café, the air is cold and smells like a freshly opened chilled Bisleri, which smells like nothing. Everything in Bombay smells like something. I stand by the door while Alex slides in next to Saskia.

"We've come to take you back to work, madam."

She glances past him toward me. "Rakhi? What's going on?"

I take a step forward. "Gauri Ma'am saying you and Merel come to office now."

Saskia holds her hand out, palm facing the ceiling. "Did she say why?"

"Some work she has."

"Is that so? Well, Merel's in the loo. I'll have to wait for her." She turns to Alex. "The bathrooms here are way cleaner than the nasty ones in the office. Have a cappuccino with us before we go?"

"Sorry. We've got to head back, too."

"She does"—Saskia tilts her head in my direction—"but you don't." She pulls her bun out of its elastic and lets her limp hair fall down her back.

"Another time."

She tucks a few strands behind her ear and smiles. "I'll hold you to it."

I wish I could just leave rather than watch this moody firanghi try to flirt. Instead, I hover near the door, stepping out of the way each time someone comes in or out of the café.

"This place is pretty nice," Alex says, his eyes darting up to the skylights in the high, slanted ceiling.

Saskia nods. "It's clean. Air-conditioned. Peaceful. If I'm going to sit around all day doing no work, I may as well do it here, yeah?"

"What do you mean, 'no work'?"

She drains her coffee cup. "Merel and I came here to do ethnographic research on this public interest case with Gauri. The Chembur case. You know, meeting with slum-dwellers, community leaders, government officials. But we've been here since May and have barely done anything. Just running random errands and editing people's submissions on unrelated files. And it's not because there's nothing to do. But Gauri can't be bothered to carve out any time for us. We can't go back to the Netherlands with nothing to show for our time here, you know?"

Alex frowns and says nothing.

"I turned down a placement in Rio de Janeiro," Saskia continues, rubbing at her eyelashes, leaving a faint blue smudge under her eyes. "At least in Brazil you can wear a swimsuit on the beach without being gawked at. Or groped." She shudders.

"But do you really want to be working in international development just so you can lie on the beach?" Alex asks. "How do you build a real understanding of a situation if you're not immersed in it?"

"The only thing Merel and I are immersed in is not being taken seriously because we're white women. It's reverse racism."

"That's not a real thing."

"Wait until you experience it."

"Easy there," Alex says. "I'm only half white."

She smirks. "Lucky you."

I scratch my elbow, wishing they'd hurry up so we can leave. Everyone in here is staring at me, standing alone in the doorway: The woman making coffee behind a glass display case of biscuits and cakes. The white man at the table next to the girls, with a laptop computer and large camera. The tall Indian woman with him, with big tattoos of birds on both of her bare shoulders.

My stomach makes gurgling noises as the South Indian thali motors through my belly. I'm not used to eating so much in the middle of the day.

Merel emerges from the back of the café, wiping her hands on her pants. "Hey, Alex! You found our hideout!" She frowns when she spots me by the door, and slides down the bench next to Alex, who tells her Gauri Ma'am wants them back at the office.

Merel puts her hands behind her head, revealing her SHAKTI tattoo, which she doesn't seem too bothered about in here. "What for? I handed in some research to her a week ago and she hasn't even touched it!"

Saskia glares at me. "You're not going to repeat any of this to Gauri Ma'am, are you?"

I mouth the word no.

Merel sighs. "Well, if there's work to do, I guess we should go, then, yeah?" She gulps the rest of her coffee and slaps some bills down on the table.

On the way out, Saskia stops in front of the beediwala and rustles through her purse. "Two Gold Flake Light," she commands. The beediwala hands her two cigarettes, which she inspects closely. "Gold Flake, I said, Gold Flake!" she shouts, stomping her foot. "Am I speaking Chinese or what?"

The beediwala hardly knows any English, I want to tell her. Especially not the weird accented kind that she and Merel speak.

Back at the office, the interns plop down at their workstations while I knock on Ma'am's door. Her glasses are sitting on the desk, upturned, and she squints into her computer screen.

"What is it?"

"Ma'am, you asked me to bring the interns back."

"Did I?" She puts her glasses on.

"Ji, Ma'am. I found them and told them to come see you."

She murmurs to herself as she clicks her computer mouse. "Listen, Rakhi, shut the door when you leave. I have to make some calls." She turns her back to me and picks up her phone.

Outside, Saskia and Merel are waiting for me at their desks, Alex sitting beside them.

"How can it be hotter in here than outside?" Merel stretches out on her chair, fanning her neck with her notebook, her free hand hanging limply at her side.

"Well?" Saskia flips her hair behind her shoulder. "When are we meeting with Gauri?"

"Ma'am is busy." I watch the interns apprehensively, as their faces fall. "You waiting."

"Until when?"

"Don't know."

Saskia tilts her chin downward. "You don't know?" She turns to Merel, who is slumped so far down in her chair she's nearly sideways. "This is bullshit. We shouldn't be dicked around like this, yeah?"

Merel nods and shuts her eyes.

Saskia turns back to me and shouts out very slowly, "ESPECIALLY. WHEN. WE. DON'T. HAVE. ANY. WORK. TO. DO." Her eyes are two big blue stones on her reddening face.

Alex holds his hands up like a football referee. "Okay, let's just—"

"You can tell your boss I said that," Saskia says to me, as if I had anything to do with Ma'am summoning them. "Teek hain? Understand?"

Unblinking, I stare back at her. I want so badly to charge at this stupid gori. To force my hands on her narrow shoulders and ram her unsuspecting body against the wall. To see her fly across the office, her ugly blond hair trailing behind her. I want to see the shock on her face when she realizes it was me who shoved her.

Instead, I turn my back and march to the kitchen, my fists scrunched so tightly my knuckles turn white.

Gauri Ma'am would fire me if I laid a hand on Saskia. She'd say I haven't done enough to reform my old ways, that I am impulsive and not ready for the working world. That I'm a threat to her employees. She'd remind me that she even went so far as to get me a therapist. She's always acting like it will take a mountain of work to make me normal like everyone else. But what about the rest of these bhenchodhs?

By the time I've unballed my fists, Alex shows up in the kitchen, smelling like the rasam we ate at lunch.

"I told those girls they were wrong to be angry with you." His voice is soft.

But it doesn't matter, does it? Saskia and Merel aren't the problem. I am.

THE ACRID SCENT OF THE mosquito coil burning in the corner of Dr. Pereira's office tickles the inside of my nostrils, and I sneeze.

"Is the coil bothering you? The mosquitoes breed in that small marsh outside during monsoon season," Dr. Pereira says, her silver nose ring catching the light.

Pulling a handkerchief from my bag, I glance at the window where her potted plants are lined up side by side on the ledge, lit up bright green in the slants of sunlight. There are so many plants—leafy ones with tall stems, spiky short ones, even one with pink-striped leaves—all pushing past one another in the direction of the light. "If you shut the window it will keep the mosquitoes out."

"I prefer to have a fresh breeze coming in. Otherwise, the air can get so stale inside. Would you rather I closed it for our session?"

My back rigid, I lean back on the blue fabric sofa. The seat is so bouncy and soft I can never figure out how to balance on it. "I don't care."

She says nothing. Just crosses one leg over the other, the green linen fabric of her kurta crumpling further. She folds her hands in her lap, her face calm. She does this sometimes. Keeps quiet until I feel the need to say something so she will stop staring at me.

I didn't know what to think when Gauri Ma'am told me she would be sending me to a therapist for stealing a crystal elephant.

"What will the therapist do to me?" I asked.

"Arre, she's not going to do anything to you. If you put in the work with her, she can help you . . . cope. With your past, the way you behave now, the stealing, the lying. With adjusting to your new life. You'll go Wednesdays at six o'clock until you show some signs of progress. Don't be late."

The following day, I met with Dr. Pereira for the first time. She fidgeted with her silver nose ring, told me that our conversation was confidential, and insisted I call her Gitanjali. Then she started with her questions: *Why do you think you're here? What do you suppose Gauri Ma'am wants you to get out of these sessions? What does progress mean to you?*

I angled my body away from her. This had to be some kind of test to figure out whether to send me to a pagalkhana. I eyed the door, the window, and the door again, mapping out escape routes. Nobody was going to lock me up with a bunch of crazy people.

"Maybe you feel angry about Gauri sending you here," Dr. Pereira suggested. "Let's talk about that."

"Why, so you can tell Gauri Ma'am?"

"Why do you think I will tell Gauri Ma'am?"

"You tell me."

The next morning, Gauri Ma'am told me that Dr. Pereira had called her to say I was severely resistant to participating in our therapy sessions, but that she would be open to continuing to see me.

Snitch. I was right not to trust her. When I told Gauri Ma'am it was a waste of money to send me to therapy, she replied that what she did with her money was up to her, not me.

And so, every week, I show up at this office to be poked and prodded by this woman who sits there, watching me smugly, as if from behind some invisible wall.

I shift my weight in my seat. "Arre, are we going to start or what?"

"You're feeling impatient."

I tell her no, I'm not feeling impatient, but what's the point of me being here if she only wants to talk about mosquito coils? "I could be eating dinner at home with Tazim right now," I point out.

"Is that where you'd rather be?"

I gaze around her office, walls bright lemon yellow, green and orange cushions dotting the sofa. A white bookcase neatly stacked, nothing like the sagging, crooked ones at Justice For All. "Yes."

"Why is that?"

"Because I've come here every week since January, and I'm no different than when I started. But Gauri Ma'am won't let me stop. And you get paid to see me, so you're never going to tell me I'm done. So what, we'll keep seeing each other until one of us dies?" I pick at the little blue balls of fuzz on the couch. I can feel her staring at me. "Maybe I should just kill myself."

"Rakhi. That is a very serious thing to say." Dr. Pereira sits upright in her chair. "I don't actually believe you want to die, but I have to ask, how often do you have thoughts—"

"Arre," I groan, cutting her off. "I don't want to die. I just want to stop coming here, but I have no choice."

She scribbles in her notebook. I crane my neck forward to try to read what she's writing, but she's too far away. She glances up from her book. "Why do you feel you don't have a choice?"

"Gauri Ma'am says I have to see you to keep my job, and if I don't, I'll never learn how to 'participate in the world as a functioning member of society.'"

"Do you understand why she says that?"

"Everyone in that bhenchodh office behaves worse than I do, but they don't have to see you."

I relay the day's events—Saskia and Merel disappearing, Gauri Ma'am telling me to bring them back, Saskia's rage when Ma'am wasn't ready to see them immediately.

"And when you brought the Dutch interns back," Dr. Pereira says, tapping her pen against her notebook, "Gauri Ma'am did not acknowledge that she had asked you to bring them. And they directed their frustration at you."

"Arre, they shouted at me. Why are you using hi-fi language?"

"How did that make you feel?"

"They get to bunk off work, treat me like garbage, and keep their jobs. But I take one stupid elephant, one time, and I'm the one who has to have my head checked every week?"

Dr. Pereira tilts her head, the early evening sun lighting up her curls so they shine golden brown. "Do you really think the only reason you're in therapy is because you stole a crystal elephant once? Do you remember when we spoke about your trauma from what happened with the paanwala?"

I roll my head back. "Not this again."

"Here, I'll jog your memory." She flips through the pages of her notebook. "You said you believed nobody would ever trust you again. That you worry you are a violent and dangerous person, and the nightmares will never stop. That you have difficulty building relationships—"

I slap my palm down on the sofa. "I never said that. I said that's what Gauri Ma'am thinks about me. That's why she forces me to be here."

Dr. Pereira nods, scribbling some words in her notebook.

"What are you writing?" I yell, rising to my feet. "Why don't you reply to me?"

"What would you like me to say?"

"That I'm not a bad person."

"I never said that you were, Rakhi."

I fold my arms across my chest, shielding myself from Gitanjali Pereira and her calm voice and her stupid questions.

After a few moments, she tells me that expressing my thoughts is the healthy way of coping with feeling afraid and anxious. "Let your thoughts out into the open so we can examine them," she says. "Maybe it will help. Like when you told me about the bad dreams, and I gave you that exercise. It helps, no?"

She might be right about the night terrors but I refuse to give her the satisfaction. Instead, I stare defiantly at the faint gray smudge on the lemon yellow wall behind her, waiting out the rest of the hour. I don't want my secrets on display any more than they already are.

By the time I get home from Dr. Pereira's, there's a teenager with a cricket bat leaning against Tazim's doorframe. I eye his patchy moustache as I slide by, and he stares back at me, looking bored.

....

Perched on a small stool beside her red gas cylinder, Tazim flips a roti and places it on top of a thick stack of them, which she wraps up in an Urdu newspaper and then hands to the boy. "Tell your grandmother she can order whenever she likes. I only need a few hours' notice." The boy nods, passing her a few notes before he disappears into the gully.

Tazim wipes the sweat from her forehead with her palm and sits down on the floor across from me.

"You're selling roti now?" I ask as she slides me a plate of dal and rice.

"Until Hanif is able to send money from Dubai."

"Any word from him?"

"Not yet, but when he calls, I'm going to tell him to come back. They're starting to hire people for that hotel. You know, the billboard just outside?"

"The Marquis? It hasn't even been built yet," I say, as I mix the dal and rice with my fingers.

"They're looking for people who went to hotel management college. But maybe they'll take Hanif since he worked in Dubai."

"College? Even the hotel kachrawala needs a degree?"

"Arre, my husband can't return from foreign just to be a kachrawala!" Tazim ladles more dal onto my rice. "You know Zeenat

Aunty? The one with the henna-dyed hair like a red cloud around her face?"

"You know I don't talk to anyone here besides you and Munna."

"Well, her family sent their youngest son to hotel management college. Now he's working at a big hotel in Lower Parel, meeting actors and pop stars. Wears a nice suit every day, makes good money. He even saw the prime minister of India once. And he left Behrampada. Leases his own flat."

"Must be nice. Yesterday the firanghis at the office asked me why I live in Behrampada. Like it's a choice." I laugh. "Chutiyas."

Tazim pauses for a moment. "Maybe they have a point. You went to school. You can read and write. You even speak English, Rakhi."

"So?"

She splays her hands out wide. "That's more than most of the people here can do. And you don't have a child to take care of, or a husband to deal with. You meet all these rich firanghis at your work."

"It's not like that, Tazim. I don't speak good English. You just can't tell because you don't speak it yourself. And the firanghis, they're not here to hand out money, or better jobs. They just come to India to do a bit of work, buy some bangles and bindis, then fly back home. They never stay or come back."

"You also have your Gauri Ma'am watching out for you. Everyone in Behrampada is afraid of crossing you because of her. You think you'd be safe living here on your own without Munna making sure everyone keeps away from you?"

"It's not that simple." If Tazim spent even a day with Ma'am and me, she'd know.

"Nonsense! Gauri is a big lady! But she won't be around forever. You're a young single girl in Bombay. You have no family to watch out for you. There's nobody to fix your marriage. If I had your life, I wouldn't be wasting my time living in Behrampada, eating here every night. You've got a winning lottery ticket and you're too stubborn to cash it in!" Tazim is scolding me the way she does with Ayub when he misbehaves.

I lean back against the edge of her cot, dal-coated fingers sitting atop my plate. "What am I supposed to do, then?"

"That new hotel next door, they'll hire you."

"You just said they want only college graduates."

"Then go to college! Zeenat Aunty's son has his own flat, Rakhi."

"Arre, Tazim, how do you know his family is not lying? For all you know he works in a—"

She raises her hand, cutting me off. "If you tell Gauri Ma'am you want to go to college, she'll pay for it."

"She's done so much for me already. Finding me a place to live, giving me a job, getting me a voter ID card. You know how hard that was without a birth certificate? Besides, I can't ask for college fees. She has her own problems right now."

Tazim snorts. "What problems? Being a famous lawyer? Having a nice flat to live in?"

"There's no money coming in at work. Ma'am can't afford to keep everyone. If I ask her for money for college, she'll fire me."

"Fire you for what?"

I stare down at the drying dal on my fingers, stringing together the words Gauri Ma'am would use. "For putting my interests ahead of the office."

"What bakvaas," Tazim blurts out. "If she fires you, who will make her tea?"

We trade looks and burst into peals of laughter. Ayub glances up from the scuffed, empty water bottle he's been pushing around the floor like a truck, and jumps up and down in front of his mother, mimicking her laugh. She pulls him in and hugs him tight as he tries to wriggle away.

Tazim eventually lets Ayub go and hands me the rest of the rotis, wrapped in a piece of newspaper she can't read. "For breakfast."

"Sure you don't want it?" I ask.

She ushers me out the door. "When you make it out of here, don't forget us."

Outside, the sky is inky and bats zigzag around the minarets of the nearby mosque. The bulbs in our lane glow bright, teeming with throngs of lusty insects.

Climbing the narrow ladder to my door, I spot a new plastic tarpaulin on my roof. Munna must have just put it up. During monsoon season, slums are dotted with blue sheets. From the train, they look like little blue jewels nestled in a pile of gray and brown rocks.

I switch on my lamp and place a bucket under the crack in the roof in case it rains tonight and Munna's handiwork is as shitty as I suspect it is. I flick the fan on. It disrupts a swarm of mosquitoes that spread out in a thin malarial cloud before exiting through the bars of my window.

As I lie awake later that night, listening to the faint cries of an argument farther down the lane, it occurs to me that Tazim might be right. The Marquis Hotel is coming up, and so are lots of other places like it. If I spoke better English, or had the right people on my side, or a diploma, I could get a better-paying job. Have a career, even. I could live somewhere else. Make so much money that I could afford my own first-class train pass.

That night, I dream of Babloo. He's begging at Bandra Station, asking me for a ticket to Bhutan, so he can go swimming in a waterfall. He's still twelve or thirteen years old. I hand him twenty rupees, but when he unfolds it, it catches fire and he howls so hard I wake with my ears ringing.

MAGISTRATE KAPURE BOUGHT EVERY LAST detail of Babloo's story.

"This boy is a menace. He has reached the point of no return," Magistrate Kapure declared at our Juvenile Justice Board hearing. And just like that, Babloo was locked up at Dongri Observation Home with the other juvenile offenders. For some reason, Kapure thought there was still hope for me, so he sent me out of the city, to the Asha Home for Destitute Girls. "To be reformed and rehabilitated," Kapure said. I didn't understand what he meant.

In the days following the hearing, after Babloo and I were separated for good, I tried to tell anyone who would listen that Babloo had lied. That it was me who had done such a terrible thing. It didn't work. Three Dongri guards wrestled my twelve-year-old self onto a bus headed to the Asha Home in Aurangabad, eight hours outside of Bombay.

Run by nuns in light gray frocks with rulers ever ready to slap you for something you didn't do, the Asha Home was a three-story house tucked into a tiny neighborhood on the outskirts of the city. We weren't allowed outside without the nuns.

Where I once roamed any street or gully I wanted and slept under orange streetlamps, I was now confined by concrete walls, low ceilings, and fluorescent lights that buzzed inside my brain. I felt the smallness of everything. I didn't belong there. I belonged with Babloo, and if he was at Dongri, I would find a way to make it back there, too.

I started seeking punishment by pinching the nuns' nipples through their clothes. Like a pickpocket, I would creep up beside them, then thrust my hand forward, squeezing down with my thumb and finger. They'd flinch and bring their arms up to their bosoms, shoulders hunched up, horrified. Babloo would have roared with laughter if he could see it. I was so bad the nuns upgraded their punishment to beltings, but even then I didn't stop. Finally, they threatened to send me back to Dongri, and I begged them to do it. But they never followed through on their threats. So I decided to do something so unforgivable I'd wind up back in front of Magistrate Kapure. I would burn the Asha Home to the ground.

I snuck into the kitchen for kerosene one particularly humid morning, but I couldn't find any. Cooking oil would have to do. Fighting off images of the paanwala on the ground, I struggled to lift the heavy jug of oil from the cupboard shelf. But my palms were too sweaty to grip the jug, and it fell to the ground, cap popping off. A pool of vegetable oil spread out across the floor, soaking the bottoms of bags of rice, coating the brooms in the corner.

The nuns heard the commotion and dragged me by the hair to a dark, empty storage closet, where they locked me inside all day. Later, I learned they made calls to people from the board of trustees, whatever that was. I was told that one of them had come up to Aurangabad to meet me. A few days later, the nuns sat me at a table in a classroom across from a large woman with very short gray hair. That was the first time I met Gauri Ma'am.

She asked the nuns to leave us alone. "So, Bansari, did you really think you could burn the home down with cooking oil?"

"That's not my name."

"Excuse me?"

"You have to call me Rakhi." I met her eyes and her face softened.

"I'm not surprised you hate it here," Gauri Ma'am said, gazing up at a picture of a heavy-lidded Mother Mary perched above the doorway. "I would, too."

I sat back in my chair, studying this woman who spoke with the kind of authority I had only ever seen from men until now.

Gauri Ma'am leaned over the table. "I know why you're here, Rakhi. I spoke with Magistrate Kapure."

I didn't say anything.

"That man who sells paan. He hurt you and you tried to teach him a lesson, didn't you?"

Wasn't it enough that the paanwala's burning visited me in my dreams? Why did I have to talk about it with this woman, too?

"You were attacked by someone bigger and more powerful than you. And still, you tried to confront the situation. You have something the other girls in here will never have, beyond a sense of right and wrong. You have a drive to correct injustice."

I chewed a hangnail loose, spitting it on the floor. "Who told you all that?"

"If you get through the next six years without getting in trouble, and if you study hard, you can leave here and do whatever you want."

I stopped biting my fingernails and lay my hand on the table. "Whatever I want?"

"I'll make sure of it. You just have to study and learn to behave."

All I wanted then was to find Babloo again. And if this Gauri Ma'am was going to bring me to him, then I would do what she said.

.... **6** ....

LATER THAT WEEK, A FIVE-STORY apartment block in Santacruz
East collapses just after dawn. By midmorning, I'm sitting at my
computer, clicking through photos of the damage. Ugly broken slabs
of concrete and twisted rusty metal poles balance against one another, while men covered in thick gray dust hunt through the rubble
for bodies.

I wonder how much they pay the rescue crews to pull people out.
When I lived on the streets by VT, there was this one group of boys
who pulled dead bodies away from the train tracks for small sums of
money. There were all kinds of bodies: college kids who jumped after
exams, drunks who staggered too close to the tracks, idiots who got
hit by trackside poles when they tried to catch too much breeze.
Those boys were obsessed with death. They talked about it all the
time. Of all the children living near VT, they huffed the most solution. They were always diluting little bottles of Eraz-ex with spit,
dabbing it onto dirty rags, sniffing so deeply you wondered how such
thin bodies could hold that much air. Babloo didn't like them, with
their red noses and their swollen, weepy eyes that couldn't focus on
one thing.

"The funny part," he once said, "is they'll most likely die on the tracks themselves. From being too stoned, or they get so fucked in the head, they jump."

"If you cleared dead bodies every day, you'd be screwed up, too," I said.

"Bullshit," he snorted. "It's a free country. Everyone has a choice about what they do."

These days, I think a lot about what he said. What if your options are so limited you don't really have a choice at all?

"Rakhi, what have you done with the housing rights books?" Kamini is standing behind me, hugging her notebook.

I point behind me to the unsorted pile on the floor. "They're somewhere in there, didi." Kamini is a few months younger than me, but I'm still supposed to call her didi. I'm the only one who finds this strange.

She pushes her glasses up on her nose then squats down to the floor. After examining three books at the top of the heap she exclaims, "How am I supposed to find what I need in this chaos?"

"Didi, Gauri Ma'am asked me to re-sort these." As if anything I do around here is my idea.

Bhavana walks past and pauses. "What are you two doing, making so much noise?"

Kamini holds up a book and rises to her feet, her black bob swinging. "Rakhi's taking forever to shelve these. What was wrong with the old way of sorting them, anyhow?"

Maybe you should ask Gauri Ma'am, I want to tell her.

"What's so urgent that you can't go through this pile yourself, Kamini?" Bhavana asks. As the third-most senior lawyer in the office, Bhavana tends to keep the younger lawyers in check, answering their questions, resolving their disputes.

"If I can find a good strategy on how we can move the Chembur appeal forward, then maybe Gauri Ma'am will let me be the junior lawyer on the file with you and Vivek."

"And how do you know she wants a junior lawyer?"

"The more brains on this file, the better, na? And I've already expressed that I'm ready for bigger files."

Bhavana's round face breaks into a smile. "Kamini, you're barely two years out of law college. It was five years before Gauri Ma'am let me touch an appellate-level case. And even that was considered early."

"I just want to be useful, Bhavana," Kamini whines, pulling her smudged glasses off her face. She wipes them clean with the hem of her shirt.

"Arre, you're still so young. Focus on what's been given to you, and do a good job. Gauri Ma'am sees everything. Your time will come." Before Bhavana ushers Kamini out of the library, she turns to me. "Rakhi, hurry up with these books, na? The rest of us have work to do."

"Yes, Bhavanadidi." As if I don't have work to do, too.

A short while later, I hear three loud bangs on the front office door. Startled, I pop my head out to see skinny little Tulsi Prasad and her parents from the Chembur slum case hovering in the doorway.

"Namaste," Tulsi calls out in a sullen tone. "Gauri Ma'am is here?"

How many times have I instructed her to knock lightly? She treats this place like she owns it. For pro bono clients, they always act so entitled in this office—asking to use our phone so they don't eat up their minutes, then talking so loud on their personal calls as though they work here—and everyone just lets them. And for some reason, even though I work here, they get treated better than I do.

When I inform Ma'am that the Chembur slum family have arrived, she clucks her tongue. "Arre, Rakhi, they have names. Send them in. And bring water."

As the Prasads shuffle into Ma'am's office, Kamini lingers outside with her pen and notebook. "Gauri Ma'am, shall I sit in and take notes for you?"

"No," Ma'am replies, putting her glasses on.

Squeezing past a sulky Kamini, I enter Gauri Ma'am's office with a tray of water. Tulsi's father's shirt is frayed at the neck, like it's been scrubbed too hard. Couldn't he pick something more appropriate to wear to meet with Gauri Ma'am? He and the mother are seated at the edge of their chairs, backs straight.

Tulsi is sitting back in her chair, her hands folded in her lap. "How can the High Court say we can't appeal this decision? You said we had a strong case."

The mother, dabbing her eyes with the pallu of her yellow sari, stops sniffling. "You told us to trust you," she cries.

It's not even noon and already she's starting with this natak?

"You did have a strong case," Ma'am says, her voice calm. "You still do. And you should still trust me."

"Then why is nothing going our way?" Tulsi asks. "We could have put our time and energy into moving on. We can't afford this fight anymore."

"Tulsi, you know I am taking this case pro bono, unlike the lawyer you had retained before," Ma'am says, her face stern. "The one who took your money and didn't file any paperwork with the courts."

"It's not just about money," Tulsi says icily. "It's been over a year since the demolition. In all the time we've wasted with this case, we haven't been able to find a new place to live, or replace the ID cards we lost. Nobody will lend me their old books, and even if they did I have nowhere to study. I've missed the medical college entrance exams again because of this case."

"Can't you just bribe a judge? Or a governmentwala?" the mother asks.

Shameless!

"That's not how we do things around here. Please, have some water," Ma'am says gently, motioning to me and the tray.

"We don't want water," the father says, standing up so abruptly he knocks the tray from my hands with his shoulder. Glasses shatter on the floor, and water spreads everywhere.

Startled, Tulsi and Ma'am clutch the sides of their chairs. Everyone stares at me.

"Hai Bhagwan," Tulsi's mother moans, her left hand hovering at the base of her throat. "When will this end?"

"Rakhi, clean up this mess right now," Gauri Ma'am orders, ignoring the woman's theatrics.

I drop to the floor, annoyed at having to pick up after these people.

The father continues with his list of demands. "We want our home back. We want our Tulsi to sit for her exams. We want—"

"Instead of rebuilding our lives, we have to keep coming here," the mother howls. "And all you give us is bad news."

As I dump broken glass into the wastebasket, I'm shocked that these people think they can come in here and break our glasses and talk to Gauri Ma'am like this. They should have been prepared. Everyone knows the governmentwalas are always ready to demolish slums. What would they have lost by being a little more careful with the belongings they couldn't do without? Why didn't they keep Tulsi's books together so they could be rescued in one go? Why wouldn't they keep their ration cards safe? It's hard to have sympathy for people who behave so foolishly.

Gauri Ma'am puts her hand up. "Please, let me speak."

"No," the mother cries. "You never have anything good to say."

Ma'am tries again, her strained voice climbing above the mother's. "I promise you we will give this one last shot. It will be our best effort yet. We will take this appeal to the Supreme Court, I give you my word."

Tulsi scans Gauri Ma'am's face. "How do I know I can trust you?"

Who does she think she is, the Queen of England? As if they have a train station named Tulsi Prasad Terminus. As if Gauri Ma'am has anything to prove to her when she's taking this case on for free.

"Tulsi, it takes years to build trust. You have not known me for long. You don't know my character. But when I give someone my word, I mean it. You see Rakhi over here?"

Determined not to peek up at them from where I am crouched on the floor, I continue gathering up glass shards.

"When she was only, what, sixteen? I told her I would hire her one day. Isn't that true, Rakhi?"

I stand up tall. "Ji, it's true."

"And when she finished school, I did. I found her a place to live, gave her a phone, sent her to English classes, helped get her identification cards. Made sure she was well taken care of. She's been with me for four whole years. So, you see, I keep my promises."

Five years. I've been at Justice For All for five years, though sometimes it feels like twenty.

"We've come so far. We just need to give it a big push now," Gauri Ma'am says.

The Prasad family gapes at me. The mother nods, her chin trembling.

....

Sometime after the Prasads finally leave, news spreads that sixteen tea plantation workers in Assam were shot dead, execution-style. One of them was known to Bhavana, and she begins frantically dialing every lawyer she knows in the northeast of India. After about an hour, she slams her phone down, swearing.

"Why are you so angry, Bhavana?" asks Utkarsh, one of the junior lawyers. Kamini whacks him on the arm because we all know how deeply Bhavana cares about the people in the northeast. Not to mention she was born and brought up in Shillong.

"What do you mean, why am I so angry? Not a single lawyer out there is willing to get involved," she says. "Lazy cowards, all of them."

Kamini asks if she called all her law college batchmates in Kolkata, and Bhavana sighs. "Every last one. Sometimes I think I should have stayed out there instead of coming to Bombay."

Alex pulls up a chair to her desk. "Who were these people who got shot?"

Bhavana winces, as though he's asked a stupid question. "They're ... tea plantation slaves," she says. "They've been trying to unionize for the past two years. I have no doubt the tea estate owner is behind this."

"Why can't Justice For All get involved?" Alex asks.

"We used to have a satellite office out in Assam, but it's closed now. No money."

"But Gauri Ma'am said she was only closing the northeast office until she secured more funding," Kamini says.

Bhavana raises her eyebrows. "Have you heard of any large transfusions of cash coming in to Justice For All recently? Because I haven't."

AFTER THE SHOPS ON M.G. Road closed up for the night, Devi and I huddled under the covered awnings where hawkers sold books and banana-shaped massagers. The skies were black and the rain fell down so hard it barely mattered that we had found cover. We wrapped ourselves in old newspapers, even though the rough, frilled edges scratched our cheeks.

"This spot is the best to sleep when it rains," Babloo said. "It takes a lot longer to get drenched."

Babloo was in charge of picking where we slept. Usually it was on the footpath near VT Station—at whichever spot was as yet unclaimed by the older boys. But the cars proved to be dangerous. At night, when the roads emptied out, there were always drivers racing, weaving dangerously, sometimes jumping the curb. That's how Pappu had wound up on crutches.

Devi and I shivered, clinging to each other under the awning. The cooler temperatures were fine when we were running around, but harder to take when we were lying down to sleep.

"You cold?" Babloo asked. When I nodded, he sprang to his feet and touched Kalu on the arm. "Come."

"I'm tired," Kalu whined.

"Get up, chutiya," Babloo said, yanking Kalu to his feet. "We'll be back."

They splashed away into the wet night with Salman and Pappu, returning an hour later with bundles of fabric.

"Here," Babloo said, thrusting some cloth at Devi and me. "To keep warm."

Devi squealed and unfurled it over our legs. "Where did you get this?"

"Don't worry about it," Babloo said, running his hands through his damp hair.

"Is someone going to come looking for it?" I asked. "Will we get in trouble?"

"This is how we live here, okay?" Babloo said. "You want to go back to Patna? Train station is right there."

I couldn't imagine going back. Babloo, Kalu, Salman, Pappu, and Devi were my family now.

Babloo and Kalu scrambled under the sheet as Devi held it up for them. Pappu and Salman followed. The six of us clung together that night, keeping one another warm and safe.

....

Even though Babloo did his best to take care of us, he was still a kid himself. He had soft, tender spots, and though hidden deep, they came to light sometimes—like the time he got thrashed by a fisherwoman. It happened during monsoon season, after I'd been in Bombay for a couple of years. Kalu, Babloo, and I were weaving through morning crowds down the Dockyard Road Station platform, which was slick and dotted with puddles. Babloo was wearing flat slippers that skidded and slid during the rains. He kept looking back to make sure we hadn't lost Kalu, who could never keep up.

And then, *smack!* Babloo rammed right into a wiry fisherwoman's right hip, sending her basket flying up in the air, and him flat onto his back. Medium-sized gray fish fell from the sky in slow motion, and for a moment all we could hear was the sound of them flopping against the platform, the tracks, commuters' heads and shoulders. People cried out "Chi! Chi!" in disgust. Bones crunched and flesh squelched as dozens of feet trampled the fisherwoman's catch.

Kalu and I watched the scene unfold with horror. Babloo continued to lie there on the ground, covered in fish scales and the briny stink of fish-water. His eyes widened when he saw the fisherwoman bounding toward him. He tried to dash, but she was faster than him, grabbing him by the shoulder. "Phatka paahije ka tula," she shouted before whacking him across his face. Marathi swearwords I had never heard before spewed from her angry mouth. Then she said something that made Kalu double over laughing, clutching his stomach. Babloo's jaw was clenched and his eyes were red. I thought they might explode out of his face.

When the fisherwoman was done slapping the shit out of Babloo, she scraped up what was left of her catch and boarded the next train.

By the time Kalu and I reached Babloo, he was crouching near the wall. "Leave me alone," he bellowed, standing up straight and swatting us away.

We hung back a few feet behind him as he made his way to a nearby tap so he could wash himself down.

"You smell disgusting," Kalu snickered under his breath.

"What's that, bhenchodh?" Babloo swung his drenched fist in Kalu's face, splattering fishy water on him. Kalu ran away, cackling.

I chased after Kalu, asking him what he was laughing at.

"That fisherwoman," he replied. "She was saying Babloo's mother farted in his mouth at birth." And he burst out in laughter again.

"Yaar, you know his mother killed herself," I whispered while I kept an eye on Babloo, who was scrubbing his face under the trickling tap. "She ate rat poison in front of him." He had told me the story once, and it was the only time I had ever seen him cry.

"So?" Kalu shrugged. "It's still funny," he said, wiping the tears from his eyes.

7

THE NEXT WEEK, VIVEK BECKONS to me while in discussion with Utkarsh. They are huddled around Utkarsh's laptop. Behind the cracked glass of the screen, a big black splotch sprawls out, like an angry spider. Gauri Ma'am will not take this lightly. She snapped at one of the lawyers, Jayshree, a few weeks ago for chewing on the end of a pen, saying that she was defiling office property.

"How did this happen?" I ask Utkarsh.

"Arre, that's none of your concern," he says, flapping his hand to dismiss me. "Just go get it fixed."

"Chup, Utkarsh," Vivek says, before leaning toward me. "Rakhi, the manufacturer is saying they'll fix it for seven thousand rupees. That can't be right, can it? Where do you usually go to get computer things fixed?"

"Sir, there are some local shops in the next lane. Let me call."

"You always have the answer," he says, patting my arm.

"I'll need to know what happened to it, though. So I can get the right quote," I lie.

"Something fell on it," Utkarsh sputters, sliding down in his chair. "A . . . glass jar."

"Empty? Full?" I press.

Snapping his head up, he glares at me. "Arre, I dropped a bottle of Old Monk, okay?" He folds his arms. "At least nothing spilled."

Vivek sighs heavily. "You know your laptop is for work only."

Utkarsh drags both hands through his bristly hair. "Sir, I'm sorry, sir. I was playing music from it and I had a few friends over. Just . . . please don't tell Gauri Ma'am, Sir."

"We won't tell anyone, will we, Rakhi?"

"No, Sir. Just the computerwalas."

After calling the nearby shops, none of whom cared how the screen broke, I report back to Vivek that Kaycee Brothers will fix it for five thousand rupees.

Utkarsh gazes eagerly at Vivek Sir. "We can pay for it from the petty cash, no?"

Vivek and I glance at each other and then at Utkarsh. "No," we say, at the same time.

Utkarsh sits upright in his chair, gripping the armrests. "I can't pay for this on my own. I don't have that kind of money lying around."

"Maybe we can take it out of your wages."

"Sir, then Gauri Ma'am will find out, and on top of that you know how little I make here—"

Vivek rubs his eyebrow. "It's okay, it's okay. We'll split it. Twenty-five hundred each and we don't speak of it again, teek hain?"

Utkarsh clasps Vivek's arm. "Thank you, Sir, thank you so much. If you cover my half, I can pay you back in installments. I promise."

"Sir, what about your daughter's wedding," I say as Vivek and I leave Utkarsh's desk. "Utkarsh broke the laptop, not you."

"It's okay, Rakhi. We'll manage," he says through his pained gaze, like he's trying to convince himself.

When I get back from Kaycee Brothers Computers, who tried to charge me another five hundred rupees when they saw the laptop, Alex is crouched over the stacks of books in the library. He glances up at me.

"There's a book called *The Right to Housing in Law and Society* by someone called Sharda. Gauri said you could help me find it."

I squat beside him and start scanning the piles on the floor.

"Gauri told me to read up on landmark housing rights cases in India. You know, build a better foundation while I'm waiting for my assignment tomorrow."

"I think Kamini is having the book," I say, after rooting around.

"Great," Alex says. "I'll go ask to borrow it."

From behind the bookshelf, I watch Alex pointing at a book on Kamini's desk. At first Kamini shakes her head no, pushing her shoulders back. Then, when Alex points to Gauri Ma'am's office, her shoulders slump, and she hands the book to him carefully. As he makes his way back to his workstation, Kamini sits in her chair, glaring at Alex, her lips pinched together, her eyebrows pulled down with worry.

....

That evening, Tazim unwraps a packet of mirchi ka salan and peas pulao.

"Arre! Such hi-fi food?" I marvel at the thick peanut gravy clinging to the sides of her metal bowl. "Have I come to your wedding?"

She slaps me on the arm, beaming. "I made all this food for Memsahib yesterday, but today she told me to take it home."

"That's new," I say. "When has she ever sent you home with her food?"

"Never. She said she and Sahib went out last night instead of eating all this, and that it shouldn't go to waste." Tazim gently stirs the mirchis around in the rich gravy. "She said their nephew insisted I take it."

"So strange," I say, laughing nervously.

Shit. How long till Alex says something about working with a curly-haired slum-dweller named Rakhi? Knots tighten in my belly and I can barely stand to look at the mirchi ka salan. When Tazim turns her back, I scrape most of my food onto Ayub's plate.

Later that night, my empty stomach growling, I lie on my mat, listening to the steady hum of the nearby Western Express Highway and the occasional bleats of the goat who lives one lane over. My eyelids feel heavy, and I drift into a short dream. Babloo and I are still kids, curled up in a dark alcove beneath the footbridge over the tracks. "This is where the street children sleep," a voice announces. It's Gauri Ma'am, leading a tour of Bandra Station. A cluster of white tourists crane forward to hear her voice above the roar of the trains. Babloo and I crawl out from the alcove, peering up at the visitors, curious. One of them is Alex but he doesn't recognize me, just pauses to stare at us while Gauri Ma'am asks if there are any questions.

"It's me," I say in the dream. "It's Rakhi. From the office."

Alex squints. "Trust me, we've never met."

I am awoken by the rattling of the little table beside my mat. It's my mobile buzzing. GAURI VERMA flashes on the glowing screen.

I answer it, rubbing my eyes. "Ji, Ma'am."

"Be at the office tomorrow morning at seven sharp." Cars are honking in the background. It sounds like she's leaving work.

I prop myself up on my elbow and try to swallow a yawn. "Yes, Ma'am. What happened?"

"Rubina Mansoor is coming to visit tomorrow morning," Gauri Ma'am huffs, sounding annoyed. "You will have to come early and tidy the office. I want everything put away, everything in order. Kitchen, library, the waiting area. And wipe those cobwebs off the bloody ceiling fans. The office should be spotless."

"Rubina Mansoor, Ma'am?" I switch on the lamp but the light doesn't help make any sense of what Ma'am is saying.

"I've called all the lawyers to tell them to be there on time and to dress in formals. They don't know that Rubina is coming."

"How come they don't know?"

"Arre, this plan all came about so suddenly. I'll explain everything tomorrow. Oh, and make sure the kachrawali empties every last dustbin when she comes in. Don't just take her word for it. Check with your own eyes to see if she's actually done it."

As Gauri Ma'am rambles on about the kachrawali, I fiddle with a thread coming loose from my sheet. What could Rubina Mansoor want from Gauri Ma'am, anyway? Legal advice? Is that how desperate we are for money—she's taking on film stars as clients?

"Ma'am, Vivek Sir knows about Rubina?"

She doesn't say anything for a moment. "No. I told you, it came about so fast."

Gauri Ma'am never used to make decisions without first consulting Vivek. Not that she always followed his advice, but she would seek it, at least.

"Just make sure you wear a nice, clean salwar kameez, teek hain? I've given you so many of Neha's old clothes, there must be something smart in there. No wrinkles, no stains. Check the legs of your pants before you put them on. Inspect every fold of fabric. And fold your dupatta nicely."

"Teek hain, Ma'am. And you called the interns?"

"Arre," she mumbles. "I don't even have their numbers on me. Call them up first thing tomorrow morning. Tell them to dress nicely. No shorts, T-shirt nonsense."

Last year's British intern wore ripped denim shorts, a T-shirt, and scuffed sandals to the office every day until Bhavana told him to stop dressing like he was on holiday in Goa.

"Okay, seven o'clock in the morning I want you in the office. This is important, understand?"

After she cuts the call, I switch off the lamp, lie back down on my mat, and stretch my arms out. It's almost one in the morning. I should go back to sleep, but instead I reach for my phone. The darkened room glows an empty green. "ALEX INTERN" is now the first name in my scant contact list. It's mostly people from the office and Munna, but still long enough to make it seem like I have friends. People to eat an ice cream with on the weekend. Imaginary cushioning to muffle the quiet roar of constant loneliness.

Perhaps I should just call the interns now. I bet Saskia and Merel are still awake. I write both girls a text message. **meseg 4m gauri**

mam: pls b at work 9am. dress in nice clothe. I add a generous **Thnk u** to the end of the message, even though they don't deserve it.

I copy the same text message to Alex, then pause. I wonder if he already knows that his aunt's friend is coming tomorrow. Maybe I could just call him to find out. No, that's a bad idea. It will look like I have an urge to speak to him late at night. I could call him tomorrow morning, but what if he's in the bath or having breakfast and then I miss him and he shows up looking like some Colaba Causeway firanghi? What will Ma'am say then? Or worse, what if Tazim's there tomorrow morning and she somehow overhears Alex on the phone with me?

At this hour, I know I should just send a text message, but my thumb presses down on the CALL button. Shit. I draw a sharp breath and hit the End button ten panicky times, then throw the phone down on the floor. My heart is pulsing. Maybe the call didn't go through.

Before I can settle back into the creeping darkness of the room, my phone's green light flashes back on and it starts buzzing.

"Hey, Rakhi? Did you just call me?" Alex's voice sounds clear, uncurdled by sleep.

"Y-yes. Gauri Ma'am saying . . ." I pull at the stray thread from my bed sheet until it is as long as my arm.

"Yes?" He sounds like he's smiling.

I swallow and close my eyes. "She saying . . . Please you are coming at office nine o'clock tomorrow."

"Isn't that our usual start time?"

He's right. "Yes. Do not be late."

"So . . . Anything else?" He draws his words out, and they hover there until I speak up again.

"And you have to dress in nice shirt and pant."

His laughter explodes over the line. "What? Do I really dress that badly?"

"No, just . . . Ma'am saying—" I sit up and flick on the lamp for clarity. I stare at my bare feet, curl my toes inward, and gather my

English words, stringing them into a slow sentence. "Ma'am say everybody wearing nice clothes. For guest tomorrow."

"Guest? It's not Rubina, is it?"

So he does know. For a second I don't say anything, stunned that there's someone at Justice For All who knows something before even Vivek.

"You knowing about Rubina Mansoor?"

"I don't know why she's coming, just that she is. She and Gauri have been talking about some kind of joint venture."

I don't say anything. A lone mosquito hums by my ear and I slap it against my cheek. I wipe the blood from my palm on my knee.

"Is there anything else?" Alex says.

"No, nothing."

"All right, I'll see you tomorrow. Oh, by the way, I never thanked you for having lunch with me the other day. That was really kind of you."

What do I say? *You are welcome?* "You are paying."

He chuckles. "That's not the point. Good night, Rakhi."

"Good night."

The line goes dead and I sit there for a few minutes, pursing my lips to keep from smiling.

8

THE ROADS ARE STILL EMPTY when I leave for work the next morning, and most of the autowalas are curled up asleep in the back seat of their rickshaws, their cracked heels sticking out into the soft light. Gauri Ma'am is already at the office when I arrive, furiously punching at her keyboard. She usually only types like this when she has a court date looming.

I cross my dupatta over my chest and around my waist, and get ready to scrub the place down. The ceiling fan blades are caked with dark gray dust and gilded with cobwebs. When was the last time Gauri Ma'am told me to clean them? Must be at least two years back. I wipe them with a cloth and the webs drift to the floor like feathers. When the blades are cream-colored again, I drag my dirty rag and bucket of water to the kitchen, pausing at Ma'am's door. She is draped in the starched black-and-white cotton sari she keeps for Bombay High Court appearances only. Her eyes dart from her computer to her notebook, over the mess of papers, books, and pens.

"Ma'am? Can I ask one thing?"

She glances up at me, lacing her fingers together and cracking her knuckles. "One thing. And make it quick."

"How come Rubina Mansoor is coming today?"

"To meet all of you," she says, as if it were completely obvious. "To see the office."

"Yes, but what for?"

Gauri Ma'am sits back in her chair. Rubbing a thick, white whisker sprouting from her chin, she sighs. "Rubina wants to help 'uplift India.' Her words, not mine."

"She is finished with acting, now?"

"I'm not sure, but my guess is she wants to reinvent herself." Ma'am pauses, as if waiting for me to say something, then stands up and starts to shuffle papers on her desk. "Have you heard of Annie Lennox?" Before I can say no, she continues. "She's a British pop star from the seventies and eighties. Well before your time. Annie Lennox once said there are two kinds of artists: those who endorse Pepsi, and those who simply won't."

"Pepsi, Ma'am?" I could use a cold drink.

She gives me a hard smile, as if she's disappointed that after all these years she still can't have a real conversation with me.

"Times are tough." She adjusts the folds of her sari, smiling to herself. "And Rubina Mansoor just might be our Pepsi."

....

Everyone arrives by nine, even the interns. Vivek's shirt is buttoned up to his neck, and a dark blue tie rests over his chest and round belly. Some of the younger female lawyers have lined their worn-out eyes with kohl. The room is humming with noise as everyone admires one another's clothing, clearly puzzled as to what is going on.

Alex's hair is combed back and there is a sharp crease running down the middle of his khaki pant legs. Tazim must have pressed them this morning. The thought of her fingers folding the fabric, running a hot iron down each pant leg, and then handing them to Alex, makes me shudder.

"Well?" Alex approaches me, his brown leather shoes clacking, while Vivek unloads a stack of library books into my arms. "How do I look?"

"Tip-top," Vivek says, eyeing his outfit. "In India, we say 'jhakaas.'"

"Ekdam jhakaaaaas, Vivek," Alex drawls, holding his palm up in the air.

Vivek high-fives him, grinning. "You speak Hindi, do you, Alex?"

"Thoda thoda," he says, sheepishly, holding his index finger and thumb to signal a small amount.

Is that his answer every time someone asks if he speaks Hindi? Why can't he just say no?

Gauri Ma'am emerges from her office and marches toward us. "Gather 'round, everyone. Now, I have told you all we have a special guest today. Our guest is someone you may all be familiar with—a public figure by the name of Rubina Mansoor."

Around the room, eyebrows jump.

"The actor?" Kamini gasps.

"That hot girl from 'Drip Drip'?" Utkarsh says, his wide-set eyes growing bigger.

The office chatter builds and Ma'am speaks again. "Yes, that Rubina Mansoor. She is coming today to see our office and to meet all of you. I don't have to tell you twice to behave professionally." Here she shoots Utkarsh a look of warning.

Vivek's face twists in confusion. "Gauri Ma'am, when did this—"

"Later, Vivek." She spins around to face me. "You—go downstairs and wait outside. Rubina should be here soon. And untie your dupatta. You look like a kaamwali." Then she walks to the window and flicks on the seldom-used air-conditioning unit, which grunts and hums as if a parade of lorries were charging through the office.

Hurrying carefully down the dingy stairwell, I undo the knots in my dupatta, smiling to myself at this bizarre situation. If only Babloo could see me now, waiting on the street to receive the Drip Drip–wali herself, Ruby M.

After fifteen minutes, a white car with dark windows rolls up outside our building. A driver in a red dress shirt rushes out to open the rear door, and then a pair of slim ankles wrapped in strappy gold sandals peek out from under the door, hovering near the ground.

Rubina Mansoor emerges. And it's as if I've forgotten how to blink. She must be forty-five, fifty even, but her hair trails down her back like plumes of thick black smoke. Her white embroidered cotton kameez and navy churidar look clean and expensive, in spite of their plainness. She adjusts a pair of wide black sunglasses on her nose, her long, pink fingernails gleaming in the pale morning sunlight.

"This is the Justice For All office?" Her voice is deeper in person than it is on-screen.

I nod vigorously and glance up at our windows. Faint outlines of faces crowding behind the glass. "Come, Madam, please," I say in slow English. I lead her up the two flights of stairs, mumbling something about the lift being out of service. There's a pinching feeling inside my nose as I try not to sneeze from her heavy, flowery perfume.

As soon as I push open the door to the office, Gauri Ma'am and her black-and-white sari fill the doorframe. "Rubinaji, come in, come in. I am so pleased to welcome you to our humble quarters," Ma'am sings in a high, almost nervous voice I have never heard in all the years that I've known her.

"No, no, Gauriji, the pleasure is mine," Rubina replies.

Ma'am ushers her inside, guiding her to the lawyers' workspace. Everyone is sitting silently in their chairs, faces glued to their computers as if they are immune to the glow of an aging film star floating through our shabby little office. Kamini tries to suppress a sneeze, fails, and shrinks into herself as she wipes saliva off the corners of her mouth, clearly mortified.

"This is my formidable, hard-working staff," Gauri Ma'am says, introducing everyone by name. One by one, they turn around in their seats, press their palms together, and dip their heads.

Ma'am moves to the interns' workstation, and Rubina cups Alex's chin in her hand. "Our future Ivy League scholar, how are you?"

"Not bad, Ruby Aunty," Alex says with a smile. "Glad to see you here."

Kamini eyes Jayshree, who nudges Sudeepthi, who elbows Bhavana, whose mouth gapes at the familiarity between Rubina and Alex.

"Aunty?" Utkarsh mouths to Vivek, who doesn't respond.

"I hope these lawyers aren't working you too hard," Rubina says.

"Well, this is only my second week, so let's see," Alex chuckles. "And there are a couple of other interns here as well," he says, pointing to Saskia and Merel beside him, their hair pulled back into neat, matching ponytails. Instead of their usual attire of rumpled kurtis, they're both wearing collared shirts tucked into trousers. I guess they got my SMS.

"With all the brilliant work you do, Gauriji," Rubina proclaims, "it's a shame you don't have more international talent here." She then approaches the Dutch girls. "Are you also Canadian?"

"No, we're from Amsterdam, actually," Merel says, tilting her head so her ponytail swings. Saskia nods, beaming.

"Beautiful. Amsterdam is one of my favorite cities in the world. You must go someday, Gauriji. Canals, tulips, bicycles—it's worlds away from Mumbai."

"I'm sure," Gauri Ma'am says.

"But there's no place better than India, isn't that right?" Rubina declares triumphantly to no one and everyone.

Sudeepthi, stone-faced, pokes Bhavana's arm with her pen. Ma'am glares at them, but gives Rubina Mansoor a tight-lipped smile and begins to steer her toward her office.

"Alex, darling, why don't you join us," Rubina suggests.

Ma'am waves her hand. "That won't be necessary. Alex has plenty of work to—"

"Arre, Gauriji. He's come all the way to India to learn something, so let's teach him a thing or two, na?"

Ma'am hesitates, then waves Alex over, her lips pressed together. "Come in, then," she says, avoiding eye contact with the lawyers.

I rush to the kitchen to fill a tray with glasses and a Bisleri that's been chilling for the past few hours. When I shuffle into Gauri Ma'am's office, Alex pipes up.

"Ruby Aunty," he says, motioning to me, "have you met Rakhi?"

Rubina twists her head a few inches behind her shoulder and smiles. "Namaste."

"Will you take tea, Rubinaji?" Ma'am asks. "Our Rakhi makes excellent chai."

Rubina says she isn't consuming dairy these days, so she'll take it black. She repeats herself to me in Hindi, slowly. "Not a drop of milk in mine, just boil the tea with water. And absolutely no sugar. You understand me, right?"

She clearly has no idea how many firanghis pass through this office with their strange diets.

"You have to be direct when you're giving them instructions," Rubina says to Alex and Gauri Ma'am, throwing her hair behind her back. "Food waste is such a problem these days."

As the office door shuts, I hear Alex mutter, "She understands English."

In the kitchen, I've started boiling enough water for two separate batches of tea when Vivek inches up to me. "Well, then?" he whispers loudly. "What's going on?"

I pull a spoon from the drawer. "I don't know."

Vivek leans against the counter, stroking his tie, as I measure tea leaves into both pots. "Rubina Mansoor, of all people, here in our office? I haven't heard much of her since that 'Drip Drip' video back in the nineties. She practically had to go into hiding after it came out, no? They were burning effigies of her in the streets."

Back then, Rubina Mansoor was a ripe, young actress who went by the name Ruby M, though she failed to snag any lead roles (the wholesome heroine parts went to her rivals) and never amounted to more than an item girl, dancing suggestively to catchy, upbeat numbers in Hindi films. For a whole year, you couldn't go anywhere without hearing "Drip Drip" blaring from a taxi, a shopfront, or the radio.

The song was a hit, but really it was the video that made it take off. Those five minutes of her writhing around a jungle, with her tiny black chaddis peeking through her wet sari, catapulted her from anonymity to sudden infamy. Newspapers referred to her as the "Thong Girl," and she even became the face of a swimsuit line for a brief period.

"Sir, she is married to a builder now. I saw in *Mumbai Mirror*."

"Which builder is this?"

"Jeetendra Arora, Sir."

"That guy whose billboards are all over the city? He's got a luxury flat in every western suburb. Arora Eternity Heights, Arora Eternity Grande, Arora Eternity Luxe . . ." Vivek's shoulders slump. "Arora is trying to get into the Fort area, isn't he? Does he want to buy our office building? They're going to kick us out, I know it. Hai Bhagwan, we'll never be able to afford anything else in this area."

Before I can reply, Kamini rushes into the kitchen with Utkarsh trailing behind her. "Rakhi, quick. Tell us. What is happening?"

"I don't know, didi. I was only told to make tea."

"What bakvaas," Kamini says, eyeing me from over the tops of her glasses. "You spend enough time around Gauri Ma'am to know what's going on."

Vivek frowns. "If Rakhi says she doesn't know, she doesn't know."

Utkarsh studies Vivek suspiciously. "Sir, how is it possible that even you don't know?"

Vivek pulls at his tie and nobody says anything.

After a moment, Utkarsh perks up. "You think they are filming something in our office?"

I pour the tea into cups while they argue over what kind of director might shoot a film in an old building like ours. Lifting up the tray carefully, I move to the doorway, but Kamini blocks me. "Just one more thing. How does the new intern know Rubina Mansoor?"

I swallow. "She is friends with his aunt, I think."

Kamini smirks. "He told you this?"

"Didi, chai-pani time. Gauri Ma'am is waiting."

Kamini sighs and steps out of my way.

"...and it's people like me who have a duty to help the rest of India rise up," Rubina Mansoor is saying as I prop open the door to Gauri Ma'am's office with my hip.

From the corner of her eye, Gauri Ma'am catches Alex giving me a sly half-wink but continues to nod along to Rubina's words.

"I want to use my name..." Rubina is saying as I set her no-sugar, no-milk, garbage-water-looking tea in front of her. She glances down at her teacup, wiping the rim with her thumb and forefinger. "My fame, my spotlight, my resources, all of it, in pursuit of the greater good. But I don't have the tools to do it alone, of course." She laughs and pushes the tea away without taking a sip. "And that's where Justice For All comes in. I would be there to drive your cause forward. To drum up support."

Gauri Ma'am is still nodding.

"You know, all these big companies have brand ambassadors. Shah Rukh did all those Pepsi ads. And just see how popular Pepsi became in India."

As I slip out of the office, I hear Ma'am cough and sputter so hard on her tea that, for a second, it seems as though she's about to choke.

After almost an hour behind closed doors, Gauri Ma'am, Alex, and Rubina Mansoor emerge. From the kitchen I can see Rubina flashing the lawyers a warm smile, revealing a large set of sparkling, straight teeth. It's even harder to believe that the item girl who once danced across the screen in a wet sari wants to work with Gauri Ma'am.

"I look forward to seeing you all very soon," she says, pressing her palms together and bowing as though she's in a temple.

Utkarsh springs up from his chair, returning the gesture, bowing lower than his waistband allows, while I try not to catch a glimpse of his underpants as his shirt rises up. The others are fixed in their seats, grinning like idiots. Even Bhavana.

"Bye, darling, I'll drop in on your aunt soon," Rubina calls out to Alex, who stands with his hands in his pockets.

As soon as the door shuts behind Rubina, Ma'am switches off the struggling air conditioner. "Is everyone here?" she asks.

"Ji, Gauri Ma'am," I say, even though Saskia and Merel seem to have disappeared again.

Sitting at the edge of the lawyers' shared worktable, Ma'am leans forward. Her face is warm and friendly, and she meets the eager eyes of her staff.

"Gauri Ma'am," Bhavana says, finally. "We're dying to know what's going on."

As the other lawyers plead with her, too, Ma'am finally puts her hands up, as though she's satisfied that she's created enough of a buildup for what she's about to unleash.

"As you all know, this has been a difficult year for us. Two of our foreign funders slashed their budgets, forcing us into a tight spot. I've had to make some difficult decisions . . . Shutting down our satellite offices, letting people go, reducing our operating costs . . ." Ma'am wipes sweat from her upper lip with her handkerchief. "But the only way to survive hard times is to get creative. This is why Justice For All will be launching a publicity campaign to boost our profile and ultimately generate financial support. And Rubina Mansoor has agreed to be our ambassador. That means she will be the public face of our organization."

Collective confusion sets in as lawyers scratch their temples and rub their cheeks. Bhavana's hand creeps up like she's not sure she wants to raise it. "Ma'am, are we investing a lot of resources into this new . . . effort?"

"No more than if we were trying to find other sources of funding."

"What will a publicity campaign cost us?" Vivek asks. "Have you done the numbers? Can we sit down and look at them? What about the opportunity cost?"

"Vivek, you leave that to me."

"Gauri, my apologies, but if this doesn't work out, what does this mean for the rest of—"

"It means you have to continue to do your work with the same level of dedication that I have always expected from each and every one of you."

The meeting ends, the lawyers disperse, and I go to the kitchen, but Vivek follows Gauri Ma'am to her office.

"And what's in it for her?" His voice is hushed, urgent. "What does Rubina Mansoor get from this partnership?"

Ma'am peeks over Vivek's shoulder and behind her, but she doesn't spot me listening behind the kitchen doorframe. "She becomes popular again. Relevant. What else?"

"Gauriji, please, we should be focusing our energy on securing long-term funding, not playing games with some fading celebrity. What if this all goes wrong? We can barely afford to pay the lawyers."

"Are you the boss in this office?" Ma'am's voice is fierce.

"No, of course not."

"Did you build this place from the ground up?"

"Gauri, please, I mean no disrespect—"

"Have you sacrificed everything for it? Friends? Money?" She pauses, her voice cracking. "Family?"

No matter how much money Vivek has given up to work at Justice For All, it will never compare to Ma'am's sacrifices with Neha. "No, I have not."

"Then do not question me. Especially in front of the staff."

"Forgive me, Gauriji."

Her door closes. There's no sound of footsteps, and I can tell Vivek is still standing in front of Ma'am's office. I hang back in the kitchen to give him some space. Eventually he sighs, long and deep, and trudges away.

EVEN THOUGH THE FLOORS OF the Asha Home were hard to sit on, I did it for six years. Hips throbbing, mind spinning through the lessons, the grammar, the songs, I somehow passed each standard. Not by much, but I passed.

Gauri Ma'am visited me a few times a year. The other girls would ask me why I had private meetings with her, and I wouldn't know what to say. Ma'am never spoke about herself. She only asked me questions about my life. *Why did you leave home? What was it like on the streets? What do you want to do when you leave this place?*

I told her everything. I told her I wanted to see Babloo.

"He made you feel safe," she once said. "He was the closest thing to family you had."

He was family, I wanted to tell her. My parents hardly existed in my mind anymore, my memories of them thin and hazy. But Babloo I thought of every day. About how we laughed at the same things. How he shared every piece of food he came across with me. The way we held hands as we left the dark, empty hallway in Ballard Estate.

It was during my last three months at the Asha School that Gauri Ma'am asked me if I wanted to work for her.

"What do you do?" I ask.

"I'm a human rights lawyer. I fight for people who can't defend themselves."

"And what do you want me to do?"

"Support me, support my team. You'll be paid. Enough to live independently. The office is in Bombay."

Bombay? A light in me switched on. "I'll do it."

"It will be hard, Rakhi. You aren't accustomed to being around middle-class people, to office life."

"I said I'll do it."

Gauri Ma'am exhaled. "I want you to take a day to think about it before you say yes. You aren't used to working under authority, to following orders."

"Arre, have you seen these nuns?"

She laughed. "You're clever. You'll go far if you continue to apply yourself."

I told Gauri Ma'am I would do whatever she needed me to do, and I would do it well. Anything to get back to Bombay. To Babloo.

"Good," she said. "That's what I like to hear."

....

My last day at the Asha Home, the nuns tried to hug me goodbye. I pushed past their scratchy gray frocks toward Gauri Ma'am. "I'm ready to leave," I told her, impatient.

"Then let's go," she said.

The coach took almost an entire day to wind its way through hills and valleys to Bombay. As Gauri Ma'am slept, read papers, and took phone calls, I broke my head on what I would say to Babloo when I finally saw him. Would I start with "I'm sorry"? Or just drop to his feet and tell him I was indebted to him for life? And what if he wasn't okay? No, of course he was okay. He was Babloo.

"I can sleep on the street," I said, after Gauri Ma'am's taxi dropped me off outside a hostel. "The rains have stopped."

She shook her head. "Rakhi, you live in a different world now."

I rubbed the back of my neck and stared down the street, eager for her to leave so I could go find Babloo.

"And I didn't give you a job so you could go back to your old ways, understand? I don't want you searching for that boy. Or any of your old friends, for that matter."

"No, but—"

"Your past will only hold you back. I'm taking a chance on you, don't forget. It would be a shame for you to throw away this opportunity."

She checked me into the hostel, took me to my room, and told me she would come gather me in the morning to take me to her office. "Get some rest," she said, from the doorway.

Instead, I waited ten minutes, then got on a train and went straight to Dongri. The remand home looked smaller than it had when I was twelve.

I ran up to the night watchman, breathless. "Is Babloo here?"

He ignored me.

"Babloo, do you know him?"

He continued to ignore me, so I ran past him, toward the gate.

"Ei!" he called out, suddenly alert. "You can't go in there. If you're searching for someone you'll have to talk to the Superintendent Sahib."

I held my chin up. "Call him, then. I need to speak to Babloo."

"Superintendent Sahib is not here. Come back later."

I returned the next day after work. And the day after that. I went to Dongri every day for two weeks until finally they told me that Mohammed had left the remand home a year ago and they were not aware of his whereabouts.

9

ALEX POKES HIS HEAD INTO the library after I've distributed afternoon chai. "Your tea is really good," he remarks. "In case nobody has ever said it to you before."

I swivel around in my chair from my computer to make eye contact with him. "Okay," I reply, hesitating. What else do I say?

He steps forward. "Did you add . . . fennel seeds?"

"No. Just tea, milk, and sugar only."

"I could have sworn I tasted fennel," he says, frowning. "By the way, I put that *Right to Housing* book back. The one I was looking for."

"Kamini is not needing?"

"No clue," he says. "Guess she can come find it here if she wants." He pulls out a book from the shelf and begins to flip through it. "Hey, listen to this. *Higher education appears to provide women with the key to many of the same opportunities as their male counterparts. They participate in the labor market at salaries and positions comparable to male graduates.*" He jabs the book with his index finger. "I was telling you this at lunch last week, remember? If you go to college, you can get a job that pays a lot more money."

Arre? This again?

"So, what are you waiting for?" Alex asks.

"Money," I whisper, so nobody outside the library can hear me talking. "Too much fees."

"You can't borrow from anyone?"

"From who?"

"Can't your parents help you out?"

Why does he think I have parents? Then it dawns on me. Gauri Ma'am must not have told him about my past. That's why he's being so nice to me. He doesn't know what kind of person I really am.

I turn back to my darkened computer and move the mouse so it wakes up. "No. There is no money."

"Sorry," he says. "I didn't realize."

Just then, Gauri Ma'am bursts out of her office, throwing her bag over her shoulder. "Bhavana," she shouts. "The retainer agreement with your Bangladeshi migrants—where is it? I need it right now. And Sudeepthi, you've got that mediation next week? Are you ready? You've consulted Vivek? Quick, print out your key points for me, I want to review them on my way to my next meeting."

Bhavana and Sudeepthi jump to their feet, scrambling to the printer.

"And where's Rakhi?" Gauri Ma'am calls out.

I slide past Alex and out where she can see me. "Ji, Ma'am, I'm right here."

"You have therapy tonight, don't you?"

Kamini and Utkarsh peer up from their desks, their faces clouding at the word *therapy*. My face burns. "Ji," I whisper.

"Arre, what? Speak up. Yes, you have therapy tonight, or no, you don't?"

"Y-yes, tonight," I stammer.

"Don't be late. I spend all this money, the least you can do is show up on time."

As the door slams, Jayshree stares at me. "Gauri Ma'am sends you to therapy? What for?"

Shit. Now every last person in the office is gaping at me, even Alex. My eyes dart to Bhavana, the only person besides Vivek who knows about Dr. Pereira.

"Oh, it's for her wrist, na?" Bhavana says, blinking rapidly. "Rakhi has a muscle strain, so Gauri Ma'am found her a physical therapist."

"All you need is Tiger Balm," Utkarsh says. "Don't waste money on therapists and whatnot."

"Homeopathy, also," Kamini says. "Works wonders."

"Arre, she's fine," Bhavana snaps. "Why are you all getting involved?"

I shoot Bhavana a look and she gives me a quick nod before sitting down at her desk.

As everyone returns to their work, I drag myself back to my workspace, my ears burning. Nobody else has to get their head checked every week just to keep their job. So why should I?

....

By five-thirty, the office is quiet and almost empty. On my way out, I pause outside Ma'am's door. "I'm leaving for Dr. Pereira's office, is there anything else?"

She is still on the phone, rubbing the dark circles under her eyes. She glances up and waves at me the way you'd swat at flies buzzing around your soda bottle.

I'm halfway down the stairs when I hear someone call my name. Behind me, Alex is slinging his bag over his chest. "You leaving?"

I nod.

"Great," he says. "I'll take the train up with you."

Outside on the street, it's still sweltering. Alex and I trudge down the lane, past dogs panting in the early-evening shade of parked cars, toward VT Station. The trains will be packed at this hour.

"It is busy," I say. "You taking taxi, okay? Or you waiting. Taking train later."

Alex appears to think about this. "Okay, well, do you want to go for a walk and take the train with me in half an hour? Get a . . ." He scans the street and spots a juice cart with pyramids of oranges, lemons, and mosambis stacked up to eye level. "Get a drink?"

I hesitate, thinking of the poking and prodding that awaits me in Dr. Pereira's office. Who cares if I'm fifteen minutes late. "Okay."

Alex buys us two nimbu panis, one salty (for me) and one sweet, no ice (for him).

"I have some good news," Alex says, with a gleam in his eye. "Gauri is changing my title to consultant. I'm not an intern anymore."

"Means?"

He uses his straw to stir the sugar granules settling at the bottom of his drink. "Consultant is just a fancy way of saying someone who provides expert advice. It'll look better on my résumé when I apply for jobs in the future."

An expert? On what? It's only his second week. This isn't going to go down well in the office. "You telling others?"

"What do you mean? It's not a secret."

"No, just . . . others not happy, maybe." I look down at my nimbu pani, dragging the straw through the floating bits of pulpy lime.

His gaze wanders for a moment. "I'm not worried about that. There's politics in every office. I'm only here until September, so it won't really impact anyone or anything. And anyway, it was Gauri's decision. I haven't been here long, but it seems like whatever she says goes, right?"

Maybe he's right. Why should either of us have to take the heat for Gauri Ma'am's decisions?

He peers over my head into the distance, pointing to a wide row of trees. "Hey, what's over that way?"

"That is Oval Maidan."

"Can we go check it out?"

My gaze jumps between the Maidan and the road to VT. I'd rather do anything than go to Dr. Pereira right now. Especially after Ma'am told everyone at the office about it. I shouldn't have to go if I don't want to. Not tonight, not ever.

"Wait," Alex exclaims. "You have some wrist therapy tonight, right? Gauri was saying—"

"No," I say, pulling my shoulders back. "Not tonight. Canceled."

Unless Gauri Ma'am wants to drag me up to Dr. Pereira's office in Borivali herself, I am going to spend this evening doing exactly what I choose.

"Come," I say, lifting my chin. "Follow me."

GEMMA AND GILES WERE THE kind of firanghis who didn't mind being ripped off for a pair of sandals in the market—they said that was the price they had to pay, as goras. That, and of course their British currency was worth so much that an extra two hundred rupees here or there meant nothing to them.

They came to Justice For All a year after I started. A few months into their internships, they asked Gauri Ma'am if they could take me to Kerala for a week.

"Imagine how exciting it would be for Rakhi to go out of town on a holiday," Gemma said, while I stood beside her and Giles in Ma'am's office. "She'll get to sleep on houseboats and visit tea estates. We'll pay for everything, it won't be much. We're happy to do it."

I couldn't believe anyone, let alone a couple of firanghis, would want to take me on holiday. It was the first time anyone in the office besides Gauri Ma'am and Vivek had paid me any special attention.

Ma'am motioned for me to leave the room, so I did, though I kept listening to the conversation from outside. "Rakhi's been through a lot. She's getting used to day-to-day life off the street, out of the girls' home. She has a lot of rehabilitating to do. She still views relationships as transactional. If she goes to Kerala with two young people, it would certainly undo much of the hard work we've already done. And you wouldn't want that for her, would you?"

After dismissing Gemma and Giles, Gauri Ma'am called out to me. "I know you're standing outside my door, Rakhi."

I inched my way back into her office and sat down in front of her desk, staring at my fingernails.

"When you were at the Asha Home, I told you that once you left you could do whatever you wanted, wasn't it?"

"Ji, Ma'am."

"Then you must trust that I am working very hard to get you there. Going on holiday with Giles and Gemma seems harmless, na? But a trip like this could disrupt the routine you've established for yourself. Perhaps it could muddle the expectations you have of people. Or complicate the emotions you feel when you're back. A number of unsettling behavioral changes could follow. And if that happened, I would have to reconsider whether I could keep you at Justice For All."

I searched her face for some clue as to how a holiday could make me do something bad enough to get fired. "I don't understand, Ma'am."

"Exactly," she said, sitting back and folding her hands on her desk. "That is exactly my point."

She told me that even though the choice was mine to make, she was asking me to trust her. There was no choice, though. I knew I would lose my job if I didn't follow her orders.

Later that day, I thanked Giles and Gemma for the invitation, but I was too busy to spare the time to go to Kerala with them. They gave me pitying looks and told me to let them know if I changed my mind. Gemma then asked if I was going out to Sai Krishna anytime soon, and if I was, could I pick her up a cold Bisleri?

I said yes, pocketing her thirteen rupees exact change. On my way out, I slammed the office door with more force than was necessary.

THE BROWN GRASS AT THE Oval Maidan is soggy in some spots. By the time Alex and I find a dry patch at the edge of the field, I have two missed calls from Dr. Pereira's office. I slip the phone back into my purse.

"Cricket, eh?" Alex plops down on the grass and reclines on his elbows. "Never really watched it."

When I was ten, there was a month when some NGO people from the U.K. taught me, Babloo, and twenty other street kids to play cricket. More importantly, they fed us lunch every day. But we also had to sit all morning and listen to stories about HIV and malaria and the nasty bugs that would come if we didn't wash our armpits and private parts. At the end of each day, the foreign NGO didis and bhai-yyas handed out fistfuls of shiny foil packets. I thought they were sweets, but later the older boys near VT Station said they weren't and wrestled them out of our hands. Before the NGO people left to go back home, they gifted us bright yellow T-shirts that spelled KIDS-PLAYUK in big purple letters.

"The game is taking long time," I tell Alex, kneeling next to him at a safe distance. "Sometimes many days."

"Oh, yeah. I knew that." He squints and peers across the Maidan.

Fringed by coconut palms, the field is hosting eight or nine cricket games this evening. Spaced so close to one another, the players' clothes are the only way to tell the games apart. The skinny teenage boys in jeans and colorful T-shirts shouting at one another are clearly not associated with the groups of older men wearing white uniforms with chest guards, batting gloves, and helmets.

As the sun drops, Alex and I watch the players bat, argue, and switch spots on the pitch. Crows swoop low until someone hits a ball and they disperse. A kid in a Kolkata Knight Riders shirt catches a ball near us. He sees Alex, pauses, and grins.

"Hello, Sir, how are you?"

"Hey, buddy," Alex replies, looking up. "Good game?"

The kid grins again, nodding his head.

"Ey sala," his teammates shout at him. "Get back!"

"Cool jersey," Alex calls out, as the kid runs back to his friends.

I pull my knees up. "You knowing IPL?"

"What's that?"

"Indian Premier League. That boy is wearing IPL team shirt. Finals was in May. Mumbai Indians winning. First time."

"First time, eh? What was that like?"

I smile. "Big party, all over whole city."

"Did you go to the game?"

Does he not know how much IPL matches cost? "No, I watching on TV with my friend at neighbor house. Thirty people coming to watch."

"Where was that?"

"In Behrampada only. Where I am living."

Surprisingly, he doesn't look at me with pity when I mention my slum. Instead, his eyes grow wide. "Thirty people? Was it a big home?"

"Arre, no. Small only. So much of people, hard to breathe." Neighbor after neighbor had filtered into the hut, and soon people were packed in so tight Tazim and I couldn't have left even if we'd wanted to.

"Thirty people in a small space," he says, eyebrows raised. "Could you imagine if someone passed gas?"

"Someone did, many times," I blurt out, smiling at the memory. The smell hung in the room for over an hour because it had nowhere to escape to, and Tazim and I giggled all night about it.

"How'd you celebrate the win? Did you go out? People in North America spill out onto the streets and party all night when we win big sporting events."

"Pataakhe," I say, my eyes itching at the thought of the burning gunpowder smell that accompanies the cascades of golden stars and white sparks.

"Pataakhe? Oh, I know this—firecrackers, right?"

"Ji," I say, surprised. "You are knowing some Hindi!"

"My mom put me in Hindi classes when I was little but it never really stuck. My dad is white, so my parents don't speak it in the home."

"Your father not learning Hindi?"

"He has no reason to."

I wonder if his mother feels the same way.

"You know, I was thinking about our conversation the other day," Alex says, pulling brown blades of grass out of the ground. "If you did go to college, what would you study?"

"I'm telling you, there is no money."

"I know, I know. But if you had the money. What would you study? Law, like Gauri and everyone else?"

"No," I say, without skipping a beat. Never. I don't want to go through all those years of schooling just to be stressed and underpaid like Vivek and the other lawyers.

"Engineering?"

"No, no, only very smart persons is becoming engineer."

He lifts a single eyebrow. "Who told you that?"

"Gauri Ma'am, her daughter is engineer." How many times have I had to listen to her boast about how brilliant Neha is? *Neha was her class topper at IIT. Neha tutored her fellow students for fun. Neha was three years into her PhD in electrical engineering on a full scholarship before she quit her studies to become a housewife to that Hindu nationalist NRI buffoon.*

"Okay, I get it, no engineering. There must be something you want to do instead of . . . what you do now."

I point at the older men in white uniforms. "Cricket player?"

Alex smiles. "Be serious, Rakhi."

How to be serious about something I've never been serious about? My gaze wanders past the clock tower, toward the big white Trident Hotel in Nariman Point. "Working in hotel?" I suggest, hoping he'll stop asking after this.

"Do you need to go to college for that?"

I nod, thinking back to what Tazim said about the Marquis. "Hotel college."

"Oh right, like hotel management. That's a booming industry in Asia. You could start out at a front desk one day, and in five years have a whole slew of staff reporting to you. Plus, there are tons of luxury hotels in India, let alone the rest of the world. You could go work in Singapore, or Hong Kong, or Bangkok. You could even work on a luxury cruise ship, I bet. Any idea where you'd want to work?"

I'd never thought about working in a hotel until recently. Maybe he's on to something. "Bombay only," I reply. Where else would I go? My home is here. Gauri Ma'am is here.

"But wouldn't you want to go away? Experience a different city? Have you ever lived elsewhere?"

I hesitate and clear my throat before I remember that Alex still doesn't know about Bihar or the Asha School, or that I lived on the streets before that. And he doesn't have to know any of it.

"No. I am living Bombay since long time."

"Where do your parents live?"

I swallow. "Far away."

"Are you married?"

I grimace and tell him no. As if I would be sitting on the Oval Maidan at dusk with him if I had a husband.

"You're a real lone wolf, aren't you?"

Suddenly aware of my hair flying around in the breeze, I try to smooth it down. "Means what?"

"You're all alone in this huge city. It's cool, though. You can do whatever you want."

Gauri Ma'am told me the same thing when she offered me the job at Justice For All. And now look at me, five years later. Being ordered around by everyone in the office. Being forced to see Dr. Pereira even though I don't want to. And I still haven't found Babloo.

"Look," Alex says. "I have an idea. The money Gauri is paying me to be a consultant—that can be yours. You can use it for application fees."

I blink twice. "How much money?"

"I'll be honest," he replies, "it's not really that much. She's only paying me forty thousand rupees for my two months here. I'd make more working full time at a coffee shop in Toronto for two weeks."

Is he serious? That's almost as much as the junior lawyers make in two months.

"So listen: show me around the city, I'll pay you a tour guide fee, and then you've earned the money. You can put it toward your school fees."

I'm not sure what to start with—that Gauri Ma'am is paying an intern, or that this intern wants to give me all this money. My scalp prickles at the thought of how badly this could go.

"It's nice to get paid, but I don't need the cash. And I was never expecting it, anyway. So, what do you say?" Alex asks, his eyes bright.

Forty thousand rupees. I've never even seen so much money at once. But Gauri Ma'am would kill me. Leaning away from Alex, I lower my gaze to the ground and start picking at the grass. "No," I say, trying not to look at him. "I am not taking the money."

"You wouldn't be taking it, you'd be earning it. You show me around Mumbai a few times a week, and we practice English and work on your applications. You can even teach me a bit of Hindi. It would be purely transactional."

Transactional. That's the same word Gauri Ma'am used to warn Gemma and Giles about why I shouldn't join them in Kerala. But Alex is saying it like it's a good thing.

The cracking sound of a cricket ball being batted hard ripples across the field. The ball climbs straight up in the evening sky, arcs high, then plummets down, landing on the grass near us with a thud. Alex springs forward to retrieve it, then skips a few steps, arching his back and lengthening his body as he lazily throws the ball back to the bright-shirted boys. The Kolkata Knight Riders jersey kid asks him to come play with them, but Alex holds his palm up to decline, nodding his head back toward me. The kid's friends whoop and make kissing noises. One of them thrusts his pelvis at us a few times like he's in some vulgar song and dance.

Alex chuckles. "No, no, not like that! Next time I'll play." He jogs back to me. "Kids," he says as he plops down.

The boys disperse across the field, back to their game, but one of them walks our way, his eyes fixed on me. A moustache sprouts above the corners of his lips. He can't be more than seventeen.

"You," he starts, pointing at me. "Where do you live?"

"Get out of here," I grunt, waving him away.

He takes a step closer, squinting his eyes. "I've seen you somewhere."

It hits me—this is the boy who came to collect a packet of roti from Tazim last week. "I live in Mazgaon," I lie. "Do you live in Mazgaon?"

The boy shakes his head no, takes one last look at me, then runs back to his friends.

"What was that about?" Alex asks.

"Nothing," I respond, shifting sideways so I'm not facing the cricket games anymore. *Shit.* If this kid goes around telling people in his family that I was watching cricket with a firanghi man, how long will it take before word gets to Tazim? I wrinkle my nose at the thought of how many more times I might have to keep lying to her. On the other hand, what kind of fool would I be to turn down a lump of cash because some little chutiya from Behrampada might see me and spin stories?

I take a breath in and release it slowly, turning to face Alex. "If I saying yes, you telling anyone? Gauri Ma'am?"

"No, of course not. It would be hard to explain, anyway. I promise this will be worth it."

I look at Alex, and then at the kid in the distance, who is still gawking at me from the cricket pitch. Forty thousand rupees. "Okay. We do it. Thank you."

Alex smiles. "Don't thank me. You're the one doing all the work."

....

Later that evening, at Tazim's, I sit on the floor rolling a red plastic bangle toward Ayub. Each time he catches it, he hands it back to me.

"No, baba, roll it, see?" I position it upright and press down on the top so it goes spinning across the concrete toward him. He squeals when it hits his toes.

I glance up at Tazim, cooking a roti over her burner. It puffs up into a perfect sphere, and she flips it onto a plate.

"No parcels today?" I ask, doing my best to sound casual as I roll the bangle to Ayub once more.

"They already came."

"Your customers pick up every day?"

"Not yet. It's hard to know if I can rely on this extra money." She slaps a roti on my plate. "Come on, eat. Ayub, give Ammi the bangle."

"The boy who came last week for roti. The one with the cricket bat. Who is he?"

She frowns. "Mehru Begum's grandson? I don't know his name. Her children and grandchildren live in Santacruz, anyway. She only ordered roti because they were all visiting the other day. Why do you want to know?"

"Asking only," I say, relieved that he won't be dropping by regularly.

After rolling out a few more rotis, Tazim joins Ayub and me on the floor, her joints cracking loudly as she sits. "Allah," she groans, softly. "Must have hurt my knee swabbing those hard marble floors."

"You okay?"

She adjusts her weight, wincing as she leans back against the wall. "Just promise me one thing. When you finally cash in that winning ticket you're sitting on, and you go and get a nice job and a nice flat, make sure Ayub isn't doing the kind of work his parents are."

I draw my knees up and hug them, wanting so badly to tell Tazim that in a couple of months I'm going to have enough money to go to college and get hired at the Marquis. That perhaps one day I'll even open my own Marquis. Or my own business. It feels like electric currents are running through my fingers just thinking about it.

I lower my head to hide my excitement. "Bilkul, Tazim. I promise you."

11

HAVING RISEN AND BATHED EARLIER than usual, I arrive at work by eight. Gauri Ma'am is already there, having a conversation with somebody in her office. I tiptoe past her open door to my workspace.

"It's a risky idea, Rubinaji," Ma'am says gently. "My office doesn't have the resources to organize a rally. Not to mention it would disrupt our regular casework, and we're already short-staffed."

I hold my body perfectly still and take small quiet breaths in and out so they don't notice me.

"A minor disruption, Gauriji. You leave the details to me." Rubina Mansoor waves her hands while her bangles jingle. "Just get your staff and peers to spread the word, and I'll handle the fine print. Actors, models, directors—they'll all join in. The newspapers will report, the cameras will come, and you and I will be front-page. People will remember us." She clinks her heavy ring on a water glass as she says this last bit.

"With all due respect, we are asking the Supreme Court of India to appeal a decision of the Bombay High Court. Rallies don't sway judges. Strong evidence and good arguments do." Gauri Ma'am's voice sounds like honey being pushed through an old sieve—cloying and strained.

"Gauriji," Rubina says, her voice just as syrupy, "you think the Supreme Court is immune to public opinion?"

There's no rebuttal from Ma'am. Just a strange silence, which lingers for a while until Rubina pierces through it.

"And then there's the question of donations for the organization, too. My husband's company will no doubt be interested. They're into all this corporate social responsibility, you know. They're the first major developers in the city to start constructing sustainable luxury buildings. Using materials that will help reduce energy and water usage."

"I've seen the billboards."

"They've won awards three years running. It's just terrible, what these other two-bit builders have done to the Mumbai cityscape, isn't it? Total environmental degradation. Not a care for the plight of this place. Only concerned with cutting corners and lining their pockets. Anyway, I know we can rely on the Arora Group to help support our cause, financially."

"Financially?" Ma'am's voice is small.

Rubina's laugh rings loudly, like bells in a temple. "Justice For All is on-brand for his company, but still Jeetendra will do whatever I say. What are men for, na? Tell me, what does your husband do?"

Gauri Ma'am clears her throat. "He's also a lawyer. Lives in Delhi. It has been a while since we last spoke."

"What happened?"

"Nothing terrible. Just divorce. He decided he didn't want to come third anymore."

"Third?" Rubina asks, amused. "Who was first and who was second?"

"Second was my work. First, our daughter."

I bite my tongue to keep from making a sound. Neha would certainly disagree with her first-place rank.

....

"What do you mean you're a goddamn consultant?" Saskia's voice thunders all the way to the kitchen, where I nearly drop the tray of midmorning tea.

In their workspace, the Dutch girls loom above Alex, who's sitting calmly in his chair, hands folded in his lap. "I mean exactly that."

"And what are you doing as a consultant that you weren't doing as an intern?"

"I'm doing research for the Chembur appeal with Gauri, Vivek, and Bhavana."

Oh no. Now it's out in the open. The steam rising from the twelve little teacups warms the bottom of my chin as I continue watching the three of them.

Saskia's head snaps back. "Chembur? How is that possible? You're just an intern, like Merel and me. In fact, we have more education than you, because we're actually in master's programs. You haven't even started yours yet."

"At Harvard," he whispers under his breath.

"What did you say?" Saskia puts her hands on her hips.

"Look, I'm sorry if this is upsetting to you, but don't take it out on me. I didn't offer myself a promotion. Gauri did."

Merel tosses her hair, huffing impatiently. "So what, did you just ask for a new title? Are you getting paid as well, for god's sake?"

Alex fiddles with a pencil on his desk. "The terms and conditions of my employment here are strictly between me and—"

"You're getting paid?" Saskia roars.

"I didn't say I was getting paid. You inferred that," Alex calls out as Saskia stomps to Gauri Ma'am's office and flings the door open. I nearly drop the tray of tea again, startled at her shameless display of defiance. I squeeze my eyes shut, waiting for Gauri Ma'am to pounce, but instead Saskia just groans.

"Of course Gauri's not here. How can you presume to lead a damn organization when you're never present?"

....

News of Alex's promotion spreads quickly. The lawyers' reactions are just as hostile as I expected.

"Why would a firanghi undergraduate be chosen to work on the Chembur file over me?" Kamini wails before disappearing into the latrine.

"Over any of us," Utkarsh shouts back.

Jayshree suggests that Justice For All can't be in that much trouble if there is money in our budget to pay an intern.

"Vivek Sir, this has to be a mistake," Bhavana says. "Will you please talk to Gauri Ma'am for us?"

Maybe Ma'am's decision is unfair, but I'm not bothered by it. Not when none of these people ever notice how unfairly she treats me.

When Ma'am finally returns to the office, it's already early evening and everyone but Bhavana, Vivek, and I have gone home. She trudges to her desk, slamming the door.

Eyes wide, Bhavana pokes Vivek on the shoulder. "Go talk to her," she mouths silently.

Vivek nods, rising to his feet. He tugs at his collar, then walks over to Ma'am's office, tapping on the door with his knuckles before entering and shutting the door softly behind him. Bhavana tiptoes to my workspace, pressing her finger to her lips as she crouches beside my desk.

After some muffled conversation we can't quite pick up, Gauri Ma'am declares, "I *am* trying, Vivek. They must learn not to feel entitled to things because of how long they have worked here. If they show me they can do the work, I will reward them. It's that simple."

"They aren't entitled, Gauri Ma'am," Vivek pleads. "But this intern? What skills does he have that you need?"

"Don't you think I did my due diligence before I hired him? He's quite smart, and writes crisply, clearly. His research skills are better than anyone's in this office. And he already has access to online research databases we don't."

"How?"

"Through Harvard. He has a friend who started the same pro-gram last year. They've given him use of their accounts."

"I suppose that's good. But the pay? Why should he get a stipend? You've never paid an intern before."

"Vivek, this is how you invest in the future of an organization. If I give Rubina's firanghi friend a good experience, she will reward us with her continued support. And who knows, maybe after he's done at Harvard he'll be interested in supporting us in some kind of way."

"Gauriji, this is wishful thinking. At least try to see this from the staff's perspective."

"You go back and tell them that anyone who doesn't like it can find a job elsewhere."

....

At the end of the week, Gauri Ma'am emerges from her office and marches toward the lawyers' workspace. "Everyone, gather round quick. Alex and Rakhi, you, too," she calls. "Did any of you assign work to the Dutch interns?"

"Ma'am, I did," Vivek says.

"Me too," Bhavana adds.

Gauri Ma'am taps her fingers on the shared table. "Anyone else? No? Good. You should all know that they have resigned."

Finally.

Vivek's eyes pop. "They've left their internships?"

"Yes, they have abandoned their posts and forsaken their work. I received an email this morning from the two of them. They have left us to work for another NGO."

Alex raises his eyebrows, as if he's amused.

Vivek takes a step toward Gauri Ma'am, touching his palm to the side of his face. "Are they still in Bombay? Did they leave anything behind?"

"Yes, they are still in the city. Rakhi, go check their desks."

Their desks are empty. Only tea stains, notepads, and an unopened pack of Orbit chewing gum. I slip the gum into my pocket, relieved I won't have to deal with them anymore. "Ma'am, nothing there," I say.

"I lent them some books," Vivek murmurs. "From my own collection."

"You call them, then," Ma'am says. "The rest of you are not to have any contact with them, teek hain?"

The lawyers all mouth yes, or nod in agreement. As if anyone here was planning on staying in touch with those two after they left.

After Gauri Ma'am leaves, the lawyers chatter and whisper, throwing stares at Alex, who is back at his desk with his earphones in.

"Those girls were hopping mad that Alex was getting paid," Bhavana mutters to Vivek. "Never thought they'd quit, though."

"As long as we don't lose any of the lawyers," Vivek replies.

....

Later that afternoon, Alex asks me if I know of a Muslim neighborhood near the office. "I saw it featured on some TV show in Canada. The hosts went around eating kebabs at different food stalls."

Bohri Mohalla, he means. He suggests we go there tonight.

"After all lawyers leaving," I reply.

It's almost seven by the time everyone clears out. I follow Alex out the door, checking behind me every couple of seconds to make sure Gauri Ma'am doesn't emerge from her office and see us. Halfway down the steps, I pause. What if there are people from Behrampada in Bohri Mohalla? Someone could tell Tazim. And then? Would she piece together that her memsahib's nephew and I are spending time together?

Alex stares up at me from the bottom of the stairs. "Coming?"

There are millions of people in this city. Seeing the kid who picked up roti at Tazim's at the Oval Maidan was a one-time thing, surely. I tighten my fists and march down the stairs before I can change my mind. "Yes, coming."

The tinny sound of the azaan from nearby Minara Masjid fills the air, almost loud enough to drown out the *caw-caw* of hungry crows. Alex and I wait a few minutes on the street, as people stream into the mosque to offer evening prayers before eating. When the sun dips behind the buildings on Mohammed Ali Road, the naked yellow bulbs hanging over the stalls light up, and the food vendors in their crocheted white skull caps and hennaed beards start to cook up endless pieces of meat on charcoal grills. The blare of car and motorbike horns and the usual market shouting punctuate the crackle and sizzle of the food stalls. Above us, hawks circle high in the sky.

"Bhaiyya, we'll have two of those," Alex says, pointing to dangling skewers of kebabs and chicken legs. He insists on calling all the food vendors "bhaiyya," because he believes it will get us quicker service. I want to tell him we're already getting quick service because he's a firanghi.

Perched on small red plastic stools in front of the food stalls, we balance our steel plates on our laps, the glare of motorcycle headlights shining bright in our faces. A group of women in black floor-length burqas sweep past us and Alex shoves his stool back to let them pass.

"I still can't believe Merel and Saskia quit," he says. "You think it's because of me?"

I peer up from my chicken leg. "Yes," I mutter. "Of course." Is this thought only occurring to him now?

Alex tears a rumali roti apart with both hands. "It's kind of sad how people don't seem to want to ask Gauri for anything. I mean, I asked for all the things she gave me. You can't just sit back and wait for things to happen."

I opt not to tell him that if he had asked for even another cup of tea without his Rubina connection, Gauri Ma'am would have sent him packing.

"People in India are so deferential to authority."

"Means?"

"They don't stand up for themselves. Don't worry—I can say that because I'm Indian."

"You are Indian?" I laugh so hard I cough on a coriander leaf that gets caught at the back of my throat.

"Okay, okay," Alex says, handing me his bottle of Bisleri. "Fair enough." He sits back on his stool and starts mopping up his bheja fry with the rest of his roti. "What is this, anyway?"

I point to a large metal platter near the hot tawa, piled high with uncooked organ meat. His eyes scan the hearts and kidneys, and then his face falls. "Brains?" He stares at his plate and then at me. "What animal?"

"Goat."

His eyes briefly bulge at the food on his plate, before a smile creeps across his face. "You know, I wouldn't eat bananas until I was sixteen. I couldn't even touch them with my fingers. Thought they were the grossest thing in the world." He pops the last bit of bheja fry into his mouth, beaming like he's won an award. "And look at me now."

"You are proper Mumbaikar now," I tease.

"Maybe I am," he says, unaware that I'm making fun of him. "What if I get a job here after I'm done at Harvard? We can keep coming back here until I've tasted every last organ there is to try."

"You coming back?" I ask, my cheeks warming at how pleased I am by this prospect.

"Why not? I'll swing by the fancy hotel where you work at the end of your shift, and we'll come down here together. You'll pay, of course, since you'll be making more money than me . . ."

"Arre," I chuckle, elbowing him. In what world would I make more money than someone like Alex?

"Think about it," he says, springing up to order more chicken kebabs.

As he points to pieces of meat, I consider what he's saying. My shoulders drop unexpectedly, and for the first time in eleven years, it's as though I have no past to hold me down, and I no longer have to fear for my future. I feel like I could push up off my feet and my whole body could float away, and it wouldn't matter which way was the right direction.

THE MOST PLEASANT I EVER saw Gauri Ma'am was in the lead-up to her daughter Neha's brief visit to Bombay two years back.

We got away with murder. Sudeepthi asked to take a longer leave than usual around Christmastime so she could spend a few weeks with her granny in Manipal, and Gauri Ma'am approved it. Jayshree spilled her tea all over a stack of Gauri Ma'am's papers, and Ma'am laughed it off, cheerfully. And when Utkarsh, newly hired at the time, said India shouldn't decriminalize homosexuality because it would open the door to legalizing bestiality, Ma'am allowed Bhavana and Sudeepthi to tear several strips off him, instead of doing it herself. She also didn't fire him, which everyone felt was far too generous.

Before Neha and her husband's arrival, Ma'am asked me to accompany her to the airport to help with bags and getting them settled. Not that I really had a choice. Their flight would arrive at midnight, and they would stay at Gauri Ma'am's house before going on to Goa the next day for a friend's wedding.

The air was cool that night at the arrivals gate. Gauri Ma'am lent me her shawl to keep warm as we waited for Neha and Yogi to come out. Next to us, bored drivers dressed in white uniforms held signs that read MCKINSEY & CO—MISS PRIYA GAUTAM and MR SRINIVAS VODAFONE.

"I think this will be a good visit," Ma'am said, twisting her gold bangle around her wrist over and over again. "We'll start fresh. She just needs a reminder of what she's left behind."

"Ji, Ma'am," I said, even though I had no idea what the disagreement between them was about. I was curious to meet Neha, at last. I had never met anyone who had stood up to Gauri Ma'am.

After watching the steady stream of sleepy travelers dwindle, we were still left waiting.

"You think something happened?" Ma'am asked me, her foot bouncing impatiently. "I bet customs is holding them up." Finally, she dialed Neha's number, grumbling about the international charges. "Hello? Hello, Neha? Where are you?"

I could hear Neha's voice on the other end of the line. "Ma? We're already at the hotel. Why?"

"What hotel?" Ma'am said, her voice rising. "I've been waiting at the gate for almost two hours."

"Yogi emailed you before we left. Haven't you checked your email in the past twenty-four hours?"

"I haven't seen any email," she said, her back stiffening.

"We decided to just go to a hotel after the flight. We've got our flight to Goa tomorrow morning anyways. It didn't make sense to drive all the way to Mahim, sleep for five hours, then come back to the airport. And you know Yogi has asthma. Sitting in a taxi twice for no reason, what's the point in that?"

I almost felt sorry for Ma'am as she let out a forceful breath. "It's been three years since I've seen you."

"Ma, stop it. We'll see you on our way out. We're flying back to Bombay on January third for a whole day, remember?"

"Don't bother coming to see me, then," she declared, her nostrils flaring. "Go back to America from Goa."

"Ma!" Neha shouted through the phone. "You're being dramatic again."

Maybe Ma'am was being dramatic, but Neha was really pushing the limit. How hard would it be just to allow herself to be picked up at the airport, given a bed to sleep in, and dropped off at the airport again?

"Because I raised you to be an intelligent person, Neha. And instead you throw away your career to be some housewife. And to a controlling, neoconservative NRI who you follow around as though you're an obedient puppy."

"Controlling? You want to talk about controlling? You're so obsessed with being self-righteous that you alienate anyone who doesn't agree with your radical opinions. You always put your work ahead of your family."

"No, I have always put you first, Neha. But I never raised you to be so apathetic. I never raised you to pick a man over your own ambition. I never raised—" Gauri Ma'am stopped and looked at her phone, her eyebrows drawing together. Neha had hung up on her.

She pinched the top of her nose and pushed out three slow, deep breaths. "Come, Rakhi," she said. "Let's get a taxi."

We rode in silence down the Western Express, Ma'am staring out the window. I wondered what else Neha could get away with if she tried. If there was anything Neha could do to make Gauri Ma'am love her any less. Were there limits? And was this why Gauri Ma'am was so strict with everyone at the office? Because she could never manage to control her own daughter?

As the taxi slowed to a stop near the main road leading to Behrampada, I slid to the door to make a quick exit.

"Wait," she said, reaching for my arm. "There's a lesson here for you."

Her nostrils flared slightly, and she swallowed. Was she going to cry? I froze, overcome with a strange mix of horror and concern.

She didn't cry, though. Instead, she caught her breath and then looked me in the eye. "Even when people hurt us," she said, "how we respond is a test of our loyalty to them."

Did it ever enter her head, I wondered, that there might be a lesson here for her, too?

ON MONDAY, GAURI MA'AM SITS me down with a pair of dull scissors in front of a stack of newspapers and instructs me to scan for stories about Justice For All.

"Ma'am, won't you know if there's a story about us? The journalist would interview you, na?"

"If Rubina gives even one sound bite to a journalist and mentions our name, I must know about it. Now stop asking questions."

When I'm done, I bring her four articles. She runs her finger over a headline from last week's *Times of India*: "BATTLE OVER FOR VICTIMS OF CHEMBUR FORCED EVICTION, HIGH COURT SAYS."

"These papers get more ridiculous every year," she murmurs. She flips through the rest of the clippings. "What's this?" She pulls a story I found in the *Mumbai Mirror*: "FORMER FILM STAR DEDICATES LIFE TO SQUASHING POVERTY."

"Vivek," Gauri Ma'am shouts. "Get in here, right now!"

Vivek appears in the doorway, eyebrows raised. "What's going on?"

"Just read this." Ma'am holds the article out to him as he sucks in his gut to squeeze past me.

"*Rubina Mansoor, one of Bollywood's nineties screen queens, is speak-*

ing out on ridding India of poverty . . . ? I don't know if she can really be called a screen queen, but—"

"Keep going." Ma'am covers her eyes with her palms.

"*'I love India, and India loves me,' the superstar said. 'I want to give back everything it has given me and more.'* What does she mean by that?"

"Read out the bit where she talks about us."

"Accha . . . Okay, okay . . . *Rubina has partnered with local human rights organization Justice For All, which operates under the leadership of Advocate Gauri Verma, a veteran human rights lawyer. 'Gauri and I both want the same things for our country, but we have different ways to get there. She fights in the courtroom, whereas I am well poised to arouse the beating heart of this nation . . .'* Arouse? What does she mean, 'arouse'?"

"Finish reading."

"*'Together, we look forward to a brilliant partnership.'*" Vivek puts the article down and rubs his chin. Both of them stare at the clipping for a moment. "Gauriji, did you and Rubina agree to send out a message that you were working together?"

"Of course not." Ma'am wrings her hands. "This is all moving so fast."

"Call Rubina up. We must control this situation before it controls us."

"You're right." Gauri Ma'am wipes her upper lip with her handkerchief before her eyes dart to me. "What are you still doing in here?"

"I was just leaving, Ma'am."

"Rakhi," she says, as I exit her office. "Good job finding this article. Never thought I'd see my name printed in the *Mumbai Mirror*."

. . . .

The next morning, Gauri Ma'am tells everyone to assemble in the lawyers' work area. "I want you all to know I'll be filming a segment for *Good Morning Mumbai* with Rubina Mansoor today," she announces. "It will air later this week."

"But Gauri Ma'am, you never do television interviews," Bhavana says.

It's true. She says TV makes obedient sheep of us all.

"Correct, Bhavana." Ma'am smiles and pulls her shoulders back. "But times are changing and we must change with them."

Kamini puts her hand up. "Ma'am, what will you be talking about?"

"Chembur, first and foremost. The slum demolition, the High Court's judgment, its decision to deny us leave to appeal. But also the work that we, that you, all do. The exposure will raise our public profile, which will in turn generate more support."

After the meeting, I stay behind in the lawyers' workspace to try a bunch of keys on a drawer Utkarsh has locked. "You lost the key I gave you?" I ask him.

"I misplaced it," he says, side-eyeing me. "Anyways, it's your job to carry the spare keys. And don't tell Gauri Ma'am, understand?"

From her desk beside him, Kamini taps Utkarsh on the arm. She's got the *Good Morning Mumbai* webpage open on her computer.

He leans over as she scrolls down the page. "My ma loves this show."

Kamini frowns and reads out the titles of the featured videos. "*Slim Down in Twelve Days with Three Simple Exercises . . . Menstruating Women Banned Entry into Religious Sites: Discretion or Discrimination?* Uff, is this really the way to go? So tacky, na?"

Utkarsh scratches the pockmarks on his forehead. "How should we know? We're only two years out of law college."

"We're not idiots, Utkarsh. We're allowed to have opinions."

....

Once the *Good Morning Mumbai* interview is posted, the office breaks out into a frenzy I can hear from the supply closet at the back of the office, where I am stacking yellow writing pads and half-opened boxes of ballpoint pens.

"Come, Rakhi," I hear Gauri Ma'am say from behind me. "Even you should be seeing this."

As all the lawyers scramble to Vivek's desk, I stand on my toes behind Utkarsh, craning my neck to see about half the screen. Vivek has cued up a clip called "Bollywood Actress Teams Up with Lawyer in Fight for Slum-dwellers." The video starts with Gauri Ma'am and Rubina sitting on chairs set next to each other on a shiny black stage, facing a thick-haired man in a white shirt, black vest, and glasses. He introduces himself as Ashutosh Gupta.

Alex moves back to stand beside me, then taps Utkarsh on the shoulder. "Hey, man, Rakhi can't see."

Utkarsh glances back at Alex and then me. "So?"

"So move."

"Chill, bro, it's in English, she won't even understand," Utkarsh says.

"She speaks really good English, actually. And who are you to decide who gets to see the clip?"

"It's okay," I croak, stepping farther back.

"She's an officewali. She doesn't actually need to know any of this," Utkarsh replies.

Chutiya. I hope he's the first to go when Ma'am has to start making cuts.

"Are you serious?" Alex says, staring Utkarsh in the face. "Step aside."

"Chup, both of you," Bhavana hisses in our direction as the clip starts. "Utkarsh, make space for Rakhi."

He stiffens but moves a few inches to the left, eyeing Alex angrily. On screen, Ashutosh introduces Rubina, then tilts his head toward Ma'am. "Gauri Verma is a human rights lawyer who newspapers have taken to calling the 'Champion of the Exploited.' Gauriji, tell us what that means."

"Well," Ma'am starts, "I don't give myself these names, but at Justice For All—"

"That's the name of your organization, right?"

"Correct. At Justice For All we engage mostly in public interest litigation, but we also believe that social and political movements, combined with public education, are crucial tools in the fight to advance human rights. In light of the Bombay High Court's decision on Chembur—"

"And for our viewers, this is a case in which you took on the government for bulldozing a slum, and lost."

"Yes. In light of this decision, which we plan to appeal to the Supreme Court of India, we are embarking on a public interest campaign alongside the litigation."

"Tell me why." Ashutosh pushes his glasses up.

Gauri Ma'am unfolds her hands. "Well, greater awareness of issues makes the process of social change more participatory—"

"Let's face it, Ashutosh," Rubina interrupts, while Ma'am's eyes harden. "How many of your friends know what happened in Chembur? Sure, they've seen the headlines, but do they truly know? And if they did, wouldn't they demand better? India is fast asleep. But who's going to wake them up? Politicians? Name me one politician who isn't stained with corruption. Religious leaders? You'll never find a guruji who speaks for Muslims, Christians, Sikhs, Buddhists, and Hindus alike. So who do the people trust? The answer, you could say, is staring you in the face." She beams and Gauri Ma'am shifts in her seat, her chin dipping down.

Ashutosh leans forward. "And what is the answer, Rubina?"

"Celebrities." Her eyes gleam, as though she's just divulged some secret knowledge. "Tell me, who else can convince a billion people to drink one brand of cola over another one, when both sodas taste exactly the same?"

Ashutosh cuts in, waving his pen in the air. "If you're talking about Coca-Cola and Pepsi, I think some might argue that they taste somewhat—"

"But not just any celebrity, you see! For the right price, anybody can sip from a bottle on camera. But with a charity, there's no money being dangled in our faces. These causes must be headed by a star who is true in her commitment and dedication. Not all celebrities have the passion and grit to do television appearances one minute, then march in the streets the next."

"And Gauriji, has Justice For All found its celebrity ambassador in Rubina Mansoor?"

There is a brief pause, as though Gauri Ma'am is swallowing an uncomfortably large pill. "Just listening to her, Ashutosh, I think you'll agree we have."

Staring into the camera, Rubina Mansoor bats her eyelashes the same way she did in the "Drip Drip" video, and I half expect her to break into a dance routine.

The segment continues with Ma'am trying to talk about the impact of forced evictions on families, and Rubina cutting her off to talk about how her husband's green buildings will save the city from environmental catastrophe. When the video ends, we all turn around to face Ma'am, who is standing behind us, her arms crossed.

Bhavana takes a deep breath. "We support whichever direction you choose to go in, Ma'am, but Rubina Mansoor? Are you sure about this?"

"Yes, I am sure," Ma'am replies without hesitation, as if she was expecting this question.

Vivek stops shifting his weight from side to side. "What if she says something that doesn't align with—"

Ma'am raises her hand. "Just stop. Rubina Mansoor isn't going anywhere. In fact, she is very much our last hope. Not just for Chembur, but for all of you. Because with her squawking on TV like this, the media will pay attention to us. Which means the people will pay attention to us. And when people pay attention to us, we can raise more funds. And with more funds, you'll all keep getting paid and won't have to worry about our office shutting down by the new year."

I hadn't realized things were that bad.

"And while I have you all here, you should know that I have taken permission from the police for us to march from the Oval Maidan to the Bombay High Court in mid-August."

Vivek looks perplexed. "For what purpose, Gauri?"

"It will be a protest against the High Court's decision to deny us leave to appeal the Chembur case," she announces, beaming.

Everyone goes completely silent. The room is still.

"For once, you all have nothing to say?"

"It sounds pretty cool," Alex says. "Are we planning on getting a lot of people to march with us?"

"Thank you, Alex," Gauri Ma'am says, probing each of the lawyers with her eyes. "And yes, by drumming up media attention on Chembur over the next three weeks, we'll get more people to join us. As we work out the logistics, you will all have additional work to do, on top of your files."

"I can reach out to different organizations," Alex volunteers. "If anyone wants to help me."

"Ma'am, I'll do it. He doesn't know the NGO world," Sudeepthi says, sneering at Alex.

Kamini raises her hand. "Gauri Ma'am, what if we disrupt traffic? The public has such low tolerance for being inconvenienced, especially when they don't even empathize with the issue. Are you concerned—"

"That's the entire point of protest," Alex interrupts, cocking his head to the side. "To disrupt business as usual. To call attention to an issue."

Kamini's mouth twists as she tries to form words but nothing comes out.

"Is Rubina a part of this protest?" asks Bhavana, rubbing at a mosquito bite on her wrist.

"Of course she is. Is that a problem?"

Bhavana clenches her jaw. "Perhaps she and her designer handbag should go visit what's left of the Chembur slum so she can more accurately understand the human rights violations she's so passionate about."

Gauri Ma'am just glares at her, as if daring her to continue.

Bhavana knows better than that, though. She lets out a long, shaky breath and casts her eyes back down to the red welt on her wrist. The rest of the lawyers, shuffling back to their seats, say nothing.

"DOES ANYONE HERE CELEBRATE RAMADAN?" Alex asks in the lawyers' workspace as I'm handing out tea.

"No," Bhavana replies, not looking up from her computer. "And you mean *observe*, not celebrate."

"Too bad. I went to this great place to eat the other day that's supposed to be a big deal during Ramadan."

"Accha?" Kamini says, turning around from her computer. "Where did you go?"

"Bohri Mohalla," Alex says, glancing at me. I avert my eyes. He's not going to tell people I brought him there, is he?

"Who took you there?" Kamini asks. "That's pakka local."

"I saw it on a travel show," he says, smiling politely. "I went by myself."

"You live close to there or what?" Sudeepthi asks.

"Not really. I'm staying in Pali Hill with my aunt and uncle."

Around the lawyers' workspace, eyebrows lift and lips press together.

"Bandra? Must be nice," Sudeepthi mumbles.

"What do your aunt and uncle do?" Vivek asks.

"He exports leather goods. She doesn't really work, but she keeps herself busy socializing. You know how it is."

"No, we don't," Utkarsh says, smirking.

"Where in Pali Hill?" Vivek asks, taking a sip of water.

"Oh, it's this building off St. Andrews Road. Blossoming Heights."

Vivek chokes on his water, then makes eye contact with me and points to my workstation. "Now," he mouths, his brow knotting.

Shit.

"Blossoming Heights is the building where that lady lived, isn't it? Motiani or some such?" Vivek whispers as we shuffle into the library. "And the husband, he worked in import-export, didn't he? Is this boy related to them?"

"Vivek Sir, you won't say anything, will you? Alex doesn't know about all that."

He drags over a chair and sits down. "Let me piece this together. The family that came to me after you stole from them—the family I lied to, saying you had disappeared—this exact same family has now sent their nephew to work at Justice For All?"

"Ji, Sir. But they didn't know you worked at Justice For All, remember? They only thought you were one lawyer working alone. So they won't find out if nobody says anything."

He says nothing, staring at my pile of moldy books on the floor.

"Please, Sir, you can't tell anyone. Especially not Gauri Ma'am."

He looks me in the eye. "All this lying, this deception. This is why Gauri Ma'am has been sending you to Dr. Pereira."

"Yes, but Vivek Sir, I didn't hire Alex, did I? I haven't done anything this time." This is mostly true, as long as he doesn't find out I'm showing Alex around Bombay for money.

Vivek goes quiet again.

"Sir, if any of them find out—Mrs. Motiani, Gauri Ma'am, whoever—you'll help me again, na?"

He chews on his lip for a moment, then speaks. "I lied for you once. I went against my own principles to do that. I want nothing but success for you, Rakhi, but I cannot cover for you again, understand?"

"Sir, but what if someone finds out—"

He rises to his feet, sighing heavily. "Then it will be yours to fix, teek hain?"

....

Since I said yes to Alex's offer, I've taken him to all the safe tourist spots that firanghis rave about: The Dadar phool gully, where he took hundreds of photos of flower vendors and their chaos of blooms and garlands but didn't actually buy anything. The Sassoon Docks on Sunday morning, where we wandered among the piles of pomfret and crabs but didn't stay long because he caught a whiff of drying bombil and almost vomited. Haji Ali, where the tide was too high to cross the causeway into the dargah, so we spent most of the evening ordering fruit creams from the juice center outside. Each time I returned home late, happily telling Tazim that work was busy—which was true, I guess.

A couple of days after Ma'am announced her rally plans, Alex and I wander to Marine Drive on Friday evening, strolling up the wide seaside promenade studded with six-story blocks of flats, coconut palms lined up in front of them like tall, swaying security guards.

"This would be a nice place to hold a protest," he says, as we wait for a vendor to hack the tops off big green coconuts with a curved black knife.

"Road is too big, na?" Marine Drive could easily fit ten lanes if drivers gave one another space. "Here, protest is looking empty. Gauri Ma'am will not like."

"Forget Gauri, Rubina will hate it more," Alex says, and I laugh.

Alex hands the coconutwala some cash and then turns to me. "How come everyone at the office hates Rubina so much?"

"She is . . . different," I say, reluctant to explain. How to get across to Alex all of Justice For All's troubles, made worse by the sudden entry of Rubina Mansoor as Gauri Ma'am's filmi new fix?

We find an empty spot on the big concrete ledge between the boulevard and the Arabian Sea. There are at least a hundred other people sitting on the ledge, gazing out at the sea as it reflects blazing orange sunlight. The tide is low now, exposing the stacks of large four-legged concrete structures (tetrapods, Vivek said they were called) that protect the city from flooding when the waves come in. A boy in dirty khakis hops between the star-shaped structures, stretching his arm to extract discarded Bisleri bottles, which he tosses into a nearly full gunny sack.

"You're right, she is different from the people at the office. She's rich, she's glamorous. She's also way less educated."

"Too much she is talking," I add.

Alex takes a sip of his brimming coconut through a pink straw. "She's a handful, but she doesn't hide who she is. I think that's her strength. She acknowledges her wealth, the world she comes from. She doesn't pretend to be virtuous and humble, like some people who work in this field."

At first I think he's talking about Gauri Ma'am, but then he goes on about his friends back home whose parents are surgeons and CEOs, who went to private schools and go on ski trips and safaris with their families every year, but still pretend to be poor because they live with roommates in the city. I tell him *poor* must mean something very different in Canada, and we laugh, slurping down the last bits of our coconut water.

My phone buzzes. It's Dr. Pereira's office. She's been calling me ever since I first skipped therapy last Wednesday. I ignore the call as usual, then whistle at the coconutwala to come here and carve a spoon out of the coconut shell so we can scoop out the creamy insides.

"You know, your English is really improving," Alex says. "You're pausing less, and your grammar is better. And you're talking more freely, too."

I take a bite of the glistening white coconut flesh to hide my embarrassed smile.

"You've got to kick that Indian English, though. Try to sound more . . . neutral."

"*Neutral* means what?"

"You know how Indian call centers phone up people in the West to sell them things? Well, they do much better if they speak American English. Or British English. I know, it's like, racist on some level, but that's the world we live in."

"Arre, I am Indian only."

"See, you just did it. 'I am Indian only.' You don't need the *only.*"

I flinch, staring down at my empty coconut. How many kinds of bhenchodh English do I have to learn now?

"Hey, what about your college applications? I should come over to your place sometime so we can work on them."

"I told you, na? You cannot come."

"You're overthinking this."

"People will talk."

"About me? What do I care what the people in your slum think?"

"About you. And me. All bakvaas things." I try to avoid his gaze and peer down at our feet hanging side by side, over the sea. His feet are big and white and his toes are hairy. My toes are dark and dry, marked with flecks of the purple nail polish Mrs. Motiani donated to Tazim last year.

Alex carves the rest of the flesh out of his coconut, then tosses the empty shell over the ledge. It bounces over the boulders until it finds its way into the sea, where it bobs on the surface of the waves. He leans back on his elbows, staring out at the red sun beginning to dip into the sparkling orange-black water.

"You've been taking me around after work and on the weekend. I have to hold up my end of the bargain and help you with your applications."

"You are paying me," I say.

"But the whole point of me paying you is so that you have money for college. I don't want to be some foreigner who comes to India for the adventure and doesn't give back, you know? It's so extractive and gross."

"It is okay," I say, clutching my empty coconut against my stomach. I'm not sure why he cares this much.

He drums his fingers on the ledge. "It'd be so much easier if we could work at my aunt's place. But they're just not the kind of people who . . . I mean . . . It would be awkward." He chews his lip for a moment then turns his face toward me. "You've never told me where your parents live."

I place the coconut shell on the ledge between us. I suppose there's no harm in being truthful about them. "My father, mother, both dead. From long time back."

Alex lifts himself off his elbows and turns his entire body away from the sunset so he's sitting cross-legged, facing me. "So, who raised you?"

"Nobody," I answer, before realizing I shouldn't have said it. He's still the only person in the office who doesn't know about my years on the streets.

When he asks what I mean, I tell him, "Nothing. Too long story."

"I don't have any place to be right now. Do you?"

Something bigger than me coaxes the words from my mouth. Maybe it's because he's genuinely interested. Or maybe it's because Gauri Ma'am isn't here to tell the story for me. "I was living on street. Near VT Station. For five years."

He just sits there, staring at me blankly. Finally, he says, "Are you joking?"

"No." My ears burn. I want him to stop gawking at me, but he presses for more detail.

One by one, I field his questions. *How did you end up on the street?* I tell him about running away from my uncle and onto a train in Patna, and arriving in Bombay. *What was it like, being on your own?* I had friends, we looked out for one another. Was it safe? No, of course not. *How did you get off the street?* I was sent to a girls' home when I was twelve. *Does anyone at Justice For All know?* They all know. *How come nobody told me?* Ask them.

Once he is out of questions, we sit in silence for a few minutes. Behind us, cars zoom up and down Marine Drive and the streetlights glow orange in the dusk. Ahead of us, the frothy tide rolls in, crashing against the boulders. A strong breeze sends a misty spray from the sea over us.

Alex turns to me once more. "And what about your friends from the street? Did they turn out okay, like you?"

I think about this, sorting through each one in my head. Pappu was long dead. We never saw Devi again after she was raped. Kalu ran away to Hyderabad. Salman and Raju, I have no idea. And Babloo . . .

I push a curl of hair behind my ear. "I don't know. It was long time back."

"You haven't tried to find them?"

"One, yes," I say, unable to meet his eyes. "My best friend."

"Where is she?"

"Can't find him now." Saying it out loud sends a shiver down my back.

"He didn't get sent to the same home as you?"

"It was home for girls only."

"And there was no boys' home for him?"

"I never saw him, I am telling you." I wish I hadn't revealed so much. At this rate he'll find out about the paanwala and Dongri, and will probably start treating me like everyone else does. My heart thunders in my chest.

Alex sits quietly for a while, wearing a grave expression on his face. "I'm sorry," he says, hesitating as if he is weighing his words. "I'm sorry you had to go through all that. Losing your parents. Running away. Living on the street. Losing your best friend. And you're doing so well, considering."

I stare down into my lap.

"Never in my life have I met anyone like you. You're going to go places. I can't wait to see what you go on to do."

"Hotel program, no? You are helping me for college."

"For now, yes. But you're destined for so much more."

A warm feeling spreads in my stomach. I pretend to scratch my cheek so I can cover my reddening face.

THE RED SKETCH PEN GREW warm in my hand as the NGO didi gave us our instructions. "Draw a big circle in the middle of the paper. Pretend it is your garden of safety."

"Means what?" Devi asked, spinning a yellow crayon around on her piece of paper.

"Draw the things you want to keep inside the circle, and the things you want to keep out, on the outside."

I drew a big juicy vada pav inside the garden, adding streaks of bright green for the chutney. Then I drew a glass of water and a glass of chai. Finally, I added a tree because it was supposed to be a garden. Outside the garden, far from its safe walls, I left the police and the older boys.

The didi who handed me colors patted me on the shoulder and took my drawing when I was done, even though I told her I wanted to keep it.

Babloo had a harder time following the instructions. No matter what the NGO didis told us to draw, he would sketch the exact same scene: mountains, birds, a waterfall, a house, and a bright blue sky with fat white clouds. "No roads," he said, holding it up for the didis to see. "Nobody is allowed here. Just me. Rakhi can come, too." Each time he finished his picture, he would ask the didis to write *Bhutan* in big letters at the top. They always let him keep his drawings, and he stored them carefully with his sleeping mat until they got washed away in the monsoon rains.

Years later, when I was searching for him around Bombay, I wondered at times if that's where he went when he left Dongri. I pictured him in Bhutan, living in a house in the mountains. Swimming in waterfalls. Lying barefoot in the warm grass, watching clouds drift through the sky, thinking of me.

"WALK FASTER," BHAVANA BARKS AS I trail behind her on the way to VT Station. "We'll be late meeting Gauri Ma'am and Rubina, and that's one less thing I need to hear about."

"Ji, Bhavanadidi," I shout over the car horns on M.G. Road, weaving through a crowd of tourists trying to order bhurji pav from the andawala.

Days after Bhavana remarked that Rubina should visit what remains of the Chembur slum, Ma'am has arranged for just that, with Tulsi Prasad as tour guide. Ma'am suggested I come, too, in case there was "any trouble." What trouble she meant, I have no idea.

This late in the morning, the commuters have dwindled, and Bhavana and I are able to spread out on a wooden bench as our train climbs up the Central Line to Chembur.

Bhavana peers up at the small rusty ceiling fan in the train. "I have pleadings to draft, clients to call, yet I'm being dragged out to Chembur so Rubina Mansoor can prance through a bulldozed slum."

"But it was your suggestion, na?"

She shoots me a sharp look. "I was being sarcastic." She sighs. "The worst part is that now we're pulling Tulsi and her family into it, after all they've been through. They don't care about Justice For All, or the work we do, nor should they. They hired Gauri Ma'am to help them fight a very specific fight, not to get sucked into this desperate attempt to revive our organization."

I sit back on the bench. "What else would Tulsi have to do today, anyway?"

"It's not easy for these people to stand up to Gauri Ma'am, especially when they've put their trust in her."

"You should have seen Tulsi shouting the last time they came to the office," I say. "Behaving like a maharani."

Bhavana sighs again, as if I've just said the stupidest thing she's ever heard. "Rakhi, none of this is Tulsi's fault. At this point, the Chembur slum case is now a lower priority for Gauri than Rubina Mansoor. It comes down to numbers: focus on one case, or on what you believe to be a cash cow that will allow you to continue working on a thousand more cases."

"Yes, but Ma'am said she is trying to get attention so the judges decide to allow the Chembur appeal."

"The highest judiciary in the country does not care that some failed actress is pretending to care about poor people. And don't even think about repeating any of this to Gauri Ma'am. Understand?"

"Don't worry," I say, airily. "Even if I wanted to, she'd find a way to get angry at me instead of you."

"You don't know it, but she treats you like her own daughter."

I want to laugh. Neha would get away with so much more than I do.

"Whatever happens to Justice For All," Bhavana continues, "Gauri Ma'am will always be looking out for you. What other boss would pay out of pocket to send her officewali to psychotherapy?"

I lean away from Bhavana and gaze out the window, not wanting to tell her I've missed my last two sessions with Dr. Pereira.

When we reach the demolished section of the Chembur slum, the sun is blazing hot. In the distance is a giant, gleaming white building that wasn't there the last time I was here. Across the front of the building, big blue letters spell out CHEMBUR GYMKHANA.

"Squash, tennis, skating rink," Bhavana says, reading the gymkhana sign. "This place is turning so upmarket." We linger beside a roadside chaiwala in the shade of a small tree, waiting for the others to show. Two small plastic cups of tea later, Tulsi Prasad finally appears.

"Where is Gauri Ma'am?" Tulsi asks Bhavana, letting her rucksack slide from her shoulder to her hand. "She said to be here at ten-thirty and it's already eleven."

"So why did you come half an hour late?" I retort.

Bhavana smacks my arm and takes out her phone. "Yes, hello, Gauri Ma'am . . . Yes, Rakhi, Tulsi, and I are all here . . . Traffic? Accha, accha . . . No, there's no video crew here, yet . . . Okay. Okay, bye." She continues to stare at her phone, her brow furrowing, mouthing the words *video crew.*

It's almost noon by the time a shiny white car rolls up beside the chaiwala. From the car emerge two men and a short-haired woman with a full face of makeup. "This is the place?" she asks the men, who are unloading a video camera and a long microphone from the trunk.

Before Bhavana can ask who they are, a silver Mercedes pulls up behind them. Alex steps out of the front passenger seat, waving at Bhavana and me. I didn't know he was coming.

Gauri Ma'am gets out from one back door, squinting into the bright sun, while the driver scurries out to open the other one, from which Rubina barks, "Arre, close it, I'm not ready." Through the window, I watch her pat the makeup under her eyes with her fingertips as she inspects herself in a round compact mirror.

Alex taps me on the shoulder. "Gauri invited me," he whispers excitedly. "She said I would get a clearer picture of what we are fighting for."

Bhavana heads straight to Gauri Ma'am. "I thought this was just a tour. Why is there a video crew?"

Gauri looks Bhavana dead in the eye. "DeshTV is filming Rubina walking around the slum with Tulsi. It will be a six-minute clip on the news tonight."

"How come you didn't tell—"

"This is Manali Singh," Ma'am interrupts, gesturing to the short-haired woman. "Manali, this is one of the lawyers on the Chembur slum case, Bhavana Bose."

Before Bhavana can respond, Rubina finally exits the car and slams the door shut. She's wearing sunglasses and a deep green cotton sari block-printed with red and yellow flowers. I wonder how many other saris her maid had to press before she selected this one as her slum-tour outfit. As Rubina adjusts her flowing pallu, Gauri Ma'am wrinkles her nose. "Are you wearing high heels?"

Rubina lowers her shades to gaze at Gauri Ma'am. "I always wear stilettos with a sari," she says, her tone flat.

"Yes, but, to a demolished slum? How will you walk through that?" Gauri Ma'am points across the road at the wide field of debris. "It's all rubble."

"I'll just get some wide shots from the side of the road, okay?" the video guy says to Manali Singh as he peers through his camera.

Rubina glares at Ma'am. "Gauri, you never said I had to dress like a laborer for this visit."

"I didn't think you'd—"

"Rakhi will go buy you a pair of slippers," Bhavana interrupts.

Ma'am's face softens in gratitude. She rummages through her purse and hands me a wad of cash. "Quickly," she says, her eyes stern.

After running down the road to several small shops, I find a stall with three packets of rubber slippers, the kind people leave outside the toilets. I buy the biggest pair and run back to an impatient Rubina.

She snatches them from my hand and closes her eyes. "These are too small. Why didn't you ask me my foot size before you left?"

"These were the biggest size, Rubina Madam."

"This is completely unsafe," she declares. "I'm more likely to fall in these than in my stilettos."

Gauri Ma'am eyes Bhavana's feet. "You can wear Bhavana's shoes. They're sturdier."

Bhavana's nostrils flare a little while Ma'am makes no effort to acknowledge her anger. Even Alex seems a little surprised at the suggestion, glancing up from his little digital camera.

"Sharing shoes is unhygienic," Rubina snaps. She offers Bhavana a fake smile. "I'm not trying to offend you."

Gauri Ma'am rubs her forehead and exhales. "Okay, either you wear the slippers or Bhavana's shoes. Just decide." The video crew trade looks but continue fiddling with their equipment in silence.

After Rubina decides Bhavana's shoes are the safer option, Ma'am takes the new slippers from me and hands them to Bhavana. Even I am embarrassed for her as she silently pulls her leather sandals off her feet and places them on the ground in front of Rubina.

"You," Rubina says, as she thrusts her stilettos at me. "Hold on to these, and don't leave them anywhere." They're the same shade of green as her sari, as if anyone would have noticed them.

When Rubina declares she is ready, one of the men hoists the camera up onto his shoulder and the other lifts the mic in the air. Ma'am motions for us to come along, but Bhavana stays where she is. "I'm not walking through the slum in these chappals," she calls out.

Ma'am comes back to our side of the road. "Fine, switch with Rakhi."

"Rakhi shouldn't be wearing these slippers in there either."

"Do I need to remind you that you have been assigned this case? This is your client. We need you here."

"Who's the client? Tulsi Prasad or Rubina Mansoor?"

Gauri Ma'am and Bhavana glare at each other.

Through clenched teeth, Gauri Ma'am tells Bhavana to go back to the office, and that she will deal with her later. Bhavana turns on her slippered heel and slap-slaps back down the road toward Chembur train station.

Tulsi then leads Rubina, Gauri Ma'am, and the video crew into the demolished slum. Alex and I hang back, careful to avoid being seen on camera.

In some areas of the tour, it's as though someone had scraped the hutments away with a knife, leaving only footprints of lives once lived there. In other areas, tiled walls and squat toilets lie half buried in rubble. We step over bamboo poles, broken doors, exposed water pipes, and bits of insulation that poke up through crevices like dingy candy floss. A now-torn poster of a shirtless movie hero flexing his muscles peeks out from under a piece of corrugated metal, though with his head ripped off he could be any actor, really.

I gaze across the landscape. This could be any slum if the government had their way. Behrampada, even. My limbs start to feel heavy. I wish I was anywhere but here.

"Are you okay?" Alex asks.

I gather myself and nod. "It is hot out. Sun is strong."

"Fifteen hundred homes were destroyed," Gauri Ma'am declares as the camera rolls.

"It's devastating," Rubina says to Manali Singh. "But this is our collective shame. We cannot keep looking away."

Who's we? I want to ask Rubina. *Some of us don't have the luxury of looking away because this is our reality,* I nearly blurt out.

Tulsi leads us to the bare foundation where her two-story brick hut once stood. Lying on its side is a red alarm clock that looks like the one Tazim has in her hut. "After the bulldozers, we came back to try to rescue our things but the police ordered us out. When my brother resisted, they beat him."

"What did you lose?" Rubina asks.

"Our ID cards, my textbooks, laptop computer, clothes, cooking vessels . . ."

"You had a laptop? What exactly for?"

"Same reasons why anyone would have a laptop." Tulsi's eyes flick from Rubina to Gauri Ma'am, as if searching for answers, but she carries on when Ma'am refuses to meet her gaze. "This demolition came out of nowhere. We'd been here since the 1990s. The city provided piped water and electricity meters. There are local schools. Politicians would come canvass during election time. My parents spent thousands of rupees to renovate our home months before it was torn down. We had replaced the tin walls with bricks and installed a private toilet."

"You thought you were safe here," Rubina says.

Tulsi blinks back tears and wraps her arms around herself.

Gauri Ma'am clears her throat and faces Manali Singh. "The government, the police, and the Bombay High Court all called them encroachers. But why was the city supplying them with utilities like water and electricity if their houses were illegal?"

"Where do you stay now?" Rubina asks Tulsi.

"With an old classmate nearby. My parents are staying with relatives in Navi Mumbai. My brother is with his friend in Thane. We are spread out in all corners of the city. We can't find anyone to take all of us. To stay together we'd have to spend our nights outdoors, under bamboo poles and a tarp, like lots of other people who used to live here. My parents and I are trying to earn the money for a rental deposit on a flat nearby."

"How much is the deposit?"

"Too much. Lowest we can find is fifteen thousand."

Rubina takes Tulsi's hand. "My dear, I want to give you a small gift. I want to give you the money for your deposit." She smiles gently, like a benevolent goddess bringing rain to a farming village plagued by drought.

What a performance. Even the camera guy grins like he knows he's filming good television.

Tulsi gasps. "I . . . I . . . Rubina Madam, are you serious?"

Rubina puts her hands on the girl's shoulders. "Yes, my dear. The courts may never acknowledge the depth of your struggle, but I do."

"Thank you," Tulsi whispers, tears streaming down her cheeks. "This is the first good news we've heard since the demolition."

Gauri Ma'am glances away. I know she wants to say something but can't, since the cameraman is still filming.

In spite of the fact that there is no shade in this field of rubble and the midday sun is beating down hard, I rub the goosebumps that have sprouted on my arms.

....

Soon after Rubina announces her donation, Manali Singh decides she has all the footage she needs. After Rubina, Alex, and the others disperse in their cars, Gauri Ma'am walks with me to the train station in silence.

"Gauri Ma'am," I start, "now that Rubina is giving Tulsi all that money—"

Ma'am stops in her tracks and holds up her BlackBerry. "I got an email from Dr. Pereira's office this morning. She says you've skipped the last two therapy sessions."

I draw in my breath.

"So it's true?"

I nod, my shoulders drooping.

"She also billed me for the sessions you missed. I'll be docking that money from your wages."

I didn't ask for any of this, I want to shout.

"From today on, I treat you like the rest of my staff. No special allowances, no overlooking your missteps. You live up to the same standards the others have to. Understand?"

"Ji, Gauri Ma'am," I mumble.

How to tell her that I never asked to be treated differently from the others?

NOBODY SAYS A WORD ABOUT the DeshTV clip the next morning. When Gauri Ma'am leaves the office at midday, the lawyers let out a collective exhale and crowd around the table in their workspace, ready to break for lunch.

"Rakhi," Vivek calls out to me, "bring a plate from the kitchen. I've got your favorite today." Whenever Vivek's wife makes baingan bhartha, she makes double for me.

"Uff," Jayshree says, as Vivek spoons it out onto my plate. "Such a nice smoky smell."

"She makes tiny cuts in the eggplant, then sticks cloves of garlic and green chilies in them, then roasts it over the gas flame," Vivek says, proudly.

"So lucky you are, Rakhi, isn't it?" Jayshree eyes me as Vivek removes two rotis from one of his metal dabbas and folds them on my plate. His wife's rotis are always dripping with ghee.

As I dig into the bhartha, Kamini cracks open the plastic lid on her bowl of cut-up papaya. "Fine, I'll start," she blurts out. "All this celebrity endorsement funda seemed harmless until Rubina threw cash in Tulsi's face."

Everyone glances up from their lunch.

"Well, it's been apparent to some of us from the beginning," Bhavana says to Vivek, who shrinks slightly as his shoulders hunch over his tiffin. "The legal system is our bread and butter, na? And yet, we are hitching our wagon to some celebrity who feels comfortable saying out loud—"

"On television," Sudeepthi interrupts.

"Yes, on television, that a lawyer can't do much for a client."

Kamini stabs at a chunk of papaya with her fork. "I just can't believe Tulsi. 'This is the first good news I've heard since the demolition'? Does she know she has the best bloody lawyer in India working for her?"

"Pro bono," I mutter, licking the charred bits of eggplant from my fingertips. How come Tulsi doesn't have to pay for the legal services she doesn't want, whereas I now have to pay for the missed therapy sessions I didn't want?

"Arre," Sudeepthi says, amused. "Where did you learn that word, Rakhi?"

Suddenly self-conscious, I shrug. "From Gauri Ma'am."

"See?" Kamini says, pointing her fork at me. "Even the officewali agrees."

The door swings open and Alex strolls in with a parcel from Sai Krishna. "Thought I'd try out the tomato onion uthappam today," he says, dragging a chair up to the table. "What are you all talking about?"

Kamini's back stiffens. "We're discussing the DeshTV clip from yesterday."

"Oh, right," Alex says, unwrapping his uthappam. "Kind of amazing that Rubina came through for Tulsi like that."

"Of course you'd say that, you're her nephew."

Alex sets down the little plastic bag of coconut chutney he was about to tear open and sits back in his chair. "I'm not Rubina's nephew. Why does everyone keep saying that? And so what if she donates a little cash to a good cause?"

"If you read between the lines," Bhavana says, "Rubina was saying that public interest litigation is not to Tulsi's benefit. She's saying that she, a wealthy actress, has more to offer than Gauri Ma'am, or us."

Alex pokes at the chutney packet. "Isn't that for Tulsi to decide?"

"Decide what? She's already retained Ma'am to argue her case."

He waves his hand dismissively. "It sounds like you're essentializing Tulsi because she's poor. Like she herself doesn't know what's best for her, but you guys do because you're educated, you're lawyers, and you have money."

Judging by the looks on everyone's faces, I wish he hadn't said that.

"Money, Alex?" Bhavana sputters. "You think we have money? We may be lawyers, but our peers who went off into corporate law are making at least five times our salaries. Not to mention we live in the most expensive city in India, so our salaries don't stretch very far. Meanwhile, you're nicely staying in Pali Hill, your Canadian dollars buy you anything you want, and your only point of reference for human rights law, let alone India, is Rubina bloody Mansoor." She bangs the table with her fist, rattling Vivek's steel dabbas and Kamini's plastic bowl.

"Bhavana," Vivek says, gently.

Alex packs up his uthappam and chutney and rises to his feet. "Okay, people, I'm just here to learn. I have no skin in whatever game this is. I'll leave you all to discuss this among yourselves."

....

Over the next couple of days, it becomes clear that the DeshTV clip is generating more attention than anyone could have predicted. Sudeepthi announces that five organizations have already confirmed they will march in the rally with us because they saw Rubina's DeshTV clip.

"Our name must be all over this," Gauri Ma'am reminds Sudeepthi when she reports that she got one of the better-known housing rights organizations to join us. "Our name, not theirs. Make sure they know that."

Bhavana suggests Tulsi be invited to participate in the rally, since her case is at the center of this movement. Gauri Ma'am agrees, noting that an aspiring doctor like Tulsi is the kind of slum-dweller the public sympathizes with. Rubina has promised that her celebrity friends will march with us. When Utkarsh and Kamini hear this, they ask Ma'am who exactly might be joining. Soap stars? Models? A-list film stars? B-list? Utkarsh points out Rubina's celebrity friends might all be old, since Rubina herself is old. Ma'am pulls down her glasses and, gazing over the rims, says flatly, "Did you get your law degrees to serve yourselves, or others?"

A little later, I'm in the middle of calling up different electronics shops across the city, asking about the price of megaphones, when Alex stops by my desk. "Can I ask you something?"

I peek past him to make sure Ma'am's door is closed. "Yes?"

"The other day, when Bhavana said that by giving Tulsi the cash for her rent deposit, Rubina was sending a message that money is more important than justice—do you think she was right?"

Alex presses on, asking me what I would have done if I were in Tulsi's position. Nobody here ever asks my opinion on anything that goes on at Justice For All.

If I were dragging a washed-up film actor, some lawyers, and a camera crew to gawk at my demolished home, I'd have inflated the price of the rent deposit to set Rubina up to offer me more. Say twenty-five thousand. A woman who wears spiky stilettos to walk through rubble wouldn't be able to tell the difference between the truth and a lie, especially when she has the chance to look like a savior on television. But why would Gauri Ma'am let Rubina make an offer like that? It's clear they both want different things out of this arrangement. Perhaps they should acknowledge they are both using each other.

"Question is wrong," I finally say. "Forget Tulsi. It is Rubina and Gauri Ma'am. If together they are working, they must . . ." What's the word?

Alex scratches his chin. "Be on the same page?"

I'm about to respond when Gauri Ma'am's door bursts open and Jayshree runs out, whimpering, to the empty interns' workstation. Then the door slams shut, as if Gauri Ma'am slammed it herself.

I glance at Alex and put my finger to my lips. We get up to peek through the library bookshelves.

"Arre, what happened?" Vivek says, pulling up a chair beside Jayshree, who is rubbing her eyes with her palms.

"She promised, Vivek Sir. She promised I could go." Jayshree's small voice breaks and she bends forward in her chair, burying her face in her hands.

Vivek tugs his crumpled handkerchief from his pocket and offers it to her. "Go where?"

She sits up and takes the handkerchief from his hand, dabbing her face. "My cousin-sister's wedding. In Hyderabad. I asked for permission months ago. And now it's on the same day as this stupid rally."

"Gauri Ma'am said you can't take the time off?"

Jayshree's chin trembles. "She said people get married every day and the office needs me more than my cousin-sister does." She peers up at Vivek. "I can't abandon my family. Not for this kind of pay. My mother would never forgive me. So I told her I quit. And then Ma'am told me to pack my things up and leave today."

Vivek blows his cheeks out and releases the air in his mouth in one long breath. "Your family comes first. We'll make sure you find work when you're back."

"Not here, Sir." She presses her lips together. "I can't work for her anymore."

They sit there for a moment until Vivek clears his throat. "For now, you go to Hyderabad, enjoy, and you call me when you're back in town. I'll make some calls, find a place for you to land, teek hain?"

Jayshree nods through her tears. "Thank you, Sir."

Vivek chews his bottom lip, his eyes fixed on Ma'am's door.

By late afternoon, Jayshree's desk is empty.

AT THE END OF THE week, Alex shocks the office by telling them he doesn't know what Ganesh Chaturthi is.

"But it's Bombay's biggest festival," Sudeepthi says. "Surely you would have heard of it."

"Aren't you supposed to be Indian?" Kamini asks. "Didn't your family teach you anything?"

Alex flinches. "What does that even—"

"And on top of that," Bhavana interrupts, "it's already the third day of Ganesh Chaturthi. There are lights everywhere. People playing with colored powder in the streets. Music blasting. Roads closed. Have you not . . . noticed?"

"There's always something going on in this city—how am I expected to keep track of it all?"

The three women walk away from his desk, rolling their eyes. "I thought he was supposed to be smart," Kamini says, loud enough for Alex to hear.

A grimace lingers on his face as he watches them take their seats in the lawyers' workspace.

"Many people, they are going to beach with Ganesh murti and putting into water," I offer, feeling sorry for him.

He lifts his chin. "They push their idols into the sea? What for?"

"We don't call them idols," Vivek says, stopping at Alex's desk on his way to the kitchen. "We call them murtis. You will surely have seen a Ganesh murti. He has an elephant head and a big potbelly. He's considered a protector, or a remover of obstacles. Hindus pray to him at the start of any new venture—buying a car, moving into a new home."

"That's right. My family's driver has a tiny one on his dashboard," Alex exclaims.

Vivek goes on to tell Alex that people believe dissolving a plaster likeness of Ganesh in a body of water will take away their hardships.

Gauri Ma'am walks by and adds that the real reason for these massive public celebrations is to distract people from the fact that the government could end hunger and poverty but deliberately chooses not to.

"Ma'am," Vivek says. "That's quite a cynical take, don't you think?"

"It's the truth, and you know it. Why else is the charity sector so big in India? To reinforce the flow of accountability down to ordinary people like us, instead of back up to people with the money and the power to fix everything."

Deflated, Vivek gazes down at his shirt buttons.

....

On Saturday afternoon, Alex and I bounce up and down in unison when a pothole wallops our autorickshaw. We're on our way to Juhu Beach for the fourth day of Ganesh Chaturthi because Alex said he wanted nothing more than to watch a million plaster elephants sail off to sea. Already, the drumming from the crowds is like thunder, growing louder and louder as we close in on the beach.

When the rickshaw stops at a light, Alex releases his grip on the back of the driver's seat. "So, I'm wondering if I have to go shopping for Friday. I didn't bring super-formal clothes with me on this trip."

A man selling big maps of India walks up to Alex, and I wave him away before he can start his sales pitch. He sucks his teeth, mutters something under his breath, and moves on to the rickshaw behind us.

"What is on Friday?" I ask.

"The office fundraising party, what else?" Alex smirks. "Why do you seem so confused?"

"There is no party for office."

"Yes, there is. Rubina is hosting it to raise money for Justice For All."

"Gauri Ma'am isn't telling me this."

"Sorry," he offers. "Rubina told me about it. I figured everyone knew, but I guess not."

I look away so Alex can't see my face fall. Gauri Ma'am can't even hold a meeting with a client without ensuring I pencil the minutes she spent with them in her calendar. How could she throw a fundraising party without telling me? And if she hasn't told anyone yet, was she ever planning to in the first place?

The rickshaw putters to a stop at Juhu Road, and Alex nudges me out of my thoughts. "Wake up. The driver is trying to tell you something."

"You have to get out here and walk," the autowala says, peering at me in his rearview mirror. "Street is closed."

Outside the rickshaw, Juhu Road extends before us, jammed with hordes of families, children, and young men dancing through clouds of pink powder on their way to the shore. Every few meters are plaster Ganesh murtis of assorted sizes and styles. Ahead of us, a big truck with loudspeakers holds an enormous Ganesh clad in a shiny yellow dhoti. Golden fireworks spray out from its sides.

Alex enters the crowd, tall and white-looking, creating an instant spectacle as he dances with his hands in the air. People flock to him, pulling him toward their friends. "Ganpati Bappa Morya," they shout, coaxing him to say it, too, while I trail behind him, mumbling the chant quietly. It's only when a group of rowdy men try to hoist him onto their shoulders that I step in and yank him down.

It takes us half an hour to cover the small, choked-up stretch of road to Juhu Beach, where I grab Alex's wrist to pull him away from the people running toward the water. We walk farther down the beach, trying to get away from the crowds, and still people swarm around us, holding giant paint-splattered balloons, crunching through watery mouthfuls of pani puri, and hauling their Ganesh murtis into the surf. Elephant figures bob out to the horizon, until the sea breaks their trunks, severs their arms, and swallows them up. Tomorrow, pieces of dismembered Ganesh murtis will wash up onshore and the NGO types will scream about litter on the beach and deliver sermons on more eco-friendly ways to celebrate.

Alex and I sink down onto an empty patch of sand, firm and compacted from being trampled on by thousands of feet. Late afternoon shadows lengthen, as if the breeze coming off the sea is pushing them farther and farther up the sand. Behind us, a panting man uses all of his body weight to crank a four-person Ferris wheel holding six children.

Alex reaches into his backpack and rustles out a small stack of crisp papers. "College application forms. For hospitality management programs in Bombay. I printed them out for you at home." He hands them to me. There are five in total.

I can barely get past the headers at the top of the forms, with their large fonts and capital letters. *Sanskriti Institute of Hotel Management. Janpath College.* SSDN *College for Women. Seva Niketan College. Lady Victoria College for Women.* They're so official looking, so imposing.

The sour, spicy scent of tangy chaat masala from the Juhu Beach snack center wafts toward us, snagging my attention. I want to throw the applications into the sea and buy something fried and crunchy.

I hand the papers back to Alex. "It is not feeling right. Tuition fees is too much, and maybe I am not getting a job in a hotel after. Then what? Gauri Ma'am isn't taking me back."

"Just trust me," he says.

"Why?"

He pauses. "I see how hard you work, how clever you are. All you're missing is someone to open doors for you. Together we're going to make this happen."

I want to believe him. "Okay," I finally say, encouraged by his enthusiasm.

"Good. Now let's eat." He rises to his feet and dusts the sand off his shorts, handing the applications back to me.

Stuffing the papers into my bag, I follow him to the cluster of food stalls perched atop a set of concrete steps. In a couple of hours, when night falls, the snack center will give off a fierce glow, a beacon of light for beachgoers ready to plow through paper plates of bhel puri, papdi chaat, and other street food.

Alex and I stand in line for pav bhaji. When it's our turn, the man at the counter slaps glistening heaps of orange-red bhaji from the hot tawa onto a paper plate, places some buttered white pav on top, and slides it toward us.

We are making our way down the steps to find somewhere to sit when a loud hiss pierces the air. Probably some hero trying to get a girl's attention. I roll my eyes and continue down the stairs.

The hiss rings out again. "*sssssssssssssTT.*"

I ignore it, but Alex's ears perk up. He turns back, scanning the growing crowd of people buying snacks and cold drinks and ice creams.

And then: "*sssssssssssssssssTTTT, Rakhi.*"

That voice—clear as water. I spin around, my eyes darting over the faces of the festivalgoers surrounding us. I don't recognize any of them, but still. Could it be? No, it's impossible. I look left and right, my hands trembling under the weight of the paper plate of pav bhaji. Then I turn back toward the sea and there in front of me—standing against the backdrop of roaring black waves lit up by the enormous stadium lights of the snack center—is Babloo.

A flash of cold hits me in the stomach while I try to catch my breath.

He looks nothing like I had ever imagined. Taller and older, with neatly combed and oiled hair, a silky, collared purple shirt tucked in at his narrow waist, and crisp pressed black slacks. Maybe this is a strange hallucination brought on by all the hungama at the beach— the throbbing loudspeakers, buzzing neon lights, people shouting everywhere. I rub my eyes with my free fist to make it go away. When I open them, he's still there, shaking his head and grinning.

"Relax, yaar. I'm not going to steal your food." He motions at the pav bhaji, now running off the plate and splattering onto the sand. It is absolutely two-hundred-per-cent-no-chance-in-hell-anyone-else-but-Babloo.

Alex rescues the plate just as it's about to tumble from my hand. "Do you know this guy?" A warm, loud whisper in my ear.

I open my mouth but the words are caught in my throat. "This," I stammer. "This is . . ."

"Mohammed." Babloo touches his chest. "But this girl knows me as Babloo. We are old-old friends."

He speaks English now?

"So I finally get to meet your friends, eh?" Alex thumps me on the back and I stumble forward. He turns back to Babloo and introduces himself. A smile curls along Babloo's lips and he looks at me from the corner of his eye.

I feel light-headed, and the beach starts to spin around me. "I . . . I must sit."

While Alex dashes up to the snack center to buy water, Babloo negotiates a red plastic chair away from a family feasting on food-stall spoils by telling them I'm pregnant. He drags it up behind me and I sink into it. Then he crouches down in front of me and flashes a wide grin. A gold-capped tooth on the side of his mouth catches the light.

"Babloo, is it really you?"

"You tell me. Do I look the same?" He stands up tall.

I nod, my breath catching. "You look nice."

He pulls one of my escaped curls taut and then lets it go, watching it spring back into its original shape. "You grew into that wild hair."

We both smile and I feel my chest expanding. Warm energy surges through my body and I spring out of the chair, wrapping my arms around his shiny purple shoulders. I laugh with relief as my eyes well up, not caring that the people he took the chair from are eyeing us suspiciously. Babloo hugs me tight, patting my upper back.

"I tried to find you," I finally say, blinking to push the tears back in. "I searched everywhere."

He breaks away from our embrace and takes a step back. "I never left."

"You were in Bombay this whole time?"

"It's a big city. Gets bigger every day."

"Yes," I say, searching his face for a trace of emotion. Why can't I find any?

"Tell me, yaar," he says, "what are you doing now, after all these years?"

"I have a job. At an office. Couldn't keep stealing from college kids forever."

"Accha? You're a working woman?" He nods in exaggerated approval and claps his hands. "Very good. And who's this hi-fi firanghi with you?" He tilts his head toward the pani puri stall where Alex is waiting in line for water. "Bet his pockets are lined with cash, na? Easy target."

I bury my toes in the sand. "No, yaar, that's just Alex. He works with me. He's from Canada."

Babloo reaches in his shirt pocket and pulls out a cigarette. It's a Gold Flake, the brand that Saskia and Merel smoke. He pushes the cigarette between his lips and hunches forward to keep the wind from blowing out his match. He used to say cigarettes were a waste of money. "Tell me, then, where do you work?"

"I work for human rights lawyers," I say, sliding a sickle of dirt out from under my thumbnail.

His eyes widen in disbelief. "You're trying to tell me you're a lawyer now?"

"No way, yaar."

"Then? You've become an NGO didi or what? Teaching the street kids ABC-123-HIV?"

"Not at all. I make chai, and photocopy papers."

He exhales a long plume of smoke. "Accha, you're the peon. Still, that's not bad."

Before I can reply, Alex reappears with a sweaty water bottle.

As I gulp the cool water down, Babloo grins at Alex again and switches back to English. "So, boss? First time in India?"

"No, man, I have an aunt here."

"You Indian?"

"Half, I guess. Mom's brown, Dad's white."

"He is from Canada," I interject.

"You already told me that," Babloo says. "You know, I was knowing Rakhi when we were small kids."

Alex's eyes brighten. "Were you one of the street kids?"

Babloo throws his head back and guffaws. "She has told you everything, then?"

"Wait, are you—" Alex touches his chin, pausing. "Are you the best friend? The boy who got lost?"

I try to stop him from saying anything more. "No, no—"

Babloo cuts me off. "I was never lost." He frowns and takes a short drag from his cigarette.

Alex grabs my shoulder. "Rakhi, this is the guy you were telling me about, isn't it? The one you've been trying to find all these years?"

I wish Alex's phone would ring, or the fireworks would start, or a fist fight would break out nearby just so he'd be distracted for a few minutes.

Babloo leans in toward Alex. "So, my friend, you and Rakhi are working at Juhu Beach today?"

"We're just hanging out. Rakhi shows me around the city. All the parts that my family avoids."

"Your family doesn't like Juhu Beach?"

"They don't like big crowds. Or the outdoors. Unless the space is . . . private."

Babloo narrows his eyes. "Where does your family stay?"

"Pali Hill. In Bandra."

Babloo's forehead smooths out and he nods, as if he suddenly understands why Alex's family are not at Juhu Beach with us. "Good area. Rakhi is taking you to all nice-nice places?"

"Awesome places. We did Oval Maidan, Bohri Mohalla, the Dadar flower market, Sassoon Docks . . ."

"Haji Ali, Marine Drive," I fill in.

Babloo taps his cigarette and the ash flies off into the sea breeze. "All tourist sites?"

Alex glances at me. "I guess. But they were cool."

"She has taken you to beer bars?"

"No—is that the same as a regular bar?"

"What about leather tanneries? Old cotton mills? Toddy shops? Wrestling matches? Construction sites? Cockfights? Teen patti? You know what is teen patti? Means . . . card games. Gambling."

Alex's eyebrows jump. "Uh, no."

"Arre, he can't go to places like that—" I start to say.

"Alex, my friend, you want to see the real Bombay?" He sounds like he's selling a pair of chappals to a tourist. Friendly, persistent. *Come, my friend, come. Looking is free!*

Alex glances at me, then back at Babloo.

"You must join me. Some places are not . . . nice . . . for ladies, you see." Babloo tilts his head in my direction. "Take my number, I will show you something different. Rakhi, it is okay with you?"

I bite the inside of my lip and force a small smile. "Yes," I say, surprised at the flatness of my voice as they exchange phone numbers.

Babloo shakes Alex's hand, then draws him in for a hug where he thumps him on the back a few times. They smile like they are old friends who haven't seen each other in eleven years.

"Too much time has passed," Babloo says to me in Hindi. "Let's catch up without this firanghi."

"Give me your number, then." I hand Babloo my Nokia and he glances up a few times while punching in his number, as though he's reading my face. He hands me the phone back and points to the bent paper plate of pav bhaji in Alex's hands. "Looks cold now. Buy a new one."

Babloo's mobile rings, loud and shrill. He holds it to his ear and turns away to face the sea. "Haan boss . . . Yes, yes, I'm coming. Be right there . . . Yes. Ten minutes." He slips his mobile into his shirt pocket. "Business."

Before Alex or I can say a word, Babloo starts off up the sand to the road. "Alex, SMS me when you're free."

Alex nods vigorously, the way he did when Gauri Ma'am first lectured him about human rights in India.

"And you," Babloo calls out to me, over a mob of children running toward a man with a candy floss machine. "Don't be a stranger."

BABLOO AND I SAW THE real Rakhi Tilak when I was nine. Two years had passed since I arrived in Bombay, but it felt like I'd been living on the street with the other kids for a lifetime.

It was during Ganesh Chaturthi. The monsoons were over, and the disappearance of the rains had given way to steamy afternoons. Me, Babloo, Kalu, Devi, Pappu, and this new kid, Raju, had gone down to Chowpatty Beach to watch families and their priests wade their enormous Ganesh murtis into the Arabian Sea. Salman couldn't join us because he was locked up in Dongri. We weren't sure what for.

The roads to the beach were a thick web of dancing and acrobatics and trucks with loudspeakers. Fistfuls of colored powder blew through the air. The group of us wove through the crowds together, following Babloo. Once we reached the beach, we pounded our heels in the sand and ran down to the frothy sea water. The waves lapped at the shore endlessly, like a stray dog licking its balls.

While the others went looking for ice golas, Babloo and I followed a man carrying a long stick with a massive swell of pink, orange, and green speckled balloons fastened to the end of it, hoping one would come loose so we could snatch it. The flock of balloons blew violently in the sea breeze, threatening to detach, and it was when they parted that I saw her. Rakhi Tilak, the actress.

Soon after Babloo gave me my name, I learned it was impossible to take a step in the city without being reminded of her. Her big eyes, rosy cheeks, and tiny chin were plastered on every bus, billboard, and TV screen. She was one of the few actors in the industry who didn't belong to a filmi family. Instead, she came from a tiny fishing village on the Konkan coast. Magazine covers proclaimed her *Rakhi Tilak, Fisher Girl with Big Dreams,* even though she went to college in Pune and claimed to have never caught a fish in her life. As her career took off, her dance scenes always managed to be exciting without crossing into vulgarity. Her costumes never showed skin, but they were always sheer, or wet, but never both. She started landing heroine roles opposite A-list actors. And when "Drip Drip," the Ruby M string-chaddi song, came out that year, the Fisher Girl with Big Dreams had gone on record as saying Ruby was simply giving the people what they wanted, and if anyone was to be judged, it should be all of us together.

Babloo and I quickly forgot about the balloonwala and watched from afar as Rakhi Tilak walked toward the shore, pious and silent, with her Ganesh murti cradled under her large breasts. Trudging behind her were a chubby woman in thick glasses carrying a few handbags and a notebook, and a big, bald-headed man with large biceps who kept an eye on the crowds of young men following closely, bouncing, dancing, and hooting at the sight of Rakhi Tilak. By then, I was old enough to know that all of them would happily drown in the sea if they could trade places with the murti for a few moments.

I elbowed Babloo. "Come on," I said, darting off toward the front of the crowd.

As we drew nearer, Babloo called out, "Rakhi Aunty, Rakhi Aunty!"

The men in the crowd began to shout her name, too, professing their love and offering their hands, as if she might actually say yes to one of them. The big bald man held them back with his tree-trunk forearms.

Rakhi Tilak floated serenely through the shouting and chaos like a tiny bubble above a freshly poured soft drink. Wrapped in a yellow sari with a modest gold border, she covered her head with her pallu. She was much smaller than I thought a movie star would be.

"Help me call her name," Babloo yelled as he gripped my hand, dragging me through the web of young men. "Bhutan ki baby! Bhutan ki baby! Over here!"

I flailed my arms about and shouted out for her. "Ey! Rakhi Aunty! Eyyy!"

That's when Rakhi Tilak, almost at the sea, stopped in her tracks and turned toward Babloo and me. Then, maybe because I was the lone girl in a sea of horny male faces, she handed her Ganesh murti to the chubby lady beside her and bent down, so her eyes were level with mine, and gestured for me to come closer.

I shrank back a little and looked to Babloo. His jaw hung down as limp as a dead fish. I turned back to Rakhi Tilak, took a few steps forward. Up close, I could see how her eyelashes resembled spiders' legs and the powder on her face cracked like the earth before monsoon season. Her mouth was painted with a thick pink ribbon of color, and when her lips parted into a smile I swore she had a snaggle-tooth, but Babloo later said I was full of shit.

"Hello, darling. Tell me, how old are you?" she asked. Her voice was mostly sweet, a little hoarse, like perhaps she was tired. She smelled of sandalwood and flowers. A tiny see-through Ganesh pendant dangled from a delicate silver chain around her neck.

"Nine," I said, my eyes darting between her face and the Ganesh pendant as it caught shards of afternoon light.

"Such a pretty girl, you are."

I raised my eyebrows in disbelief. This woman must be mad.

"What's your name?"

"Rakhi," I told her.

"Really? Or you're doing some masti?"

"No, Rakhi Tilak Madam, I swear. It is my real name. My chosen name. My parents named me Bansari, but here in Bombay I go by Rakhi."

"What do your parents think of your new name?"

"They . . . they're dead."

With a clenched half smile, she reached for my hand and squeezed it. "You know, when I was in college, I read a book that said that you're not born only once, on the day your mother gives birth to you, but that life forces you to give birth to yourself, over and over again."

I had only just learned how people had babies, thanks to some NGO sex education didis. Whatever Rakhi Tilak was saying sounded yuck. Like your body folding up and twisting inside your privates and then out again, but then you'd come out as someone different. As I reeled from the hideous image in my brain, she let go of my hand, removed the Ganesh pendant from her neck, and placed it around mine.

"It means that you are in charge of your destiny. When life gets hard, remember what I told you," she said, fastening the necklace. Then she straightened up, adjusted the pallu of her sari, took the Ganesh murti back, and carried on walking toward the surf. The crowd followed behind her, but I stood still, men bumping into and shoving me in all directions. I didn't care. The grin on my face was so huge I could feel it in my toes.

Babloo thumped me, hard, on my back. "Stupid! Why didn't you tell her to adopt you?"

I drew my hand back to slap him but he dashed away, and then I chased him down Chowpatty Beach until we were out of breath. We found Kalu, Devi, Pappu, and Raju sucking away on orange ice golas. They didn't believe the story of my encounter with Rakhi Tilak until I showed them the pendant.

"Anyway, why would she call you pretty?" Kalu snorted, his lips and tongue stained bright orange. "You have big curly hair and frog eyes."

The new kid, Raju, laughed, and Babloo whacked his ice gola to the sand because he was too recent an addition to our group to be laughing at me.

Weeks later, Raju yanked the pendant from my neck and disappeared with it.

"HOW WAS GANESH CHATURTHI YESTERDAY?" Tazim asks me on Sunday afternoon, while I sit on her floor rinsing rice in a metal pot.

"Same as always," I say, avoiding eye contact. "Lots of people."

"I've never been," she remarks, sitting down beside me with a wooden chopping board in front of her. "Always someone to feed, something to clean." She starts slicing off the hairy tops of small red onions with a blunt knife.

"Must be boring by yourself, na?"

"A little." I swirl the rice around with my fingers, flicking off the weevils that float to the top.

Tazim blinks and gives me a knowing smile.

"What?"

"Nothing. Some people were talking at the water pump this morning. Said they saw you at Juhu with a handsome fellow."

Handsome fellow? I draw in my breath, suddenly fearful that she might know about Alex, but when I study her face, she's smiling. I breathe out. "There were lots of people on the beach. Doesn't mean I was there with all of them."

Tazim puts her knife down on the cutting board. "Okay, tell me. What are you hiding? Who is he?"

"I . . . went to Juhu Beach by myself . . ." Her eyes don't show a hint of suspicion so I carry on. "And I bumped into an old friend there, by chance."

"Accha?"

I clear my throat. "We were childhood friends." She knows I lived on the street, but I've never told her much about that time. Like most people, she'd never understand why we had to do what we did. "His name is Babloo. It's been eleven years since I've seen him."

"Does he live in Mumbai, still?"

"Yes. He gave me his phone number."

"Is he handsome?" She giggles.

"Arre, Tazim, I'm not going to marry him!" I splash some of the starchy rice water at her. "It was nice to see him, though."

"Then? Why do you look so heartbroken?"

"I've just always wondered what happened to him. He looks fine, but something still worries me."

Tazim tilts her head to one side and locks eyes with me. "Then you must go see him. Go."

"What? Right now?"

"Rakhi, you are still young. You can do these things."

"You're only two years older than me."

She reaches for the pot of soaking rice and grabs it from me. "Go, now! I'll keep some food aside for you for when you get back. Go!"

I jump up. "Chalo, I'm going. Thank you, Tazim."

"Don't thank me," she calls after me. "Just invite me to your wedding!"

"I swear it's not like that," I call back as I race down the gully to Bandra Station, dialing Babloo's number.

. . . .

I wipe tiny beads of sweat from my palms onto the knees of my salwar as I wait outside Joggers Park, where Bandra West meets the

Arabian Sea. The track by the seaside is lush and breezy. At this hour it teems with walkers, and I watch as hefty gray-haired ladies motor past the trees and bushes in their gleaming white trainers, moving their arms back and forth like steam engines. Their maids do a damn good job of cleaning their shoes.

After twenty minutes, I spot Babloo climbing out of an autorickshaw, fifty feet away. The sight of him for the second time in one weekend is just as staggering as it was the first. His shoulders are still narrow, like a boy's, but his nose and cheekbones are sharper than I remember. And then there is his combed hair, thick and straight, and his clean skin. When we were kids, he exercised his freedom not to bathe often and instructed me to do the same. "To keep the perverts away," he said. I'd obey, proudly showing him the dusty progress of my feet and legs.

Babloo lights a cigarette as he strolls my way. His walk has matured into more of a strut, all loose hips and self-assured stride. He stops a meter in front of me and nods a hello. He pays the park entrance fee for both of us, and we walk in silence toward a bench facing the track. He takes a seat beside me, crossing one leg over his knee, draping his right arm over the back of the bench.

"So," he says, stretching his neck to the side, "now that the gora is gone, tell me what happened to you. Since, you know, the last time I saw you."

I take a deep breath. "They took me to a girls' home."

"I heard. Asha Home, right?"

He knew? My mouth opens and closes as I struggle to find the words to respond. "How? Who . . . who told you?"

He frowns and takes a drag of his cigarette. "That's where they sent most of the girls who didn't get stuck in Dongri."

I spread my fingers out against the heat of my collarbone and pause to gather myself. "If you knew where I was, why didn't you contact me? Write me a letter, even? I was there for six years."

"You didn't contact me, did you?"

"They wouldn't let me." My face starts to feel prickly.

"We could barely read back then, let alone write. Remember?"

"They didn't teach you to read in Dongri?"

"I was in jail. You think they offered to let me dictate letters to you?" He picks up a pebble from the bench and flings it at a nearby pigeon pecking at a blackened banana peel. The pigeon flutters a few feet in the air, then floats back down.

I take a deep breath and try to keep an even tone. "Did you ever wonder if . . . if I was . . ."

Babloo leans forward, resting his elbows on his knees, and looks at the ground. "If you were okay? Every day."

The tears well up, too fast for me to blink them away. We sit in silence, watching the walkers power past us. Ducks honk and flap their wings in the shallow pond inside the park.

"What was it like in Dong—"

"Come on, yaar, what's the point? The important thing is that we are both alive, healthy, and happy now. You are happy, aren't you?"

I take a moment to think of an answer that sounds believable, and realize that I've been happier this past month than I have been in years. "Yes, I'm happy," I say. "I'm really happy."

"Good. I'm glad," Babloo says, flicking his cigarette butt toward the pigeon with the banana peel.

For a while we exchange details about where we live, what life is like now, but I can't help but feel as though he's not telling me something.

As he's going on about the layout of his new flat in Ghatkopar, I interrupt to press him once more. "Just tell me what happened to you, yaar."

He chuckles. "You don't give up, do you?" He lights another cigarette. "I was fine. Stayed in Dongri until I was eighteen, made it out in one piece, got a job, a flat. Made some money. End of story."

"Were you okay when you left Dongri?" He can't be telling the truth. That place is rough. Everybody knows it. Gauri Ma'am has been fighting with the state for years on how they run the remand homes in Maharashtra, and she says Dongri is one of the worst.

"If anyone was going to survive that place, it's your Babloo," he says, smiling.

I sit back against the bench and stare at my palms for a moment. "Then why did you lie to the judge?"

"Yaar, you would have been killed in Dongri. I was doing you a damn favor."

"Yes, but why? I deserved to be there more than you did. It was my stupid idea to get that madherchodh paanwala back in the first place."

Babloo grazes his fingers across his crown, nudging pieces of windswept hair back into place. "Perhaps. But look at you now. You got an education. You work an office job, and you spend Saturdays at Juhu Beach with American guys. Things worked out for you, no?"

My cheeks tingle. "He's Canadian."

"Canadian, American, African—whatever he is, he's lucky to have you," Babloo says in the same tone he used to taunt the police officers the day I arrived at VT.

I can't help but smile. Even after all these years, he is still the same old Babloo.

"Giggling, are you? See? You can't hide these things from me."

"Arre, shut your mouth." I jab him with my elbow. "It's not like that. He only wants a tour guide, and he's helping me practice English and apply to college."

Babloo presses his lips into a thin line. "If you say so."

"Babloo," I start. Then, after a sigh, "Are you sure you were okay all those years?"

"This again?" He leans in toward me, his chin jutting out. "I have my own flat. My boss pays me good money. Have a few girls here and there. So don't you worry about me. Your Babloo is first-class."

That night, I lie on my mat, mulling over every beat of our conversation. His manner was the same—confident and dry. But something was keeping him from opening up about what had happened to him over the past decade.

I turn onto my side, gazing up through the window of my hut. I could never have imagined him growing up to be like this, with his own flat in Ghatkopar, a job, and shiny new clothes. It's like someone handed him a brand-new life.

I think back to when we were at Chowpatty Beach and I met Rakhi Tilak all those years ago. What did she say? We give birth to ourselves over and over again. Until now, I never really thought about whether that could be true.

BABLOO, PAPPU, AND I WERE crouching on the footpath, counting out our coins to buy biscuits, when Kalu stumbled around the corner, covering his eye with one hand. Trails of blood trickled from a wound on his other arm, which hung loosely at his side.

We bolted up at the sight of him.

"They tried to take my money," Kalu whimpered as I lifted his hand away to check his face. His eye was swollen shut and a gash ran from his forehead to his cheek.

"Gently, gently," Babloo barked at me. "Who took your money, Kalu?"

"The older boys. I didn't give it at first. Then they pinned me down and hit me in the face with a stick."

"Rakhi, go—" Babloo started.

"Chemist. I'm going right now," I said, scraping up our pile of coins from the footpath, hoping it'd be enough for bandages and medicines.

"The one beside the dried fruit store. Not the one nearby. Their securitywala will just chase you away."

I nodded and dashed off. Kalu was an idiot for trying to stand up to the older boys on his own. I once heard about some new kid who didn't want to hand over his money to them. They pinned him down and melted a plastic bag all over the kid's body, burning his flesh. He survived, but he was theirs after. Years later, Gauri Ma'am would explain to me that the older kids hurt younger, weaker kids because they too were hurt when they were small, and cycles like this are hard to break.

As the sun went down, I perched on the footpath next to the public garbage bin overflowing with food wrappers and plastic bottles. On my other side was Kalu, newly bandaged and cleaned up. He was too worn out to find someplace else to sit, and the *caw-caw*ing of the overexcited crows didn't seem to bother him, so we remained there, waiting for Babloo, who had gone to sort out the situation with the older boys.

I leapt to my feet when Babloo returned. "What did they say?" I asked, the words catching in my dry mouth.

Grim-faced, he paused. "I told the older boys I'd give them a hundred rupees a week if they left us alone."

"How are we going to get them so much money?"

"We'll manage."

Kalu shook his head and glared at Babloo with his one open eye. "You could have offered less money, chutiya. How are we supposed to eat? Or buy medicines next time someone beats us? Now we're fucked."

Babloo shook his head. "Trust me, I bargained them down."

"Down from what?" I asked. "What the hell could they have asked for?"

"A car?" Kalu asked, laughing.

"A bar of gold?" I said.

"You, Rakhi," Babloo said, watching the crows diving in and out of the bin. "They asked for you."

18

ON MONDAY MORNING, WHILE I'M out filing documents in family court for Sudeepthi, I decide that no good can come of telling Gauri Ma'am that I've finally found Babloo.

When I started seeing the therapywali, Ma'am said I had a "strong fear of engulfment." Those were the words she used, as if I would understand them. "Means what," I asked.

"Means you have trouble forming relationships because you're afraid of being weak, of disappointing others, of being hurt. Your parents died and left you alone, your family didn't care for you, and that boy Babloo deserted you, for all we know. You didn't make a single friend at the Asha Home, and you don't really have any friends now."

"Did Dr. Pereira tell you this? She doesn't know anything."

Ma'am knotted her brow and frowned. "I've told you. Dr. Pereira is a professional, she doesn't report back to me. You don't have to be a doctor to deduce these things. And don't forget, I took a big risk with you, bringing you here straight from the Asha Home. Your success depends on how you take care of your mental health. No more sniffing around town for this Babloo boy. He's gone. Let yourself grieve for him, and then carry on with your life."

"What if he finds me?"

She sighed and pressed her fingers to her temples. "Then we'll deal with that when it happens."

....

When I return to the office in the afternoon, I notice a plastic Sai Krishna dabba of half-eaten dal khichdi drying out on Gauri Ma'am's desk. She must have been called away suddenly. As I pack up what's left for her to eat later, I spot her datebook sitting there, open to this week.

I have an urge to read it, then stop myself, remembering how Ma'am is always saying people in India need to respect each other's privacy. But though Ma'am insists on referring to me as an assistant, I'm still her peon, as Babloo said. And peons always know and guard the secrets of their sahibs. It's the best part of the job, Tazim likes to say.

Like that time Mr. Motiani went to Singapore on a business trip, and Mrs. Motiani made Tazim destroy the evidence of her late-night affair with her diamond seller's thirty-year-old son, Ricky Shah. Tazim had to scrub out the stains from Mrs. Motiani's bedsheets, and send the driver out to buy new liquor to top up what Ricky had guzzled from Mr. Motiani's crystal whiskey set.

I pick up the datebook, running my finger over the smooth pages.

Monday—2 p.m.: Jeetendra Arora. Meeting at Nariman Point

Why is she meeting with Rubina Mansoor's husband, the building developer? I scan the pages for more information.

Friday—8 p.m.: fundraiser party at Arora Splendour Towers (Lower Parel)

So Alex was right. But Arora Splendour in Lower Parel? I haven't even heard of that one. How many buildings does this guy have his name on?

I keep flipping pages until I find a "Fundraiser" to-do list. I skim over the tasks she's set for herself at the top. Finishing her speech for the party, picking up her black silk sari blouse from the tailor, buying thank-you cards, sending Arora her donor retention plan.

My eyes stop, though, when I see a task with my name crossed out: ~~*Rakhi help with serving, cleanup, etc?*~~

And then, right under it: *Ask Rubina to ensure waitstaff speak English.*

She wanted me to wait on her and Alex and all the other hi-fi guests at her party, and then she decided I wasn't good enough. Which is worse?

Slamming the datebook shut, I stalk out to the kitchen with her leftover dal khichdi. I shove it into the fridge, hitting a sticky old jar of lime pickle that rattles and tumbles over, its lid popping off. Bright orange oil spills out, dripping down to the rack below.

Just then, Alex comes into the kitchen and leans against the wall. "I got a text from your friend Babloo. We're hanging out tonight. You and I didn't already have plans, did we?"

"Oh?" Babloo is calling Alex? Why isn't he calling me?

Alex gapes at the mess in the fridge but doesn't offer to help. "So, we did have plans?"

"No plans. I will come with you and Babloo." I grab a rag from the sink and start to wipe away the lime pickle.

"Wait," he says, pulling out his phone and punching out an SMS. "Let me just see if—"

Immediately, his phone starts ringing. "It's Babloo," he says. "Hello? . . . Yeah, yeah, I'll give it to her." He holds the phone out. "He wants to talk to you."

"Yaar," Babloo says on the other end, after I wipe my oily hands. "You don't want to come tonight. I'm taking him out with friends. No ladies allowed."

He must be joking. "Very funny."

"Really. Not tonight."

"Arre, Babloo, what difference does it make if I come?"

"Next time, teek hain? Look, I have some work to do. Call you later." The line goes dead.

Alex scratches behind his ear. "Everything okay?"

I hand the phone back and offer Alex a smile, which disappears quickly. "You go with him."

"You sure?"

I pick up the rag again and start rinsing it out in the sink. "Yes, I am sure." What else can I say? I've only seen Babloo once since Juhu Beach and now he wants to see Alex and not me? And who are these friends of his? What if Alex gets into some kind of trouble and Gauri Ma'am finds out?

"Awesome. Okay, I have to finish drafting a research brief for Gauri before I leave. See you tomorrow."

"You enjoy with Babloo." I pause and then turn back to Alex. "Be careful."

"Of what?"

"This is Bombay, na? Always, you have to be careful."

He backs out the kitchen door and whispers loudly, "Maybe you should work on your college applications tonight." He smiles, and then heads back to his desk.

Work on them how? If I knew how to write a college application I would be there by now. I turn the tap off and throw the wet rag into the sink, where it lands with a heavy slap.

....

The next day, I'm switching out Vivek's aging computer monitor, watching the dust particles float in the morning light, when Alex trudges into the office, rubbing his forehead. Dark circles bloom under his watery, red eyes. Before I can ask him about his night out with Babloo, Gauri Ma'am whisks him into a meeting with Rubina Mansoor. "The rally is only nine days away, we have lots to do," Ma'am says, slamming the door behind her.

Vivek glances at Gauri Ma'am's closed door, then slumps back in his chair and twists his gold wedding band around his fleshy finger, eyeing it intently.

"Sir," I say, careful not to startle him. "Your monitor is plugged in again."

He doesn't respond.

"You can use your computer now," I say, louder this time. When he still doesn't reply, I tap his shoulder. "Are you feeling all right?"

He snaps out of his thoughts. "How much do you think I could get for this ring?" he asks, holding up his left hand.

"Sir, what for?"

"My daughter's wedding plans are getting complicated. The groom's side wants us to hire a violinist for the wedding reception," he says, rubbing his forehead. "Tell me, do you even know what a violin sounds like?"

"No, sir," I say.

"I figured," he sighs. "My in-laws bought this ring for three thousand in the late eighties. Must be worth at least twenty-five thousand now. Think I could get that much?"

No moneylender is going to give him anywhere close to that amount, but I don't want to disappoint him. "Sir, I don't know."

"It's quite heavy," he murmurs, stroking the ring, wedged deep in his finger.

"Sir, I think first you have to worry about how to get it off your hand, na?"

His frown melts. "Rakhi, Rakhi," he says, chortling so hard he starts hacking into his sleeve. "Always so quiet, and then blunt as a hammer. What would this office do without you?"

I smile, scratching behind my neck. "You'd order chai from outside?"

He sighs, wiping a tear from the corner of his eye. "Everyone is so tense right now, especially with the rally next week. Perhaps we all need a little humor in our lives."

....

Alex leans against the kitchen counter, watching me add milk to afternoon tea. "So, last night, Babloo took me to the liquor store and we bought a bottle of Black Label and—"

"Who is paying?" I set out nine small cups on a tray.

"Babloo paid. I told him to just buy whatever he usually drinks, but he insisted on getting the expensive stuff."

I'm still annoyed from yesterday, but he doesn't seem to notice. He goes on about how he went to Babloo's new flat and they sat on the floor drinking because the sofa and chairs hadn't arrived yet, and then Babloo's friends came over and they finished the bottle and ordered fish pakoras that arrived wrapped in newspaper.

I pour the last cup of tea and then turn to face Alex. "That's it? What about cockfights and teen patti?"

"Well, one of the guys—his name was Suresh—he said he was part of a gang."

"Arre? Alex, what you are—"

"No, it was actually pretty cool," he insists, lowering his voice. "I mean, at first I was nervous. He showed me a little compartment in the heel of his boot where he keeps a small blade."

I fold my arms. He cannot be serious.

"I get it," he continues. "These guys have to be able to defend themselves. Some of them started telling me their stories, like how they got into this gang, where they came from. It was fascinating. There is so much goddamn money in this city and the only way some people can access it is by joining gangs. So you can't really fault them, you know?"

"You should not spend time with this kind of people. You don't know them. They will do anything. They will wait until you are drunk, then take your money, watch, shoes."

He lifts a cup of tea off the tray and blows on it. "I thought Babloo was your best friend," he says, watching me from behind the rim of his cup.

"Yes . . ." I start. I want to tell Alex that he has to be careful be-cause even in this kitchen I could pick his pocket and he wouldn't notice. Instead, I smile. "There is no problem. You do what you want."

Alex takes another sip of tea and pours the rest down the sink. "Good, 'cause I'm seeing him tonight."

"Again?" I can feel my smile wavering. "Where you are going?"

"Not sure. He said it would be a surprise. I asked to bring you and he said no girls allowed."

Just yesterday, Babloo said I could join them next time. What are they doing together?

After I distribute the tea, I phone Babloo from the latrine but he doesn't pick up. I lean against the stall door, thinking of what to say.

wat secret u r keeping from me?

He replies in an instant. **secret?**

alex said no rakhi 2nite

arre chill ya . . . tension mat lo . . . alex toh safe hoga

u tek care him, boss will b angry w me

acha? alex says u r keeping secret 4m boss . . .

Someone's footsteps fill the bathroom, and I flush the toilet and head back into the office.

THE DAY BEFORE THE JUSTICE For All fundraiser, Gauri Ma'am summons Vivek into her office and tells him about the party in a low voice. I stand in my usual hiding spot by the kitchen, listening.

"Are staff invited?" Vivek sounds hopeful.

"No," she whispers, "it's not for the staff. I mean, it's not really for any of us. It's for Rubina to feel like she's really contributing. And, of course, to bring in some money."

"But, Ma'am, surely you must tell everyone."

"When it's over. So I don't have to tell them they can't come."

"And the intern? Sorry, the consultant? Alex?"

"Of course Rubina had to invite him. But he knows not to say anything. And anyways, he's not really staff, so what's the problem?"

"Gauriji," Vivek says, sighing. "Throwing a secret party to raise funds for Justice For All without telling the staff . . . It's not right."

"Desperate times, Vivek. Why can't you just trust me?"

"The staff are fed up. And you know they don't hold back."

"Bhavana giving you trouble?"

"Arre, no, Gauri, it's not Bhavana. It's everyone. It's me, too. I don't agree with any of this. We have to focus on our cases, our clients, and not blindly follow this actress into this fantasy world. What if she—"

"What, Vivek? The worst thing that happens is we don't raise any money, and so it will be as though we did nothing at all. We don't have the money to keep going like this beyond the new year. We'll have to find cheaper rent, cut back to a skeleton crew."

"Respectfully, I disagree. The opportunity cost—"

"My god, Vivek, just stop it, all right? I cannot keep having the same discussion with you every two days."

There is a long pause, and I slip to the far end of the kitchen before Ma'am's door opens and closes, quietly.

....

I'm washing the cups from afternoon tea when Babloo phones me saying he wants to take me out for dinner. "To catch up properly," he says. "Chill marna, you know?"

"Sure, why not?" I reply, trying not to let the relief sound in my voice. We haven't met since Joggers Park, but he's already seen Alex twice.

The bus from Ghatkopar Station hits every pothole in the road on the way to a restaurant called China Corner. As I step off the bus, I marvel at the unexpectedness of this moment. Less than a week ago Babloo was missing or dead for all I knew, and now he and I are going for Chinese food in the central suburbs.

China Corner looks like Sai Krishna, bright with white-tiled floors, and is filled with round-faced Gujarati families reaching over big plates of food. Babloo waves at me from a yellow booth. "I've already ordered for us both," he says, grinning.

As soon as I sit down, a young waiter in a stained yellow uniform appears, balancing plates of food so big I worry his tiny wrists might snap off. He swiftly places the plates in front of us before giving Babloo a fast, blank rendition of what's on the table. "Sir, your order, sir. One chicken chow mein, one chicken manchurian, two sweet-corn soup, one veg fried rice, one chili chicken, four spring roll, two Thums Up. Aur kya, sir?"

Babloo gazes at the food and then at me, smirking. "You want anything else?"

I stare at the spread of food and ask if anyone else is joining us.

"Just us," he replies, digging a fork and spoon into the chow mein. He twists them a bit and shovels a pile of shiny noodles onto his plate.

I shake my head no and the waiter disappears in a blur of dull yellow fabric. I reach for a spring roll. I've never tasted one before. The shell breaks when I bite into it, flaking like a crunchy samosa. "All this food for two people? And so much chicken?"

"Times have changed," Babloo says, through a mouthful of noodles. "Eat up."

"Remember what happened to Kalu? With the chili chicken?"

When we were living on the streets, some tourist gave Kalu fifty rupees and he decided to buy himself sticky, bright orange chili chicken from a small take-out place outside Bombay Central Station.

Babloo snickers. "He wouldn't share because he said he'd earned the money himself, na?"

"And then he got the runs," I add, chuckling.

"And shit his shorts in the middle of the street!" Babloo wipes a tear away from his eye. He sighs. "It's been so long, hasn't it?"

Around us, families tuck into piles of rice, noodles, and chicken, parents barely noticing as their squealing children dart between irate, silent waiters. Bollywood dance songs blare out of the tinny speakers, and Babloo bobs his head to the beat. We look like we fit in. I don't think any of these people would ever guess we used to sleep outside VT Station.

"My flat is right behind this restaurant," Babloo says. "Building is called Rajshree Castle Housing Society. You can come by anytime, whenever you need anything. Door is always open."

My face warms at his generosity. "Sometimes I wondered if you had run away to Bhutan. Remember how much you used to talk about going there? You even had the route planned out. And you said I could come, but only if I bought my own ticket."

He continues to eat his noodles, avoiding my gaze. "Did I?"

I swallow. "Yes, remember that time in Ballard—" .

"Anyone would be stupid to leave Bombay, especially for a place like Bhutan. This is where the money is."

Either a hole has been ripped in his memory, or he doesn't want to talk about what happened between us, so I change the subject. "Tell me then, what is your work? Don't say 'business-shizness.'"

"Business-shizness is correct, though." He wipes his mouth with a paper napkin and crumples it into a tiny ball. "I work for a guy. He takes jobs from his clients. I do the things he asks me to do."

"Is your boss a goonda or what?"

He pauses a little too long, and I swallow my next mouthful of spring roll a little too fast.

"Babloo," I sputter. "Are you serious?"

"Don't behave like some nun locked away in a convent."

"But crime, though? Why would you—"

"Arre, leave it, yaar. Unlike you, I'm not a high school pass, so no bloody office is going to hire me to do tip-tip on the computer all day."

"You could do other things," I offer, but he puts his fork down and folds his hands.

"Like what, serving food at a Chinese restaurant? Like this bhen-chodh?" He gestures at a gaunt, middle-aged waiter swatting a grimy blue rag at the table next to ours.

I sit back against the booth. "You don't have to hurt people, do you?"

He throws his head back and laughs so loud the boy beside us looks up from his plate, noodles dangling from his oily lips. "No, yaar, I don't have to hurt people. I swear, you're still as naïve as you were when I first met you. Remember? You thought those VT police would buy you food if you only asked."

"Shut up," I say, stirring the ice in my Thums Up with a straw. "So what do you actually do if you don't hurt people?"

"I collect hafta from illegal hawkers in Goregaon."

"Tax?"

"Something like that. Hawkers who operate on city land have to pay the police every week. I collect it, charge extra, and give a portion to the police."

"Why can't the police just collect it themselves?"

"They're lazy chutiyas. Anyway, it's easy money."

"And if the hawkers don't pay you?"

"Then I make sure my guys give them trouble."

"So you *do* hurt people—"

Babloo drops his spoonful of chicken manchurian on his plate. "You going to tell your human rights lawyers on me?"

"No, no," I stammer. "Of course not."

"Look," he says. "Everyone is out here trying to make enough money to eat. Hawking is illegal. But people come and set up and sell anyway. And I collect the hafta, and the money gets distributed to others. It's a system. And it works."

I consider this. "Do you like doing it?"

Babloo rolls his head from side to side, stretching his neck. "The money is fine. But honestly, I'm too good for this. Hafta in Goregaon is at a rate of twenty rupees per hawker per day. In Bandra, where your gora friend lives, it's a hundred."

"So you want to collect hafta in Bandra?"

"No, yaar, I want to stop collecting hafta. I want to move up the ranks, you know? Bring business in. Make decisions."

"I don't understand."

"Forget it." He tears the top off a plastic packet of red chili sauce with his teeth. "So, missing your firanghi tonight? He talks about you so much. Buk-buk-buk, Rakhi this, Rakhi that."

"Shut up, Babloo."

"Arre." He smirks. "Getting so angry?"

I want to tell him that I found Alex first. Like that time I pinched an old man's wallet and everything in it—from the cash to the lone photo of a stern-mouthed woman with surprised beady eyes— belonged to me.

I shovel a spoonful of chili chicken into my mouth. "I'm not angry," I say as I chew through the crunchy stickiness. "Anyways, good you're babysitting him. It gives me a break. He's too much."

Babloo nods along. "So tell me, when are the two of you getting married?"

I hurl my crumpled napkin at his face and it disappears behind his shoulder.

He squeezes the last bit of sauce onto his noodles. "Your firanghi won't stop SMSing me. Not sure what he's searching for, but it looks like he thinks your Babloo is the one to find it for him."

I take a sip of my soda and frown, staring at the grains of fried rice strewn across my plate. "Where have you taken him?"

"Relax, he's safe with me."

"Are you sure?"

Babloo pauses, chow mein dangling from his fork. "What's the problem?"

"Yaar, he's my colleague, not yours. If anything happens to him, if any of your goonda friends try anything, it's my gaand, not yours."

"Sure you're not just jealous?"

"Of what, chutiya?" I look him in the eyes and he sits back.

"Relax," Babloo says. "We got together at my place on Monday, then to a beer bar Tuesday."

"A beer bar? The ones with those dirty dancing girls?"

"Yes, Memsahib, the ones with those dirty dancing girls."

I picture Alex, sitting in a smoky bar with no windows, peering up the skirts of costumed bar-balas thrusting their hips to item songs. Then, clinking glasses with Babloo, while his other hand is wrapped around some girl's sweaty bare waist.

Fidgeting with a napkin, I try to sound uninterested. "Where was the bar?"

Babloo doesn't bother looking up while he mixes the last of the chow mein with the rest of his chili chicken. "Near Mira Road. Far from here. New place. Opened last month."

"Why did you take him there?"

Babloo shrugs. "He's a man."

I sit back. "Well, did he like it?"

Babloo holds my gaze as he sets down his fork on his plate so gently it barely makes a sound. "He's a man."

I WAS TWELVE WHEN DEVI was gang-raped by the older boys. She was taken to hospital, bleeding and unconscious, and we never saw her again.

"I told Devi to be careful around them," Babloo said, kicking pebbles while I sat beside him on Mint Road, poking at a half-eaten Chicken Maharaja Mac that some firanghi had placed on the ground beside us.

"Didn't I tell her?" Babloo asked. "You'll be next." His voice was more hoarse than usual.

"Bullshit," I murmured, pushing the chicken sandwich around in its carton. It left a thin smear of white-orange sauce and a trail of bruised, light green leaves.

"Don't act tough," he said. "You know what happens to girls here."

He was right, but I didn't want to admit it. We were the same age, Devi and me. Sure, she was always trying to hang around the older boys, but it didn't matter. They would have done it anyway.

"Listen," Babloo said, his voice quiet. "I can help you." He caught my gaze and lifted his chin.

"Help me how?"

"Break you in." He clenched his fists and pulled his elbows back, like he was ramming his body forward. "Protect you. As . . . your boyfriend."

I scraped a tiny white seed off the sandwich bun and rolled it between my thumb and finger. I knew exactly what he meant.

"Think about it." He stood up, dusting off the back of his shorts. "And give me that thing if you're not going to eat it." I didn't respond, so he reached down to grab the rest of the sandwich.

If I said yes, maybe I'd have Babloo forever—to protect me, to love me the way boyfriends love girlfriends. If I said no, I could end up like Devi—dead, for all anyone knew. What was there to think about?

It happened just once, in the damp unlit corridor in an empty old building in Ballard Estate. The floor was cold and gritty so Babloo took off his shirt and spread it out for me to lie on. I concentrated hard on not looking at him, but each time I snuck a glance, he was looking away, too. His skin was flushed and he cleared his throat a lot.

Afterward, he wiped himself off, pulled his pants up, and said that now I didn't have to worry about being kidnapped and sold as a child bride to an eighty-year-old sultan in the Gulf. I didn't know what the Gulf was, but it sounded bad. We walked back to Mint Road together, loosely holding hands. Neither of us said a word. Not because there was nothing to say, but because there was so much to think about. What now? Were things different between Babloo and me? Or would they stay exactly the same?

Finally, I spoke up. "You know Bhutan? How do you get there? From Bombay."

"Not easy. You take the train to Siliguri, then a bus to Bhutan. I already looked into it. I'm going the first chance I get."

I gazed at him, a slow smile building. "Should we go together?"

"Save up, then. It's expensive." He let go of my hand and gave me a light slap on the shoulder. "I'm not paying for your ticket."

THE EVENING OF THE FUNDRAISER, I sit on Tazim's floor helping her parcel rotis for her customers before dinner. Ayub lies on the cot he shares with Tazim, singing ABC.

"Ten for Masooma Begum, six for Azizbhai's sister-in-law, and sixteen for Munna," Tazim instructs over the noise of Ayub's song as she slaps the rolled-out dough onto her hot tawa.

"Why so many for Munna?" I ask, folding paper around a stack of rotis. "He has a wife, only."

"So what if I toss him some extras? Maybe he will remember next time I fall short on rent."

"You could give Munna a thousand rotis a day and he would still kick you out." I breathe in deeply to catch the scent of the fresh bread. "Arre, we'll eat soon, na?"

She says yes and tells me to stir the dal as she waits for the roti to puff up.

As I reach for the metal spoon to disrupt the thickened layer at the top of the pot, my phone rings. It's Gauri Ma'am. She sounds frantic. "Rakhi, Rakhi, where are you?"

I cover my ear with my other hand to drown out Ayub's ABCs. "Ma'am, I'm at home. What happened? Everything okay?"

"Go to the office immediately, turn on my computer, and print me out a document saved on my desktop as 'Fundraiser Speech' and bring it to a building in Lower Parel called Arora Splendour, to the top floor. Just past the Sai Baba Mandir. Doorman will let you up." As she's speaking I can hear Rubina in the background, shouting at someone about cocktail napkins.

"Ma'am, when do you need it?"

"In less than an hour. Drop whatever you're doing and leave now." The line goes dead.

Tazim smacks the puffed-up roti off the open flame onto a plate and turns off her burner. "So Gauri Ma'am is asking you to work now? At least eat first, na? What difference will ten minutes make?"

"All of it," I say, springing to my feet.

"She'll be angry with you whether you're late or not," Tazim says, as I peel the hot roti from the top of her stack and dart out the door. "They shit on us because they can," I hear her yell as I run to the station.

Forty-five minutes later, after printing out the speech, I'm on the train up to Lower Parel, smoothing out Ma'am's notes.

Good evening, everyone. My name is Gauri Verma and I am the executive director of Justice For All. Thank you all for joining us. We would not be here tonight without the support of my dear friend Rubina Mansoor and her generous husband, Jeetendra Arora, who in his own right is moving mountains to make our beloved city more livable. When Rubina first started planning this fundraiser, she told me she would invite the crème de la crème of Mumbai society, and just looking at you all tonight, I can see that she was indeed correct.

The what of Mumbai society? I skip past the long description of why she started the organization and what it stands for. There must be something more interesting in here.

Justice For All has had another superb year, continuing to be on the forefront of human rights work in India. As you are all aware, we are seeking leave to appeal a decision of the Bombay High Court that centers on the right to housing for people living in a slum in Chembur. This work would not be possible without my excellent staff.

I snort out loud. She would never call us "excellent" to our faces.

My employees work hard. And they do it for a fraction of the average lawyer's salary because they believe that every person is born with the same inalienable rights and freedoms; that human rights are based on dignity, equality, and mutual respect, regardless of caste, religion, or how much money you have in the bank.

I skip down the page.

Despite our successes, Justice For All is now facing funding challenges unlike anything we've seen before. Although we have mostly been funded by international donors, over half of the funding that we need to sustain our operations will end at the end of this year. This is not because the quality of our work has changed. And it's certainly not because the need for our work has decreased. Rather, the growing economic crisis has dramatically reduced our foreign funders' budgets. The world has begun to view India as a middle-income country that does not require outside assistance.

So what Ma'am told Vivek was true. She's going to have to let most of us go if she can't get funding quick.

Your individual contributions and networks can make a dramatic difference for us in this critical period. Each lawyer in our office

costs on average fifty thousand rupees per month. If each of you
gave only twenty-five thousand rupees, our office could continue
to operate for an entire year.

I sit back against the train bench, stunned. How is Ma'am going to
convince Rubina Mansoor's hi-fi friends that human rights are important just so she can pay the rent and not fire anyone else? Maybe
she shouldn't have kept this a secret. I could have taught her a thing
or two about begging.

When I burst into the wide, high-ceilinged lobby of Arora Splendour, I pause at the sight of a giant, menacing chandelier looming
over my head. It's far too big and heavy to just be dangling from a
thin chain.

The security guard scans me up and down, asking me what business I have there.

"I have to go to the party on the top floor. Arora Sahib's flat. To
deliver something. It's important." I shake Ma'am's speech at him.

He straightens up. "You'll have to phone someone to come get
you."

Gauri Ma'am doesn't answer her phone, so I dial Alex, who picks
up on the second ring.

"Rakhi," he yells, over the chatter of voices and music. "I was just
thinking about you. I'm at that secret fundraiser party I told you—"

"Alex, I know. I am in lobby," I shout into my phone. "Gauri
Ma'am left her speech at the office. I have it. Come down."

In moments, Alex strolls out of the lift, shining bright like a
movie star, dressed in a dark blue shirt and black pants. His glossy
black shoes clack loudly on the mosaic of black-and-white floor tile.

I hold out the speech. "You take to Gauri Ma'am. I am going."

"Just come up for a second. I bet you've never been to a party like
this before."

"Gauri Ma'am saying no staff."

"But she's expecting you. Bring her the speech, and then you can
leave. Come on. The food's good."

Even though the roti I crammed into my mouth at Tazim's stopped the gnawing in my stomach, it still feels empty. "Teek hain. Two minutes."

Alex tells the guard not to worry, I'm with him.

As the lift doors open to the top floor, I smooth the pieces of hair around my face with my hands.

"Don't worry," Alex says, "the lights are pretty dim inside."

He's right: I've never been to a party like this. In spite of the low lighting, the women shimmer from top to bottom in silk saris and salwar kameez. The men are paunchy, in their starched collars and suit jackets. Waiters in black shirts whisk large silver trays of food around the room. The ceilings are high and the flat is huge. There must be at least a hundred people here, if not more. I can feel myself shrinking.

One waiter, holding a tray of paneer cubes topped with tiny green leaves, bumps into me as Alex leads me through the crowd. The waiter's eyes widen and he grabs my elbow. "Who are you?" he whispers loudly in my ear, over the loud din of laughter and music I don't recognize. "What are you doing here?"

Before I can answer, Alex turns around and reaches for my free arm. "Hey man, she's a guest."

"Sir, you're sure?" the waiter says, not letting go of me. "We've been instructed this is a private event, and to report any intruders."

"Yeah, I'm sure. We work together. And we're friends. Back off." His eyes shine like he's had a few drinks.

The waiter draws in his breath, then releases my arm.

"These people," Alex says, as the waiter walks off. "Can you believe—"

"Alex," I interrupt, waving the speech in the air to get his attention. "Where is Gauri Ma'am?"

Before he can reply, I feel a poke on my shoulder. When I spin around, it takes me a moment to recognize the person grinning at me.

"You could have at least worn something nice, na?" Babloo says.

His hair is slicked back and there's a small diamond stud in his left ear. Underneath his thin blue shirt, a white banyan glows like an X-ray.

"How did you get in here?"

Babloo points at Alex. "This guy invited me."

Alex squeezes Babloo's shoulder. "Ruby Aunty said I could bring a friend."

They hold their glasses up and clink them. The brown liquid inside Alex's glass splashes on his hand, and as he shakes it off they laugh like old friends.

Now I feel like more of an intruder than when the waiter tried to throw me out.

Babloo grins. Gauri Ma'am will for sure notice this guy who, in spite of his nice clothes, is missing a layer of fat and muscle to disguise him among these pale rich folk.

"I would have asked you to come, too," Alex goes on, "but it wouldn't have been fair to the other people at the office, you know?"

But it was fair that you were invited? I want to say.

"Plus," Alex continues, "this is a good opportunity for Babloo to meet people. Put feelers out. Start something new."

I turn to Babloo and switch to low, hushed Hindi. "Who are you trying to meet here? You know these people will throw you out the second they find out you're not one of them."

Alex cuts in to say something about introducing Babloo to people and then whisks him away out onto the terrace, leaving me to stand by myself with the speech rolled up in my hand.

This isn't good. I scan the room for Gauri Ma'am. There's no telling how she'll react if she finds out Babloo is back in my life—and now in Alex's, too. From a distance, I watch Alex introduce Babloo to Jeetendra Arora. They are lit up by the warm glow of hundreds of tiny white lights strung across the terrace. Babloo leans in to say something to Arora, who suddenly frowns, then takes a step back. Through the bobbing heads and shoulders, I watch Arora turn his back on Babloo and join a conversation with a different group of people. Babloo pinches his lips together the way I remember him doing whenever things didn't go his way.

As if this party wasn't already tense enough, I spot Mrs. Motiani in an emerald salwar kameez standing only a few feet away from me next to a gleaming white piano, laughing with a woman in a fuchsia sari. *Shit.* I can feel the hair on my arm rise. Head sunk low and shoulders hunched, I shield my face with my hand and slink away toward the door, trying to blend into the shadows and occupy as little space in this room as possible. I should have known the Motianis would be here. Why didn't I think of that before I followed Alex upstairs?

On my way to the door, Gauri Ma'am interrupts my line of sight and barrels toward me. "Finally," she snaps, pulling the speech from my hands. "What took you so long?"

Before I can step past her, Rubina appears, looking very tall and thin in a deep purple sari with a gold border. Her hair is tied back into a big ponytail so tight it appears to be pulling at her face. "Your office girl showed up at last, did she, Gauri?"

I shift my weight from one foot to the other and point to the door. "Ma'am, I'll go now," I say.

"Arre, wait," she says, bringing the papers close to her face. "It's so dark I can't even tell if you've printed it all."

"Listen, we're already running behind schedule. I don't want people to lose interest." Rubina cocks her head to the side, appearing to think. "Why don't you let me handle it. Give me the speech so I can get a couple of ideas."

Gauri Ma'am clutches her papers to her chest. "You've already been so generous. Thankfully, I have my notes and am ready to go."

"I would be honored, Gauri."

"We can both say something, if you wish."

Rubina throws her head back and laughs. Her purple lips make her teeth look very white. "Nobody comes to a party to be bored twice."

"But I am the face of my organization. If these people are going to donate money, they should at least see the people doing the work."

"Then where are your staff, Gauri?"

"Rubina." Ma'am's eyes are pleading.

"Trust me, these guests are my people. If it's money you want, I know how to squeeze it out of them," Rubina says, holding out her palm.

Defeated, Gauri Ma'am hands her speech over to the nautanki-wali she herself agreed to partner with. While Rubina skims the pages, Ma'am's forehead becomes knitted with worry. Her eyes pass over Babloo, who is still by the bar with Alex. I hold my breath as Ma'am cranes her neck to get a better look. Thankfully, Rubina starts tapping her finger on a cordless microphone, and Ma'am's attention snaps back.

Once Rubina begins Ma'am's speech, leaving out a few details about the work Justice For All has done, I mouth to Ma'am that I'm leaving. She just nods, too worn out to ask me for much else.

As I shuffle out of the party, I can hear Rubina improvising the part in Ma'am's speech asking for a donation of twenty-five thousand rupees from each of the guests. "Only twenty-five thousand rupees," she says. "Think about that. The cost of a new smartphone for your kids, or a couple of silk salwar kameez with modest embroidery. You know, the kind that you might wear once to the temple before you gift it to your maid's daughter for her wedding. Don't cover your face, Kiran, my dear, you know I'm talking about you!"

The crowd roars at Rubina's joke as I slip out of the flat, shutting the door behind me. I punch the button for the lift over and over until it arrives.

If Gauri Ma'am had just told me about the party ahead of time I would have made sure she had her speech printed before she left the office. I wouldn't have told anyone else about it. And I would never have asked to come.

....

Babloo holds out a small leaf bowl. "I've already paid," he says, over the noise of the car horns.

"Good," I reply, snatching the bowl from him.

He called me this morning, telling me to meet him at a pani puri stall near S.V. Road. I didn't want to come, still annoyed about him being at the party last night, but he was pushy.

"This monsoon has been so dry," Babloo says, squinting into the sun. "You know grape farmers out in Nashik are killing themselves because their crops are drying out?"

"I didn't know."

It hasn't rained in days. Not even a single ten-minute shower. Even the muddy water in the potholes has disappeared. I gaze up at the sky, light gray and flat. We still have a month of monsoon to go. Soon, some big cloud will creep in and new patches of black mold will bloom in forgotten corners of the office. Behrampada will flood. Everything will turn bright green and leafy, and grapes will grow and those farmers in Nashik will have died for nothing.

The panipuriwala plucks a round, crispy puri from the tower behind him and pokes a hole in the top with his thumb. Then he pushes in a dab of aloo and chana with some imli chutney, dunks it in the pot of masala water, and drops it in my little bowl. Taking care not to spill any precious liquid, I raise the puri to my lips. The entire thing collapses inside my mouth, sour and spicy.

"So, tell me," Babloo says, wiping a dribble of water from his chin. "Why are you so upset with me?"

"I'm not upset," I say, turning away from him to face the pani-puriwalla.

"You're lying."

"Fine. It's not fair that Alex is my friend but you get to go to these parties with him."

"Uff! It was my one chance to be near that spicy Ruby M. I was hoping she'd be wearing her see-through sari, though," he says, starting to hum the tune of "Drip Drip."

I tell him to be serious, so he stops his song and shrugs. "Fine. Last night was a career opportunity for me."

"How? You want to be a waiter at hi-fi parties? Or are you going to build flats for Jeetendra Arora? I saw you trying to talk to him on the terrace."

Babloo shakes his head while the panipuriwalla drops another puri into his bowl. "Don't worry about it. You're way too caught up in making sure Bombay stays crammed with slums."

"What are you talking about?"

"All that bakvaas last night. These lawyer people you work for, it's like they don't care about the city at all. They're happy to let it sink under the weight of all these people and their rubbish."

"What nonsense are you talking?"

"All that fundraising—for what? So next time a builder tries to put up a flat, some rag-picker can complain that they were there first? Tell me, how many more people can live on that land if it's a tower? It's stupid, what you're all trying to do in Chembur."

"Arre, those Chembur people lived there. How would you like it if your home was bulldozed without warning?"

"If you build a shack out of garbage on land you don't own, then you should expect it to be torn down." He crunches through his puri. "I just can't believe you, of all people, are a part of this movement."

"What movement? This is my job. This is how I earn money."

Babloo scratches the side of his face and shrugs. "I guess I had higher hopes for you."

"What about Alex? He works for Justice For All, too, but I don't see you blasting him."

"Arre, he's just here for time-pass. So he can say he worked in India. And anyways, if he really cared about this human rights social-justice nonsense, he wouldn't be so willing to enjoy all this money and wealth he was born into. Eventually you have to choose. You can't have both."

"Choose between money and caring about other people? How do you come up with this rubbish?"

The panipuriwalla interrupts us with two more puris, then asks us if we want more.

"No," we both say, in unison.

THE FIRST FIRANGHI I EVER really spoke to was Derekbhaiyya.

After a year on the streets, I was used to the NGO didis turning up every so often to teach us things, but never with a gora. One day the NGO didis brought with them a very tall man with golden hair, crooked teeth, and a tattoo on his leg of a strange insect that peeked out from above his white sock. "Yeh ek octopus hai," he said to me, grinning. (Years later I would ask Vivek what an octopus was, only to find out it wasn't an insect at all.)

"Derekbhaiyya is here to learn more about you so that people can help you better," the didis said. "And he speaks Hindi. Say hello."

We did. After the NGO didis left, Derekbhaiyya pulled out a brand-new football from his rucksack and held it out. Babloo seized the football, and Devi, Kalu, Pappu, Raju, and I kicked it around until at least ten more kids showed up. Kalu kicked it far into another lane and the boy who went to retrieve it never came back.

"You'll need to bring a new ball," Babloo informed Derekbhaiyya, as the group dispersed.

And so, the next day, he turned up with another football, gleaming white and green. It had never been kicked around, so we kicked it good and hard.

"I'm here for research purposes," Derekbhaiyya said one afternoon after he had bought us all Amul elaichi milks. "I'm not with an NGO, or government, or anyone like that. I'm here for purely academic purposes," Derek continued in decent Hindi. "I want to make very clear to you all that I won't be paying you for participating."

"Arre?" Babloo slammed his milk carton down, incensed. "Not even a pair of shoes?"

"I don't want you to feel pressured to show me things, or make up stories about your lives because you think I want value for money."

Some of the other kids got up and left.

"You're free not to participate."

The worst kind of firanghi was a kanjoos firanghi, and that was Derekbhaiyya. I rose to my feet, but Babloo put his arm out.

"My friends will stay," he said in a stern voice that signaled to the rest of us not to argue with him.

Over the next few weeks, Derekbhaiyya spent time with us, except Babloo created an alternative life for us. A life in which Babloo pretended he spent a rupee on a newspaper every day. "We may be poor, but we care more about this country than anyone." Playing along, I peered over Babloo's shoulder at the front page, running my finger slowly over the words.

Derekbhaiyya appeared baffled at first, but Babloo was convincing, so Derekbhaiyya just nodded, writing in his notebook. He was so impressed he didn't even think to check if we could read.

As Derekbhaiyya followed us around, we spun false stories about how we lived. One day we were pious Hindus who only ate the food Derekbhaiyya brought us after we recited a prayer. Babloo chanted fake hymns in Marathi so he couldn't understand.

O holy garbage we eat,
We pray to you
And the wasteland

Of this city.
Thank you, ugly white man
For being such a fattoo.

Devi and I collapsed into giggles, and Babloo explained to a puzzled Derekbhaiyya that she and I were shy about praying in front of him, and asked him to turn his head. He did.

When Derekbhaiyya left, I asked Babloo why he bothered making up all these stories when we weren't even getting anything out of it.

"These chutiyas come here, take pictures, videos, collect stories about us, then go off and get paid all kinds of money and we never hear from them again. I'm tired of it."

"But Derekbhaiyya was nice. He bought us food, at least."

"Nice? That bhenchodh didn't want to pay us because he thought we'd lie and screw up his work. He's definitely not working for free. Why should we?"

I mulled this over in my head. "So we gave him what he paid for?"

"Bullshit for bullshit," Babloo said, grinning. "It was a fair trade."

THE SAI KRISHNA COOK CASTS thirty pale uncooked samosas into the hot dark oil, where they bob up and down until he coaxes them onto their other sides with a slotted metal spoon. I watch him fry the samosas to a bubbly golden crisp, then set them on newspaper, double-bagging them. I hand him the hundred-rupee note Gauri Ma'am gave me, hugging the warm paper sack against my chest as I hurry back to the office. Ma'am hasn't bought us all samosas in years. Even Alex has been strange today. He strolled into the office this morning beaming, and when he waved at Gauri Ma'am, she actually smiled and waved back.

As I quietly prop open the front door with my foot so I'm not accused of kicking it, Gauri Ma'am calls out to me. "Come, Rakhi, hurry up and pass out the snacks. Even you must be here for this announcement, too."

I drag a small knife through the paper bag and dump the contents onto a large plate before setting it down on the table in the center of the lawyers' workspace. I pull a chair over and set it beside Gauri Ma'am.

"I want to thank you for your hard work over the past month,"

Ma'am says, clasping her hands on her lap. She scans the circle of lawyers biting into the still-warm samosas. "We should all be very proud of ourselves." She holds out her hands and starts to clap. A reluctant wave of delayed applause rings out as people balance their food on their laps to free up both hands.

"Many of you do not know this, but our new friend Rubina Mansoor and her husband, Jeetendra Arora, held a private fundraising event for us at their home on Friday night."

The lawyers turn to each other, confused, some of them mouthing the words *fundraising?* and *what?* Alex picks fallen bits of peas and potato off his lap and tosses them into his mouth.

"I am so very happy to report," Ma'am continues, grinning, "that we have raised a hefty sum of money, half of which came from the Arora Group."

"How much?" Vivek says, his mouth full.

"Enough to fund us for the next two years. It buys us time while we seek more secure funding."

Vivek, mid-swallow, coughs a few times, and a piece of half-chewed samosa hurtles out of his mouth and onto the floor.

Two years? All those glittery guests of Rubina's have that much spare cash floating around? Did she have to bribe them with free use of her flat for their next functions or what? Everyone else erupts in excited murmurs and small claps.

"This is a good thing," Ma'am says, eyeing the soggy morsel in the middle of the circle. "All this money doesn't mean we get a break, though. The Chembur rally is this Friday, only four days away. Thanks to all your efforts, it will be one of the biggest protests this city has seen in the past five years. We've confirmed that seven other NGOs and many members of the human rights law bar are joining us, and, through Rubina, we expect to have celebrity support too."

"Which celebrities?" Utkarsh asks. "Anyone good? Or all aunty types?"

Ma'am tells us the list isn't confirmed yet, then rattles off twelve names that have never been on the A-list. Still, all the lawyers, Utkarsh included, break into smiles, exclaiming how exciting this is. It's quite something for Justice For All to pull off.

Later that afternoon, a large cardboard box arrives at the office addressed to Gauri Ma'am. She signs for it and motions at me to get a knife. While she opens the small envelope attached to the box, I slice open the brown packing tape in the waiting room. The noise of the stiff cardboard tearing draws the attention of a few lawyers, and soon they're all crowded around me as I crack open the box to reveal an enormous white photocopy machine.

"Arre," Gauri Ma'am says, turning over the note from the envelope. "It says, *Best wishes from the Arora Group.*"

While Gauri Ma'am and the lawyers gloat about how much time and money we'll save in printing flyers for the rally, and managing file work in general, I spot Vivek at the back, staring at the copier sitting in a mess of cardboard, polystyrene, and paper. He purses his lips and says nothing.

....

While distributing morning tea, I see Kamini frowning at her computer screen, Utkarsh gleefully hovering beside her.

"I swear I have never seen this video in my life," Kamini cries.

"Arre, come on," Utkarsh says as he hits PLAY. "There's nobody in the country who hasn't seen 'Drip Drip.' What kind of sanskaari rock have you been living under?"

She shields her eyes with one hand and punches Utkarsh on the arm with the other.

"Drip Drip" was a hit song from a film that nobody remembers. I do, though, because Babloo made us watch it five times. It was about two men competing to win the heart of a woman who was set to marry a third guy. There was some detour to Thailand, a wise but dying grandfather, and an overprotective brother in the army. Of course, the only reason Babloo made us watch the film over and over was because of Rubina Mansoor, who only appeared as an item girl in "Drip Drip."

As I draw closer, I hear the familiar chorus I haven't heard in years:

My heart is like a glass of water
On your parched lips
Giving you life, waking you up
Drip drip, baby, drip drip
My heart crashes into you like a wave
Begging you to feel it
Drip drip, baby, drip drip
Drip drip, baby, drip drip

Drenched in monsoon rain, Rubina, in her see-through white sari, draws her hand sensuously down her face and over her chest. She swings her hips and turns, revealing the outline of her black thong. Behind her, a group of male dancers in white banyans and shorts are also soaking wet, but you can't see their underpants. In the background, palm trees sway and a small waterfall burbles.

"Such a vulgar video," Kamini moans. "Just see how they're dehumanizing her."

"Dehumanizing?" Utkarsh tilts his head as the camera moves up to Rubina's breasts.

"They've reduced her to a collection of body parts in order to titillate men like you," Kamini sneers.

I don't know what *titillate* means, but she spits each syllable out with such disgust it must be bad. The camera zooms out to show Rubina's full body. She turns so we can see her tiny black chaddis peeking through the wet sari again. The men in the white shorts pulse to the music, eyeing her as she dances. She arches her back and a dancer pretends to bury his face in her chest.

"This whole song and dance is completely nonessential to the narrative of the film," Sudeepthi sputters from her desk. "Women's bodies used merely for entertainment—it's sexist. And completely wrong."

"It's Rubina Mansoor, the new face of Justice For All," Bhavana chimes in from her desk.

"Arre, her ass is more recognizable than her face," Sudeepthi groans. She and Bhavana exchange knowing glances before chuckling.

She isn't wrong, I think, as I set teacups down by Kamini and Utkarsh.

"You think the common man cares about the exploitation of women's bodies for entertainment? You're all just overthinking it," Utkarsh says, his eyes still glued to the screen.

Before Bhavana can reply, Alex walks into the lawyers' workspace. "What are you guys watching?"

"Stop the video," Kamini hisses at Utkarsh, snapping him out of his trance. He pauses the video on a shot of Rubina bent over, her breasts heaving at the camera.

Alex blinks at the screen, while the lawyers trade looks and fidget nervously. "Really?" he says, raising his eyebrows. "Do you all think this video is appropriate for the workplace?"

He has a point. Nobody would be watching "Drip Drip" if Gauri Ma'am were here.

Bhavana folds her arms and smirks. "If this video isn't appropriate for us to watch in the workplace, as you say, how on earth is it appropriate for this woman to be the face of Justice For All?"

"Wow," Alex says, shaking his head as though he can't quite believe what she said. "First of all, you're watching an actor playing a role. The role is not the face of Justice For All, the actor is. And second, I thought you all were supposed to be these progressive human rights lawyers. Instead you're all crowded around a computer, judging a woman for being brave enough to show her body."

"Brave, or desperate?" Sudeepthi mumbles to Bhavana.

They snicker so loudly Vivek marches into the lawyers' workspace. "I can hear all of you from my desk."

"Come on, Sir," Bhavana says, pointing at the screen, still frozen on Rubina's breasts. "Even you must agree that this is all so . . . absurd."

"What, this video? That's one way to describe it."

"Not just the video. I mean that, overnight, an irrelevant celebrity craving attention can just . . . take command of Justice For All."

"Bhavana, we have to be supportive—"

"Of what, Vivek Sir? All these lawyers here, with so many years of education and experience, and our mouthpiece is the thong girl from the 'Drip Drip' video?"

Vivek waves his hands in the air, clearly frustrated with Bhavana, whose fists are balled up. "Say what you will, but I am grateful for Rubina. You all have jobs for the next two years because of her. So turn that video off, and all of you, get back to work. You too, Rakhi. Don't make me call Gauri Ma'am." He glares at us, sweat forming on his temples. I've never heard Vivek speak so forcefully to anyone in the office.

"Sorry, Sir," Kamini offers, sheepishly.

Vivek sighs. "It's okay. The important thing is that everyone is going to be fine. So let's focus on what matters—our work."

. . . .

The day before the rally goes surprisingly smoothly until Alex and I go to Om Digital Prints around the corner to pick up our signs and giant banner.

While we wait for the clerk to check our order, Alex turns to me. "What do you think of 'Drip Drip'?"

I shrug, halfheartedly. "It's dirty . . . so people like it, na?"

"I didn't ask what other people think. What do you, Rakhi Kumar, think?"

What do *I* think? I can't hear that song, or see that video, without thinking of Babloo as a kid, mimicking Rubina's moves for the rest of us. We would roar with laughter as he pulled his shorts up his bum, swaying his hips hard and fast. The way his hand would graze his collarbone, coy and delicate, during the hook, and then at the chorus, thump his chest to the beat, the rest of us would cheer and laugh. And he would perform it over and over, no matter how many times I asked. When I watch "Drip Drip" I don't see what the others see, because all I can see is Babloo.

Before I can reply, the store clerk interrupts. "It's all here. Finished."

"We must be checking parcel at the store before we leave," I tell Alex, as he hauls the boxes onto our flimsy metal dolly.

Alex groans. "Come on, there's still so much to do at the office. It's a waste of time unpacking and packing and then unpacking it all again."

The store clerk narrows his eyes. "Sir is right, everything is fine. We double-checked it. No, triple-checked."

I start to protest, knowing he's full of shit, but Alex pleads with me to just trust the clerk. Fine, I tell Alex, and pay for the printing.

Back at the office, I smack my hand on my forehead when I unroll the large red banner over the table. What was supposed to say STOP DISPLACEMENT NOW! instead says STOP PISPLACEMENT NOW! I knew we should have opened the box in the shop.

Alex scratches his chin, offering solutions as if this isn't his fault. "Why don't we just touch it up with some red and white paint?"

Just then, Gauri Ma'am sails in, sees the banner, and shouts at me, Alex, and Vivek, who happens to be passing by, about how she'll be damned if all the work she's put into this protest goes down the drain because of a garbage-looking sign. She calls up Om Digital Prints, demanding a new sign within the next hour, threatening to sue them. When that doesn't scare them, she tells them she will call the BMC and have their electricity cut. They tell her a new sign will be delivered to the office by eight o'clock this evening, not a second later.

Over the next few hours, we run through the sequence of events for the rally with all the lawyers. Bhavana reviews Tulsi's speech for the tenth time, reading it aloud to Gauri Ma'am, who makes last-minute changes and reminds her that "it is imperative that Tulsi not be late, or get lost." As Bhavana calls the Prasads one final time to confirm where and when they will meet us, Ma'am's phone rings.

"Yes, Rubina, tell me," she says, standing in the lawyers' workspace, nodding as she listens, her eyes gleaming. "It will be a stunning visual, yes . . . I'll inform them," she concludes, and hangs up.

That's when she declares to all the lawyers that there's a change to tomorrow's program: they will all wear their advocates' robes during the rally, which she says will create a striking image for the papers to run the day after. Her announcement does not go over well. Some of the lawyers protest, saying it's bad form to wear their robes outside the courtroom, that the rules don't permit it. Vivek suggests it could backfire, that they would look undignified.

Ma'am smacks the table with her palm. "Your robes are so much more than a dress code you have to follow like good little colonized subjects. Every victory, every defeat I have had at the Bombay High Court lives in my robes," she says, her voice growing louder. "They're a bloody battle uniform. And right now, we're at war." She breathes heavily, searching the lawyers' eyes as if daring them to argue back.

Vivek speaks up, his voice gentle. "Okay, Gauri Ma'am. Everyone will show up in their gowns tomorrow. Let's not discuss this anymore."

. . . .

At eight, long after everyone else has already left for the evening, Ma'am is about to pick up the phone to shout at the printers for the fourth time today, when the replacement banner arrives.

I spread the banner out over the table. STOP DISPLACEMENT NOW! I peer up to see if she's satisfied.

Chewing her thumbnail, she sinks into a chair. "Do you think we're okay for tomorrow?" She stares at me, eyes wide, like she's scared of something. "Because, you know, this could all just . . ."

"Ma'am, everything is ready. The banner was the last thing—"

"It's so much more than the banner," she replies, taking off her glasses. "I've taken us in a whole new direction. And nobody trusts me. Not even Vivek."

I pull on a corner of the banner to flatten a wrinkle. "If they didn't trust you, they would have left by now."

Gauri Ma'am closes her eyes. I have never seen her this overwhelmed. "We're ready, then?" Her voice is small, and when she opens her eyes she gazes at me like if I say we're not ready, she'll cancel the whole thing.

"Ji, Gauri Ma'am. We're ready."

She lets her breath out, then pauses. The sound of her ticking wristwatch fills the air. She pulls her shoulders back, stands up, and walks back to her office.

22

ONCE THE LAWYERS, GAURI MA'AM, and I collect our supplies from the office and meet at the northern tip of Azad Maidan, the sun is mounting in the sky. Every few minutes it seems as if someone is frantically looking for Gauri Ma'am, or Gauri Ma'am is frantically looking for them. By eight o'clock, hundreds of people have gathered behind us: Rubina's glossy, slim-ankled friends, other NGO and activist types, some communists, assorted law students. All the lawyers from Justice For All are in their black advocates' robes; the other lawyers marching with us refused to wear theirs.

"These gowns were a poor choice," Kamini says, peeling off strands of sweaty hair stuck to the sides of her face. "It's so hot, already." Tugging at his collar, Utkarsh groans about how black wool doesn't suit the Bombay climate.

"It's only for this morning, and then you can all take your robes off," Vivek says, taking a long swig from a bottle of water.

I smile, comfortable in my white cotton salwar kameez. This is the first time being an officewali instead of a lawyer has ever paid off.

Alex appears, snapping pictures of the lawyers with his digital camera. "You all look so grand in your legal regalia. Gauri and Rubina were right. People will stop and notice."

People will notice any big group of people marching through traffic, I want to say.

"Arre, Vivek," Gauri Ma'am says, pushing past a group of NGO workers to get to us. "There you are. I've been searching for you everywhere. It's Tulsi."

It seems Tulsi Prasad and her parents still haven't shown up. Gauri Ma'am has been trying to phone her all morning. She even sent Bhavana out to where Tulsi is staying to look for her.

Typical Tulsi, holding everything up.

"We were supposed to start twenty minutes ago," Gauri Ma'am says. "If she doesn't show, I'll have to change my speech. Incorporate all the points I had written for Tulsi's speech. Bloody hell."

Just then, Rubina inserts herself between Ma'am and Vivek. "We don't need the Chembur girl. Nobody knows her."

"I think Rubinaji means nobody knows Tulsi was supposed to come," Vivek offers, balancing a sign that reads HOUSING IS A HUMAN RIGHT on top of his shoe.

Just then, Ma'am's phone rings. "It's Bhavana," she mouths, disappearing behind Utkarsh and Kamini. Rubina turns to greet her friends Cookie Singh and Natasha Gidwani. I recognize them from the papers. Cookie is a presenter on *India's Got Talent,* and Natasha is a fashion designer. They dispense flimsy hugs, kissing the air beside each other's cheeks. Light bounces off their freshly blow-dried bronze hair. "Babe," they coo at one another, their voices long, drawn-out. "Babe, it's so good to see you." "You too, babe."

When they're done with their greetings, Rubina demands I find them each a signboard to carry. I tell her the signs have already been given out, and there are none left.

"What good is a media snap of Cookie and Natasha if they're not carrying a signboard?" She points at Kamini and Sudeepthi. "You two. Hand over your signs, please."

Kamini and Sudeepthi eye each other, and then Rubina.

"I carried this sign here myself," Sudeepthi says, chin raised. "And I will hold on to it for the duration of the rally."

"Me too," Kamini says, strengthening her grip around her sign.

Rubina's eyes bulge. "Arre, what is this nonsense? I am the one who organized this rally. If I give you an order, you carry it out."

Kamini steps forward, about to respond, when Gauri Ma'am barrels back toward us. "I spoke to Bhavana. She said Tulsi isn't coming." She pauses, then turns to Rubina. "Apparently, her family went to see a flat today. They were worried it would get snapped up if they didn't go right away. Did you know about this, Rubina?"

Rubina waves Gauri Ma'am away. "Of course not."

This huge big rally, all for Tulsi, and she doesn't even show up?

"Arre, they wouldn't be moving if you hadn't given them that money on the slum tour," Ma'am cries.

"Accha," Rubina says, hands on her hips. "And you think I told them to go at this particular time, on this exact day? That was their choice, not mine!"

Gauri Ma'am opens her mouth to reply but Rubina holds up her hand. "Listen to me, Gauri. Do not let these people derail us. There is so much momentum behind this rally right now." She gestures at Cookie, Natasha, and her other actor, model, and fashion friends, whose giant sunglasses cover half their faces. "They've all come out to spread our message."

Gauri Ma'am nods intently, staring past Rubina's friends to the swelling crowd. She exhales, then rolls her shoulders back. "Hand me the megaphone, Rakhi. We're starting." She points to Rubina's friends. "Anyone remotely famous who doesn't have a sign needs one right now. Sudeepthi, Kamini, Utkarsh, Alex, Rakhi, did you hear me?"

....

Photographers and video cameras swarm near the front of the rally where Rubina stands, flanked by Gauri Ma'am and Alex. Rubina's friends fan out beside them, their signs bobbing in the air, followed by the lawyers in their billowing black gowns, attracting attention from gawking bystanders.

"Look behind us," Kamini says, as we depart Azad Maidan. "The crowd is growing." Vivek, Utkarsh, and I turn back to see that the gathering of NGO people and students behind us has doubled in size.

Rubina begins to lead a chant she says she wrote even though it's only six words. "Justice for who?" she calls into the megaphone. "Justice For All!" we respond. At first the lawyers say it quietly, somewhat reluctant. Within minutes they're shouting it at the sky, lifted by the energy of the crowd behind them, like every doubt they've ever had about Rubina has evaporated in the hot sun. Vivek nudges me to shout louder, and I do. It feels good to scream out loud and with abandon.

Rubina continues to lead the chant as the crowd stomps beneath the shade of the peepal trees on Fashion Street, where vendors are already setting up their stalls of export surplus clothing. Some bystanders whistle, some clap, though it becomes clear they're jeering at Rubina when one hawker, in the middle of selling copper bangles to tourists, loudly belts the chorus of "Drip Drip." His voice carries above the clamor of the protesters, but Rubina and Gauri Ma'am are too caught up shouting into the megaphone to notice. Part of me wishes they had heard it.

As the rally moves through the morning, we pass people waking up on the street. "Housing is a human right!" Rubina chants, her fist punching the air. Under two poles and a tattered sari, a sleepy baby is so alarmed by Rubina's voice on the megaphone that she screams and screams as her startled mother holds her close, covering her ears. Still, she wails so hard I worry she might just pass out. The mother's other ratty-haired kids stare at us in open-mouthed wonder, and I suddenly have the urge to disappear from this entire natak. A procession of people with homes—some of them high-rise luxury flats built on the remains of slums—shouting about how housing is a human right.

I stop chanting, as though one less voice in this sea of protesters might lower the volume for the baby. None of the protesters notice, so delirious are they with purpose, their eyes blazing bright as they charge forward.

"Justice for who?" Rubina calls. "Justice For All," the crowd hollers back. And in that moment, I know this crowd of hundreds is just chanting the name of the organization. A gust of wind carries dirt from a construction site off the side of the road, pelting my face with grit.

23

AT THE START OF THE following week, Gauri Ma'am is in such a good mood you'd think Neha was leaving her husband and returning to Bombay. Her laughter is unrestrained and her face is constantly beaming. "Rakhi, my girl," she says, handing me a pair of scissors, "take a break from your other duties today. I want you cutting out all the news stories about the rally." She points at a stack of papers outside her office.

I heave the newspapers onto my desk, running my fingers over the headlines. HUNDREDS RALLY FOR RIGHT TO HOUSING. TRAFFIC SHUTDOWN IN SOUTH MUMBAI FOR PROTEST. STARS TAKE TO STREET FOR SLUM-DWELLERS. There we are on the front page of every paper: Rubina with her fist in the air. Swarms of people so big, M.G. Road was shut down both ways. Ma'am delivering her speech outside of the Bombay High Court.

One of the articles features a quote from Gauri Ma'am in which she mentions she has a Chembur slum client called Tulsi who missed out on sitting her medical school entrance exams because of the demolition. It was the only time Ma'am mentioned Tulsi's name after she cut all the other references to her from the speech.

"I still can't believe that Tulsi didn't show up," I say to Vivek, who has dropped by my desk to look at the news coverage. "This whole case started with her. And after everything Ma'am has done for her, she chose that moment to go see a new flat? Without Justice For All introducing her to Rubina Mansoor, she wouldn't even have the money for a flat deposit."

Vivek considers this, frowning and staring into space as though maybe I'm right. Then he shrugs. "Rakhi, her family's entire life was derailed. And now they finally have a chance at a safe place to live. A chance to start over. So what if they chose to go see that flat during the rally? Shouldn't they be free to make those choices on their own terms?"

I bristle at his question. What about me? Shouldn't I be free to make choices on my own terms? Why does that shameless Tulsi get a chance to start over and I don't? I want to ask. Instead I murmur a yes, running my scissors down the length of the paper.

....

Gauri Ma'am's good mood fades by the middle of the week, when she gathers everyone together in the office for an announcement.

All around me, I hear whispers about what might be going on. They're too consumed with the possibility of a raise or the reopening of our satellite offices to notice the dark cloud hanging over Ma'am.

"Vivek has something to share with all of you," Gauri Ma'am says, once everyone is silent. Bhavana and Sudeepthi lean forward expectantly in their chairs.

Standing beside her, Vivek takes a deep breath. "Thank you, Gauri Ma'am. I first want to say that you all are the reason why I come to work every day. But, as you know, sometimes we have to make hard decisions when new opportunities present themselves. I'm going to be leaving Justice For All. I've accepted a position as the assistant director of the International Centre for Rights and Democracy."

Every face in the circle falls. The deep rumble of a lorry backing up through the laneway outside fills the air. Still, nobody says a word.

"I'll be leaving in the middle of September," he continues, "which should give Gauri Ma'am and me enough time to transfer my files."

"Mid-September? That's only a month away," Bhavana says with a pained look on her face.

"Why are you leaving us?" I blurt out, my voice trembling. "What have we done wrong? Tell us and we'll fix it."

Everyone turns to gawk at me but I don't care. He can't leave us. Vivek glances at Gauri Ma'am, but she nods her head, motioning for him to answer the question.

Vivek smiles. "Well, Rakhi, we must all keep growing, that's all. Even when you're as old as I am." He chuckles, as everyone else sits stone-faced.

"We will all miss Vivek dearly," Gauri Ma'am says. "But he will go on to do important work. That is the thing to remember. And as the new funding breathes new life into Justice For All, we will be hiring more staff here as well. In this way, we are all evolving, together and apart."

Bhavana, who looks like she might burst into tears, springs from her chair, its legs scraping against the floor, and pushes past Vivek. She flings the office door open and disappears through it, leaving us to listen to the sound of her feet shuffling down the stairs.

Gauri Ma'am stares at the door left ajar, then excuses herself, leaving Vivek standing in the middle of the circle while we watch Ma'am go into her office and shut the door behind her.

"Sir," Sudeepthi says, after a few quiet moments pass. "What's the reason? Be honest."

"It was time," Vivek says, with a half smile.

I watch Vivek fielding the lawyers' frantic and worried questions. Gauri Ma'am took him for granted and now he's leaving. I hope that this new job pays better. That he'll never need to find out how little his gold wedding band is actually worth.

"Vivek Sir," I say, interrupting Kamini, who's asking if he's given thought to who's getting his files. "What does it mean, *evolving*?"

"Means . . . changing. No, maturing. No, no, more like expanding. Or maybe unfolding."

"Unfolding," I say. "Like a piece of paper?"

"A crumpled-up piece of paper. Yes."

"I am happy for you, Sir."

He smiles and nods, placing his hand over his heart.

Later that day, I pull out the college applications from my desk drawer, smooth out the wrinkles and creases, and start scribbling down answers to the questions.

Summer came early the year everything changed.

It was only April and already waves of heat were shimmering up off the road as if it were mid-May. I had been in Bombay for five years by that point, and I'd come to learn the rhythms and patterns of the changing seasons. The thickness of mosquito swarms during monsoons. The bright blue sky on a clear winter day. The cranky impatience of policewalas in the summer.

Babloo and I sat on the sun-baked footpath by the paanwala's stall, coughing on dust kicked up by the street sweepers. With his index finger, Babloo rubbed beads of sweat from his upper lip, which was starting to sprout hair. At twelve and thirteen, we had crossed over to the age where begging didn't yield the results it used to. There were smaller kids now. Much cuter than us. Kalu had taken up selling peanut chikki on trains for a few weeks, but most of his day's earnings were garnished. We survived by finding odd jobs and picking pockets.

"Let's get some water, yaar," I groaned, lifting my hair off my sticky neck.

"First, see this," Babloo said, pulling out a shiny rectangular slab from his pocket. In his grubby palm it resembled the silvery kaju barfi the NGO didis handed out for Diwali, but when I poked at it with my finger, it was hard like metal. "I yanked this from some bhenchodh college kid on the train." He unwrapped a little white cord with white pebble things attached at the ends, and let it dangle to the floor.

"What does it do?"

"No clue, yaar."

The paanwala, whose stall was a few meters from where we sat, grunted at us. "Saala, it's an MP3 player. You listen to music with it," he said, as he assembled a row of betel leaves on a metal platter in front of him.

Babloo called back to him. "Is that so? Did you make it yourself? Tell, tell, what else have you invented? Some kind of electronic paan, maybe?"

"Get lost, chutiya," the paanwala said, throwing his towel over his shoulder.

Dancing around the stall on his toes, Babloo continued to taunt the man. "Arre, vah! Rakhi, did you know we were in the presence of a computer wizard? Maybe we should call Bill Gates Sahib over from America? You can teach him some things, na?"

I laughed, too, pointing and shouting "Bilget Sahib, Bilget Sahib!" even though I had no idea who this person was. "Babloo," I whispered. "Who's Bilget Sahib?"

"Arre," Babloo shouted. "Bill Gates is the paanwala's baap, didn't you know?"

His nostrils flaring with rage, the paanwala rolled up his sleeves with his betel-stained hands, then tore the silvery rectangle from Babloo's grasp, threw it on the ground, and stomped on it with his heels. There was a sickening crunch, as if the silver rectangle was a little bird whose tiny bones had snapped all at once. The paanwala motioned to a small, garlanded photograph sitting on his stall, of an older man with a tight-lipped face and startled-looking eyes. His father, no doubt. "Have some respect, bastards."

Babloo, horrified at the quick death of his stolen treasure, charged at the paanwala's stand and upturned the metal platter of betel leaves. The plate crashed down to the ground, spinning around a few times before finally landing with a clang on the pavement. The framed photo of the dead paanfather tumbled down with it, glass shattering.

The paanwala lunged at Babloo, twisting his skinny arms behind his back. Then he dragged Babloo off into a narrow laneway and threw him against the wall, kicking at his crumpled body. I ran behind them, launching my body into the paanwala's and pounding at his back with my fists.

The paanwala turned to me. He swung his arm around my neck, forced me up against the opposite wall, and pushed his body hard against mine. His vinegary sweat stung my nose. I heard the sound of his pant drawstring being pulled loose.

"It's your turn," he growled, as he shoved his free hand down my underpants.

I screamed no, then sank my teeth deep into his forearm, piercing through skin, into flesh. His blood tasted like salt and metal. I kept my jaw there as he howled, until he finally loosened his grip.

"Kuthi," he shouted, clutching his arm, his eyes widening at the blood dripping down his hand and onto the laneway.

I broke away, pulling Babloo up from the ground by his shoulder, and together we ran.

Later that evening, Babloo and I shared a packet of Parle-G biscuits. My cheek was still stinging from where it had been scraped raw when the paanwala shoved my face against the brick wall.

"Don't worry," I told him as he pressed lightly on his fat lip with his finger. "Each time the paanwala goes to take a piss in that lane, he'll see his blood spattered all over the ground until the rains start."

"It's not enough," Babloo murmured, lowering his head onto my shoulder. He was only this affectionate when he was sad and vulnerable, but I happily accepted it, resting my head on top of his. "We have to get back at him."

"What if we stole his betel leaves?" I offered, biting into a biscuit. I brushed away the crumbs that fell into Babloo's hair.

"Betel leaves aren't worth much. Think bigger."

"Steal his money?"

"How? He keeps it in his pocket."

"I've got it," I said. "We could burn his stall down. All his betel leaves, coconut, tobacco, supari—gone. And then he'll be poor and have no job and he'll have to go back to his village."

Babloo sat up straight and turned to me, eyes lit up. "See how clever you've become!" He plucked the last biscuit from the packet and lay his head back down on my shoulder.

I smoothed the empty Parle-G wrapper in my hands. The chubby, fair-skinned child on the label stared back at me quizzically, her hands upturned as if to say, *Really, Rakhi? You're going to set this guy's stall on fire?* I crumpled the wrapper in my palm and threw it down the lane. This little Parle-G shit would never have to do the kind of things Babloo and I did. She'd never have to make anyone pay for what they did to her, because nothing bad would ever, could ever, happen to someone like her.

THE NEWS OF VIVEK'S DEPARTURE has turned the lawyers into somber shadows of the people in black robes who were shouting in the streets just one week ago. Gauri Ma'am has been especially distracted and avoidant, like she knows the staff blame her. I wonder if she realizes she pushed Vivek away.

When Gauri Ma'am is out at a meeting, I tiptoe to Alex's desk so as not to attract attention from anyone else. "What does this mean?" I whisper, pointing to the word *rusticated* on the Lady Victoria college application.

He sets down his bottle of Fanta, takes the pages from my hand, and scans them. "It's just some rules about the college. It says that smoking and alcohol are strictly prohibited on campus, and if they find you consuming them you might be fined, punished, or . . . rusticated? I think they mean kicked out."

I nod, reaching for the papers, but he presses them to his chest and looks up at me. "Do you really want to study at a place like this? Seems pretty strict."

"Arre, you printed for me."

"Okay, but why are you reading the college rules? Shouldn't you be focusing on filling out the applications first? They're asking questions like why you want to apply. You should be crafting responses so I can review them."

I've never applied for anything in my life. How would I know how to turn the notes I scribbled into proper answers?

"I cannot do all on my own," I say, firmly.

He takes a gulp of his orange soda. "Okay. So let me help you. Come to my place tonight."

I roll my eyes. "Oh, really? Your aunt can help, too?"

"My aunt and uncle left for their farmhouse in Lonavala yesterday morning, actually. Something about hill station air. Which means the flat is empty tonight and we have the perfect opportunity to work uninterrupted. I'm only here until September. If we don't start now, we'll never do it."

A fly crawls into his bottle of Fanta, buzzes around in tiny circles in the bottleneck, and then falls into the last inch of flat soda. Wings drenched in orange liquid, it tries to wrestle its way out, but fails.

"So, what do you say?"

That fly will be me if I'm spotted at Blossoming Heights.

The sound of someone humming the tune of "Drip Drip" pierces the air. It's Vivek. He nods as he passes Alex and me, continuing his song. He's looked happier in the past two days than he has in months. It's like he's become a new person.

As Vivek's humming fades, I take the application from Alex's hands and roll it up. "Okay, I will come to your home tonight. When I finish work. Maybe it will be late."

"Text me," he says, and turns back to his computer.

....

Later that evening, Gauri Ma'am, Vivek, and I are sorting through Vivek's loose documents on the big table in the lawyers' workspace, and putting them in their corresponding files. Now that we have the copy machine from Arora, Gauri Ma'am made Vivek and me scan and save all his documents before he transfers his cases to the lawyers. Then, once we scanned everything, Ma'am suggested we start sorting them into the correct folders.

Outside the window, white lightning flashes against the bruised sky. I hope I make it up to Pali Hill without getting caught in the rain.

"Ma'am, can I finish this on Monday?"

Gauri Ma'am takes off her glasses and pokes at her fleshy lower lip with the tip. "Why so impatient all of a sudden?"

"Ma'am, it's raining . . ."

"No, it's not."

"Ji, but it will. See outside." The sky is almost black now.

"Arre, Gauri, let the girl go," Vivek says. "Behrampada floods during heavy downpours."

Gauri Ma'am looks perturbed at Vivek jumping in. "Her home is on the second floor of the hutment," she snaps. "Why would it flood?"

I feel my throat getting dry. "Actually, Ma'am, there's also Tazim, my downstairs neighbor," I say. "I want to make sure she is safe."

"Call her, then."

"Ma'am, Tazim doesn't have a mobile."

Ma'am puts on her glasses and stares at me without blinking, like she knows I'm lying about something. I try not to move a muscle in my face.

"Gauri," Vivek says firmly. "Let Rakhi leave. It's late."

Ma'am sighs. "Chalo, go home and take rest. But Vivek has a lot of paperwork that needs filing, and we have two weeks to do it. You'll have to come in tomorrow to get a head start."

I nod and hurry back to my desk, checking to make sure they're not watching me before I pull my college application forms from my drawer and stuff them in my bag. "Thank you, Ma'am, thank you, Sir," I call out, running down the steps to the street.

Before I make it to VT Station, though, the low-hanging clouds finally burst. Rain starts to come down in fat drops, and my flimsy purple umbrella twists and flips in the wind. Once I'm on the Bandra-bound train, I watch the palm trees outside bending sideways in the wind.

Water sprays into the compartment and I move farther inside the car, away from the window, shielding my bag with my body, so my college applications don't get wet. I peek at them inside my bag, safe and dry. Tazim will be fine. She can handle a little rain. If her hut floods, I can let her into my place when I return from Alex's. The applications shouldn't take too long. If we finish them tonight, I can submit them soon, and in a few years, who knows? I could be working at the Marquis. No more human rights funda, no more lawyers, no more bhenchodh interns.

....

When the bus from Bandra Station reaches Pali Hill, it's already nine. Around me, autorickshaws pass through deepening puddles, churning muddy waves. I take a deep breath at the sight of Blossoming Heights. The rain is pounding the flower-covered compound wall, and fuchsia petals litter the ground like offerings at a temple.

I text Alex from the street.

He writes back immediately: **tell guard ur coming to 606. u have to sign in.**

The watchman inside the lobby has a white moustache and a navy blue uniform. He's reclining on a plastic chair behind a wooden table, eyelids lowered, though he straightens up as my slippers squelch across the marble floor. Thankfully, he's not the same watchman from the last time I was here, when Tazim and I carried Mrs. Motiani's Persian rugs to the courtyard for cleaning.

Clearing my throat, I inch up to the desk. "Ji, I'm going to six-zero-six."

He gazes up at me through sleepy eyes, his hands resting on his stomach, fingers interlaced. "Who are you here to see?"

"Motiani Sahib's nephew."

The watchman narrows his eyes as I drip water onto the ground. "What work do you have there?"

"Delivery," I say, without hesitation. I pull the dampened college applications from my bag for him to see. "Office delivery." He would never believe I was visiting Blossoming Heights as a guest.

The watchman frowns and slides the register book toward me. I print my name, the date, and the time on its blue curled pages. He telephones the Motiani flat to say there is an office delivery, then points me to the lift.

My heart beats fast until I get into the lift and the shiny metal doors slide shut, revealing the dull reflection of a girl, her drenched salwar kameez clinging to her body. Until now, the thought of being anywhere near this place again made me shudder. And now I'm here, to do what I need to do to start a new life. My lip twitches, and I try to suppress a smile.

I press the doorbell and jump at the ear-splitting shrieks of an animal in distress coming from the other side of the door. It's Mrs. Motiani's dog, Tango, snarling like he's a street dog and not a ball of white fluff who shits on marble floors. When the door swings open, Alex—barefoot and wearing red shorts and a gray T-shirt that says TORONTO RAPTORS—is holding the teeth-baring dog back by his turquoise collar. Tango's eyes are black and sparkly, and he lunges forward like he wants to take a bite out of my leg. He couldn't remember me, could he?

I stand in the doorway while Alex drags the dog into a different room and shuts the door, quickly. The flat hasn't changed since I was here with Tazim. Same large paintings, same naked white statues. It seems different at night, though. There's a soft, honey-colored glow everywhere. And it's so quiet you can't hear anything but the dog whimpering from his room.

Alex laughs. "That was Tango. He's always a little hyper around new people, but I've never seen him bark this much." He pauses, staring me up and down. "Why are you all wet?"

I pull the soggy fabric away from my body. "It's raining."

"It is?" He walks to the window in the sitting room and pulls back the curtain. Tall shadowy trees sway back and forth, and bursts of lightning flare up across the dark sky. He stands there with his hands on his hips, peering out the window. "They keep the air-conditioning on and the windows shut all the time. I didn't realize the rain had even started."

I stay by the doorway and kick my sandals off, pushing them to the side. The hard marble is cold under my muddy feet.

When Alex returns to the hallway, a puddle is forming at my toes. "Let me get you something dry to wear. My aunt has tons of old clothes."

I hold up my hand. "No, no, please."

"Relax, she'll never notice," he says, and disappears down the long corridor into another room. He returns with a thick, peach-colored towel that feels like a cottony cloud, a green T-shirt, and some stretchy black pants that look like churidar, and points me to a bathroom with beige walls. Inside, there is a giant mirror, a bouquet of dried flowers by the sink, and a Western toilet. I bend down to examine the white roll of toilet paper hanging from a bar nailed to the wall. I rip off a square and press it against my cheek. It's soft, spongy—nothing like the thin, scratchy toilet rolls I buy for the interns from the chemist's shop.

Tugging at the wet drawstring of my salwar, I let my pants slide down my legs to the floor. I peel my top off and let it fall, too. I step out of the mess of clothes, and hoist a muddy foot into the washbasin. I don't want Tazim to ask Alex why there are footprints all over the flat when she comes in on Sunday. The water from the tap flows out fast, starting warm then growing hot.

As I scrub the dirt off my toes, I catch a glimpse of myself with one leg swung over the bathroom counter, my hair wet and matted. I peel a wet curl off the side of my face. If staring at myself in the lift mirrors made me smile, the sight of myself washing my feet in Mrs. Motiani's bathroom makes me want to laugh.

The T-shirt Alex brought me smells like Dadar flower market without the market smell, and the black churidar are stretchy and hug my legs and thighs. With these clothes on, I could pass for one of those college girls who crowd around tables at Café Coffee Day, sipping on tall, frosty drinks.

I peek outside the bathroom. Alex is reclining on a low white sofa in the sitting room, strumming a guitar. "Have a seat," he says, and points to the laptop on the coffee table. "I opened the website for the Sanskriti Institute of Hotel Management. We'll start with their application and go from there."

I set my wet clothes down on the floor in a neat pile, making a mental note to wipe up the water seeping out from them before I leave, and sit down on the sofa in front of the glowing laptop. Across from me, Alex stops and starts the same tune.

The college's website features a photo of a man with a big white chef's hat, and a woman in a black suit with her hair pulled back, smiling behind a tall wooden hotel desk. I imagine them waiting on people like Rubina Mansoor, and bringing drinks on a tray to firanghis like Saskia and Merel.

I pull out the notes I scribbled earlier and start typing them into the computer.

Myself Rakhi Kumar. I am wanting to study for the hospitality program. I am 23 years and work in human rights office of Advocate Gauri Verma. I know maths and tiping and speaking English. I like to helping people. I helping many peoples from foren—Enland, USA, Canada, Duch. They come to India and think it is bad place. If I work in hotel management I can show foren people India is best in the world.

When I read what I've typed, I want to give up. Why do I need to write down all the reasons why I want to do this program? How would they even check that any of it is true? I could say I've taken Russian or South African firanghis on slum tours and they would never know. Isn't it enough that I'm willing to pay a college to learn? I stare at the screen and try to think of more things to write, but the sound of Alex playing his guitar is distracting.

His phone buzzes and he sets the guitar down and bolts up from the sofa. "Hey, Babloo, what's up, man? . . . Nothing, nothing. With Rakhi, actually . . . No, my place. Why?"

Great. I haven't spoken to Babloo since we got pani puri on S.V. Road almost two weeks back, but now that he knows I'm here he's going to want to talk to me. I turn back to the computer and stare at the smiling Nepali chef on the website.

After a few moments, Alex returns. "Rakhi? Babloo wants to talk." He tosses the phone to me, sits down on the sofa, and picks up his guitar again.

I shuffle to the far end of the corridor so Alex can't hear me talking. Still, I whisper into the phone. "Yes, what is it?"

"Yaar," Babloo says, guffawing so loud I have to hold the phone a few inches from my ear. "Even I haven't been invited up to Pali Hill, myself."

"What do you want, Babloo?"

"Can't I say hello, hi, how are you? What are you doing at Alex's home this late?"

"Working on something."

"On what?"

"He's helping me apply to college." I brace for him to laugh at the thought of me attending college, but instead I hear him take a drag of a cigarette.

"You shouldn't be spending time alone with him like this, in his home. You're not from his world."

My back stiffens. "You think I don't know that already? Or have you forgotten I knew him first?"

"Calm down. Just remember, if you ever need anything, you come to me first."

"What could I possibly need from you?"

"Arre, why are you yelling? I'm just looking out for you. As always, isn't it? This boy, he's not the one for you." He keeps laughing, which only makes me angrier.

"And he is for you? Taking him to drink whiskey and eat pakoras with your friends? Going to dance bars, hi-fi parties, all that non-sense? How are you any different from me?"

Babloo stops laughing and his voice becomes hard. "I know more than you, I've done more than you, and I've seen more than you ever will. End of story."

"And what, I'm just some idiot office girl? You think because you were gone for so long I put my life on hold for you? That I was just waiting for you to come back?"

He doesn't say anything, and in the silence that follows I realize that what I just said is true.

"Like you said, he's only a tourist. Here for a good time, that's it."

My voice is straining. "Just let me go, yaar."

"Fine, then. Go." The phone goes dead.

Back in the sitting room, Alex is stretching his fingers to hit the right notes on his guitar. Water streams down the window panes, turning the outside world into a vague blur of nighttime blacks and streaks of streetlamp yellow.

I hand him his phone. "Can you read my application now?"

He stops strumming. "How many lines you got?"

"Six."

"That's it? Add some more. Whatever comes to mind. Then we'll edit it."

Sinking into the sofa, shoulders slumped, I spend the next half hour adding more bakvaas about firanghis and hotels and India.

When I tell him I'm done he takes the laptop away and returns with printouts, two bottles of Coke, and a bowl of peanuts. As he reads through what I've written, he squints. Purses his lips. Frowns.

"Is this true? You want to work in hotel management because you care about what tourists think of India?"

"I am showing you around, na?"

"All right," Alex says, finally. "You're going to have to think about it some more. I've written down some notes. But here's my advice: You need to make this personal, or else you sound like everyone else applying for this program."

"What does it mean, *personal*?" I put some peanuts in my mouth. They're coated in a sweet and salty crust. I shiver and pull my knees up. Even with dry clothes on, this flat is still so chilly.

"You've got an interesting story."

"Because I am living in Behrampada?"

"Well, that's one part of it."

"Lots of people working in these hotels come from the slum, only. So I am just the same as other people." I hug my knees to stay warm.

Alex asks me if I am all right.

"It's cold. AC is on high," I say, rubbing my arms.

He runs into the hallway and returns in a second. "Okay, turned it off." He then walks to the giant windowsill and slides the massive window open with both hands. The drumming sound of heavy rain fills the room, and I inhale the warm, misty air curling past us.

"Better?" He sits back on the windowsill.

I rise from the sofa to stand beside him, peering out the open window. There are iron bars to keep us from falling out. Or to keep burglars from coming in. Because of the sheets of rain, it feels like we are behind a giant waterfall. The tree-shaped shadows sway against the dark sky.

Alex reaches his arm between the bars and out the window, holding his hand out. Big, fat raindrops splash on the surface of his palm. He closes his eyes and inhales deeply, then lets his breath out slowly before he opens his eyes again. "I feel so awake right now."

I take a seat next to him. "You are awake." Firanghis are always trying to create meaning in ordinary things.

"No, I mean full of energy or life or whatever. I feel whole, if that makes sense."

"Means?"

"I haven't really told you this, but when we hang out, I don't feel like such an outsider."

I scratch the hollow of my throat, unsure of what he means.

"Back home, I'm not white enough to fit in. Kids used to imitate my mom's accent. She stopped cooking Indian food because I got teased at school for smelling like spices when she did. Even now, people laugh when they hear Lalwani-Diamond, like it's fucking gibberish. And then I come to India, thinking these are my people, but here I'm not Indian enough. I barely speak Hindi, I don't know the culture. To everyone here, I'm just a white guy. And either people are weirdly drawn to whiteness, like my aunt and uncle's friends, or they're repulsed by it, like everyone at the office."

He wipes little beads of condensation off his Coke bottle with his fingertip. I didn't realize there was something he was insecure about. I decide against telling him that people in India also think his last name is funny.

"People insist on categorizing me as white or Indian, and that's made me second-guess how to even categorize myself. I'm just tired of people trying to put me in a box, you know? I just want to . . . break free. Do you know what I'm saying?"

I read the wariness in his eyes, the worry on his forehead. It looks familiar. "People are seeing what they want to be seeing, only. And nobody is believing you when you are saying they are wrong."

"Yeah, sort of." Alex nods. "You can probably relate to being labeled. Babloo told me what happened when you were kids."

"Told you what?"

"About the guy who sold paan. And how you both got locked up after."

That chutiya Babloo. He disappears from my life and never looks for me, even though he was here in Bombay this whole time. And when I finally find him again, he tries to take away the first real friend I've had since him. I draw my legs up to my chest, forcing out a strangled laugh. "It's not important," I say, but what I want to tell him is that it's my story. And it's not for Babloo to tell.

For a while, neither of us says anything. Outside, the shadowy figure of a bat darts back and forth, between the tall trees. I can hear the rain bludgeoning every leaf on every plant in Pali Hill.

Finally, I unclench my jaw. "Why you are talking to Babloo about me?"

"It just came up in conversation." He holds my gaze like he's waiting for me to say more. I don't respond but the silence between us grows so uncomfortable I have to say something.

"It was a big mistake," I blurt out. Gusts of wind throw fat droplets of rain at the windowsill and onto our arms and legs. They do nothing to cool down my overheating body. "I was . . . I was only twelve years."

"You don't have to justify it to me. I'm not judging you."

"I had to survive."

As I say it, I feel warmth spreading all over my body. I've never willingly spoken about the paanwala incident to anyone. It's like there's a muscle that has been tight and tensed up for eleven years. Until now.

"Every time I learn more about you, I'm convinced you have everything you need to succeed in life." He goes on about how I'll have to keep in touch when he leaves, tell him what I end up doing, that maybe he'll come back to work in India after he's done at graduate school.

"You are serious?"

"Yeah, why not? I'll come stay at the hotel you're working at. And you can give me a discount rate since you'll be running the place by then."

I don't say anything, overcome by a pleasant sense of dizziness.

He swings his feet around and down onto the floor. "It's getting late. Let's try to get a rough draft done for all of the applications. I'll proofread them as we print them out."

I take a deep breath in, inhaling the clean, earthy smell of the rainstorm outside. "Okay."

THE SANDWICHWALA OUTSIDE ST. XAVIER'S College sold us the
kerosene for fifty rupees and nothing less.

"This guy is ripping us off," Babloo said.

"It'll be worth it," I replied as I handed the sandwichwala the cash
I'd pinched from a firanghi lady haggling for a pair of wooden bangles on the Colaba Causeway.

The rusty canister of kerosene was heavier than it looked. I could
barely drag it more than a few inches, so Babloo sighed and gripped
the other side of the handle. We staggered off, the kerosene hanging
between us. Even though his arms were as skinny as mine, they were
much stronger somehow.

"It's because girls are naturally weak," he remarked.

"What bullshit, yaar."

"Prove me wrong, then," he said, letting go.

The kerosene dragged me down by the shoulder. I had to tell
him he was right before he'd pick up the canister again. We lugged
it back to the paanwala's stall and hid until he went for his afternoon shit, leaving his stall under the watch of a distracted sugar-
canewala.

"Lift with your legs," Babloo urged as we struggled to heave the tin up to the paanwala's little table while staying hidden.

"What do you mean, 'legs'?" I hissed back, glancing back over my shoulder to make sure none of the people milling around nearby had noticed us.

"Okay, now tip it."

Our twelve- and thirteen-year-old frames were no match for the physical rigor of this prank. The kerosene glugged out of the tin too fast to save it. Babloo twisted his body so that at least some of it splashed over the table of paan leaves and betel nuts. Then we poured the kerosene over rags, stuffing them into the cubbies of the stall. The rest of the liquid spread quickly across the road, filling the cracks and potholes.

"Quick, hand me the matches," I whispered, my heart leaping in my chest at the mental image of the paanwala's wares burning to the ground. That would teach him to mess with Babloo and me. I smirked at the thought of him being left penniless. Chutiya.

That's when I saw the paanwala trudging back from the public toilets. I seized Babloo's hand before he could get a spark. "Shit, he's coming back."

We scrambled out of the way, diving behind a row of parked cars on the other side of the street. Squatting behind the mud-caked wheels of a white Maruti van, we waited, our breathing shallow. The crunch of gravel under the paanwala's leather chappals was loud, in spite of the traffic noises in the distance.

I tugged Babloo's shirt. "Yaar, let's run."

But then there was the sound of a match flaring up. The paanwala was lighting his beedi. I held my breath as he let the burning match fall to the ground. The kerosene on the floor ignited, flames creeping up to the stall.

Babloo and I hit the ground, chests to pavement, and peered from behind the Maruti to see the paanwala's pant leg on fire. But as he rolled on the ground to quell the flames, he was only rolling in the kerosene we had spilled.

I pushed myself up to run away but Babloo swung his leg over mine and dug his elbow into my back. "No," he hissed. "Stay down."

"Babloo—"

"Trust me."

Pinned down under the left half of Babloo's trembling body, I watched helplessly as the paanwala flopped and thrashed about on the ground, like a fish in an empty bucket.

Then came the sound of running feet. More feet joined in. Someone yelled about getting water to put out the flames. Voices rang out calling for an ambulance, a doctor, a fire truck.

Eventually, the tan trouser legs of policewalas appeared and Babloo sprang to his feet. I lay frozen on the ground, too stunned to move. Without wasting a second, he put his hands under my arms and hoisted my stiffened body off the ground, dragging me away with adult strength.

For a brief moment I glanced back, only to see the entire paan stall engulfed in flames.

MY EYES FLY OPEN AS I force myself out of my nightmare. In my dream, my face had melted off like candle wax. Shaking, I touch my cheeks, my nose, my lips to make sure they're still there.

But before I can sit up in the dark to start Dr. Pereira's night terror exercise, I realize I'm gazing up at a high, plaster ceiling instead of a tin roof. Blinking rapidly, I reach around me for my little cassette player so I can hold my crystal elephant, but my palms skim along smooth sheets, not rough fabric. And I'm lying on something that feels like a soft piece of bread, instead of my thin mat.

Shit. I'm still in the Motiani flat. I tense up immediately, throwing the covers off me like they're covered in spiders.

Then I remember that even though I'm still at Blossoming Heights, it's Saturday, and I'm only there because Alex and I worked on my applications until three in the morning and he wouldn't let me catch a bus back to Behrampada.

"Arre, I will be fine. Don't take tension," I said.

"No way, it's not safe. You can stay in my room and I'll take my aunt and uncle's." Then he handed me the applications that he'd marked up.

There they are, sitting on the table beside the bed. I pick one up and flip through the pages, reading what I've written about why I want to study hotel management.

"What kind of life do you want?" Alex asked me last night. "I don't just mean what kind of job you have, or where you live, or how much you make. What do you want your life to look like?"

I didn't know how to reply. Nobody had ever asked me that before.

I fall back on the bed, stretching my arms out. This mattress is so big I could roll over twice and still not fall off. The rain has stopped. Green parrots chatter outside and steamy morning sunlight starts to break through the trees.

In the bathroom, I splash cool water on my face, which jolts me back to the fact that I shouldn't linger here, even though the Motianis won't be back until tomorrow night. Still, I can't help but marvel at the privacy, the spotlessness, the soft light. There's plenty of time for me to head home to change before I go back to the office to continue Vivek's filing.

After I leave the bathroom, I'm still thinking about returning to bed when I turn in to the corridor and freeze. Tazim is there, standing in the kitchen with a broom in her hand. The look of horror on her face grows as her widening eyes move from my loose, messy hair to the green T-shirt belonging to the memsahib of the house.

Tazim's grip on her broom loosens and it falls, rattling on the marble floor. We both stand there for a moment, staring at each other. Neither of us says a word.

"Y-you don't work on Saturdays," I stammer.

"The boy is by himself this weekend," she replies, her voice barely rising above a whisper. "What are you *doing* here?"

Before I can say anything, she turns her head to the kitchen, her eyes landing on the empty Coke bottles and bowl of peanuts perched atop the otherwise-spotless marble countertops.

"Please, let me explain," I say, extending a clammy hand toward her.

She steps back. "I told you never to come to my work again."

"There's a reason. Alex—you know, the Motianis' nephew—he is one of the firanghi interns at Justice For All. We were just working late yesterday and—"

"Liar!" Tazim roars, cutting me off. I've never heard her shout before. "I can see for myself what you've done. I want you out of this flat, right now."

Trembling, I careen down the hallway and back into Alex's bedroom. I move fast, throwing on my wrinkled salwar kameez from last night. The cool dampness of the fabric momentarily soothes my prickly skin as I sweep the college applications into my bag.

There's no sign of Tazim in the hallway, so I dart to the front door, slip on my sandals, and yank the heavy door open, careful not to let it make a sound as it closes behind me.

Just as I am about to press the button for the lift, a hand grabs me by the wrist.

It's Tazim, nostrils flaring, breath heavy. Stunned by her aggression, I let her march me down six flights of stairs, her braid flying behind her. The sound of her bare feet slapping down on the concrete echoes softly in the stairwell. I should have guessed the Motianis would call her in on the weekend to clean up after Alex.

Down in the lobby, the night watchman is slouched in the same spot he was in the previous evening. He rubs his drowsy eyes and frowns when he sees the Motiani family's bai dragging me away. He starts to get up, but Tazim holds her hand out. "There is no problem, she is my helper."

The night watchman pauses, then swallows her answer whole, slumping back in his seat with a yawn.

Tazim leads me outside, through the courtyard and gates. It's only once we are standing in front of the fuchsia flowers on St. Andrews Road that she lets go of my wrist, leaving behind a stinging red welt.

"Tell me. How long has this been going on? How long have you been lying to me?"

"Tazim," I plead. "Please don't do this—"

"I will lose my job if Motiani Sahib finds out you came back and—" She stops herself and wrings her hands.

"Listen to me." I raise my palms up in front of me as though I am approaching a pack of growling street dogs. "Nobody will take your job away from you."

"Do you understand how hard it was to convince them that you left town? They questioned me for days to make sure I wasn't lying. They still have all your information, you know."

Of course. The background check Mrs. Motiani insisted on before I spent the day scrubbing the grime and dog hair from her Persian rugs. I had to write down my name, phone number, and give them a photocopy of my ID card.

"Even so, they're away for the weekend, na? So, what's the problem? They didn't see anything."

"But *I* saw you. And if Mrs. Motiani suspects anything happened while she was away, she will ask me, and I will have to answer! And then she will fire me because I told her you left town in January, and also because I am the only reason you are in Pali Hill."

"What do you mean, 'only reason'? I just told you I work with Alex. He's my friend. I came here to see him, not to see you."

"What, is he your boyfriend?" Tazim snorts. "Are you moving in? I see you've already helped yourself to Mrs. Motiani's clothes."

"Enough," I say, wincing. "Nothing happened. We were working late. I just fell asleep, I swear."

"If it's men you need, there are hundreds of them in Behrampada. Better yet, go down to Kamathipura, that way you can get paid for something you just gave away for free."

I can see the cords straining in her neck. I never knew this kind of rage simmered inside her.

I lower my voice, trying to appeal to the Tazim I know. "You told me to make something of myself, didn't you? You told me I'm the one who has a way out of this life."

She throws her head back and cackles. "Accha? And this is how you do it? Using other people to get ahead?" she says. "You were already a chor, but now you're a randi, too."

A head on a bicycle turns at the word she just used, and tires screech. A small crowd begins to gather: other maids reporting for Pali Hill duty; a magazinewala watching us from the awning of his little stand; even his middle-aged customer in her floor-length caftan is gaping at us, eager to take in the scandal erupting in front of her.

"Enough with the randi nonsense, we're just friends—" I start.

"If anything is missing from the flat," Tazim continues, "anything at all, you'd better tell me now. I know your type. You don't care about the difference between right and wrong."

"You don't know what you're talking about."

"You're the one who sleeps at my family's house, as if you own the place!"

I recoil at the words coming out of her mouth. "They're not your family! You're their servant, understand? You clean their shit!"

She takes in a sharp breath. "If I lose my job because of you, it will be Ayub who suffers. I won't be able to pay for his school fees until Hanif sends money from—"

"Your husband's gone. He's never coming back. And you'll always be an overworked bai, and you'll never have enough time or money to take care of Ayub, and that's why he'll never amount to anything. Because of you."

That's when she raises her hand and slaps me across the face.

Shocked, I touch the spot where she hit me. My ears start to pound. I could tear her to shreds right now. She's so much weaker than I am. Better suited to chasing a child and swabbing a marble-floored flat than to fighting. Women like her never learn how to defend themselves. They only know how to clench their jaws and bear the pain the rest of the world brings them.

I take a step toward her and draw my hand back, but she just stands there, her breathing ragged. Tears spill from her clenched eyelids. I watch her lean toward the wall, putting her hand out for support. Quickly, she draws her hand back to avoid crushing the flowers. Even in this state, she has to mind the petals because those flowers matter more than she ever will.

There's nothing left to say. I lower my hand, then drive it into the thickest cluster of blooms on the wall and tear them out by their stems, leaving a small, naked patch on the wall that exposes the ugly, blackened stucco underneath.

Then I turn and sprint down St. Andrews Road.

WHEN I ARRIVE AT THE office later that morning, still reeling from my fight with Tazim, Gauri Ma'am has located three extra boxes of Vivek's papers to be scanned and filed. "I gave Vivek today off," she says. "I told him you would sort through everything." Then she disappears into her office to make phone calls.

At noon, I get an SMS from Alex: **just woke up, figured u left.**

Relieved he didn't hear the fight, I text him back saying I had to go into the office this morning. He responds a few minutes later.

those days will be far behind u soon. be proud of all your work last night. cant wait to see how high u will fly in a few years!

I clutch my phone, smiling. I think back to what Babloo told me last night, about Alex only being a tourist. He was probably just jealous Alex chose to see me instead of him.

I spend the rest of the day scanning Vivek's extra files, trying to push my fight with Tazim out of my head. A chor and a randi, she called me. As if that's all I am to her.

Judging by how long it took Tazim to get over the crystal elephant incident, I'll have to avoid her for at least a week. As the day goes on, I remember what Gauri Ma'am said to me about Neha. Even when people hurt us, how we respond is a test of our loyalty to them. Maybe I should give Tazim a few weeks to cool down, then tell her she was right. I shouldn't have been at Pali Hill, even if I was invited. Maybe it doesn't matter who's right.

By the time I've sorted and scanned the last three boxes of files, it's already evening. Why does Vivek have so many files and how come he's never bothered organizing them? Maybe he thought he'd always be at Justice For All.

Just then, Alex sends a text.

if ur still at the office, can u scan/send me the marked up applications? i want to spend some time tomorrow reflecting more about what u wrote.

I reply yes, return to my desk, and pull out the applications Alex marked up with a red pen last night. As I'm shuffling them into a neat pile, Ma'am pulls a chair up to my desk and sinks into it with a thud, as if her knees have given up on her body. The dark circles under her eyes look grayer than normal. She removes her glasses and wipes them with her dupatta. "It's hard to imagine this place without Vivek."

"Maybe it's time for him to leave," I suggest, laying my arm on the applications to conceal the header. "Like he said."

She rubs her chin. "Just as things are ramping up. The timing is unfortunate. We could have really used him around here. But I suppose even the most determined people in this field can lose their drive."

I grit my teeth, wanting to tell her that she pushed him out and all this is her fault.

"Anyways," she says, struggling back to her feet, "call Sai Krishna and order me a dal khichdi. And tell them to go easy on the salt or I'll be dead by Monday. And order yourself whatever you like."

"Ji, Ma'am," I say, realizing I've been too distracted to eat any-thing all day. I watch her start to walk away before I dial the Sai Krishna number from memory, calling in for two dal khichdis. The first time she said to order whatever I want, I did, but she said I or-dered too much and then deducted the cost off my wages to teach me a lesson. So now, if she offers, I order the same thing she does.

After I hang up the phone, I swivel around in my chair to see Ma'am standing over me, my Sanskriti Institute application in her hand.

Shit.

Her brow knots as her eyes move slowly but steadily across the page, as though she's reading every single word. Finally, she moves the papers away from her face. "So . . . you are applying to the hospi-tality program at the Sanskriti Institute of Hotel Management be-cause . . ." She pauses. "You want to show India to tourists?"

"No, Ma'am." My hands are trembling.

"No, what?" she snaps. "No, you aren't applying to the hospitality program, or no you don't want to show India to tourists?"

How do I explain my way out of this? "I . . . I—"

"These papers are yours, are they not?"

I stare at the pattern of folds and creases in the application clasped in her hand. There's no way out of this. "Ji, Ma'am," I say, steeling myself for what's to come.

Gauri Ma'am flips the pages over to where Alex has scrawled his comments in red pen. I haven't even read them yet.

She starts to read aloud.

"This is a great start, Rakhi. Take a few days, and focus more on your lived experience and how it makes you unique." Ma'am looks down at me, then back at the paper, and continues. *"Be honest with yourself as to why you want a new career. Talk about how you grew up, what you learned on the streets, and why you feel underutilized in your current role."* Ma'am says "underutilized" as if she is asking a question. *"We'll nail it, I promise. Alex."*

I feel like a rat caught in one of those sticky traps I set in the corners of the office. I would chew my leg off to escape this situation if I could.

"Is there something you want to tell me, Rakhi?"

I gaze up at her. "No, Ma'am, it's nothing. I wasn't going to send it in."

"If you are so unhappy here, why did you not just come to me?"

"Ma'am, I am happy. I swear," I say, trying to keep my voice from trembling.

She lowers herself down into the chair again, tossing the application onto my desk. "You know, when I met you at the Asha Home, you were the only child who stood out to me. All those wild, chatty girls were only interested in someday marrying the first boy to come along. And the well-behaved ones wanted to pledge their lives to Jesus and rot away in a nunnery. Everyone at the school told me you were hopeless, you know that? Hopeless."

I'm too nervous at how calm Ma'am is to care about what the nuns thought of me.

"But when they told me your story, I saw something in you. A fighting spirit. A fierceness. The people who were supposed to care for you had abandoned you. Every door had been slammed in your face and yet there you were, still surviving. Clawing back so hard that you needed to rein it in so that you didn't go down the wrong path. You reminded me so much of my Neha. Clever, independent. You deserved another chance. Tell me, Rakhi, isn't that what I gave you? Another chance at life?"

I know "yes" is the only answer she wants to hear, so I tell her yes.

Ma'am stands up, removes her white cotton dupatta, and lets it unfurl. I watch her as she silently folds the translucent fabric twice over until it's smoothed out and drapes it across her broad chest. Then she speaks again, looming over me. "Tell me, where are your friends from the street now?"

"Friends?" Does she know about Babloo? "I don't know, Ma'am."

"You know why you don't know? Because you made it to a place they could never dream of. Do you know where girls from the Asha

Home go after they reach eighteen? One or two extraordinary ones a year will get jobs in call centers. The rest of them, the lucky ones, they get work as maids or cooks. And the unlucky ones? They're in some seedy brothel, wishing their boyfriends hadn't decided to turn around one day and start pimping them out." She folds her arms across her chest. "So if you're not happy here, you would do best to reflect on what else you might be doing." Her voice is sharp and prickly.

I take a breath and look up at her. "Ma'am, you said yourself, I can't be an officewali my whole life. Remember? It's why you sent me for English lessons."

She frowns, her tightly cropped hair catching the glare of the fluorescent lights overhead. "You may not realize it, but good administrative help is what allows us to fight for what is right in this country."

"You said it. I'm not lying." She knows I'm right.

She waves her hand. "Chalo, put this nonsense away and focus on your work. Not only do you need this office, but this office needs you." She adjusts her dupatta once more and turns to walk away. "Bring me the dal khichdi when it arrives. It's been a long day."

Is this what big-shot lawyers do—ignore arguments when they know they're losing? I rise to my feet and, before I can stop myself, the word spills from my lips, loud and strong: "No."

She looks at me over her shoulder. "Excuse me?"

"Ma'am, you are wrong. You always . . ." How to put it? "You always say . . ."

"What do I always say?" She's staring me down now.

I breathe in and out, trying to untangle the words caught in my mouth.

Gauri Ma'am nods. "I thought so," she says, and starts to walk back to her office. I watch her wide hips swaying from side to side, her limp dupatta floating behind her shoulders.

Somehow, I find the words, and I shout them at her back. "You always say that women should be able to make our own choices in life, that nobody can make them for us. You said that to *The Times of India* five times, to the *Hindustan Times* three times, and *The Indian Express* once. I cut out the articles. Go see them if you don't believe me."

Gauri Ma'am turns toward me. "And how is that relevant?"

"I am a woman, too, na? What I do is my choice, isn't it?"

"Oh, really?" Ma'am speaks with an unnatural stillness and a tight-lipped smile as she walks back to my desk. "Who is going to pay for your college tuition? No, forget that, who is going to pay the application fees? Who is going to take care of you while you study so you can afford to eat? So you can afford a roof over your head?"

"I will figure it out. I've made it this far in life, haven't I?"

"Arre, Rakhi. I know exactly what this is about." She snorts. "It's this Canadian fellow, isn't it? You think I haven't noticed the two of you sneaking around after work? You think I don't know that he takes you out and pays for your meals and is putting all these naïve, half-baked ideas in your head about your future? Smarten up, for God's sake. He doesn't know what life is like in India for a girl like you."

"Maybe not, but he believes in me. He knows I can do more with my life."

"Explain to me how folding hotel linens is more valuable than being a part of a movement to better this country."

"That's your work, not mine. Alex says—"

"What does a kid like him know? These firanghis, they come here saying they care so much, but tell me, do any of them stay? No. They use their internship experience to get into graduate school, or get jobs in Switzerland or New York, while we're still here doing the same thankless work for a fraction of the pay. Just look at those bloody Dutch interns. Happy to hobnob with other expatriates in rooftop bars, spending the same kind of money in one evening that someone as senior as Bhavana earns in a week. They live in an alternate reality from you and me."

"Alex isn't like that."

Ma'am closes her eyes and sighs. When she opens them again, she gives me an exasperated look. "Rakhi, what exactly is going on between you and this boy?"

"Nothing. We are friends." I focus hard on not blinking. "Apart from Vivek, Alex is the only person here who cares to talk to me about something other than making their chai and running their errands."

"You're sure there's nothing more?"

I clench and unclench my fists. "I'm not allowed to have a friend now? I'm too hopeless for that, too?"

"Don't be ridiculous. These people are different. You don't understand the way they interact, the expectations they have of others, the nuances with which—"

"What is it? You think I'm not good enough to be friends with a rich person? A firanghi?"

She holds up a finger, as if to warn me. "Lower your voice or—"

"Or what? You are the one shouting about equality in the courts, in the papers, na? You are the one who says we should all be treated equal. Rich, poor, street kid, Muslim, Dalit, widow. But you think I shouldn't be allowed to apply to college because I am poor. You think I can't be friends with Alex because he's from Canada. And everyone thinks you are such a big social-justice-wali lawyer! The media, everyone who works here, even that Rubina Mansoor. But you're just a liar. A fraud."

Gauri Ma'am's face has turned pale but I feel unstoppable.

"You're not even qualified to run this office."

Ma'am is biting the inside of her cheek the way she does when she's thinking hard. When she finally speaks up, her voice is as light as the cobwebs in the corners of the office. "If that's how you feel, Rakhi, then you don't believe in this organization."

"So what if I don't?" I put my hands on my hips, gripping my flesh hard.

"I can't have employees who don't believe in the work we do, the direction we are going in, or the leader at the helm."

We are both silent for a long time, the air filling with the sounds of horns honking and engines revving outside. Finally, Ma'am speaks.

"If you have nothing left to say, that's settled. Turn in your mobile phone."

"My phone?"

"It's office property. Or have you forgotten that I pay your phone bill? I'll also need your key to the office now that you no longer work here."

It's as though I've been kicked in the chest. "Gauri Ma'am, no. You can't fire me. What will I do?"

"Ask your friend Alex. Or better yet, ask yourself. You're an independent woman, after all."

I meet her eyes again, and she stares back, her gaze steely. I should be pleading with her, getting on my knees and begging for my job. But I can't. I won't.

"Your phone," Ma'am says.

As I place my blue Nokia in her outstretched palm, something in me shifts. I've been dreading this moment for so long, and yet I feel nothing.

"And the office keys?"

I fish them out of the drawer and drop them into her hand. Before Ma'am can say anything more, I grab my bag and the college applications from my desk, then dash out of the office. I don't bother turning around to look back.

As I march away from the office, the shadowy old buildings in the narrow laneway seem to be growing taller, looming over me. I pick up my pace but I can't shake the feeling that the city is closing in. What did I just do? I want to go home to Behrampada and lie down on my mat, but I don't have it in me to face Tazim right now. Directionless, I keep walking, my nerves raw. Eventually, I sink to the footpath under the glow of an orange streetlamp. Where to go?

There's Alex's flat. But I can't just show up at Blossoming Heights without calling. And what if the Motianis are back from Lonavala?

Who else would take me in right now? One of the lawyers from the office, maybe? Where in Sion does Vivek even live? Or Bhavana or Sudeepthi? I wouldn't begin to know. In this crowded place full of millions of people, I am suddenly very alone.

I close my eyes. I feel as lost as I did the day I first arrived at VT Station when I was a kid.

Of course—Babloo. Brimming with a fresh burst of energy, I spring up from the curb and sprint through the darkened streets toward VT.

....

Rajshree Castle Housing Society stands apart from the rundown buildings beside it, with a fresh coat of pink paint. The interior is just as spotless. Not a red paan stain in sight. Babloo really has made it. From the streets to Dongri to a flat in the central suburbs. I bet some firanghi would love to make a movie about him. The kind that hardly gets shown in India, even though the rest of the world is buzzing about it.

There's no night watchman in Babloo's building, and no way to know which flat Babloo lives in. I mill about in the lobby, waiting for people who might know him. Moths fly in through the open door and buzz loudly around the tube light on the wall, zapping themselves into a suicidal crisp.

A family with three sleepy-looking girls comes in. They don't know who Babloo is. Next come a couple of men with suitcases. They don't know him either.

After about an hour, some young guy with a pockmarked face says he knows Babloo, but he eyes me suspiciously, his eyes lingering on my breasts. "Who are you?"

"I'm his sister," I blurt out. "Visiting. From our village. I forgot his flat number."

The guy nods and takes me up a few flights of stairs to Babloo's door, then continues on his way, whistling. He glances at me over his shoulder. "Came all this way without luggage, is it?"

I resist the urge to slap him as he laughs to himself and enters one of the flats.

There's no response when I knock on Babloo's door. I press my ear to listen for footsteps or stirring. I keep knocking, louder and louder, until my knuckles go red and warm. "Babloo," I yell into the door, even though he was always a light sleeper. "Open up!"

A woman in a nightgown bursts into the hallway. "It's one in the morning, get out of here," she yells.

I ignore her, and continue banging on the door until she threatens to call the police. I lean against Babloo's door. I'm so tired it's hard to see straight. Where could he be?

Exhausted and parched, I'm ready to go home to Behrampada. Tazim will be asleep by now. I can lie down for a few hours and leave before dawn so I don't see her.

Back at Ghatkopar Station, the trains have stopped running so I sit on the steps outside, counting my change to see if I have enough for a cold drink and a taxi ride. Three hundred and four rupees. Will that be enough?

I swing my bag from side to side, hoping to find some hidden coins. The sound of metal clinking prompts me to dig into the bag with my hands. I pull out a one-rupee coin and a key with OFFICE SPARE written in black ink on its face.

Tears of relief spring to my eyes. I kiss the spare office key then run toward the taxi stand. Even Gauri Ma'am will have left the office by now. I can let myself in, retrieve my phone, and stay there till morning.

When the taxiwala drops me off outside the Justice For All office, I spot the glow of a lone canewala's neon-lit stand a few buildings away. I still haven't had anything to eat or drink all day. Licking my dry lips, I hurry toward the stand, pressing eight rupees down on the metal counter. The canewala feeds long stalks of sugarcane into the machine, two, three times over, until they are dry as dust. A tiny stream of frothy, light green juice dribbles onto a giant slab of ice and into a glass that fogs up from the cold liquid. The canewala hands me the drink, and the sugar hits my brain, jolting me awake. I drink the entire glass without a breath.

Sugar coursing through my veins, I hurry back to the office as rain starts to fall in fat drops on my head and through my hair. I slide the spare key into the door, which unlocks effortlessly. Leaving the lights off, just in case, I tiptoe in. Someone outside could be looking in. I move slowly through the dark, careful not to trip over the boxes filled with Vivek's old files that I didn't put away.

When I hear something rustling a few meters away from me, I back up against the wall, holding my breath. The rustling gets louder, until a small rat scurries out from under a desk, along the wall, and into the kitchen. I let out a sigh and run my hands through my damp hair.

The clutter in Ma'am's office makes it hard to feel around for things. My hands reach her desk and run over her pens, books, a teacup, a food spill that's hardened and dried.

I pull open drawers until I finally find my phone.

I cradle it in my hands and turn it on.

Five text messages from Babloo.

stay @ ur office 2nite ... dnt ask why
pick up d fone
where r u
call me
r u home?????

What is going on? Why is he so desperate to reach me?

After I dismiss all the sms alerts, chills graze my neck. I have forty-three missed calls. They're all from Babloo.

THE SANDWICHWALA WHO HAD SOLD us the canister of kerosene ratted Babloo and me out.

After the police booked us, they took us to the remand home in Dongri, a building surrounded by tall, mossy stone walls. Separating us immediately, they took my clothes away and handed me a scratchy blue uniform. After they registered me as a juvenile detainee, I was taken to a barrack to sit with a hundred other girls on a cold tile floor. That night, I stared up at the sterile glare of a tube light until it flicked off and the guards told us to go to sleep.

The nightmares started my first night at Dongri, and they were so vivid they would haunt my thoughts all day. They were always the same: the paanwala's clothes were on fire, and the flames spread everywhere—the ground, the cars, the trees, the buildings, the gargoyles perched atop VT Station. Eventually, the flames would come for me, but I couldn't move my legs. I couldn't escape. I would wake up on the floor, drenched and shivering.

The days were punctuated by fights at the long line of taps where we bathed with buckets and rags, and fights at mealtimes when the girls who had been there longer tried to bully the newer ones. The guards only intervened when things got bloody.

I didn't see Babloo until the morning of our hearing at the Juvenile Justice Board, two months after we arrived at Dongri. How funny he looked, with his hair combed and his neat blue uniform shirt tucked into his shorts. I was no better, with my curls tightly yanked into two thick plaits smelling of rancid oil.

"Ssst," I whispered to Babloo as soon as I saw him. "Get us out of here. This place is the worst."

The wooden bench at the JJB was hard and splintery and faced the magistrate, a stern, moustachioed man named Kapure. As the hearing started, Babloo and I were seated together, with our advocates, Chitradidi and Josephbhaiyya, on either side of us. Each time I moved or squirmed or shook my leg, Chitradidi pinched me. I hadn't sat still in over five years.

Josephbhaiyya said there were supposed to be two social workers on the board with Magistrate Kapure. We waited for them to show up, but they didn't. No one in the room wanted to schedule a new date, so they continued without the social workers. Nobody asked Babloo or me what we wanted.

Eventually, I stopped listening entirely and focused instead on little details around me. Chitradidi's maroon nail polish was chipped on every single finger. The pimples on Josephbhaiyya's forehead formed a perfect circle. A big fly landed on Magistrate Kapure's oiled combover, rubbing its front legs together. The beige paint on the wall was peeling off, leaving two naked patches that reminded me of a big fish and a tree. As if fishes lived in trees.

Magistrate Kapure called for our pleas and I said I didn't do a single thing to the paanwala or his stall, and they must have mistaken me for someone else, just as Babloo and I had agreed to do if the police ever caught us. Kapure pressed his temples as if to ward off a headache, took a breath, and held it for a moment.

"And you knew Mr. Talpade?"

"Who?"

He brought his pencil down on the table so hard the tip snapped off. "The paanwala. The man who's lying in the hospital with burns all over his body because of you."

"No. Never seen him before."

"Even though his paan stand has been in the same place every day for the past eight years?"

I flinched, trying and failing to shake the image of the paanwala thrashing on the ground, flames creeping up his body.

"Even though you said you have lived near VT Station for the past five years?"

I wiped my cold and sweaty palms on my ugly blue Dongri frock, wishing this stupid hearing would be over.

When it was Babloo's turn to speak he smiled at me, then faced Magistrate Kapure.

"And how do you plead, Mohammed?"

Babloo puffed out his chest. "I did it. I burned the madherchodh paanwala."

I laughed nervously. Was he playing a prank on everyone? This wasn't part of the plan, but I trusted him. He would do the right thing for us. Chitradidi, on the other hand, seemed shocked. Eyes wide, she peered at Josephbhaiyya, who shook his pimpled head and rocked in his seat a few times before he stood up tentatively. "Magistrate Sahib? Please, one moment, sir. If I may speak with the boy."

Magistrate Kapure nodded, got up, stretched his arms behind him, and strolled out of the room. Josephbhaiyya clasped his hands together, flashing a sweet, tight-lipped smile at Magistrate Kapure's back. When the door swung shut, Josephbhaiyya spun around to confront Babloo, gripping his narrow shoulders. "Yaar, what are you doing?"

Babloo ignored him and stared ahead.

Josephbhaiyya pulled Babloo off the bench and into the hallway. They were gone for a few minutes. When they came back in, Josephbhaiyya took Chitradidi aside, whispering.

Babloo glared at me, unblinking, and put a finger to his lips. I didn't understand what was happening. How was this going to set us free from Dongri?

Magistrate Kapure returned and asked Babloo once more for his plea. Sweating visibly now, Babloo swallowed and again said he did it. He gave up every last detail. The green-and-black pattern on the kerosene tin. The many canisters of fillings laid out on the paanwala's table when we doused it in fuel. The precise shade of the paanwala's tan pants that day.

And then Babloo explained his motive. He was taking revenge for the paanwala crushing his little silver MP3 player.

"MP3 player?" Magistrate Kapure repeated, narrowing his eyes.

"Yes."

Babloo didn't leave out a single point—except for me. He told the entire story as if I never existed. Chitradidi shushed me each time I tried to interrupt.

When Magistrate Kapure asked Babloo whether I had assisted him, he replied, "She's much too stupid to help me pull off something like this. Just look at her."

My cheeks burned as though he had slapped me across the face.

"This chick is in love with me," he continued. "Follows me around everywhere. Watches too many romance films. It's sad."

Kapure, Chitradidi, and Josephbhaiyya all turned their eyes toward me. It was as if someone had stripped off my Dongri frock and now everyone in the room was staring at me. I jumped to my feet, but Chitradidi caught me by the wrist. "I'm not stupid," I shouted as she struggled to pull me back down to the bench. "And I'm not in love with you!"

Babloo shrugged. "You see? What else can I say?"

I wriggled away from Chitradidi, pointing my finger at Babloo. "You're a piece of shit," I screamed. "And your mother was a randi and I'm glad she killed herself in front of you because that's what you deserve."

Babloo bent his head back, as if he was examining the ceiling, but otherwise showed no reaction. Magistrate Kapure ordered Chitra-didi to shut me up. She dug her fingernails into my arm and hissed at me to stop shouting.

Sobbing quietly, I sat back on the wooden bench. Chitradidi tried to pat my shoulder, but I whacked her bony hand away.

When the hearing was over, Josephbhaiyya escorted Babloo out of the room.

"Why did you do that?" I yelled at him.

"Just trust me, yaar," Babloo called out over his shoulder. "You'll be fine."

I clenched my fists and screamed so loud Chitradidi dropped her papers all over the floor.

That was the last time I saw Babloo.

27

GAURI MA'AM'S EMPTY OFFICE GLOWS green from the light of my phone. Eventually, the screen light times out, shrouding the office in darkness again. I sink into Ma'am's seat. It's so much softer than the chairs the rest of us use.

Forty-three missed calls? I squeeze my knees together tight, staring at the phone, which I hold in my clammy palm as though it's a small, sick animal. The muffled sound of rain crashing down outside comes through the office's thin windowpanes. Lightning strikes, and I jump in my seat.

I take a deep breath, exhale, and call Babloo. After one ring it goes straight to his voicemail.

Leave a message.

His voice is flat. Like he doesn't want anyone to know who he is. I hang up and call back.

Leave a message.

Maybe he's in a lift and has no service. No, that's impossible: it's almost four in the morning. He should be in bed. Perhaps his battery died and his phone isn't plugged in.

Leave—Leave—Leave—Leave, he blurts out each time I call.

My tongue feels heavy and dry. Where could he be?

Suddenly, my phone starts ringing. I jerk back and it slips out of my hand and onto the floor. I fall to my knees and scramble to answer it before I can even see who's calling.

"Rakhi?" It's Vivek. At this hour? "Hello, Rakhi? You are okay? Tell me, you are okay."

"Sir, ji, Sir, I am okay." Confused, I wait for him to reply.

"Oh, thank god." I can hear him let out a big sigh. "Thank god, thank god," he murmurs. "Where are you?"

What is going on? Did a bomb go off somewhere? "Sir, I'm at the office."

"Office still? Have you been home at all?"

"N-no," I stammer, not sure if Gauri Ma'am has told him she fired me. "I haven't been, sir."

"Rakhi, there was a major fire last night."

"What do you mean? Where?"

"Behrampada's been gutted. Five hundred hutments gone."

....

Bombay swirls around me as my taxi drives up to Behrampada, rain trickling sideways across its windows. The wet roads shimmer orange from the streetlamps. It is almost five in the morning. Dawn will break soon.

I hung up on Vivek after he told me what happened. Then I unlocked Ma'am's cabinet and grabbed a handful of bills from the petty cash box, just in case. Vivek called back a few times but I didn't pick up.

Five hundred hutments, he said. I think of the zari workshops, with their threads of silver, jars of tiny beads, and panels of silk, and the boys with thin fingers who embroider the kinds of saris and lehengas their mothers and sisters could never dream of wearing. The goats lingering in the narrow gullies. The metal cabinets lined with wads of cash. Shit. I had six hundred rupees stuffed into my cassette player. And that crystal elephant.

And then I remember Tazim.

Tazim and Ayub. Oh my god.

I bolt upright, clutching the sides of the passenger seat in front of me while my knuckles whiten.

"Are you going to vomit in my car?" The driver, an elderly man with a skullcap and a long white beard, gives me a worried look in his rearview mirror.

"No, no," I say, between shallow, panicked breaths. "Just drive."

The taxi drops me off on the west side of Bandra Station, and as I race across the footbridge to the east side, the smoke stops me in my tracks, stinging my nostrils. I scrunch my eyes shut as though someone has thrown a fistful of sand in my face, but the smell of smoke conjures up the paanwala in my head. He thrashes about, covered in flames. My breath disappears. I can't do this. What do I care if this place is burned to the ground?

But I can't just leave Tazim behind. I push away the images of the paanwala and open my eyes, steadying myself on the handrail of the footbridge. Then I turn my back on the sleepy west and its clean sea air to face the smoke and grit that hisses out from whatever is left of Behrampada.

When I make it to the other side of the bridge, the sight that greets me stops my heart. The flames are low and sparse, most of the hutments black and gray, hollowed out and collapsed. It's hard to tell how far the fire has got. Even with the rain, the smoke is thicker here, so I press my damp dupatta against my mouth. I can make out a string of water tankers, but I don't see anyone putting out the rest of the flames.

Faint wails rise up above the smoke and embers. Hundreds, no, thousands of people have gathered on the paved road outside the slum, some sitting with their heads in their hands. Makeshift shelters have already popped up along the footpath. Tarpaulins and cardboard and saris.

What was the word Vivek used to describe Behrampada? *Gutted.* Like a dead fish, its insides emptied and strewn about on the outside.

....

Once I push my way through the crowd, a throng of men blocks me from entering the path to my laneway. I recognize one of the slum leaders and some of the men from the mosque.

"You can't go in," one of them commands, holding out his arm to stop me.

"This is my home," I shout. "I need to find Tazim."

"All the huts down this lane are gone," another says.

Desperate, I break past them and make a run for it, toward the blackened narrow laneway leading to my hut. I make it into the gulley, climbing over debris, but someone catches up to me, grips me by the shoulder, and drags me back to the road, saying it's not safe.

As the morning sun peeks up over the ravaged slum, I pace through the crowds, scanning faces for Tazim's, listening to snippets of conversation about personal items people took, how quickly the fire spread, which huts were still safe, and who was still missing. Neither Babloo nor Alex pick up their phones when I call.

At the first aid table across the road, wounds are being wrapped and chests are being listened to. A young nurse with a long braid is bandaging a boy's shoulder.

"Do you know Tazim and Ayub?" I ask her, frantically. "Tazim is my height, long braid like yours. Ayub is four . . . No, five. He has big ears. They stick out. Have you seen them?"

The nurse taps the boy on his shoulder and motions for him to leave. She calls for the next person, then turns to me. "Please, take a deep breath, drink some water." She hands me a paper cup and I slap it to the ground. Water splatters all over our feet.

An older man in a white coat steps toward me. "If you're looking for someone, you go to the police, not first aid." He then uses his clipboard to shove me away from the growing line of wailing children.

For the next hour, I wait on the road outside Behrampada. By seven in the morning, my phone loses battery. It doesn't matter. I have to find Tazim. If our huts are gone we'll need to find someplace new together, soon. Close to here, so Ayub can stay in his school and Tazim won't be too far from Pali Hill.

The thought of the last time I saw her makes my skin crawl. The tears, the insults, the angry words. The people on the street watching us scream at each other.

Beside a water station, two women discuss a mutual friend who found her missing children just an hour ago. "Wandering around Kherwadi, can you believe they went that far?"

I feel a jolt of energy go through my body. What if Ayub wandered off, and Tazim is searching for him? I down a cup of water and head to the train station.

....

By early evening, after combing Bandra, Khar, and Santacruz, I return to Behrampada, empty-handed. I searched everywhere for Tazim and Ayub: in grimy dark valleys beneath the concrete flyovers; the lengths of the train station platforms. Not a single person had seen a small boy named Ayub or his mother looking for him.

Outside Behrampada, the number of makeshift shelters has tripled. Two rival political parties have set up kerosene stoves and tables, their banners unfurled behind them. Long lines have formed for plates of rice and dal. I wait in the shorter one, which seems to be moving slower, because a fight has broken out ahead of me.

Later, as I'm shoveling the last bits of rice and dal into my mouth, I see my landlord Munna trudging by, heavy-footed. I've never been so relieved to see him.

I spring to my feet, calling his name.

"Have you seen Tazim?" I scan his face, my eyes bright and my voice hopeful.

He pauses and gives me a sympathetic look, a look he's never given me before. "She was found."

I take a step back. "No."

"She didn't make it out in time. Seems she suffocated in the smoke." His voice is worn out.

"It must be someone else."

"Rakhi, they found her ration card on her body."

I press a cold palm to my chest to calm the hammer blows to my heart, but it doesn't work. "And Ayub?"

"He's fine. He's with some of the neighbors. Mehru Begum, I think. Make sure someone contacts Hanifbhai in Dubai," Munna says.

"Hanifbhai is not even in Dubai. His number is disconnected. We don't even know if he's still—" My voice cracks.

Munna starts to reply but a man approaches to ask if he's seen his neighbors. As I stand there in the crowd, shoulders slumped, hands hanging limply, the din of ongoing wailing and shouting stops. I can't hear anything anymore.

What am I supposed to do without Tazim? Who else is there to laugh with about the day's drudgery? Who else can I really trust? She was my friend. And still, this whole time before Alex came, before Babloo returned, I thought I was alone. How could I have been so stupid?

I should have been in Behrampada, not banging on Babloo's door or breaking into the office. I could have searched for her when the fire started. I would have lifted her onto my back and carried her out. I could have saved her.

Piercing the roaring silence in my ears is the cry of "Khala, Khala."

Startled, I whirl around to see Ayub, sitting cross-legged underneath the shade of a sooty sari tied to four sticks. He jumps up, zipping toward me, wrapping his arms around my legs. I can feel his warm cheeks through the fabric of my pants. Gently peeling his fingers off the backs of my thighs, I crouch to the ground to face him.

The skin under his eyes is puffed up, and his lower lip is cracked and bleeding.

"Are you okay?"

He doesn't respond, just reaches for me, throwing his arms around my neck. I let him hug me, his small body hot against mine.

An older woman with a bruise blooming on her face limps toward us from where Ayub was sitting. "You're Tazim's neighbor," she says, adjusting the dupatta hanging over her head.

"Her friend," I say, craning my neck past Ayub to see her.

"You'll take him? I can't run after a small child with my foot like this." She points to a bandage around her ankle.

I pause, taken aback. "I can't watch out for him either. I don't have any place to live."

"Teek hain," she says, gripping Ayub's wrist and pulling him off me. "I'll tell my son to take him to the police station. They'll find Tazim's family."

"Tazim has no other family. Hanifbhai is in Saudi Arabia, but we haven't heard from him in months . . ."

The bruised old lady clucks her tongue in sympathy. "Then the police will have to take him to an orphanage until they find someone."

My chest tightens. "They'll throw him in a remand home."

"Tell me, is that my problem?" She pushes the frizz from her forehead to stare me in the eye.

I don't respond. Ayub's eyes are wide open, like two big saucers. He is scared and alone. Does that make him my problem? I swallow the lump in my throat. Ayub gazes up at me, pleadingly. The thought of him in a blue Dongri uniform, bruises creeping over his face, lice crawling through his hair—I can't bear to look at him anymore.

Quickly, I stagger away from Ayub and the woman. I can hear him calling my name, but I keep moving, stepping through overturned plates of rice, over old people lying on the ground with their hands outstretched. Past stunned voices recounting heroic escapes, devastating losses. Of the thousands of people in this slum, these are the people who got to live, while Tazim died. I want to scream with what's left of the strength in my body.

Ahead of me, a cameraman points his camera at a red-lipped reporter holding a microphone. A small crowd of people gathers to watch.

". . . fire officials say twenty-two fire engines were deployed," the reporter says in song-like Hindi.

Behind her, a young woman cries out: "What twenty-two fire engines?"

The cameraman shifts his weight but keeps filming.

"There is no word on the cause of the fire, but witnesses say the fire spread due to multiple gas cooking cylinders igniting, one by one," the reporter carries on. "One resident told me she heard explosions every three seconds."

"For two hours," the woman wails. "For two hours my home burned and nobody came."

The reporter doesn't blink. "The Mumbai police are reporting a death toll of thirteen people. Names will not be released until all victims' families have been notified. I can tell you that some of the dead are children—"

The crying woman howls over her. "My home, my ration card, my husband's new television, my children's schoolbooks and uniforms—everything is gone."

The cameraman signals to the reporter to wrap it up.

28

TWO YOUNG MEN IN SKULLCAPS keep shouting about time limits at the makeshift phone-charging station set up by Garib Nawaz Masjid. "Everyone gets fifteen minutes, not a second more!" I get in the line, which grows longer by the minute.

Twelve people wait ahead of me. I count them over and over again, noting more details, like the torn blue banyan the man in front of me is wearing. And the fact that the guy in front of him is missing a shirt. It's not enough to keep my mind from wondering how Tazim died.

I hope she didn't feel any pain. That it happened in an instant, that she didn't have time to be afraid. More than anything, I hope Hanifbhai finds his way back to collect Ayub.

After my fifteen minutes of charging time is up, I dial Babloo. He picks up on the first ring.

"There you are," he says. "I've been calling you and calling you. Kept going to voicemail. Are you okay?" His breathing is quick.

I don't know how to answer him. My friend is dead. I just turned my back on her son. "I'm in Behrampada. You've seen the news?"

"I saw. Five hundred huts gone."

"They are saying thirteen people are dead." My voice chokes.

"Leave that place and come to my flat, immediately. Third floor. Flat Thirty-seven." The phone goes dead.

Something in his voice wasn't right.

Now that Tazim is gone, what reason do I have to stay here?

I take one final look at what's left of Behrampada. I don't know any Muslim prayers for the dead, so I whisper into the smoky air the only thing that makes sense: "Goodbye, Tazim. Forgive me."

As the words exit my mouth, I realize there may be too much to ask forgiveness for.

…………

Babloo is talking on the phone when he opens the door to his sparsely furnished flat. He presses a finger to his lips, leads me to a plastic-covered couch, and points to a half-eaten packet of poori bhaji on the coffee table before he disappears into the bedroom, closing the door behind him. After I've finished off what's left of the food, I hold my bag to my chest and sink into the sofa, exhausted.

The sound of Babloo's muffled shouting seeps through the walls. "You should have told me, madherchodh," he yells. I can't make out the rest.

There's a remote control resting on the plastic-wrapped seat beside me. I flick on the small television to a Hindi news channel, where a husky-voiced reporter in a blue blouse is reporting from the Bandra Station footbridge.

"The fire department received a call about the blaze, I'm told, at two in the morning, local time." The reporter stares into the camera. "One witness tells me he received minor injuries while rescuing his eighty-three-year-old mother from the flames."

I change the channel to some singing show where a pudgy boy with thick eyelashes is standing in the spotlight on a shiny black stage. Three celebrity judges seated behind a big table are telling him he has a nice voice. "The voice of an angel," one of them says, to great audience applause. I lean forward. It's Rakhi Tilak. I haven't seen her face in years. Like Rubina, she slipped under the radar a long time ago.

The bedroom door swings open and Babloo walks out, shoving his phone into his shirt pocket. He stands in front of the TV, peering at the screen. "Is that Bhutan ki Baby? Rakhi Aunty? She's old now. Even you're looking better than her." He reaches for the remote and switches off the TV. My eyes cling to the blackened screen.

"You should have picked up your phone," he says. "I called you so many times."

I slump farther into the sofa.

"Why have a phone if you don't answer it? You're so careless. You haven't changed at all." He throws the remote control to the sofa.

"I didn't have my phone on me."

"Like I said. Careless."

"Why are you making such a big deal about my phone? My home just burned to the ground. What could be more important?"

He turns to stare out the window at the dusky evening sky. I can hear him breathing heavily as he rakes his fingers through his hair.

I grip one arm of the sofa. "Babloo? What were you calling about?"

"Arre, forget it."

I get up and walk up to him, so close I can smell the cigarettes on his breath. "What did you do?"

"I said forget it."

"I asked you a question, bhenchodh." My voice is trembling.

He flinches. "I don't know why you're so surprised. Slums are destroyed all the time."

I pinch the bridge of my nose and squeeze my eyes shut for a moment. I can't believe what I'm about to ask. "Did you set Behrampada on fire?"

"No. I'm still working the hafta scene, remember?"

"Then who did?" I say, my voice raised. "Someone you work with?"

He doesn't reply so I grab the remote control from the couch and hurl it against the wall. It makes a dent in the plaster.

"What's wrong with you?" He throws me on the couch.

I pick up a clock from the side table and raise it in the air. "Tell me what you know or I'll destroy everything in here."

He lunges forward, prying the clock from my hands. "If I tell you, will you stop behaving like this?"

I nod.

He puts the clock down and smooths the front of his shirt. "Boss got a job, so our guys did it. Happy?"

The hairs on my arms stand up. "Your guys? Then you must go to the police!"

He sneers. "Do you realize how many people had to be bought to pull off something this big?"

"The police knew?"

"Police, ambulance, fire trucks. For the right price, they can be counted on to take their sweet time. Why do you think they took so long to put out the fire?"

It was all planned out, and so many people were in on it. "My— my friend died," I stammer, my voice breaking. "Her name was Tazim. She lived in the hut below me."

Babloo sinks down on the sofa next to me and rubs his face with both hands. "Do you understand how much money that land is worth? It's being completely wasted, suffocated by those huts. By people who think they have a right to be there. People who never bought the land in the first place."

"That's my home," I say.

"So you'll find another one. You're a fool to think a place like that wouldn't get torn down eventually. If it wasn't Arora, it would have been someone else."

I feel my pulse quickening. "Arora? Jeetendra Arora?" I search his eyes as I put the pieces together. "Your goonda friends set my home on fire and killed my friend so that Arora builder can put up another hi-fi flat?"

Babloo throws his hands into the air as if he's talking to a child. "Don't be so naïve. That's the price of living in a place like Behrampada. It's prime land by the train station. The eastern suburbs are growing. That's where Bombay's future is."

My shoulders collapse. It's all clear to me now. "That's why you went to the party with Alex. To see Arora."

He stares up at the ceiling fan spinning above us. "Total fattoo, that guy. He didn't like that I was there. Said someone might catch on. That he has a reputation to protect. Bhenchodhs, all of them. One day I'll leave and start my own thing. Get some people I can trust. You can work for me, too."

My fists tighten. "You're a real chutiya, you know? I can't believe I thought you turned out okay."

He pulls a cigarette from his shirt pocket and lights it up. Little wisps of smoke curl from his lip before he exhales it all through his nose. "Why all this drama? You're alive, you're safe, and you have somewhere to stay. Who else in that bloody slum can say the same? You've been through worse before. Or have you been spending so much time with your lawyers and firanghis you've forgotten you're a street kid?"

"Those lawyers and firanghis would never set a zhopadpatti on fire. At least they're trying to fix this place. Those firanghis come here every year to work for free. Even Alex. That's how much they believe in the work."

Babloo throws his head back and laughs. "We don't need people like Alex coming from outside to try to fix India. What's broken here is broken everywhere."

"That's because you don't care about fixing anything. All you know how to do is take. You should be ashamed."

"Ashamed! About what? Stealing from the people who treated me like a bastard in my own country? I don't owe anyone anything."

"It's not just about stealing. My friend died in the fire. And it's because of you."

"This is what it feels like to lose someone," he snarls, staring straight ahead at the wall. "Now you know." He pours himself a whiskey, then sits back down on the couch.

"I already know. I lost my parents. And I lost you, too. This whole time I thought you were dead or in the gutter somewhere, but still I searched for you every day. You didn't even bother to look for me."

Babloo snorts into his glass and tips his head back, draining his drink. "Lost me and walked straight into your nice little school in Aurangabad, is it? Reading books, singing songs, eating three times a day. You know what I was doing? Getting beat by bigger boys. Getting beat by the guards. Being forced to skip meals for fighting back. Getting sick. I got TB, did you know that? Coughed up blood for weeks. Almost fucking died."

"I never asked you to lie at the JJB."

He leans back in his seat, rubbing his top lip over his teeth. "You think I told that magistrate I set fire to the paanwala because I loved you, na? Because I thought you were something special?"

"Didn't you? You made me your girlfriend. You said you wanted to protect me."

"I was thirteen. I wanted to fuck a girl. You were right there. It was so easy."

I wanted to fuck a girl. My face burns like I've been slapped across the face. *It was so easy.* For once, I have no comeback. No snide remark will undo what he just said.

He sets his empty glass down on the coffee table and looks up at me, calmly. "You want to know why I took the blame at the JJB?" He doesn't wait for me to answer. "I met some other boys at Dongri. They worked for the guy who's my boss now. They were impressed by our whole paanwala scheme. Wanted someone who wasn't afraid to take risks. Said if I stayed behind with them in the remand home, proved myself to them, I could join them when I got out. So that's what I did. I had to look out for my future. And just see," he says, gesturing at his flat. "It paid off."

I gaze into Babloo's hardened face, searching for the boy I used to know. Who has he become? Or was he always like this and I just couldn't see it? Tears spring to my eyes, and I blink them back.

"Listen," he says. "The two of us, we've been through enough together. We were meant to find each other again. Stay here. I can take care of you."

Up until today, I would have said yes. But now that I know what happened, how could I ever trust him again? So, I rise to my feet. "I don't need you to take care of me."

"You don't have anywhere to live, remember?"

"I'd go back to the streets before I'd stay with you," I fire back.

He cracks his knuckles. "Now that you know about the fire, I can't let you leave. I can't risk someone tricking you into squealing about Arora or my boss."

I glare down at him, defiantly. "Who says I need to be tricked?"

In one swift movement Babloo twists my arm behind my back so I can't move. "You're not going anywhere, in that case."

"Babloo, let go." I squirm, trying to break free, but he's so much stronger.

"I call the shots," he says firmly. "Not you."

I don't say a word.

"Understand?" He tightens his grip, pulling me so close I can feel the warmth of his breath on my ear. His mobile buzzes. He stares at the name and answers it with a rapid "Yes, boss," before pressing a finger to his mouth, motioning for me to sit on the couch, and slipping into the bedroom.

That's when I grab my bag and fly out the door and down the stairs to the lobby.

I hear Babloo shouting my name, his footsteps not far behind me. For once, though, I'm faster than him, jumping into the lone autorickshaw parked outside the building.

"Drive, drive, drive," I command the autowala, a young guy who can't be more than seventeen. "Don't stop until we get to Bandra. Pali Hill."

The autowala cranks the engine alive, turns the handle into first gear, and we take off. I crane my neck out to make sure Babloo is far behind. He stands in the middle of the road behind us, his arms outstretched, palms up to the sky, growing smaller and smaller as we speed away.

29

I SEND ALEX A MESSAGE, and he is sitting on the curb outside of Blossoming Heights under the glow of a streetlamp when I get out of the autorickshaw. He looks at me quizzically. "Are you wearing the same clothes you had on Friday?"

"My home. It is burned. All gone."

He stands up, asking me if I'm serious, but I cut him off, talking at a rapid pace. "It was Arora. Rubina Mansoor's husband. He is wanting to build flats over Behrampada. He hired Babloo's gang, they are burning it down." I stare at Alex, breathless, as he narrows his eyes.

"Slow down. You're trying to tell me your slum burned down and Jeet Arora is responsible? My aunt and uncle's friend?" He tilts his head and stares at my sooty arms. "Are you feeling okay? Did someone give you drugs?"

"I swear. Babloo himself is telling me."

Alex frowns. "This doesn't make any sense. Arora's reputation is far too clean for that. He's not some shady developer. And he's given so much to Justice For All. I think he knows it's wrong to burn a slum down."

"Babloo told me. He is not lying."

"You probably heard wrong."

"I am not wrong." I wring my hands. "Alex, please."

He takes a step closer and lowers his voice. "Even if you were right, which you're probably not, those people are connected to my family. Do you think I would ever associate with people like that?"

Is anyone who they say they are? Is Babloo the same boy who was my best friend? Is Gauri Ma'am the Champion of the Exploited?

"My home is gone. Please. You have to help me."

"Well, you can't crash here. My aunt and uncle are returning in an hour or so."

"Arre, not to stay. I need help. We have to tell Gauri Ma'am, police, anyone. They have to know that this is what happened to Behrampada."

Alex shifts his weight from foot to foot, kicking at a fallen leaf on the footpath. Then his eyes widen, like he has an idea. "Wait—I owe you money, don't I?" He digs into his pocket, pulls out his wallet and hands me every bill in it. "I haven't paid you for showing me around."

I take the money and count it. "Fifteen thousand, two hundred," I say, my voice flat. He said he'd pay me forty thousand rupees.

"I'd give you the full amount but I haven't got paid for August. That should cover it to date, right? So at least you can find a place to stay for the next little while."

"Still," I say, stuffing the cash into my bag, "I am needing more than money from you. We have to tell to Gauri Ma'am."

He scratches the side of his head and looks both ways on the road. "It's dangerous to spread unfounded accusations against people with good reputations. Think of how many lives you could ruin with a rumor like that."

"My friend, Tazim, she is dead. *Tazim.*" I say her name slowly for him, to let it sink in, but he only looks confused.

"Do I know this person?"

"Tazim, yaar, Tazim. Your bai. Maid. She is cleaning your flat every day."

"Her? She didn't come today. Wait," he sputters, "she's your friend?"

Tazim cleaned his clothes, made his bed, boiled his tea, swabbed his floors, and he doesn't even know her by name? I am losing whatever patience I had with Alex.

He blinks a few times and digs his hands into his pockets. "I'm out of my element here. Can we wait for my aunt and uncle to return? They know people. They'll know what to do."

"Arre, not them. They are friends with Arora. I need your help. I can't do all this alone. Come, we will go to the police together. They will be listening to you, not me."

He wraps his hands around the back of his neck. "Wait. Aren't the police here corrupt or whatever?"

"Arre, this whole thing is corrupt. Arora burns down Behrampada, he is bribing the ambulance and police so they take too long, and then is bribing government people so that he can buy the land at a lower rate and build towers for rich people."

"If the police are in on it, why would we even go to them?"

Exasperated, I throw my hands up. "Then first we go tell Gauri Ma'am. You must help me."

"We can't go to Gauri until we're sure what you're claiming is true. She'll hit the roof if she finds out we're just spreading hearsay. I'm not exposing myself to that kind of drama. Let's get ourselves sorted, let's—"

"Arre, Alex."

"Trust me, we have to be careful about this. Reputations are on the line."

People have died, I want to scream. Instead, I nod. "Fine. You take one day. But then you must help."

He swallows. "Okay."

Leaving out the fact that Gauri Ma'am fired me, I tell Alex I won't be at the office tomorrow, and we agree to meet up again tomorrow evening at Bandra Station. I take off down the road. When I glance back at Alex, he's sitting on the curb again, dragging his fingers through his hair, staring back at me.

"This is it," I call out to him. "This is the real India."

THAT NIGHT, I SLEEP ON a bench in Bandra Station for a few hours until the Railway Police kick me and everyone else who had the same idea out of the station. The others return to the east side of the station, where the displaced residents of Behrampada are fighting for space on the crammed footpath. I wander out the west side instead, up the wide, empty road, in search of quiet. I only have to make it until evening before I meet Alex again. What was it that those Dutch girls said? You can't find an inch of peace in Bombay.

I sink down on the road, and stretch out between two motorbikes parked outside a stationery shop. I wish I was back in my hut, in Behrampada, listening to the muezzin's call to prayer at dawn.

At five in the morning, my phone buzzes. It's an unknown number.

"Come to my flat right now." It's Gauri Ma'am, whispering. "I'll explain why when you get here."

She then proceeds to give me directions to her flat, as if I don't already know where she lives. Not to mention where she banks, what she eats for breakfast, lunch, and dinner, who her tailor is, and how much he charges to stitch her blouses.

"And make sure nobody sees you. Don't call back on this number, or on my mobile."

Alex must have called her and told her everything. I feel a great weight has lifted off my shoulders knowing that Ma'am knows the truth about that bhenchodh Arora. Maybe this is a turning point for Gauri Ma'am and me. She'll realize she actually needs me, that I have something to offer her. Perhaps she'll even take me back.

Gauri Ma'am answers the door of her flat by opening it just a crack and peering nervously out into the hallway. Then she pulls me in swiftly by the elbow and slams the door shut.

"Did anyone see you come here?" Her voice is fierce and low. "Did you see any police downstairs? What about on the road? How did you get here?"

"Ma'am, I saw some traffic police when I was on the bus . . ."

Gauri Ma'am nods and chews on her lip. "Sit," she commands, pointing to one of the chairs at her big wooden dining table.

It's a few years since I've been to Ma'am's flat. It's large and open. Two bedrooms, with one for Neha, who never visits. The walls are covered with paintings and carved wooden masks and heavy woven tapestries. And photographs of Neha. Onstage graduating from college, onstage receiving school awards, smiling on the beach, studying at the dining table. No wedding day pictures, though.

On the wall beside me, there's a framed photo of Ma'am's orange cat, Zoey, who died last year. Diabetes. Ma'am spent ten thousand rupees on Zoey's injections and medicines. For fifty rupees and a vada pav, I'd have found her a new cat.

Ma'am takes a seat opposite me and crosses her arms across her puffed-out chest. "I got a call from the police. That crystal figurine you stole in January. The one Vivek had to help you out with. You took that from Alex's family?"

"Ji, Ma'am. That was the Motiani family." Why is she asking me about that? We have more important things to deal with.

"Well, the family are saying you turned up at their house again a few days ago and that you stole more things."

"Stole what? What did I steal?"

"A laptop, some cash, some gold necklace."

"That's—that's a lie! You know I wouldn't do that."

"We both know what you're capable of," she says, sternly. "What's more, you no longer work for me, yet here I am spending the early hours of a Monday morning dealing with your petty theft issues. Tell me why I am doing this."

"I didn't steal anything from anyone, Ma'am. But there are way bigger things going on right now, if you'd just—"

"What bigger things?"

"Ma'am, Behrampada burned down Saturday night. Tazim died in the fire."

"Your downstairs neighbor Tazim?" She sighs and presses two fingers into the space between her eyebrows. "If I'd had a way to contact you, I would have called as soon as I heard about the fire. But then Vivek told me he reached you and you said you were fine. You broke into the office to take your phone back, did you?"

I don't work for her anymore. I don't have to answer her questions. I stay silent.

"Look, I don't want you to get in trouble. I called you to tell you the police are searching for you. The Motiani family filed a theft complaint against you."

As if the police would care about a false theft complaint over a developer scheming to burn down an entire slum. "Bas, that's it?"

Gauri Ma'am stares at me like I've just insulted her intelligence. "Don't you think that's quite significant?"

I blink. So Alex hasn't told her yet. "Gauri Ma'am, do you not know? About the fire?"

"What about it?"

"Behrampada was set on fire deliberately. Arora ordered it." I scan her eyes, which don't register the horror I thought they would. "Rubina Mansoor's husband," I add.

"You're trying to tell me that Jeetendra Arora is responsible for Behrampada being burned down?" Gauri Ma'am's lip twitches. "And

you would know this how? Have you become an investigative journalist overnight or what?"

"Babloo told me."

She jerks her head back. "Who the hell is Babloo?"

"My old friend. From the streets. You know, the one from the JJB?"

"Arre, that fellow you keep searching for? What else have you
kept from me?"

"Yes, that Babloo. He's back. He works for a goonda who took the
job from Arora. Babloo didn't set the fire. But a guy in his gang did.
Orders from their boss. I don't know the boss's name, but I can lead
you to him. I know where they eat, what beer bars they go to. I have
Babloo's address."

I wait for her to thank me for telling her the truth, but she only
rubs her forehead again. "What else did this Babloo chap tell you?"

"That Arora wants to build luxury flats on top of Behrampada,
but first he had to set it on fire and make sure it all burned down."

She doesn't say anything.

Deep lines form on her glistening forehead. She stares at me, and
for a second, it's as though her eyes are filled with sorrow. "Jeetendra
Arora did this?"

"Ji, Ma'am," I say, desperate for her to believe me.

"Who else knows?"

"Alex. Call him up, he will tell you everything I told you. He's
going to help us."

She waves me off. "Alex is leaving India today. He emailed me late
last night."

My mouth falls open. "I just . . . I just saw him last night. He
didn't say . . . We were supposed to meet today . . ."

"These firanghis, you just can't count on them. I should stop the
internship program. More trouble than it's worth."

I ball my hands into fists to keep them from trembling. How
could he just leave like that? What happened to wanting to help me?
Wanting to do the right thing? He said I would go places and I believed him. Just ate it all up. How could I have been so stupid?

"Don't look so worried, Rakhi. Alex is the least of your troubles right now, believe me."

I release my fists. "So you'll help me? We'll tell the police about Arora burning down the slum?"

"The sun will be up soon. You should leave now. I won't say anything to the police about you being here. But you can't stay."

"Why, because the police think I stole a laptop from the Motianis? Who cares about that? This Arora thing is much more important."

She pulls her shoulders back. "Breaking the law is no small matter. And I cannot keep bailing you out. Especially when you have proven to be so untrustworthy."

"And if the police find me? You'll defend me, na? And you can prove the Motianis are lying to cover this up."

Gauri Ma'am purses her lips.

"Ma'am?"

She swallows and hesitates, as if she is picking her words carefully. "If what you're saying about Jeetendra Arora burning down Behrampada is true, I can't do much for you."

"Why not?" The pitch of my voice rises. "Would you rather I go to jail for some stupid theft I didn't do?"

"Didn't you escape Dongri for what you did to the paanwala?"

"So what? Arora gets to burn down Behrampada and nobody can say anything? Hundreds of people lost their homes. People died. Tazim died."

"Life isn't fair, Rakhi. Sometimes we get out of sticky situations without a scrape, and sometimes we have to pay for things we didn't do."

"When have you ever asked a client what they've done in their past before you take their case? You're happy to represent Tulsi and she doesn't even want your help!"

Gauri Ma'am rubs her hands over her cropped hair. "Listen, Rakhi—"

I stand up. "How can you act like some big important lawyer for people without a voice, when you refuse to help your own people when they need you? How can—"

"The Arora Group has too much money to be held accountable for things like this," she blurts out, her nostrils flaring.

"Not if they have someone like you fighting them."

"If I take Arora on, I break my relationship with Rubina Mansoor."

"Rubina Mansoor? Two months ago you didn't even know her."

"Justice For All is hanging on by a thread. She has brought in so much money, raised our profile tenfold. Without private donors we are done. Everyone will be fired. Bhavana, Sudeepthi, even I won't have a job. And we won't be able to provide legal services to thousands of people. Should I be sacrificing everyone's well-being for you?"

I smack the wooden table with both palms. "Yes! I have been loyal to you. I have served you, done everything you told me to. You treated me like your child, and I had to obey you like you were my mother. Even when I didn't agree with it. You owe me this."

Gauri Ma'am juts her chin out. "Rakhi, I'm sorry if you thought our relationship was anything more than it was. I was your boss, not your parent. And I compensated you, more than fairly, for your work. I'm afraid I don't owe you any more than that."

The words flow easily, like water from a tap. "You are worse than Jeetendra Arora and the selfish people who step all over other people for their own gain. You are worse because you pretend to care."

I glare at her, daring her to reply.

Instead, she folds her hands in prayer. "Just go, please." Her voice is soft. "For your own good, leave the city. You won't find another office job, or get into college, or do whatever it is you've been trying to do, as long as you're wanted by the police."

So that's it. After all this, she's throwing me out. It feels like my skin has been torn off. "Where am I supposed to go?"

Ma'am reaches for her purse and throws a thick wad of hundred-rupee notes on the table. "Get on a train, go somewhere far from here. I am sorry I could not do more for you."

I reach for the cash quickly, almost as if she might change her mind in the next minute and take it away. "And what am I supposed to do, Gauri Ma'am?"

Her red-rimmed eyes shine. "You can do whatever you want." She stands up, walks to the door, and holds it open for me. "Goodbye, Rakhi."

....

I stare out ahead of me at Chowpatty Beach. The tide is low and the early morning waves are quiet, measured, far away.

After I left Gauri Ma'am's flat, I started walking. Down footpaths, under flyovers, through gullies, until I arrived here.

Desperate to sit down, I stumble toward the water, away from the city, its tall buildings, its lights, its pulsing energy. I kick off my sandals, the coarse wet sand soothing the bottoms of my hot, achy feet, and sink down to the glassy stretch of beach where the waves would usually be.

After everything I've done for Gauri Ma'am, how could she say I was only her employee? How could she have told me to disappear like that, with an untouched bank bundle and a weak apology? Even Bhavana said it—she treated me like her own daughter. But of course Ma'am already has a daughter. How foolish I was to believe I was anything more than an officewali to her.

I reach into my bag to count the cash she gave me, the bills rippling in the gentle sea breeze. Ten thousand rupees. It's a lot, but it's also nothing. Even with the money Alex gave me, is it enough to start over?

Just then, my phone buzzes with an SMS. It's Alex.

hey. told my aunt and uncle what u said about arora and they were pissed. they said they know u, that some shit went down

with u and them? u never told me. i cant afford to get mixed up in ur drama. flying home tonite. good luck w everything. peace out. -alex

My first instinct is to dial his number but another SMS comes through from him.

disconnecting this number.

To think this firanghi, who is escaping on the first plane out of India when I need him most, told me he was going to give me what I needed to do better, be better. To think I ever believed him.

On Saturday, I was sleeping in a big, soft bed in Pali Hill. I had forty thousand rupees coming my way. I was going to apply to college, go work in a nice hotel, make good money. I had finally found Babloo, after so many years. But instead of being the best friend I remembered, he revealed himself to be nothing like the Babloo I thought I knew. And now I have no home, no job, nobody. Nowhere to go. Nothing to be.

Then I close my eyes and I see Tazim's face, smiling and kind. Nobody seems to care that she's gone. Gauri Ma'am, Babloo, Alex, they barely registered her death. And yet she was the closest thing I had to family. Was her life so meaningless? What does that say about mine?

That's when the full weight of the past two days slams into my chest so hard I break into loud, uncontrollable sobs. Pounding the sand, I scream into the wind. My hair whips about my face, wet with tears, mucus, spit, and sea spray.

The Monday morning beach walkers keep a safe distance from me. Even the seagulls avoid me, crying as they dive at bits of snack paper littering the beach. I remain sitting there until my tears run out. By then the tide starts to come in, and I have half a mind to let it engulf me. To throw Gauri Ma'am's bhenchodh money into the breeze and let the wind carry it across Chowpatty Beach.

A strong, frothy wave rolls up the shore, splashing my lower half. As it retreats, smoothing the sand, it deposits a small Ganesh murti beside me. The sea has scrubbed the pink from his cheeks, claimed a leg and an arm. For having floated in the Arabian Sea for the past three weeks, though, he doesn't look so bad. I peer closer at the string of waterlogged yellow and orange marigolds, now decaying, tangled around his trunk. But lying on his back in the sand, Ganesh looks up at the sky, his right hand upturned in blessing. I untangle the slimy marigolds so they lie flat on his potbelly, then prop him up so he is sitting up on the shore, facing the city.

The sea brims at my feet and I edge back.

When life gets hard, remember what I told you, Rakhi Tilak said to me once, all those years ago, on this same stretch of sand.

The midmorning sun is gentle, floating up into the milky purple sky. The day is starting for everyone else, but mine has yet to end.

Rising to my feet, I shake wet sand from the bottom of my salwar kameez and start to head back toward the city.

EPILOGUE

WITH HIS ELBOWS POINTING OUTWARD, a sandy-haired American named Kenny holds up his iPhone, struggling to fit all of VT Station into the frame. He leans so far back that his chin disappears into the glistening folds of his strained neck.

"How do you fit the whole darn building . . ." he mutters to himself.

"Come," I say, tapping the damp fabric of his T-shirt, "I'll show you where to click the best photo." Leading him across the street, I tilt his phone camera back, nudge it slightly to the left. "Now try."

As Kenny attempts his shot again, motorbikes swerve past him, just another road obstruction. With one eye on his phone screen and the other eye on the early evening traffic, I hold my arm out to block cars from getting too close to him.

Kenny snaps his shots of VT, then proudly shows them to me and his wife, Lorna. "Will you look at that," he exclaims.

"The sky is all peach-colored, and with the lights on the building, and the cars whizzing by, it's just . . ." Lorna trails off, dazzled.

VT is the second stop on my Bombay street life tour. I've been doing them for almost three years now, all on my own. As I lead the tour group through the halls, two French women named Claire and Delphine argue about whether the station is built in the Indo-Gothic or Indo-Saracenic style, then ask me to settle their dispute. I've done enough tours with firanghis all into this architecture funda to know that whatever Indo-Gothic and Indo-Saracenic are, they're the same thing, but instead I wave my hand in the air to cut the French ladies off. "All these small-small things you can read about in your guide books. With me, you're going to learn what living on the street was like. We didn't care what style a building was, just that we could rest or play in it."

I show the firanghis which platform I arrived at when I was seven, which pillar I leaned on. I tell them about how me and the other kids I ran with watched films being shot here at all hours of the night. There's a more recent Hollywood film about Bombay street kids they are all very excited about. "Does that sort of thing really happen in India?" Lorna asks me, wide-eyed. "You know, the crime and all that?"

I haven't seen the film, but when I think back to how we pranked Derekbhaiyya, I doubt if any firanghi could know enough to tell an accurate story about Bombay street kids. "Real life is worse than movies," I say casually, as Lorna hangs on my words. "That is why you have come on this tour, na? To hear real-life stories." She nods, happily, as we continue through VT. The only real-life stories I tell my tour groups are my own, never the ones about the other kids. Those are not mine to tell.

As we retrace the steps Babloo and I took as the police chased us, through a maze of laneways all the way to Mint Road, I give the firanghis a beat-by-beat demonstration of my first moments in Bombay.

"The boy who befriended you at the station, what happened to him?" Kenny asks.

"Don't know," I reply. "Haven't seen him in years." I never saw Babloo again after I ran from his flat in Ghatkopar. He's probably up to the same goonda shit, extracting hafta from street vendors. Or maybe he's gone off to start his own gang, like he said he would. I don't know. Either way, he's not a part of my life anymore. Hardly anybody from that time is.

After I show my tour group the tiny movie theater where we spent our earnings, then the dabba where we'd sometimes wipe tables, I take them to the Gateway of India, with its crowds of tourists posing for pictures in the bright sun, and explain how we'd startle a flock of pigeons to create a distraction so we could pick pockets.

"Seriously?" Claire says, touching her waist pouch, slung lazily around her hips.

"That's why I am telling to you, keep your money hidden. Put that thing across your chest."

"Listen to Bansari," Delphine says, flipping her hair. "She knows what she's talking about."

Firanghis always pronounce it *Bahn-SAHR-ee*, no matter which cold, strange country they come from. I don't mind, though. It's my name. I haven't gone by "Rakhi" since that morning at Chowpatty Beach after I left Gauri Ma'am's. After I shook the sand from my salwar kameez, I thought about what that bhenchodh Alex asked me the night I went to Pali Hill. *What kind of life do you want?* I wanted a new one. The chance to start over, to shed my skin. But what was underneath? As I stepped off the sand and into the city, the answer was clear: I wanted the life that was paused the second I arrived in this city. To be the person I wasn't allowed to grow into. Who was Rakhi, anyway, but a name given to me by someone who betrayed me, over and over again? If not for Babloo, I would never have stopped being Bansari.

At the end of today's tour, I lead my group back to where we started, and take them to a bhuttawala roasting corn on an open flame.

"Remember what I taught you about street food," I announce, as the firanghis order corn rubbed with fresh-cut pieces of lime dipped in chili powder and salt. "If it's fried or roasted, it's good. No chutney, no yogurt! And no fresh fruit or vegetables unless . . . ?"

"Unless you wash and peel it yourself," Kenny responds triumphantly, as Lorna wipes kernels of corn off his chin.

"I've been craving vegetables ever since we got to India," Delphine says, holding two cobs of corn as Claire pays the bhuttawala. "How do you know all the best spots?"

I give her a coy smirk. If all those years of listening to foreign interns complaining at Justice For All prepared me for anything, it's being able to anticipate what firanghis want. And after leading my tours for the past few years, I've figured out that firanghis will tip well if you do three key things: predict their needs, meet those needs, and reassure them that those needs are completely reasonable. So when I meet my tour groups outside Rhythm House, I have a cooler of ice-cold bottles of Bisleri ready for them, and little disposable wet wipes they can use to refresh themselves no matter the weather. They like things they can throw away, and they always assume something is unsanitary, even if it's not. Most will want to buy coffee because they're still jetlagged (but not the milky South Indian kind), and a clean bathroom even though they use paper, not water, to clean their behinds, so I point them to that café with white walls that Saskia and Merel used to disappear to.

As I bid the tourists farewell, reminding some of them of how to get to Leopold Café, and navigating the rest back to their hotels, the tips start to flow in. A few behave as though they're handing me drugs, awkwardly slipping some bills into my hand and nodding solemnly. I return their gaze, dipping my head in a show of quiet gratitude. Others, like Kenny and Lorna, clasp my hands in theirs.

"We just can't believe the life you've had," Lorna says, her eyes gleaming. "What a success story. You should be so proud of yourself."

I smile as she lets go, leaving a five-hundred-rupee note in my hands. *If only you knew, Lorna.*

"Thank you again, Bansari," Kenny calls out as they slide into a taxi. "God bless!"

I wave, watching their taxi zoom up M.G. Road.

On my way home, I make my daily stop at the bhurjiwala near vt

Station, and tell him to prepare the usual fried egg pav as I count the kids milling about nearby.

"Bansarididi's here," one of the boys yells to his friends, his voice hoarse. "Come, come!"

"Arre, Sanjay," I say, as his friends dash to the bhurjiwala's stall. "Is that cough gone yet? Or do you need to see a doctor?"

I fish in my bag for a throat lozenge, and hand it to Sanjay, who is too busy eyeing the bhurjiwala cracking eggs over the hot tawa to worry about the rattle in his throat. I can tell he hasn't eaten all day.

There's a core gang of ten kids who come every day, and a group of stragglers who show up if they're in the right place at the right time. Sanjay is the leader—loud, clever, and quick on his feet. He reminds me of the old Babloo. When I started the tours, I considered collecting donations for an NGO working with street kids, but the thought of even having to set foot in an NGO office—of getting caught up in another NGO mess—made my skin crawl. So now I take a cut of my earnings and feed the kids near VT myself. The bhurjiwala charges me half-price, since it's a daily thing, and because the pav is a bit stale by the end of the day. Feeding the kids isn't much, but I know what hunger feels like, and at least it gives them one guaranteed meal a day.

The bhurjiwala hands me my own fried egg pav wrapped in newspaper. As I unwrap it, I catch a glimpse of a small advert featuring a woman with thick, glossy hair smiling up at me like she knows something I don't. MASSAGE EVERY DAY AND KEEP SCISSORS AWAY! I smooth the paper out and nearly choke on my fried egg pav. It's Rubina Mansoor, hawking something called "Cold-Pressed Extra-Virgin Coconut Oil for Hair and Scalp." Only big actresses with lush, silky manes get to be the face of hair oil products. I suppose this is a step up from shouting about housing as a human right with Justice For All. I wonder how long she lasted there.

I learned Justice For All shifted offices two years back when I was planning my tour route and found myself in front of the Maitreya Building. As I darted past, careful not to linger, I noticed new curtains in the second-floor window—Ma'am would never have spent money on those. The next time I was on a computer, I searched Justice For All's address and saw they moved to Masjid Bunder, probably to save money on rent.

One time I saw Gauri Ma'am as I was showing my tour group the quiet spots in Ballard Estate, where the other kids and I used to sleep after the office workers emptied out. Just as a trio of English ladies was marveling at how much the "tree-lined boulevards" and "Renaissance-style architecture" of Ballard Estate had an "elegant London feel," I caught sight of Ma'am hustling down the wide footpath, past the war memorial, digging through her bag. I froze, ignoring the sounds of my chattering firanghis, and for a moment she stopped rifling through her things and stared straight at me. Quickly, she shifted her gaze to something farther in the distance, and barreled ahead. I've gone over that encounter in my mind so many times. Sometimes I wonder if the lines in her forehead softened when she saw me, or if I imagined it.

After I finish my fried egg pav, I crumple the newspaper with Rubina Mansoor's coconut oil ad tight in my fist and toss it on the footpath. The sky has now gone from orange-pink to purple-gray, and I have to get to the bakery before it closes. I hurry back to VT and edge my way onto a Central Line train to Mulund, where I live now. Mulund is on the northeast edge of the city, next to Thane district. And most importantly, I don't have to pass Bandra Station, or Behrampada, to get there.

After the fire, I would pick up a newspaper every day, scanning the pages for news of what happened to Behrampada. I couldn't bring myself to go back and see what was left of it being bulldozed for some bhenchodh Arora luxury tower. After six months, I finally saw a tiny article—six lines only—buried in the paper saying that fire officials had closed their investigation of the 2011 Behrampada fire without confirming the cause, although residents continued to claim foul play. I read and reread that part again. *Residents continue to claim foul play.* Not "former residents" or "people who lived there." Just "residents." Armed with the hope that the people hadn't been pushed out, that the place hadn't been razed, I rushed to the Bandra Station footbridge and felt my heart soar when I caught a glimpse of where I used to live. Behrampada was still there. Arora hadn't burned down enough of it to clear and purchase the land, and the people of Behrampada had simply rebuilt over what he had destroyed.

One big change had come, though: the Marquis billboard was gone and in its place was a sparkling blue-glass building, fenced in by tall walls and even taller palm trees. I gazed out at the Marquis Hotel, casting a long shadow in the morning sun. What was life like for the young people employed inside that curved glass building? In spite of being armed with English and a degree, were they still having to say *yes sir,* or *no madam,* or *please sir, let me fix it?* Were they throwing heaps of food into the trash while just a few meters away were families who would be happy to eat the fruits that went untouched at the breakfast buffet? I shuddered, took one last look at Behrampada, and got back on the train. Going to college so I could work in a luxury hotel had been a bakvaas dream that was never really mine. Just a fantasy cooked up by someone I was foolish to trust.

But I know better now.

The train finally reaches Mulund Station, and I shuffle onto the platform with everyone else. The bakery outside the station is thankfully still open when I get there. "One kilo coconut biscuits. And one pineapple birthday cake," I say to the bakery uncle behind the counter.

"Any message?" he asks, removing a square slab frosted in pale pink icing from behind the foggy glass.

"Happy Birthday, Ayub," I say, smiling.

"I don't have enough icing left for that," he says. "Just 'Ayub' is okay?"

I nod. "But write '8' on there."

The bakery uncle squeezes a nearly empty bag of green frosting, slowly decorating the cake in his thin, wobbling cursive.

Three years ago, I left Chowpatty Beach and went straight back

to Behrampada to find Ayub. When I did, I promised him I'd keep
him safe with me. I didn't want him to have to make the kind of
choices I had to when I was growing up.

We quickly found a place to live in a slum in Mulund East, far
from everyone I knew. As I suspected, the police never came for me.
I got Ayub into a school, and took some odd cleaning jobs here and
there so I wouldn't have to dip into the cash Alex and Gauri Ma'am
gave me. Once I started making money on my tours, I decided it was
time for us to live somewhere safer. Someplace not at risk of being
destroyed by the government or some chutiya builder. Arora's billboards kept multiplying around the city, like cockroaches in the rainy
season. I tried to ignore them, but once they came to Mulund, I
shifted Ayub and me into a three-story chawl nearby, so he could be
close to his school and his new friends. Our one-room kholi is on the
second floor, and big enough to fit a small bed, a mat on the ground,
and a tiny kitchen.

The day we moved into the chawl, Ayub and I sat on the veran-
dah, taking in our new surroundings. "Bansari Khala," he started,
fiddling with the neck of his T-shirt. "Is my abba dead, too?" I told
him no, he wasn't dead, he was just in a different country. Traveling
for his job, I lied. Ayub smiled to himself, happy with that answer.
But I lay awake that night, tossing and turning at the thought of having to lie to him about his father forever.

The next morning, I looked up Vivek's new office, and went there
while Ayub was in school. It had been a year since I'd last seen Vivek,
but he beamed when I showed up, and gave me a hug. I noticed he
hadn't sold his gold wedding band.

When I told him everything that had happened with Hanifbhai,
Vivek said it wouldn't be easy, but he and his staff would do everything they could to bring him back from the Gulf. It's taken longer
than we expected to find him, but we know Hanifbhai is alive and in
a safehouse in Riyadh.

The biggest delay has been getting his passport replaced. When I went to Vivek's office last week, he told me the passport would be ready in a matter of months, and then Hanifbhai would be home.

"Ayub will be so happy," I said, breaking into a grin. "You've done so much, Vivek Sir. And I've put aside the money for his plane ticket, so we can bring him home as soon as he's allowed to travel."

"I'm proud of you, Bansari, for supporting Ayub and Hanif through this. You've really grown," Vivek said.

"Sir, I'm the same person you knew at Justice For All."

He chuckled, then asked me if I'd consider coming to work with him. "We could really use someone like you on the ground to work in our human trafficking unit."

My face warmed but I shook my head no. "I'm doing well, Vivek Sir. I'm making good money with the tours. And . . . I like it. I get to tell people my story. The way I want to tell it."

"I suppose I can't compete with that," he said.

Balancing the cake box so the icing doesn't smear, I walk through the courtyard of our chawl, greeting people I know. The kids Ayub plays cricket with. The ladies who run a crèche for small children. Like Behrampada, it's noisy in the chawl. Doors are always kept open—a shut door means nobody's home. Every evening, you can smell what vegetables people bought at the market, as well as who is using fresh methi leaves and who is using dried. After dinner, the old people gather on their shared gallery-like balconies to talk loudly about elections, TV serial plots, and everyone who lives in the chawl. For a long time they talked about me and Ayub, until I finally joined them and told them everything they wanted to know, from how Ayub and I were related to why I wasn't married.

I'm making enough money now to afford a small flat nearby, but I don't want to leave the chawl just yet. The people here know me, they know Ayub. There are some chutiyas here, but then there are chutiyas everywhere, from the hutments shrinking in the shadow of five-star hotels to the marble-floored flats of the rich.

"Bansari," one of the women on the third floor calls down to me from beneath towels drying on her laundry line. "Ayub's up here watching tv. Should I send him down?"

"In ten minutes," I say, pointing to the box of cake. "You come down, too, and bring your boys." Ayub's friends always pass out sweets on their birthdays.

I set the cake down on the small table inside our kholi and flick on the lights. With a few minutes left before the room fills with Ayub's friends, I slide my sandals off and sink down on the narrow cot for a brief moment of peace. I eye the walls—the butter yellow paint browns in some places and peels in others. My gaze shifts to the box of cake and the biscuits, and I can hear snatches of Tazim's voice in my head, chattering about her son's eighth birthday. If she were still here she'd be cooking up his favorite dishes for dinner, asking me to flip the rotis while she added a sizzling tadka to the dal. Sometimes it hits me that I am here, in this Mulund chawl, because she is gone.

Staring down at my tired feet planted firmly on the cool concrete floor, I take a deep breath in, then let it out. That firanghi Lorna said I should be proud of myself. And she doesn't even know the half of what I've been through. Even to me, my story sometimes seems hard to believe. How often my whole world has cracked open and crumbled. How many times I've had to pick up the pieces, shake off the dust, and start again.

When Hanifbhai returns, I'll let him and Ayub have this kholi and move into my own. I have the money for it, though I know better than to believe the money will always be there. Anything can happen.

Maybe I'll get sick of looking at sweaty, squinting firanghi faces all day, or maybe they'll stop wanting to go on street life tours and I'll have to pivot to something else. Maybe I'll call up Vivek and help him rescue all the Hanifbhai types who were foolish enough to put their trust in those who promised them better lives. Whatever happens, one thing I know is for sure: I will do whatever I want.

After my first year of law school in 2009, I spent a summer in Mumbai, working at a human rights law organization. In June of that year, a major fire tore through a slum named Behrampada.

According to reports, almost three hundred huts were destroyed in the fire. Three people died, twenty-nine people were injured, and two and a half thousand people were left homeless. Officials did not determine the cause of the fire. Residents and housing rights advocates alleged foul play, pointing the finger at builders. Behrampada's proximity to Bandra Station and a major commercial hub in Bandra East made it a gold mine for private developers. Some media reports suggested that the blaze spread by accident, after a cooking fire caused multiple adjacent cooking cylinders to explode. I even read a report suggesting the residents set the fire themselves, to stave off an impending demolition drive.

After I returned to Canada, I sometimes searched for news of what had become of Behrampada. As in *Such Big Dreams,* its people rebuilt after 2009. But the slum caught fire again in 2011, gutting as many as seven hundred hutments.

In the years that followed, I thought about Behrampada often.

What really caused the 2009 and 2011 fires? Were they set deliberately? If the fires were accidents, what role did the municipal and state governments play in permitting the kinds of conditions that allowed for this level of destruction? What was it like for the people who had built homes and communities for themselves in a space that was constantly at risk of being expropriated for commercial gain? What myths contribute to our ideas about who is entitled to occupy land, and who isn't? Halfway across the world from Mumbai, I couldn't find answers to any of these questions. That's when I started writing what would eventually become this novel.

Though I have spent time in Mumbai and the novel is loosely inspired by the Behrampada fire of 2009, *Such Big Dreams* is a work of fiction. All the characters in this book are creations of my imagination, and any resemblance to actual persons living or dead is purely coincidental.

For dramatic purposes, I have taken liberties with the timing of Ganesh Chaturthi, which usually takes place in late August or early September.

ACKNOWLEDGMENTS

THANK YOU TO MY EXTRAORDINARY agent, Stephanie Sinclair, for believing in this book first, holding my hand through every new twist and turn, and hustling hard and smart.

To my editor at Ballantine, Chelcee Johns, thank you for your enthusiasm and thoughtful insight, and for helping me to finesse this story. Thank you to my wonderful team at Ballantine: Sydney Collins, Elena Giavaldi, Ada Yonenaka, Sarah Feightner, Frieda Duggan, Caroline Cunningham, Emily Isayeff, Courtney Mocklow, Morgan Holt, Kim Hovey, Jennifer Hershey, and Kara Welsh.

Thank you to Anita Chong and my team at McClelland & Stewart.

For their assistance with earlier edits, thank you to Daniella Wexler and Jade Hui.

I would never have been able to write this story had I not been given the enormous opportunities I had at Windsor Law, the finest law school in Canada. A big thank you to Chris Waters for your support.

I am fortunate to have lived and worked in Mumbai in my early twenties. Thank you to the staff at Railway Children and the Human

Rights Law Network for showing me what social justice in action looks like.

I started writing what would become *Such Big Dreams* after signing up for a creative writing class at the University of Toronto's School of Continuing Studies. That decision set me on a course that changed my life. Much of this book was workshopped there. Thank you to Lee Gowan and the instructors who each played a critical part in imparting skill and knowledge. Thank you to my fellow students, whose early readership helped shape this story.

I am grateful to Helen Walsh, Zalika Reid-Benta, and Diaspora Dialogues for the opportunity to take my manuscript to the next level under the mentorship of Shyam Selvadurai, which was a dream come true.

It took me ten years to finish this book. To my dear friends, thank you for sticking it out with me. Especially Shikha Sharma, Morgan Koch, and Sarah Kromkamp, who have always treated my ambitions as though they were their own.

My parents are the picture of determination, and I drew on their example to carve out space for myself in a world I knew very little of. Thank you to my father, Jagdish Patel, from whom I get my sense of humor and love of storytelling, and my mother, Reeta Patel, from whom I get my curiosity and hunger for reading.

Thank you to my mother-in-law, Kajori Datta-Ray, an expert fact-checker, for your love and support.

My sister, Priya Patel, can pinpoint the origin of every single inside joke in this story. Thank you for your constant reassurance, which kept me going on this journey. I wrote this book for us.

And lastly, thank you to the incomparable Sumantra Datta-Ray, who can be counted on for absolutely everything, from triple-checking the price of gold in the 1980s, to having all the answers, to sustaining me in ways I never knew I needed.

SUCH
BIG
DREAMS

....

Reema Patel

A BOOK CLUB GUIDE

A NOTE FROM THE AUTHOR

Dear Reader,

I am thrilled to be able to share *Such Big Dreams* with you and your book club!

So much of Mumbai has been captured in literature, by global and local storytellers alike. In spite of its layered history and vibrant, cosmopolitan spirit, the city is a place of stark contrasts. Gritty yet glamorous, it famously houses both Asia's largest slum as well as some of the most expensive residential properties in the world. Contrasts like these are abundant; they also make for a setting that is ripe for the kind of conflict that makes a good story.

Such Big Dreams is the story of Rakhi, a twenty-three-year-old office assistant and former street child who wants so much more than her current life of working menial, thankless tasks at the cash-strapped Justice For All, a human rights law organization. Firmly stationed at the bottom rung of the office hierarchy, Rakhi is closely tethered to her boss, renowned human rights lawyer Gauri Verma, who monitors her every move under the guise of concern.

Rakhi's desire for a different future and Gauri's desperation to keep Justice For All from collapsing make them vulnerable to two characters: Alex, a Harvard-bound Canadian intern with a savior complex, and Rubina Mansoor, a fading Bollywood starlet who promises to lure big donors in exchange for becoming the public face of Justice For All. All four characters and the people around them become tangled in a dangerous web of chaos and deception as they all strive for what they want.

I wrote this book after working in Mumbai's nonprofit sector because I wanted to explore the conflicts that arise when people compete for scarce resources. How do these conflicts take shape when power, vanity, saviorism, and corruption are thrown into the mix? How far are we willing to go to do what we think is right? Who get to be heroes and who become villains?

I hope I'm able to transport you into this story world, to a crowded metropolis in which scrappy slum dwellers, big-shot lawyers, vainglorious entertainers, and naïve foreigners alike are forced to make difficult choices to keep going. In your discussions, I hope you're able to examine your own assumptions about how these characters should behave. You may even find yourselves asking what you would be willing to do to survive if you were in their place.

—Reema Patel

QUESTIONS AND TOPICS

FOR DISCUSSION

1. How might *Such Big Dreams* cast light on or add complexity to themes that have traditionally been overlooked in the American canon, such as race, misogyny, and class?

2. Did reading this book challenge any aspects of your view of the ways in which certain social and political issues have, in the past, been represented or painted over in mainstream literature and other art forms?

3. Describe Rakhi and Gauri Verma's relationship. What was it like in the beginning, and how did it change over the course of the book? In what ways did it change, and why?

4. Why do you think Rakhi and Alex are drawn to each other and agree to this deal? If you were in either of their positions, would you have agreed to it? Why or why not?

5. In what ways are Rakhi and Alex different? In what ways are they similar? With whom do you sympathize and identify

more? Did you find yourself taking sides as their stories unfolded?

6. The Mumbai setting is intrinsic to the story. Discuss the ways in which it functions as a character in the novel and how each of the human characters relates to it.

7. Do you think it was important that Rakhi reunited with Babloo even though it didn't end well for their friendship? Did Rakhi need to learn the truth about Babloo? If you were Rakhi, would you have wanted to learn the truth?

8. In what ways does the past influence the present in *Such Big Dreams*? How do the characters try to repress or escape the pain of their histories? What does the novel tell us about the relationship between past and present? How does this affect their relationships and help them heal?

9. Loyalty comes up often and in various ways in *Such Big Dreams*: Rakhi's loyalty to Gauri Verma, Gauri's loyalty to her work, Alex's supposed loyalty to Rakhi. Which do you feel has been tested the most and what surprised you?

10. In the epilogue, we see that Rakhi is now choosing to go by her given name, Bansari. Why is this significant? What do you think led to her decision?

11. Discuss the title, *Such Big Dreams*. How do you think it relates to the overall story? How does it apply to each of the characters in the book?

PHOTO: © IKONICA

REEMA PATEL holds a BA from McGill University and a JD from the University of Windsor. After working in Mumbai in the youth nonprofit sector and in human-rights advocacy, she has spent the past ten years working in provincial and municipal government. *Such Big Dreams*, her first novel, won the Penguin Random House Student Award for Fiction at the University of Toronto's School of Continuing Studies. She lives in Toronto, where she currently works as a lawyer.

ABOUT THE TYPE

This book was set in Caslon, a typeface first designed in 1722 by William Caslon (1692–1766). Its widespread use by most English printers in the early eighteenth century soon supplanted the Dutch typefaces that had formerly prevailed. The roman is considered a "workhorse" typeface due to its pleasant, open appearance, while the italic is exceedingly decorative.

RANDOM HOUSE BOOK CLUB

Because Stories Are Better Shared

Discover

Exciting new books that spark conversation every week.

Connect

With authors on tour—or in your living room. (Request an Author Chat for your book club!)

Discuss

Stories that move you with fellow book lovers on Facebook, on Goodreads, or at in-person meet-ups.

Enhance

Your reading experience with discussion prompts, digital book club kits, and more, available on our website.

Join our online book club community!
f **g** randomhousebookclub.com

Random
House
Book Club ™

Because
Stories Are
Better Shared

RANDOM HOUSE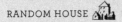